# Cherokee Reel

ᏗᎾᏍᎪᎥᎢᏍᏜᎯᏴᎠᏗᎡᏉᎦᎯᎢᎦᏚᎳᏫᏗᏑᎬᎹᎠᏛᎣᎢᎲᎫᏛᎧᏖᏖᎣᎵᏂᏃᏎᎣᎤ

## JAMES A. HUMPHREY

## This is a work of fiction.

Any semblance between original characters and real persons, living or dead, is coincidental. The author in no way represents the companies, corporations, or brands mentioned in this book. The likeness of historical/ famous figures have been used fictitiously; the author does not speak for or represent these people. All opinions expressed in this book are the author's, or fictional.

## CONTENTS

DRᏐᎣⁱᏕᎣᏢᏯᎪᎫᎬᏝᏗᎮᎪᏂᏝᎳᏍᏩᎷᎷᏰᎳᏸᎣᎻᏣᏸᎥᏸᏋᎿᏂᏃᏈᎣᵛ

# DEDICATION

To the memory of my paternal grandmother Ella Waters,
great grandfather Andrew Waters (Dawes Roll Signees,)
and my ancestor Aney King who survived the Trail of Tears.

Grandmother Ella inspires my stories.

VI

# PREFACE

Public knowledge of Cherokee history, culture, and language is sparse. A partial reason for that limitation may be awareness.

The author, a citizen of the Cherokee Nation, inspired by his paternal grandmother, presents these story elements through fiction as an entertaining learning experience. He attempts to explore her world with dignity, appreciation, and respect. Cherokee is his "in progress" second language and while not having been raised in the culture, the author's intention is to present information and events from the Cherokee worldview.

Readers may determine their own opinions about his success.

### *Please be aware:*
*Cherokee Reel* unfolds during violent years of Indigenous history. Those sensitive to turmoil may be offended by the events portrayed in this narrative.

VIII

# ᏣᎳᎩ

# ᎠᎵᏍᏚᏯᏍᏗ

ᎠᏕᎶᏆᏍᎩᏍᏗᏍᎩᎥᏯᎠᎵᏍᏆᎯᏳᎢᏓᎢᏕᏍᎠᏗᏝᎠᏐᏣᏍᎦᏍᏫᏝᏥᏉᏎᏲᎢᎣᎯᏳᎩᎦᏇᏙᏗᏰᏅᎯᏃᎤ

## JAMES A. HUMPHREY

## CHAPTER ONE — Lisa

ᎠᏛᎿᎣ'ᎢᏍᎣᏆᎩ�YᎠᏎᎮᎬᏓᎠᏨᏣᏔᏕᎢᎬᎷᎿᏣᏬᎣᏓᎯᏃᎩᏋᏋᎳᎭᏃᏓᎣᏫ

Lisa Waters preens atop a second-story staircase and views a color riot of dancing couples. "Who am I, Ezra?"

"You're the social queen of Fort Smith, Arkansas. I think maybe the entire state." The anointed's husband slips a hand around his spouse's corseted waist and guides the twenty-six-year-old onto the stairway.

At the base of the steps, in an immense ground-floor parlor, adorned and posturing dancers prance and promenade.

"Look. Everyone important dances to my music." The hostess claps both hands with satisfaction.

Women in spinning hoop dresses follow the leads of prominent Native American, mixed-race, and Anglo men.

Formal but politically uneasy guests crowd the floor and step with partners to the rhythm of the music.

The rising star of an aggressive legal, political, and financial western center, Ezra Waters grins at his partner. "When you invited these people, I thought many would decline."

"Why? They enjoy a Cherokee Reel." The hostess pretends a pout.

"No. This ex-slave band plays a plantation cake walk. Listen. Do you think our musicians mock their old overseers?"

Wife strokes her man's arm. "Dance now, husband. Talk politics when I'm not here."

Ezra nods. "Tonight, I'll speak of tea parties or female-friendly gossip."

Lisa pats his hand. "I love you for saving my party. You found waiters and performers."

"Hired is a better word. The fiddler is Judge Steel's blacksmith." The attorney points discretely. "His name is Moss. He recruited the others." The husband kisses his wife's forehead. "Never forget your father freed me. The man disliked the idea of owning a human. So do you."

"Or woman." Lisa scans the dancers. "Most of these people own slaves. Even John Ross. I'm glad the president accepted this invitation despite my liberated beliefs." She slips an arm around her husband's waist. "I hope he comes with his new wife. I so want to meet her."

***

Music inspires an animated gown collection that spins, swirls, and sways .

With hand fans, embroidered bonnets, and flushed faces, guests parade in a square.

At the corner turns, each male, on the inside, displays individual style, from flourish to foolery.

A violinist, guitar strummer, and spoon rhythm man, all talented freedmen hired for the festivity, surround a pianist and create the reel.

Fort Smith and Gibson army officers, rich Arkansas River shippers, and prosperous rice and cotton plantation owners socialize, hosted by the town's burgeoning legal establishment.

Treaty Party representatives lift knees high as they corner the cakewalk. Wealthy new arrivals compete with the Gateway to the West's society to display grace and precision.

As oil and vinegar in a glass jar, supporters of these feuding political positions do not mix. They cluster on each square's side with others of similar affiliation.

Partygoers sip raspberry brandy, watch the Cherokee adaption of the traditional plantation cake walk square, and support each other's politics.

Most whisper condemnation and eye those with opposing points of view.

A few budding temperance advocates refuse the hired freedman waiters, who present glasses on silver trays. They raise noses at those who sip and enjoy brandy.

Judge Bennett Steel, the preeminent adjudicator in charge of Arkansas federal courts and Ezra's mentor, with his gracious full-blood Choctaw wife, entertains a non-dancing clutch in one corner of the room.

***

The host couple and stars of the festivities descend the stairway to join the guests. "After President Ross lost Quatie on the trail that winter, I am surprised he remarried," Ezra replies as he notices a flurry of movement at the front entrance.

Lisa accepts a brandy. "I don't see anybody here who walked the northern route."

"Unfortunate that Ella isn't attending." Husband slips his hand around his wife's waist and guides her toward arrivals.

"My sister's celebrity might have enlivened this party. People flock to meet the Cherokee Rose. But I'm worried. I haven't heard from her in months." Lisa holds her gown's hoops forward. "Ross's first spouse sounds the same as my sister. They say Quatie gave her blankets to a sick child."

"Then she died of pneumonia." Ezra finishes the thought as he follows his wife toward the entrance. As the hosts pass, party guests turn and stare at an arriving couple.

The attorney extends a hand. "President Ross. Welcome to this home and to Fort Smith."

"And to the United States of America. It's far from Tahlequah, Mr. Waters." The dignitary removes a black top hat. "My last correspondence from Justice Steel tells me you are his indispensable man. My business contacts say you've both done commerce on the river successfully."

"Thank you, sir. The judge signed my free papers back in Georgia when I was young and educated me in the law. I consider him my father, and I'm pleased he speaks well of me." Ezra shakes the hand of the leader of the eastern Cherokees and a political hero of new immigrants to the territory. "As for your nation's shipping needs, I admit to many contacts on the Arkansas. May I introduce my wife, Lisa?"

Ross sweeps his hat toward his companion. "And this southern belle is my bride, Mary Stapler."

Attired in an ornate fashionable gown, a young and striking woman clings to her thirty-seven-year-old famous husband and smiles at the hostess, one of the few in the room near her age. "I am so pleased to meet the social queen of Fort Smith. John, why don't you and Mr. Waters work this political crowd as you always do? She and I must become friends."

Lisa nods agreement.

Ezra guides the President to the initial group of well-wishers, who surge to greet their champion.

"Your home is scrumptious and perfect for entertaining." The first lady squeezes her white-gloved hands together with pleasure. "It's metropolitan, social, and sophisticated."

The hostess beams satisfaction.

Mary leans closer. "I cannot tolerate Tahlequah—such a territorial place. John built me what he calls Ross Cottage in Park Hill. It's the only home livable for miles."

"My friends say that bungalow is a two-story house with a fine view and a mile of fenced driveway." Lisa smiles at the younger woman. "I understand it's nicer than residences in this town."

"The president loves to entertain his people. I relate, but we were married in a more metropolitan Philadelphia, not snooty society. I'm a proper Quaker raised by family in Brandywine."

The hostess rocks with the music as she listens.

"Without slaves in our home," she adds. "I hear your waiters and musicians are hired freedmen."

"Yes, my husband was born a slave. He rejects the condition."

"With my childhood religious training, I appreciate that point of view, but I am aware this territory demands an attitude readjustment."

"We Presbyterians enjoy less discipline than your Society of Friends. Ezra and I came west from Georgia with the Cherokee removal." Lisa winks at her guest. "Adjustment is a mild word for a forced march. This is his home, and he is content."

"Speaking of satisfied spouses, who in that tall man in uniform with my husband?"

"That's Colonel Mathew Arbuckle, commandant of Fort Gibson."

Both women watch the lanky officer greet President Ross.

Lisa gossips into a handkerchief. "Ezra provides legal service to the post. He says the army will replace the commander."

Mary enjoys the tidbit and points a fan at a guest whose icy stare follows John's progress through the room. "And that shorter stocky fellow? I don't believe he supports my husband."

"That's Standhope Watie, an old settler and plantation owner, a New Echota signee." Lisa's voice lowers. "He and your spouse lead different sides of this political talk. But they shook hands in Washington after signing that treaty."

"No handshakes tonight." Mrs. Ross watches the opposition's head nod to several followers.

The dissenter's leader presses a path to the door without acknowledging his opponent's presence.

A freedman waiter balances a silver tray laden with refreshments and interrupts. "Excuse me. Someone wishes to speak with Madam at the back entrance."

"The rear?"

The attendant leans close and whispers into Lisa's ear. "A woman. Says she's your sister, but we believe she smelled your brandy. The lady's drunk and filthy."

"Oh!" Lisa turns to Mrs. Ross. "Mary, there's a detail in the kitchen I must handle. Please excuse me. Let me introduce the charming wife of Judge Steel before I go."

"Yes. I heard she is a full-blood. How interesting!"

***

Moments later, the freedman waiter ushers his employer to the rear door of the home. "We insisted this person wait outside. Because of the smell."

Lisa steps into the backyard and lifts the hem of her hoop gown above the soil.

With shoulders propped against the house's wall and legs spread around a liquor bottle, a woman slumps on the dirt. Her hair hangs in strings from a worn woolen hat, and her clothing stinks of alcohol and trail dust.

"Ella!" Lisa's voice breaks. "You're drunk!"

"Not near enough, little sister." The sibling waves an empty H and H jug in the air. "Got any whiskey?"

The younger drops to both knees. "Oh no! You can't handle liquor. Where's Dideyohvsgi?"

"The old shaman died in Georgia, as I should have." Ella's giggle bubbles across alcoholic lips. "You know what he said before he passed?"

"How can I help you?" Lisa grasps her sister's hands.

The woman slobbers and laughs. "That's funny! No. My hero stuck an eagle feather in my hair and asked me who I am. I told him I am the Cherokee Rose. He made me promise to never forsake the eastern mountains. Then the old man died." She grins and drools at the corner of the mouth. "The next morning, I forsook."

Ella passes into a drunken stupor.

Freedman musicians, on break, step from the house.

The fiddler freezes as he spies his employer's wife. "Mrs. Waters, can I help?"

"Yes. Please. This is my sister."

"Let's take her inside and put her in bed."

"Not in this condition." Younger sibling fusses. "She's drunk and hasn't had a bath in weeks. We can't let guests see."

The big musician slips muscular arms underneath the limp form and lifts. "What's her name, Mrs. Waters?"

His employer blocks the rear entrance. "Ella. You may not believe this, but she is not a lush. Her detachment on the northern trail called her Cherokee Rose for many good deeds."

"I'll take her where it's warmer." Moss moves toward the back door.

"No. Somebody will see. Wait while I get money. Rent a room somewhere in town and watch over her until the party ends."

"I can't go. Mr. Waters pays me to play the fiddle for the guests."

Lisa points at a rear property stable. "I am your employer. Please carry her. You'll find a grain storage pit with door covers. No one will know she's there."

"After the company clears, should I move her to a bedroom?"

"No, Mary Ross stays tonight. The president leaves on a political junket. I don't want the first lady disturbed." Lisa follows the fiddler and his burden to the stable. "After you finish playing, take her to a hotel. I will pay well."

"No need. Your husband provides work, and I owe the man plenty."

The drunk woman in the fiddler's arms, as he carries her weight toward the grain storage, focuses on her sister's party finery. "And who do you pretend you are?"

Lisa glares at her sister.

The older sibling giggles. "Who am I, Dideyohvsgi asked? Like you, the daughter of our father and a Cherokee." Ella and the fiddler disappear into the shed.

Lisa turns to the house. "True, Big Sister, but I'm pretending to be a White debutante."

***

The following morning, the sun colors the night's atmosphere gray.

Wife sleeps with husband in a second-level bedroom on the opposite outskirts of Fort Smith from the town's new military fortification.

The property includes a stable and a rose garden enclosed by an expansive picket fence. Beyond the house, the Arkansas River curves and cuddles the land within an arc.

Lisa wakens and shakes Ezra's shoulder. "I think a bird broke the window."

She slips from bed and into a robe. As Ezra stirs, the wife pads to the room's viewpoint.

Below, Moss hurls a second stone. which smacks the pane. She recoils. "Your fiddler's chunking rocks."

Lisa opens the upstairs frame and leans out into the darkness.

"Something awful happened!" A rock clenched by fingers pauses.

"Shh. You'll wake the guests. Come to the back door."

Moments later, the couple sits at a kitchen table as the fiddler shakes with nerves and tells his story. "She's dead."

Lisa's voice cracks. "Who do you mean?"

"She bathed and went to bed. I was outside the rooming house, but your sister slipped past me to Miss Harley's. Only place that has liquor so late."

"Miss Harley's?"

"Yes, Lisa." Her husband grasps her fingers. "It's a brothel."

"She wanted a drink." Moss looks at the two. "I couldn't stop her once she got there, Mr. Waters. Nothing I could do."

"Tough men there." Ezra clasps his wife's hands between palms. "Freedmen can't go into that establishment. They might have hung you."

"But I peeked in a window." The fiddler's eyes tear and his lips tremble. "A man whipped your sister with a pistol."

"Oh!" Lisa faints. Her forehead impacts the table.

"Until she died, Mr. Waters."

The spouse assists his wife. "Moss, wait while I get her to the room and waken someone to stay with her. Then, take me to Miss Harley's."

***

Later, morning daylight floods the bedroom as Lisa's eyelids flutter open. She focuses.

At the end of the bed, Mrs. Ross, in mourning attire, sits.

"Mary, my husband?"

Her companion leans forward and clutches the older woman's hands. "So sorry to hear of your sister. Ezra said you knew. They say she's dead. He went there to supervise a murder investigation."

Lisa bursts into grief tears.

The younger woman gathers her hostess friend into her arms. "Cry. Let the hurt out."

"She suffered on the trek here," a mourning heart blubbers. "She and an old shaman returned to Georgia. Too extreme for anyone. I should have gone with her."

Mrs. Ross comforts, "That didn't kill her. Ezra said a freedman saw it. The murderer pistol-whipped your sister when she refused his advances."

"She was not a prostitute!" Lisa's spine shudders. "She had to have liquor. That pulled her inside."

"The witness mentioned that the killer was prosperous, dressed as a planter, with one of those new Patterson Colt revolving pistols." Mrs. Ross's eyes open wide, and immaturity surfaces. "He could have attended the party." She covers her mouth.

"Did Moss know him?"

"Said if he ever saw the man again." Mary Stapler nods affirmative. "He got a good look."

Lisa grasps her friend's hand. "I didn't have the strength to do things my sister did. But she died a helpless alcoholic. I want to keep this mess private."

"Quiet?"

"Yes. Ezra understands. He's an attorney and a businessman. No need for a scandal that damages our lives. Can you imagine what people would whisper if they knew Ezra's sister-in-law passed drunk in a bawdy house? I will speak to my husband. We must conceal this."

"I understand." Mary grips her friend's hands. "At your party, you called it attitude adjustment."

"You and Moss know of this. The others work with Ezra, and he can control them. So does the fiddler. Please, promise to not talk of this embarrassment."

"If that is your wish, Lisa."

"It is. Don't even tell your husband."

"Do you want your sister's murderer punished?" Mrs. Ross raises her eyebrows.

"Ezra's a lawyer. I understand trials and couldn't live with the publicity. They called my sister a hero. A trial would destroy her legacy."

"John left with supporters after your party last night. He doesn't know." The president's wife smiles.

Lisa and Mary Stapler hug each other.

"My lips seal forever, unless you release me from this oath." The most prominent lady of the Cherokee Nation cements a lifelong friendship.

## CHAPTER TWO — Moss

DᎡᏔᏚᎣᎢᏏᏚᏗᎷᎩᎪᏚᎬᏓᏆᎠᎵᎶᏎᎳᏔᏛᎱᏌᎷᎪᎦᏜᎣᏆᎲᎨᎩᎬᏎᏪᎦᏂᎯᏃᏛᎤ

Months after the party, slushy snow falls upon the crook of the Arkansas River. Fort Smith endures a harsh winter.

Shuttered windows block the chill from the home, but both owners snuggle in blankets.

Moss offers a tray. "Sir, your brandy."

The husband lifts the small decanter and pours a glass half full. "Care for a drink, Lisa?"

The woman shakes her head no and looks at the freedman server. "I'm so glad you accepted this employment."

"The one thankful, Mrs. Waters, is me. Fiddling did not keep food on the table."

Ezra serves a second. "Join me for a whiskey. My wife doesn't want any."

"Yes, sit." His partner smiles. "Play warm music for this snowy night."

Moss steps to the fireplace and captures a violin from where it leans against the brick. He sips the liquor, lifts a bow, and strokes a smooth melody.

The sister listens, thinks of her sibling, and sways to the rhythm. "The whiskey in a drunkard's cup is never meant for me." Her mind invents the words to flow with the music.

"You have a wonderful voice." Moss smiles as musical notes pause. "Let's try that again." He tucks the instrument under a chin and slides the bow across vibrating strings.

"The whiskey in a drunkard's cup is never meant for me." Lisa's eyes moisten as emotions release memories of her sister. "It kills my body and my soul and is a sight to see. I must abstain from all these things to free this Cherokee."

Moss holds the last note, and the song lingers in the warm interior air. "A Tsalagi Reel, Ms. Lisa. Your heart shapes the words, and my Louisiana rice-field fiddle makes the melody."

Ezra reaches for his wife's hand. "You miss your sister, and so do I."

The moment ends with the sound of a timid knock.

"I'll answer this time of the night." The musician stretches for the violin's case.

"Put the instrument away." Lisa drops her blanket to the floor. "Let me get the door." She cracks the entrance. Frigid air blushes her cheeks.

A slave girl in the wet rain and snow mix trembles from the freezing dampness. "Please don't scream. I was told to find someone here."

Beyond the freezing form, several men and women slaves shiver in inadequate, tattered clothes and wait.

Ezra and the fiddler join Lisa.

The woman in the bleak night spies the musician's violin case. "You must be Moss. They said you was here. Save me."

"What's this?" Ezra's voice rings with irritation. "What are these people doing here?"

"These folks are you and I, Mr. Waters. Do we help? Do you?"

"At this time of day?" The attorney pulls his wife from the entrance.

The waiting woman's eyes tear. "Mister Moss?"

"They need a place to shelter. These families are escapees. Catchers are close."

"To here!" The house's owner attempts to shut the door. "Don't hide anyone!"

"Get rid of them." Lisa stands on tiptoes to view the slaves over Ezra's shoulder. "Or help them."

The large freedman studies Mr. Waters. "Dangerous men with dogs and whips follow."

"And firearms." Ezra looks above and beyond the group for pursuers.

From a hall closet, Lisa grabs a coat. "The grain bin in the stable. Remember hiding Ella? Take these runaways while I get blankets."

"Catchers will check the stable." Moss's eyes enlarge.

She pitches her wrap to the woman, whose hands tremble as she catches the warmth. "The ice and rain may wash away the scent. I'm sure there is little time."

Ezra stares dumbfounded at his wife and shuts the door.

"My daddy was a slave, and he escaped to free you when you were young." Lisa kisses her husband. "His memory won't allow me to abandon these people."

"Sometimes you're as good as your sister." Her spouse smiles.

"I'm not. Ella takes everyone to the fireplace, but I don't want to dirty my rug." She leads upstairs. "And this is only one time. The Cherokee Rose made her house a hostel."

***

With arms full of blankets, moments later, Lisa and Ezra join Moss inside the stable.

The fiddler holds the grain bin's ground level cover open. In the large dugout, its wall surfaced in brick, the slaves huddle together.

15

"Take these and wrap yourselves." Cherokee Rose's sister passes warmth to outstretched hands. "We have plenty more."

The freedman looks at his boss. "I'm sorry, Mr. Waters, to get you involved in this."

"All's right this time." Lisa checks if each has a blanket. "These people are runaways. My attorney husband knows that's against the law. His ex-slave past says the laws of man are not always for everyone."

"Anyone say from who they're running?" Ezra looks at the fiddler.

"My master was a Cherokee planter." The woman from the door stiffens. "His name is Vann. But others belonged to different owners."

"Vann's enough threat. The man's rich and powerful," the attorney warns. "Why do they run tonight?"

"It's a revolt. Territory organizers planned this for months. My cabin was a safe house, but I was working." Moss shakes his head with determination.

"This makes me complicit." The respected legal mind surveys the small crowd in the grain bin.

"Call it our runners' protected pit." Lisa smiles at her husband.

The freedman sweeps an arm wide. "It was supposed to happen next week, but this weather swayed someone to start tonight."

"Who's that?" Ezra pushes the point. "The one in charge?"

"Don't know. Safe houses only know who recruited each place." The fiddler glances at Mrs. Waters. "A guy in the band convinced me."

"My father fought with Joseph Vann years ago," Lisa grimaces.

"He is a tough old timer. I'm sure slave catchers are on the trail now." The attorney looks outside in several directions.

"What if they catch us helping these people?" Lisa's voice trembles in fear.

"I'll stay." The musician crowds the couple toward the stable's entrance. "Go back. You don't know we are here."

"You're a brave man." Ezra pulls his spouse's arm.

"No! We mustn't let anyone discover this place tonight." His wife's speech chatters from the temperature. "Come up to the house, Moss. Freedmen are safe. But let's conceal these doors under hay."

***

A long evening extends into the early morning darkness.

Snow mixes with rain, and mud slops around the shod hooves of horses that plod to Lisa and Ezra's home entrance.

Six armed riders in wool coats and wet, dripping hats pulled over eyes shift upon their mounts in the wet and slop.

The Waters' place awaits, dark, calm, and unalarming.

Inside, Ezra and Moss stand on each side of the fireplace. Both hold loaded Leman percussion rifles and listen.

Lisa, in a heavy winter night robe, rocks before the fire. She steals glances at the door.

In the rain mix, a short, stocky rider dismounts, looks at his companions, and then steps onto the Waters' porch. "Men, a freedman attorney owns this place. They could have runaways inside, but if they do, be gentle. He's a protégé of Judge Steel."

The intruder draws an extended barrel US Navy issued Patterson Colt revolver from his belt's holster.

The mounted lawmen draw their pistols or check weapons. Many rest long guns on their knees.

Short and stocky pounds on the front door with the butt of his pistol and waits.

The woman of the house opens the carved wooden entry and peeks out. "Gracious! Ezra, it's Standhope Watie. Sir, what could you want so early in the morning? We have not seen you since our party. More raspberry brandy?" Lisa giggles into her fist against the frost. "I so hope you enjoyed a glass the other evening."

"Mrs. Waters." The man removes his hat, and water drips onto the porch. "A little whiskey warms the night, but my lawmen are on business."

Ezra, without his rifle, joins his wife. "Mr. Watie. This is most irregular. Who are these gentlemen, and what brings you to my house?"

"Lighthorse. We're trailing escapees from the Vann plantation."

"You don't need that big gun, sir, and you're dripping." She bluffs hospitality and swings the entrance open. "Please come inside the house. This is horrid weather."

The horsemen's leader holsters his Patterson and turns to his men. "You fellows stay here."

Inside, the three stand together in the foyer at the base of stairs.

Atop the steps in the darkness with both percussion long guns, Moss waits.

"Slaves ran from plantations west of here near Webbers Falls. The Lighthorse chase a group headed for Texas. I look for a few moving east. You folks heard or seen runners tonight?"

"Why, goodness no." Lisa pulls her robe tighter around her throat. "You know this family doesn't even own a slave."

The wet, stocky man pauses. "Or harbor any?"

"That's against the law, Watie." Ezra's voice steels. "My profession, I remind you."

"Now, husband, you can't be a grumpy barrister this early in the morning." The attorney's wife smiles at their visitor. "Please, tell your men to tie their horses in the stable, and I'll make everyone chicory coffee. It's fresh off the boat from New Orleans."

Standhope Watie stares at Ezra for a moment and glances at Lisa. "No thank you, Mrs. Waters. We must move on and finish our work."

As the threat exits the front door, the owner of the house draws his breath deep into lungs and closes the entry.

Husband and wife freeze. With ears to the wood, they listen to the catchers grumble and ride away.

Ezra looks up the stairs.

Moss stands ready and uncocks his weapon. "I couldn't see him but intended to blow his skull off for a free future."

"How many people escaped tonight?" Lisa turns from the entrance.

"My, I mean, our group was only part of around a hundred fifty. Most of those went for Texas." The man extends his rifle to Ezra. "Only a few head for Georgia."

"That's a large rebellion." Its owner unloads the long gun's percussion cap. "I expect repercussions."

"Are we in danger?" Lisa's anxiety stimulates, and she wrings her hands.

Mr. Waters looks at his employee. "I think not. No one knows of this except Moss. He will not talk."

"Thanks to your chicory coffee invite and that demon's hurry to whip slaves." The fiddler pauses for a moment. "And that sweet grain hole in your stable."

"I'll make it hot." She turns toward the kitchen. "For us and those in the bin. We can't risk bringing runaways inside to a proper table."

***

More than a month later, repercussions from the slave escape invade Fort Smith and the Water's secure home on the bend of the Arkansas River.

Lisa smiles with pleasure as she compares her living room Christmas tree to the illustration in a new Clement Clarke Moore book, A Visit from St. Nicholas.

She adjusts a wax candle tangled in a popcorn string but twists to her husband's voice.

"Proper decorations." Ezra eyes the holiday symbols. "Those candles are stylish since that book came out, but to me, they're a fire risk."

"Not if you don't light the wicks, honey." Lisa dances away from the observation. "And they are so fascinating. See this Christmas tree?"

The man does not look.

His wife notices. "How was work today?"

"Fine. Did you hear the news?"

"What's that, dear?" Lisa's attention turns to her husband.

"The Cherokee National Council passed a law on December the second called 'An Act in Regard to Free Negroes'."

"Let's not talk of this. It doesn't sound in the Christmas spirit." She wipes both hands with her apron. "Does Fort Smith care what the Indians in the territory do?"

"Judge Steel does." Ezra removes his coat. "This new statute bans freedmen from the Cherokee Nation, except those freed by their own owners. It's effective in January."

"That means you." Lisa stares at her attorney. "My father was an escaped slave before he released you."

"But your mother was full blood." The husband points out. "And the act's ambiguous. She owned me, and the action was joint."

"So that makes you exempt from the ban?"

Ezra sits in a stuffed chair. "Judge Steel expects so. This is a reaction to that mass runaway when Moss hid his people."

"The judge knows that?" Lisa's voice rises with alarm.

"No. But he thinks the act infringes on freedman rights."

"So?"

"My partner suggested I move to Tahlequah and open a new law practice."

"And leave Fort Smith?" The socialite's forehead wrinkles with concern. "How do you manage or sell your river businesses?"

"Keep our enterprises, of course. The judge is an associate. We do little." Ezra shrugs. "It's financing and paper signing. I could do that from the territory."

Lisa collapses into a chair. "Sounds as if you wish to go?"

"I've thought of it. In Fort Smith, Judge Steel administers justice and interprets the law. Here, he will always, and I'm only an important help man. I prefer to carry out my own plans, not aid someone else's."

"You need to move!" His wife stands and claps her hands together.

"Yes, honey." Her husband coughs. "I do."

"Then I choose to go." Lisa smiles. "Mary Stapler Ross needs social competition. I hear Park Hill far outshines homes in this town. But it'll be a friendly, correct, social battle, and I'll need help."

"I promise to do whatever it takes for you to love Tahlequah." Ezra nods.

"I mean actual logistic support." The socialite wife laughs. "New music is costly. You take care of that detail, but I will need a fiddler in my band if I choose to play my Cherokee Reel."

"I asked." The attorney mimics playing a violin.

"You're a dear husband." She beams pleasure and anticipation. "You know what I wish before I even think it."

***

Later that afternoon, Lisa rides into her rear stable, where the large freedman waits. "I wasn't expecting you. I can unsaddle my horse."

"Yes, you can." Moss reaches for the mount's bridle. "But I'll do it for you. Go to the house and get warm."

The rider dismounts, grabs a bucket, and strides toward the grain bin.

"No, Miss! Not much left in there." The man attempts to take the pail.

"Must be enough for a treat!" She bends and lifts the wooden cover.

A field hand stares upward at the base of steps within the pit.

Lisa freezes and then turns. "He's why you didn't want me to lift this door!"

"Yes, I put the man in last night." The fiddler drops a chin.

"Why? You know it's illegal and risks everything!"

"I had nowhere else to hide the fellow."

"Ezra's going to be livid!" The wife stomps a foot. "An attorney cannot risk hiding runaway slaves. My husband will fire you."

"Not if you don't tell, Ms. Lisa."

"What are you saying?"

"I have been protecting runaways here for weeks. I am a stop on the underground railroad called the Cherokee Reel."

"What's the connection to the song?"

"The song's an escape. The tracks are another dance with a different melody. I and many others help escapees slip out of the territory." Moss nods to the hidden slave and closes the bin's door. "I move runners east to the river where conductors shelter other flight routes through Georgia."

"And if catchers like Stanhope Watie discover this?"

"This musician will never fiddle again."

Lisa rests on the empty grain pail and stares at her employee. "And you could never play our Cherokee Reel at another party?"

Moss shrugs and scratches the back of his neck.

The woman sits silent for a moment. "I won't say a thing to Ezra."

The fiddler nods agreement.

"Promise to stop playing this song when we move to Tahlequah." Lisa stands and her lips firm.

The large freedman drops his head and studies the ground.

## CHAPTER THREE — Tahlequah

**ᎠᎡᎢᎣᎤᎥᎦᎧᎨᎩᎪᎫᎬᎭᎮᎯᎰᎱᎲᎳᎴᎵᎶᎷᎸᎹᎺᎻᎼᎽᎾᎿᏀᏁᏂᏃᏄᏅ**

An early historical Cherokee council meeting site grows into a rural outpost of civilization.

Ezra Waters, partnered with Judge Steel, profits from that growth.

Their company buys property, lays out streets, and sells lots as affluent indigenous planters and tradesmen realize the commercial and residential promise of Tahlequah.

Merchants, blacksmiths, and wheelwrights service forty-niners who rush for California's gold.

Trade in cash explodes.

To the partnerships' pleasure, the National Council erects a Supreme Court building south of the main square.

The town's fortunate location during the stampede westward provides ample customers as miners search for their fortunes on the West Coast but resupply in the territory.

Business thrives.

Lisa, wife of attorney-at-law and territorial representative for Steel and Waters Development Company of Arkansas finances a dozen stores, two wheelwrights, and a dentist's office that grow and prosper near her temporary house.

She and her husband build out of town.

The National Council establishes *The Cherokee Advocate*, a newspaper published near the Park Hill residence following the demise of *The Phoenix*.

The tribal government contributes land to the Masons to build a two-story meeting space with a first-floor gathering hall for the Sons of Temperance.

Ross Cottage, belonging to the Nation's leader and Mary Stapler, is a southern cottage in proximity to the town, with an apple orchard of a thousand trees, stables for many horses, and outbuildings for slaves who work the fields.

The president's people, a mix of politician visitors, Indian agents, relatives, missionaries, and a cross-section of immigrants from the water and land route forced removals from Georgia, visit his place, and the grounds swell with people.

Ezra Waters' new home, two miles from the executive's property and built by Steel and Waters, promotes the company's prestige and Lisa's friendly social and economic rivalry with Mary Ross.

Lisa hosts the prosperous, prestigious, or powerful, often connected to Ezra's financial interests, with lavish socials that feature the finest silver, hired freedmen servers, and music by Moss and his fellow musicians.

***

During a late evening, after a well-attended social, servants tidy their living room. Lisa and Ezra sit and sip nightcaps as he studies a newspaper.

"Another successful party, my dear. Thank you." Spouse beams.

"Kiss you, sweetheart. Mary Stapler was envious of the pumpkin bread I served. I heard her tell someone."

"Your Cherokee delicacy." The husband clears his throat. "But there's something I want you to consider."

Wife sets her glass on a side table and turns her attention to her husband's serious tone.

"Times are changing. People's moods are more polarized and antagonistic. Social events create business, but I believe we need to be careful."

"Of what?" Lisa smiles.

"We cannot appear too frivolous. Our guests have problems, major concerns, and it suggests we have none." Ezra grins in return. "It separates us as elitist."

"What do you mean?"

"Drunkenness, for one. Arkansas and Missouri whiskey dealers flood the Flint, Sequoya, and Going Snake districts with liquor. Slave trade traffic is another. Escaped slaves overwhelm the Lighthorse. Our people, as in the United States, are split over slavery. The Cherokee national debt burdens grow. We raise too much cotton and not enough corn."

Lisa twists in her chair. "Should we not have parties?"

"No. That's not what I suggest. Your socials are very good for business. But we both need to be more connected."

"I'm listening."

"Yes." Ezra pats his wife's hand. "Turn your social graces to temperance meetings in Tahlequah. Maybe get involved in the movement to close Fort Gibson or sponsor a few Cherokee Agriculture Society competitions. I must do the same."

"And outshine Mary Stapler Ross!" Lisa claps her hands in delight.

"I thought you and she were friends." The businessman furrows his brow.

"We are competitive companions."

"Modern women in the United States rise above this empty, social-plantation mentality." Ezra folds his newspaper.

"Something on your mind, husband?"

"This paper is the *Anti-Slavery Bugle*. It reports a speech by an ex-slave during an Ohio women's rights convention in Akron. Her name was Sojourner Truth."

"What did she say?" Lisa captures the periodical.

"She demands equality. This former enslaved person combines abolitionism with female freedom."

"They tolerated her?"

"Those who believe labor earns fair treatment did."

"And that's where you wish me involved?" Lisa looks at her partner.

"No. I want you to find your own way." He pauses. "Your father and I are freedmen and your mother, Cherokee. Trouble comes to this Nation and to the United States. Sojourner Truth understood."

"Ezra, you scare me."

"Let me read what she said, 'That man over there says women need to be helped into carriages, and lifted over ditches, and to have the best place everywhere. Nobody helps me to any best place. Ain't I a woman?' Sojourner Truth, this slave-now-free, stands for the rights of human beings."

With her husband's words in mind, but in secret during the day, a gathering convenes in Lisa's parlor disguised as afternoon tea.

"I am supposed to be searching for an impressive cause." Lisa leans closer to Mary Stapler. "Ezra believes we become elitist."

"Men!" The wife of President John Ross squeezes her friend's hand. "They give us little credit for intelligence. My husband is different. He involves me. Too much. These petty squabbles between old timers and newcomers bore me."

Both women look up and greet a new guest.

"Moss! So pleased you could come." Lisa shows a chair. "Sit and have tea. Everyone should be here soon."

"Could I help serve, Ms. Waters?"

"No! I will do my hostess duty." Liza rises and curtsies.

The freedman chuckles.

"We cannot allow my hosting the first meeting of Tahlequah's Keetoowah Society to appear pro-slavery, even to our loyal members."

Several local women join the social.

"Especially with a speaker of your stature." Mary Stapler beams at Moss.

The talk progresses.

This small group of committed and dedicated Tahlequah attendees sip tea as the fiddler begins his appeal.

"Mrs. Ross and you distinguished representatives meet in secret. Why? Because pro-slavers, plantation owners, even a few of your husbands, hang those who endorse freedom. You might rot in jail, or worse, for your beliefs." The freedman surveys his audience.

The women listen with complete attention.

"For years, I and others provided shelter and guidance to escaped slaves en route to freedom. A few of you knew of this. Many of your affiliated groups aid our efforts. Thank you."

Approval murmurs throughout the assembly.

"The United States splits. So does the Cherokee Nation. There is talk of rebellion in the South. Factions in the North suspect secessionist southerners will provoke war and divide the union."

Tahlequah's Keetoowah Society concentrates on the fiddler's words.

Several women shift their weight and glance at others.

"Groups such as this create anti-slave-owner loyal leagues. Advocates call them Pin Indians."

Mixed approval changes to anticipation.

"My mission today is to encourage you to reconsider your ideals." Moss folds his hands together. "And form a new alignment with your eyes focused on the future."

Mary Stapler Ross clears her throat. "We chartered our society to support traditions, fight slave ownership, and assert the rights of the Cherokee people and our Nation under the laws and treaties that govern the United States. Even though I am not Indian, my husband is the Nation's leader. I cannot speak for the president, but I know him well. He owns slaves, but if the politics east of the Allegheny Mountains split into factions, he will be anti-slavery."

The members sit in silence as each woman considers her own ideals.

"The Keetoowah Society maintains the old ways." Lisa breaks the solemn atmosphere. "As a child, I knew a man of tradition. He was a shaman named Dideyohvsgi . He was raised with blood law. The practices he supported died in Georgia, as he did, in his beloved eastern mountains." She surveys her audience for approval. "I am only half-Cherokee, but this adventure sounds fun. I vote we become Pin Indians!"

***

Moments later, as the members cast ballots, Mary Ross leans closer to her hostess. "Someday, you know, Ezra will discover you are involved in this cause."

A woman officer announces the count.

"Ladies, the tally establishes Tahlequah's first Keetoowah Society is unanimous against slavery."

Polite applause welcomes the conclusion, but many women hold their breath.

The vote counter nods her approval. "But to become Pins, the total is nine to one against the motion."

Moss leans to Lisa. "Thanks for trying."

His employer's wife furrows her eyebrows.

The freedman pats her shoulder. "Pin ideals don't fit your personality, no matter how much excitement they offer."

***

As months progress, Lisa's husband's wealth buys status through philanthropy, including a seat on the Cherokee Female Seminary dais for its inaugural celebration.

The event begins a mile north of her ally and social competitor's residence at Park Hill.

Both women enjoy prominent exposure as the president addresses gathered dignitaries.

"Yesterday, May 6th, we opened our school for men." Ross scans a crowd of attendees and points into the distance.

In the woods, a massive public building of brick and stone two and partially three floors high features columns on multiple sides.

Four miles distant, another houses the Male Seminary.

The crowd welcomes opening day for the female school.

Chairs line the portico, and the president stands behind a speaker's podium.

Mary Stapler Ross and Lisa sit together in the second row with other dignitaries, including many members of the Nation's council.

The crowd of attendees applauds with polite restraint.

"Today, we extend educational opportunity to our outstanding women." The speaker nods his head and seeks approval.

The applause gains enthusiasm.

"Miss Chapin, principal of Mount Holyoke Female Seminary at South Hadley, Massachusetts, designed our curriculum."

Several attendees stand.

"We offer algebra, botany, grammar, geography, and arithmetic, not to exclude Latin and vocal music."

Mary leans closer to Lisa. "John drones on today. Did you hear what the scholars did to the new administrator?"

"No, what happened?"

"She's from Holyoke. The morning after she arrived, Miss Whitmore woke to a greeting from our pupils costumed, painted, and feathered as wild plains Comanches. They say she reacted scared, out of her wits!" Both women cover their amusement with embroidered hankies.

"Wasn't last night wonderful?" Lisa covers her mouth so only her companion hears.

Mary Stapler leans to listen.

"The dance in the men's hall and parlor was exquisite. The Fort Gibson musicians were glorious!"

"Gorgeous, thanks to you for those azaleas and bush honeysuckle arrangements." Mrs. Ross pats her friend's gloved hand.

Ezra's wife conceals another laugh. "And General Belknap and Fort Gibson for the band. Remember that tall and lanky general at my party? This officer replaced him as my attorney predicted."

"Your husband's as big a celebrity as mine." Mary pretends attention to John Ross's speech. "How is Ezra?"

"Disgruntled. Judge Steel needs him in Fort Smith for a few weeks. Wants him to try a political case. Do you recall that short, stocky fellow at my reel that slipped away without shaking hands with your husband?"

"Yes, Standhope Watie." Mrs. Ross turns her awareness to her friend. "John hates him."

"They have charged him with murder. Judge Steel needs my lawyer to prosecute."

"The Treaty Party will blame the president." His wife watches her spouse with no focus on his speech. "I'm not sure you want Ezra to be identified against them."

"Or me?" Lisa claps her hands. "*The Advocate* asked me to cover the trial. They say it's old timers against new arrivals. I agreed."

"You didn't?" Mary Ross's eyes widen with amazement. "Dangerous, but that means you get to go with your prosecutor to Fort Smith."

"Yes, I'm so excited. While he's in a dreary courtroom, I can shop the recent fashions from Boston!"

34

# CHAPTER FOUR — Watie

## ᎠᎡᎢᎠᎣ'ᎢᏍᎣᏖᏯᎠᎫᎬᏖᏯᎠᎲᎷᏫᏍᎷᎬᎷᎠᏖᎣᎯᎲᎫᏯᎡᏖᎡᏂᎻᏃᎠᎣ

Judge Bennett Steel hears testimony in United States Federal
Court, Fort Smith, Arkansas.

In solemn black robes, the judiciary of the Forty-Second Circuit
Court listens to opening statements delivered by his protégé and
business partner, Ezra Waters, attorney-at-law.

"The state presumes the killing of James Foreman will not
be denied." The prosecutor leans against the decorative rail that
encloses the jury.

With both hands tight on the wood, he leans forward for
emphasis. "We are aware of the high character that Standhope Watie
bears in the community and the deep sympathy manifested in his
behalf."

The accused sits with his newly returned from an Eastern
law school attorney nephew, Elias Cornelius Boudinot, son of the
murdered Cherokee leader, Elias Boudinot, Senior.

The defendant's eyes focus on the prosecutor's lips and words.
Hatred permeates the man's stare, and he does not blink.

"You jurors have a high duty." The prosecutor nods to the
twelve tribal men in the jury box. "With your solemn oath governed
by law and evidence, you must decide the fate of the accused from
the case's merits and not public opinion."

Several attendees seated near Lisa jump to their feet, and their cheers fade with Judge Steel's gavel.

Mrs. Waters, *The Advocate* reporter, scoots further away on her bench from an enthusiastic clapper.

Boudinot rises and pats his uncle's shoulder.

He turns to the jurors. "The prosecuting lawyer stated the degrees of homicide."

The nephew spreads his arms. "We do not deny the killing of James Foreman."

Ezra glances at Lisa, who, with her head lowered, sketches a fresh-from-Philadelphia hoop dress on her notepad.

"Justification is our defense." The attorney nods at his uncle.

The opposition nods understanding.

"We will prove that on the 29th of June, 1839," the lawyer smiles with satisfaction, "the notorious John Ross and a band of wicked conspirators whose names are a disgrace to humanity conceived a diabolical plot to murder, in a base and cowardly manner, the best friends of the Cherokee Nation."

Most of the courtroom's occupants erupt with cheers and applause.

"Officers!" Judge Steel pounds his elevated platform. "Empty the room!" As officials herd disruptors to exit doors, the bench notices Lisa. "Except for members of the press."

The defense waits with Watie as the court empties, then turns to the jury. "In pursuance of their infamous designs, on the morning of June 22nd, assassins took the lives of Major Ridge, Elias Boudinot, and John Ridge. The prisoner at the bar only escaped by prompt notice and his superior courage."

Ezra and his clerk listen to Boudinot from the prosecution's desk.

"On that day and the next, several hundred Ross proxies gathered. They received Ross's reward and protection for their brutal outrages, for acts creating Christian widows."

The defense attorney points at Standhope Watie. "They disposed this man and his old settler followers, their chiefs and the best blood of their tribe, to sustain the tottering power of its President!"

Groans from the press attract the speaker's attention.

He directs his words to the public through their printed stories. "Those activities continue to disgrace the Cherokee from then until today."

Lisa stares at the defendant.

The leader on trial turns, notices her attention, purses his lips, and winks in return.

"Not satisfied with declaring this hero an outlaw, we intend to prove they tracked him, waylaid this famous champion of the people, and made every try to take his life until James Foreman, the Major Ross conspirator, was slain."

The nephew pauses and allows the jury time to digest this claim.

"This is a case where a man acted in self-defense—this defendant was that individual!"

Murmurs ripple through the courtroom, and a muffled voice from the rear floats forward. "Justice is mine, sayeth the Lord!"

The comment pierces Judge Steel's decorum.

He pounds his gavel. "Quiet! The defense needs no discussion from the well. Continue please, Boudinot."

"Thank you, your honor." The young defense attorney sits. "Gentlemen of the jury, this case is simple. This great leader of our people defended himself." The nephew nods conclusion to the bench.

"Mr. Waters. Call you first witness." Judge Steel settles in his chair.

"The prosecution calls J. P. Miller." Ezra turns and watches a ruffian-dressed, full blood step to the stand.

Moments later, eyewitness testimony fills the courtroom.

"Watie, his brother John, and I were traveling from Honey Creek in the Nation and stopped for a drink in England's Grocery Store. James Foreman picked up the prisoner's mug, drank, and motioned. 'Here's wishing you live forever.' He handed the glass back empty."

"What did the defendant do?" The prosecutor looks at the jury.

"He smiled and looked the insult in the eye. 'Jim,' he says, 'I figure I can drink with you, but I understand a few days ago, you were going to kill me.' Foreman spits on my friend's boot and tells him plain, 'If you say!' Then the fight started. Watie slings his glass at Foreman's chest. He straightens from the bar with a whip in his hand. The two struggle for the weapon and crash through the door. Outside, Foreman grabs a plank."

"A board? From where?" Ezra stops the witness.

"A pile by the entrance." Miller shifts his weight in the chair with the break in his thought. "England's Grocery was fixing a window. That's when Foreman got sliced. I didn't see the knife until Watie slid off his horse. Jim stumbled a few paces in pain. He says, 'You ain't done it yet.' So, Stand pulled his Patterson Colt and fired."

"Then what happened?" Ezra stares at the defendant.

The man on trial watches the well reporters. He glances at the opposition and returns his stare to Lisa.

"It was over." Miller chuckles. "Jim walked across the field a hundred yards, then fell over a fence and died."

"When Foreman picked up the board, did he threaten with it?" The prosecution stands by the jury box.

"No. He only held it."

"What part of his body was stabbed?" The questioner steps near the witness.

"I saw the blood. On the back."

"But you did not see the knife. Did I understand you?" Ezra leans closer.

"Because Jim was looking at me."

"Or was he facing you?"

"That's right."

Waters pauses and peers at the jury box. "And you were on England's porch? Was James Foreman returning?"

Miller glances across the room at Standhope Watie.

"I don't think so. He was a John Ross man, searching for prey. Tough fellow, a paid assassin, everyone says."

Judge Steel demands fairness and interrupts.

"Strike that last comment from the record. Its speculation and hearsay."

Ezra calls several other witnesses who testify to Watie's violent nature and history.

Testimony presents the plantation proprietor as a prominent, rough, well-armed slave owner and fervent chaser of runners, accustomed to violence.

The defendant's service as a captain in the Lighthorse, and as a member of the Cherokee Council, enter the record, despite Ezra's resistance.

Lisa sits enthralled by the contrast.

The prosecution politically aligns with Georgia's recent arrivals headed by John Ross.

They confront established New Echota signees and old settlers.

Elias Cornelius Boudinot begins the defense.

He calls B. Nicholson.

"A few days before the death of James Foreman, a large armed group came to Maysville. Jim led and claimed they searched for Watie. He said Stand threatened his life, and he brought the men to put him out of the way."

"Did he say why they intended to kill?" The nephew stands beside his uncle.

"Yes." The witness stares at the defendant, who smiles and nods his head. "He was along when they murdered old Major Ridge and knew Stand's desire for revenge.

"Do you know of other threats James Foreman presented?" The defendant's advocate walks closer to the box.

"I do." B. Nicholson leans forward. "That assassin killed at least two men. He carried violent feelings toward the Treaty Party. When the order to arrest the killers of Major Ridge and your father was issued, he fled and demanded shelter at my house."

As the man completes his words and returns to the well, Elias Boudinot turns to Judge Steel. "The defense enters evidence. We submit the report of the United States Secretary of War and the Indian Commissioner of Twenty-five November, 1839."

He lays a sheaf of papers on the bench.

"This, along with its supporting documents, concludes that Mr. John Ross conspired with others to take away the lives of prominent men of the Treaty Party, namely Standhope Watie!"

Ezra leaps to his feet. "I object to this evidence!"

He looks to the bench. "How can proceedings of Indian councils be testimony in federal court?"

Boudinot strides toward the bench. "These offer public history to the country! These documents communicated to officials of the United States by the conspirators under the seal of the war office. They describe the danger the Treaty Party faced from John Ross and his partisans!"

Judge Steel looks at Ezra. "Gentlemen, this trial is in recess while I review precedents. Will both attorneys join me in my chambers?"

***

With most of his magistrates and the jury out of the courtroom, Lisa sits alone with the press.

Standhope Watie stands and speaks to his guard. He holds a palm over his mouth for privacy. "That woman in the reporter's section is my niece. Can I say hello?"

The prisoner's escort hand shackles Watie's wrist to his own and nods permission.

The defendant steps to Lisa and leans forward as she withdraws from his pungent breath. "I'm watching you, Mrs. Waters, and dreaming of poking you and sweet Mary Ross someday."

The law officer yanks Watie away, "Shut up! That woman ain't your niece! Sorry, Miss."

***

Moments later, the press section and others stand as Judge Steel reenters the courtroom and resumes the trial.

"By precedent, this evidence is admissible."

The magistrate looks at his protégé. "Proceed, please."

Ezra stands. "The prosecution concedes danger to the Treaty Party."

The speaker glances at the defendant. "We concede the report by James Arbuckle, the Commandant of Fort Gibson."

Judge Steel looks at his jury. "That document named Foreman as one of Major Ridge's and Elias Boudinot's murderers."

Murmurs ripple through the courtroom, and the defendant smiles with satisfaction.

***

Later, the defense attorney addresses the jury with concluding remarks, "Gentlemen, I leave this matter with you. I trust this man's life into your hands with perfect confidence."

Lisa, Ezra, and the others listen to the nephew of Standhope Watie as he stands beside his uncle with one hand upon the defendant's shoulder.

"But the prisoner wishes and expects me to speak in his favor. He has that right. I embrace the opportunity."

Judge Steel, experienced in summations, settles into his chair.

"As this gallant deed, this justifiable homicide, becomes known to the general citizen, a sympathetic public will rise and manifest horror toward John Ross's murderous scheming and gory assassins."

Supporters outside the walls yell favorably, and their catcalls penetrate the proceedings.

"You may save the innocent person present with us from the sins of the forever departed."

Elias Boudinot, with passion and fervor, continues the arguments of his case.

"Europeans and Asiatics have been enslaved," the attorney concludes. "Africans are born for slavery, so tamely do they wear the chain. But the Cherokee Indian—now before you overcome by superior force, worn out of his native soil, rooted from the earth, and annihilated—but subjugated, never! Uncle, I turn to you. In a few moments, by a most intelligent and Christian jury, you must stand acquitted." Elias Boudinot freezes in silence and allows his cumulative words to impact the tribunal, then sits.

Judge Steel nods at Ezra.

The prosecutor begins his summation. "I cannot undertake imitating the vain eloquence of the last gentleman. He speaks of everything but the case. Was he defending Standhope Watie or prosecuting John Ross? He carries us from the lowest values to the third heaven. Gentlemen, you are governed by law and evidence, not by popular excitement."

Several hoots and catcalls from the audience outside the courtroom penetrate the room.

"You are to decide a single question." Ezra ignores the distraction and points at the defendant. "Was there a present necessity for him to kill James Foreman?"

Lisa catches her husband's eye and smiles encouragement.

The prosecutor looks at the jurors. "If you believe such a condition existed, no one will subscribe to an acquittal more than myself. If not convinced, no matter how painful the task becomes, you must pronounce a verdict of guilty."

As Ezra returns to his seat, Judge Steel instructs the jury. "Gentlemen, the law of self-defense is summed up in a few words. If you, from the evidence, construe that Standhope Watie had reason to apprehend that his life stood in immediate danger from James Foreman, or that he suffered pressing threat of bodily harm, you are bound to acquit. If you retain a reasonable doubt of the prisoner's guilt, you must weigh in his favor. Please retire and consider your verdict."

Ezra steps closer to the bench as the jurors file out of their box for deliberations.

He covers his lips for privacy. "They look Treaty Party, Judge."

Steel nods. "His Eastern legal school nephew said, 'the sympathetic will rise and manifest horror toward John Ross's murderous scheming and gory assassins.'"

Both eye the last juror as he exits.

The judge conceals his mouth. "I fear truth and the rule of law may be buried under the weight of public opinion."

As the participants and press representatives within the courtroom gather their belongings, Lisa hugs Ezra. "I'm glad that horrible man's fate is with his peers and not me."

Her husband grips her hand. "Not I. You are more than just."

As the married couple moves to the courtroom's exit, the bailiff bounces into the room from the jury's door and surprises the departing. "Judge Steel! Sir, they have a verdict."

***

Moments later, the foreman of the jury reads the decision, "Not guilty!"

Pandemonium shakes the hall outside as supporters celebrate.

Elias Cornelius Boudinot steps near Ezra. "You lost, you uppity nigger."

Lisa's husband shoves the young defense attorney to arm's distance and stares at Standhope Watie.

The leader of the old settlers spits on Ezra's boot. "We're coming for you, your slave sympathizing judge, and John Ross. If I had my Patterson, I'd beat the two of you senseless and send you both to hell."

## CHAPTER FIVE — Fort Gibson

ᎡᏗᏓᎧᎣᎢᏍᎤᏞᎩᎠᎫᎬᏇᏖᎠᎢᎦᏍᏬᏓᎦᏕᎷᎻᎯᏝᎣᏘᎲᏚᏍᏯᎾᏓᎨᎿᎢᏃᏀᎤᏫ

Moss meets his bosses at the front entrance to their
home upon their return to Tahlequah. "Mr. Ezra! You made the
newspapers with that mess in Fort Smith." The fiddler carries a rifle.

"I'd call it a travesty." The attorney climbs from his carriage and
offers Lisa help.

"No matter what you hail it, that verdict's causing trouble
around these parts." The freedman holds the horses so that the
wheels stay still.

Mrs. Waters slips to the ground. "What happened?"

"The not guilty verdict stirred up the old settlers. The Treaty
Party burned a straw dummy of John Ross in the middle of town
two midnights ago. I have been staying evenings in your place just
to make sure nobody burns your house."

"This scares me. I want to live in peace and enjoy our life." Lisa
turns to her husband. "Do you think we're safe?"

"I don't know." Ezra looks at his Tahlequah home. "Judge Steel
suggested we go to Fort Gibson until this blows away."

"Take me with you." The freedman pats the weapon slung over
his shoulder. "An extra-long gun might help."

"More than that. You and I both need to learn how to defend
ourselves. Times are changing. Too many guns and not enough
law. The professional teachers are army." The husband slips an arm

around his wife. "Lisa, we gather what we need and leave in the morning."

"And take Moss with us?"

"Yes. With that rifle."

"This gun's becoming part of my being, Mr. Waters, as my fiddle."

***

Thirty miles southwest of Tahlequah, at the convergence of the Arkansas, Verdigris, and Grand Rivers south of the Ozark Plateau, Fort Gibson controls river navigation.

This stockade outpost on the Texas Road from Missouri to Mexico, established to keep peace between the Cherokees and the Osages, evolved into prominence during the Indian removals.

As Lisa and Ezra seek refuge from the turmoil in Tahlequah, the fort maintains law and order commanded by Captain Braxton Bragg, Company C of the United States Third Artillery.

The couple waits in the commander's office. "This officer placed his battery into a line gap which beat the Mexicans at Buena Vista."

Ezra leans near Lisa. "In support of Jefferson Davis and the Mississippi Rifles."

"The Secretary of War?"

His spouse pays attention. "How interesting."

The room's door swings open.

A commander strides in, flanked by an adjutant.

"The same." Husband glances at wife as he rises to his feet.

Captain Bragg, a future Confederate general prominent at Shiloh, nods to the woman and extends a hand of greeting to her partner. "Good day, sir. Please pardon my tardiness. Colonel Albert Sidney Johnston and the Second Cavalry arrived from Saint Louis. I was arranging their quarters."

Ezra grasps the soldier's palm and stares into eyes that peer from dark hair and a full beard. "The unit just formed by Congress? That explains the noise."

"Much action for this quiet western post. Johnston rests his horses and men. They travel to Fort Belknap in Texas to police that country against Indians." The commander pauses as he gazes at Lisa. "Not Cherokees, wild ones on the frontier."

The wife shuffles in her chair.

"Mr. Waters. I received a letter from Judge Steel in Fort Smith. He suggests you and your spouse need refuge from the turmoil of Cherokee politics. Is that correct?"

"It is, sir. He and I align with President Ross and the new arrivals. Treaty Party old settlers threaten to burn our house and exact vengeance for my prosecution of Standhope Watie."

"I read in the paper that he was not guilty?"

"The jury so concluded. But that did not pacify his followers. They ravage the Nation to avenge the murders of Major Ridge and Elias Boudinot."

"Steel is a federal magistrate. I will honor your request." Bragg leans back in his chair. "You may take refuge in our walls as long as you consider necessary."

"Thank you."

The commander bends forward. "My duty is to inform you the winds of change sweep the Indian Nation as it does my own United States. The correspondence indicates you are a freedman and a business partner. I respect that status, but others may not. I recommend extreme care."

The office entrance sweeps open, and several dusty Calvary men interrupt.

"Excuse us, Captain Bragg. No one guards the door." A higher ranked officer removes his hat with a flourish toward the couple. "We were not aware you were busy."

The fort's commander snaps to attention and salutes. "We are concluding, Colonel Lee."

Lisa observes the West Point graduate's polish and natural aura of authority.

The commandant of lesser rank turns to the husband and wife. "Allow me to introduce the officers of the Second Calvary; Johnston's second-in-command, Colonel Robert E. Lee; Majors J. E. B. Stuart, and George H. Thomas; Captain Edmund Kirby Smith; and Lieutenant John B. Hood."

The attorney stands and clicks his heels together. "Gentlemen. We wish you the best in Texas."

***

Days later, Lisa rocks in a chair on the porch of the married officers' quarters outside the Fort Gibson stockade, and in the dawn's light, watches the Second Calvary parade, a formal departure for Fort Belknap.

Moss sits on the ground with his back against a post.

"Look at that precision. Magnificent men and horsemanship. A sight, don't you think?"

"Yes ma'am. Until you realize they go to kill Indians who don't know they're coming."

Lisa remains in silence for a moment and considers the freed-man's words. Her interest in the parade fades. She changes the subject. "How are your shooting lessons going?"

"Mr. Ezra hired a genuine expert to teach me." Moss pauses and looks up at his employer. "A scout employed by the fort."

"An old settler?"

"No. He came from Georgia. Says his name is Frogger. He fought in the Second Seminole War. Claims he's a half-son of Billy Bowlegs, who had two wives. I'm not sure which one is his mother."

"Oh, my goodness. How does Ezra find these people?"

"Same way he found me, I expect." Moss stares at the Calvary but coughs with the dust. "With respect and kindness."

"I wish I had my husband's mind." Lisa fans her nose with her hand.

"He's a special fellow, Mrs. Waters, but shooting lessons ain't everything the man tells me."

"What else?"

"I should have told you, but I was hoping Mr. Ezra would be here."

"What do you need to tell him?

"Bowlegs was in Tahlequah a couple days ago. A mob of old timers torched your place. Burned it to the ground." Moss pauses and studies Lisa's reaction. "Standhope Watie organized the whole thing."

Lisa sits in silence as the dawn's light glints off tears in both eyes.

"Things are more important in life than a big residence and people who dance to your fiddle. Don't you worry. I'll tell my husband."

***

At midday, the pair visit the post's store, a small one-room space tucked near a stockade guard house. A large hand-painted sign above its door reads, "Groceries—Provisions."

The woman pauses and peers across the fort's yard at the dragoon guardhouse. "My goodness. Look at that young man."

With a board roped to his neck marked "Whiskey Seller" and a heavy pack on his back, an offender stands on the top of a cask with an empty liquor bottle in each hand extended at arm's length.

Two soldier guards play cards on a second barrel nearby.

"The army's trying to control drunkenness." Ezra glances at the guardhouse.

"They should close those alcohol shanties in the woods," Lisa stares at the sweating in the sun trooper and continues, "not torture somebody's child."

"Soldiers keep the brothels profitable." Husband opens the store's entrance.

Wife smiles at her partner as she enters the establishment.

Inside, the first counter features firearms surrounded by baskets of produce.

"Acorn squash!" Ezra's partner inspects a gourd. "We have brown sugar. Let's have fresh vegetables for dinner tonight." Her eyes glance at the weapons for sale and fixate upon one gun.

A small hand-printed sign reads, "Patterson 5-round Texas model."

With a polished wooden grip, the fourteen-inch-long pistol features a cylinder before a single-action hammer with a hexagonal seven-and-a-half-inch barrel.

"Ezra?"

At the tone of his wife's voice, the freedman turns his attention to her gaze.

"Is that the one that killed my sister?"

Her husband steps closer. "Yes, similar. That's what witnesses and Moss said."

"They told me he beat her to death with it." Lisa's words quiver.

The man notices his spouse's hands shake. "Come. Let's pay for our things and leave."

"And walk by that poor boy on the barrel?" Lisa breaks her fascination with the weapon. "The entire world hurts. I wish I could just listen to Moss's fiddle and dance this cruelty into history, but I can't, can I, Ezra?"

"Soon. We will move off this post to a better life, I promise." Husband hugs his partner.

***

Several days later, the two waken to a soldier's warning late at night.

He pounds on the door of their constructed quarters. "Inside the stockade! By order of Captain Bragg!"

"Your robe." The groggy husband hands her the garment, stomps on his boots, and holds a curtain to peer out the window.

In the darkness, soldiers rush from cabin to barrack rooms and wake occupants.

Several sleepy residents stumble toward the fort's barricades.

"Leave everything, dear. No time. Something's happening." Husband opens their cabin's door and looks.

A private with an army issued rifle stops beyond the porch's planks. "Personnel, including civilians, inside the walls! We expect an attack."

"By whom, soldier?" Ezra takes Lisa's arm.

"Don't know, sir." The young man checks his weapon. "Comanches maybe? My orders are to get everyone to safety."

"No hostiles this far east. Must be someone else. Watch your step, honey." Spouse extends a hand.

With her husband gripped for comfort and security, Lisa steps off the porch and joins others moving toward the fort's open gate.

***

Within the secure palisade, Mrs. Waters sits in a wood rocker on an elevated and covered boardwalk that stretches around the compound's interior.

An extended roof shades the soldier's quarters, rooms, and offices from the intense territorial sun. This night, it offers a cover and a sense of security.

Ezra drops to a seat beside his wife, and both watch the activities in the compound.

The last few stragglers, civilians herded by soldiers, flow into the fort followed by a herd of army mounts controlled by Cherokee scouts.

As the animals pass the gate, troopers roll two twelve-pound cannons from the center of the enclosure into the opening.

Other dragoons turn wagons over on both sides of the cannon to block the post's entry. Men with rifles use their wood plank beds as a protective wall and wait. Anxious eyes peer into the dark, but nothing moves.

The dirt road into the fort extends from the artillery past the other buildings outside the stockade and disappears into woods.

From the trees' depths, muffled and distant voices carry to Fort Gibson in the still air.

The flames of a large fire rise above the treetops.

As Lisa and Ezra watch, torchlights glow deep in the forest, and angry cries gain clarity as they move closer.

An armed mob, with many participants on horseback, ford the Neosho River between the safety of the walls and the woods.

Captain Bragg joins his troops at the gate's barricade. "These demonstrators carry arms. No one fires upon this threat unless I command! We will not start this fight!" The fort's commander steps past the cannon and the defensive wagons and walks several paces in front.

Treaty Party members, full bloods of varying status, many in farmworker garb and others in black boots and plantation hats, follow their leader toward the gate. Many carry torches that light the night. Most have pistols strapped to their waists. Others tote rifles, and a few flourish pitchforks.

Several veteran Cherokee Lighthorse mix with the assemblage.

The group's voices swell, "Close this abomination!"

Standhope Watie, on horseback at the head of the mob with two Colt Patterson revolvers on his hips, rides toward the stockade.

The large group's participants behind the leader carry bed linens painted with bold letters. "No more shanty towns!"

Another reads, "Fort Gibson—den of drunks!"

Captain Bragg raises his right hand. "That is close enough. I know you, Mr. Watie. Do you speak for this mob?"

"I do."

"This is after hours. My post is closed. You may secure an appointment. Meet with me tomorrow in the light of day if you wish. Now, take your people and disperse."

"You see those flames in the woods?"

"I do, sir."

"That is Shanty Town burning. Why? You and your soldiers pollute Cherokee lands with whiskey and prostitution. My folk tire of the debauchery. We come to burn this pestilence to the ground!"

Lisa leans to her husband. "That man intends us harm."

"That may be the real reason he's here." Ezra pulls the blanket around his wife's shivering shoulders. "Watie likes his liquor and loose women."

"I realize you are a member of the Cherokee council. Many of your men are Lighthorse. I know you are aware officers and soldiers of the United States of America sworn to defend property and lives staff this post." Bragg draws his sword. "You will not burn these walls, and you must disperse. Lieutenant, prepare the cannon! Riflemen, ready!"

Watie turns his horse to face his mob. "This man's artillery turned the tide at Buena Vista for Colonel Jefferson Davis and his Mississippi Rifles! A few of you were there when the Mexican Army attacked his battery. I am not such a fool. Disband, men!"

Rumbles of protest roll through the crowd. Someone cups a hand around his mouth. "Two pieces ain't turning us into cowards!"

"Twelve pounders loaded with grapeshot!" Captain Bragg raises his sword. "Prepare to fire!"

"Go home, boys!" Watie waves a Patterson Colt toward the road into the woods. "We burned their shanties and whiskey. That's enough for one night."

# CHAPTER SIX — Threat

DRᎦᎣꞋꙆᏚᎣᏇᏴᎩᎪᎴᎥᏘᎪᎲᏎᏫᏗᏒᎬᎷᎿᏍᎤᏴᎯᏚᎩᎾᏸᎾᏂᏃᏇᎤꝸ

An hour's ride from the Verdigris, the Neosho presents its water. Across a river ford, four corner blockhouses connect wood palisades that sit with its entries controlled by heavy wooden gates.

Stables rest on a hill nearby.

A campus outside the fort with barracks for dragoons and a lookout post elevate above the tributary where officer quarters, a chapel, and a schoolhouse shine with new whitewash.

Beneath trees and shrubs, a small cemetery lies in peace.

Gibson's main gate, manned by two sentries, remains open daily.

A general store with an entrance to Cherokee land and one within the palisades functions as part of the stockade wall.

Outside, many customers' horses and wagons stand tied while their owners barter.

Lisa, day-dressed and toting a parasol for sun protection, steps from the porch of her new log cabin quarters.

Moss offers his hand to aid. "Morning, Mrs. Waters."

A distant steam whistle announces a steamboat on the Arkansas River.

"It is nice weather. Ezra told me I need an escort. I believe it's unnecessary."

"Maybe. After that Treaty Party debacle the other night, he wants security."

"I don't want to remember. My friend Mary Stapler Ross arrives for a visit. You will recognize her?"

"Of course. Who's going to forget the wife of the president of the Cherokee Nation?"

"Well, she's arriving on that steamboat."

"Still way downriver. Hasn't passed the bar."

In the distance, a deck signal gun booms.

"Now it has. That gun signals as they entered the Grand River." The fiddler walks with his charge to a waiting, new fresh-air Landau carriage pulled by a matched pair of Clydesdales. "Mrs. Ross is going to admire this." He opens its side entrance door.

"Let's hurry. I want Mary to see it on the landing." Its owner beams as she settles into the stuffed rear comfort.

Her driver climbs into his place and grasps the team's reins. He shifts the barrel of a holstered pistol strapped to his waist from under his leg.

His passenger notices the cartridge belt. "That's very inhospitable to Mrs. Ross."

The chauffeur guard clicks the two Clydesdales into movement. "Mr. Ezra pays me to carry it. I am much more comfortable now that I know how to use it."

***

At the river, a shelving layer of rock provides a natural dock.

Lisa's carriage approaches.

Several officers from Fort Gibson wait for the riverboat along with a crowd of soldiers, families, merchants, friends of incoming or outgoing passengers, sutlers waiting for merchandise, and assorted bystanders.

The bottom near the landing's low, fertile soil, cleared of canebrake, trees, vines, and underbrush by the fort's founder years before, extends to the dock.

This day, as other days that await a steamboat's arrival, the landing bustles with excitement.

The fort offers gaiety and society to a large section of the country and the Cherokee Nation.

Young women of the tribe mix with soldiers and officers of the post, and budding romances between couples waiting at the landing add a festive atmosphere to the group.

Older troops married to Indian wives and their families mingle in the crowd, contented and prosperous from their nuptial alliances.

Lisa and Moss sit in their carriage and gaze downriver as exhaust of the steamboat's engines announces its arrival.

"Exciting, isn't it?"

"Sure is, Mrs. Waters. This is a fine landing. It's the only dock with access to the interior of the Nation."

"My mother's people have been agitating for years to remove this post. They want this place for Cherokee use."

"Makes sense to me." The driver turns the carriage to offer Lisa a better view. "The frontier's moved into the plains. To Fort Dalton and places more useful to the military."

"Ezra and the infantry planners call that strategic."

The crowd's excitement rises as the steamboat jangles her bell and ties to the dock.

Two ramps drop, and passengers jostle to come ashore.

Several young officers from West Point and recruits to fill vacancies in the troops descend the ramp.

They mix with returning neighborhood merchants who carry fresh goods they traded in eastern exchanges for furs and skins.

A second slope unloads newspapers, crates of bonnets, dresses, and finery for the ladies at the fort. Deckhands and soldiers unload boxes of military freight.

Mary Stapler Ross waves from the steamboat's rail.

Lisa stands and swings her parasol in recognition.

Two burly, rough-hewn men with pistols and rifles go with the first lady, one on each side.

Moss guides the Clydesdales closer to the passenger ramp, and the president's wife rushes to meet her friend.

The fiddler helps the arrival into the rear.

"It's so good to see you. Delighted you came." Lisa makes room for her old ally.

"So am I!" Mary grasps Lisa's hands. "My parent's home was exile. I'm so glad to be back. John sent for me at last. I haven't seen home in months!"

"Fort Gibson's not Park Hill, but we're safe. Ezra and I have a log cabin. The place is charming and quaint, but not extravagant."

"My husband told me. It is kind for you to let me stay a few weeks."

The two rough Cherokee bodyguards stand at the carriage's wheels. and their eyes dart across the assembled crowd.

Lisa notices their vigilance. "Gentlemen, no one knows the wife of the president arrives. It's an exciting secret. Come. Ride with us back to the post."

As Moss flips the reins and the carriage moves away from the landing, Mary Ross clears her voice. "You haven't heard. They assassinated Judge Steel."

Lisa's vocal tone trembles. "Ezra doesn't know."

"Night before last. They shot him on the streets of Fort Smith as he walked home from court."

"They?"

"Old settlers, thugs, hired assassins, Treaty Party radicals— who knows for sure? They are the same." Mary grasps her friend's hand. "But I realize this post is safe. The United States government guaranteed John, and he arrives tomorrow."

"I fear for Ezra. He went upriver to check a cotton shipment at one of his warehouses." Lisa grips the first ladies' palm. "But I expect him back this afternoon."

Moss turns his head. "Don't worry about your husband. If something happened, we would know."

Mary Ross squeezes Lisa's fingers with confidence. "Things aren't that terrible. John told me our Cherokee agent sent a glowing report to the Commissioner of Indian Affairs. He reported our population as over 21,000, with 102,000 acres of crops. Fifteen hundred pupils attend school with native teachers."

"Thanks to you and your husband." Lisa nods agreement.

"And to generous donors such as you and Ezra." Mary looks at her two guards. "But I have security. John's people split worse than the north and south."

Moss pulls the team to the porch of Lisa's cabin. "War clouds in the United States are too heavy to float themselves over the Arkansas, I figure."

"I think you're right." Lisa accepts his hand in support as she steps from the carriage.

The fiddler helps Mary Ross descend and climbs aboard the front to grasp the Clydesdales' reins. "Be back. These men need mounts from the army. They have orders to join the president and escort him into the palisade."

"We're safe, Moss. Go. No one's going to make trouble near the stockade." His boss steps onto her porch. "Mary and I need to talk fun instead of politics."

***

John Ross arrives with Mary's hired guards as the sun sets.

After dinner, the Nation's leader, his wife, Lisa, and Ezra sip coffee in the living room.

"Our quarters are nothing comparable to Park Hill, Mr. President." The hostess rocks in her chair.

"Our home is opulent, thanks to my beloved." The tall dignitary nods. "But even with my security men, not as safe as Fort Gibson."

"Thanks for a respite." Mrs. Waters beams at her lawyer husband.

"Yes, for safety." John looks at the attorney freedman. "This stockade's time is gone. The council met in Tahlequah to protest this place. And they are right. I agree with them. The post is secure. But this country around is ripe with whiskey peddlers."

"Watie and old settlers attempted to force that issue." Ezra points at the president. "The post rolled out its cannon."

"Put a stop to that, I expect." John chuckles. "Lawful means are the only acceptable recourse. We petitioned the United States to do away with the post."

"Which costs us our safe home." Lisa stares at the politician.

"We Cherokees could occupy and clean up the place." The president nods in return as he appreciates an antique urn upon the Waters' hearth.

"The Cherokee Temperance Society's happy." Mary Stapler looks at her friend.

The attorney agrees. "So's the Agricultural Association. They see apple, plum, pear, and peach orchards in these bottom lands."

Near the Nation's leader, the vase explodes from a bullet's impact. Glass flies near the fireplace as the boom of a rifle's discharge shakes the interior.

Ezra dives for his spouse, and his weight knocks her from her rocking chair to the floor.

A second blast of powder smoke from another opening bursts into the living room, and shattered window splatters Mary Ross's dress.

She screams and leaps to protect her husband, which flattens him behind an armchair.

The youngest Waters cringes into a fetal position as several more barrel explosions make visibility poor within the smoke-filled cabin.

Hazy air clears, and the woman sees Moss. He holds a Colt revolver in each hand. "I got them! Those two guards for Mrs. Ross. One at each window!"

"Anybody hit?" Ezra stands in the haze.

"I'm unharmed." The hostess rises to her knees. "Mary?"

"Shocked and terrified. They were after John!"

"This old man is fine. Arm's sore." The president holds his chair to help. "For seventy years, I duck well."

"Everyone, stay here. I'll check for others." Moss cracks the cabin's door and peeks out. He steps onto the porch as several dragoons from the fort under the command of a youthful lieutenant arrive.

"Where were you fellows a few minutes ago?" The fiddler holsters his pistols.

Waters joins the group. "Someone tried to assassinate the president. He's unhurt. They failed."

"You men spread out. Restrain anyone with firearms!" the officer commands, and his troops obey.

Moss walks, with Ezra behind him, around the cabin's corner to a shattered window.

On the ground, in misery but alive, one of the two guards paid to protect Mary Stapler squirms with a chest wound. Blood spurts from his ribs, and he babbles in intense anguish. "Shoot me! The pain!"

The freedman rams his boot's heel on the assassin's rib cage. "Who hired you?"

"Go to hell, Nigger!"

The fiddler pushes harder, and the injured screams. "My God, stop!"

The president joins the two as his protector stomps on the murderer's wound.

The man shrieks, "The Treaty Party! Standhope Watie's crowd!"

"Let him die." The Nation's leader grabs the freedman's arm. "No torture."

"And damned if he doesn't." Moss watches blood gurgle from the gunman's lips.

"I wish the lieutenant heard." Ezra looks for witnesses.

"A couple of freedmen's testimony won't fare well in Treaty Party court."

"Is that the assassin?" Lisa joins the group with Mary Stapler at her heels.

"No need for you, my dear." The attorney stops his spouse. "We have it under control."

"Oh no! That's my guard." The first lady covers her mouth.

"And mine." John embraces his wife. "Without Moss on alert, this would have ended with our blood."

"I'm doubling your pay." Ezra grasps the freedman's shoulder.

"I don't do this for the money."

"And we must hire you help. Times have changed."

"That they have. This fiddler feels I'm one of those Pinkerton railroad men."

"Good. But never lose your music." Lisa hugs her friend. "That keeps you human as the rest of us instead of dead as that evil on the ground."

63

# CHAPTER SEVEN — Shelter

**ᎠᎡᎢᎣᎤᎥᎦᎧᎨᎩᎪᎫᎬᎭᎮᎯᎰᎱᎲᎳᎴᎵᎶᎷᎸᎹᎺᎻᎼᎽᎾᎿᏀᏁᏂᏃᏄᏅ**

Frogger Bowlegs and Moss crouch together with backs against a reddish-purple spring flowering Redbud tree and rifles propped across their laps.

Their horses' trail reins and graze on a nearby green rise.

The two survey a small political gathering of new settlers where Ezra and John Ross, with their wives, sit in an open carriage parked in a valley.

"Why you so fond of them people, Moss?" Bowlegs chews a grass stem.

"They gave me work when there was none." The freedman watches his charges. "He's important. The man's a leader, an attorney. He's a self-made man with my skin color. A wonderful human."

"His wife's not of your kind. She's a Cherokee. That why they support Ross no matter what?" Frogger shifts his revolver pistol from under one leg for comfort.

"Don't convince yourself of that." Moss turns his gaze to the companion. "The lady's a good friend to Ross's wife. They believe in the same things."

"Such as holding slaves?" Bowlegs spits a brown mess of chewed tobacco away from the two, and the slime splatters the soil.

"Ross owns many, but not Ezra and Lisa. She says her father was against it and even owned her husband at one time." The freedman clears his throat. "They freed him when they lived in Georgia before the removal."

"At least they ain't White. I fought those types of soldiers in Florida, but they won. Hate them people. I only work for you now."

"You were scouting for their army before we hired you." Moss gazes at the Seminole.

"To buy food. Don't mean I liked it." Bowlegs spits another mouthful of slop to the ground. "Whites despise each other more than us. Southerners hate their own families up north, brothers, fathers, cousins. But I can't blame them. I loathe equally."

*** 

President John Ross, on his feet in his carriage at seventy years of age, looms tall above an assembly of local Cherokees and listens to one.

The man's voice rings above the noise. "Our lands lie west of Arkansas, south of Kansas, and north of Texas. We are on the highway there. And a supply depot if conflict comes. The United States battled our people for decades. It is time we stand against their attempts to dominate!"

John Ross spreads his arms. "No. The Cherokee fought that country's expansion for generations. Today, we keep quiet. Let the Whites settle their own affairs. They may resort to war. We stay neutral and grow and prosper in peace."

"While the Yankees take away our slaves?" A second voice rises in protest.

"I own workers and soon return to my beloved Park Hill. The United States does not want my field hands!"

"Most slave holders are old settlers, and most are half-breeds!"

A man shakes his fist in the air. "The rest of us poor full bloods work these valleys for food and our families!" The rear of the group stirs. "You plantation people don't speak for me!"

Lisa leans close. "John doesn't have the total support he once had."

"This slave business is dirty." The president eyes an angry audience.

Mary leans to her friend. "My husband does not agree with my Quaker ways, but he's neither north nor south. His Cherokee half is his entire soul."

The speaker motions palms to the ground for peace. "The ordained missionaries of the Presbyterian Board and most of our Indian agents support the southern point of view. I say they cannot sweep us into a choice, even as an act of faith. Most denominations urge me to advocate for them. No! I side with neither north nor south, nor Presbyterians or United States government representatives, but only for our people!"

The two wives smile at each other as most of the new arrivals attending the political gathering cheer their longtime leader.

Mary Stapler twists to a cough and pats her lips with a white handkerchief.

Spots of blood soil the cloth as Lisa watches her companion conceal the stain in the folds of her dress.

The first lady leans forward. "John and Ezra travel to speak with a group tomorrow. They won't be back for two days. Ask someone to saddle you a horse after dark. I have something to show you."

Her friend nods understanding and agreement with eyes that twinkle expected excitement.

***

That evening, fireflies blink in the shadows under the trees as Moss leads a couple of saddled horses to the front of the Waters' cabin.

His boss steps onto the porch in riding gear. "Two mounts? Mary will have her own."

"Mrs. Waters, with Ezra gone, do you think I let you and the president's wife ride out into the night without protection?"

"It's exciting." Lisa pats a revolver strapped around her waist. "Your lessons taught me how to use this new pistol. Don't spoil my fun."

"Have to, ma'am. You're just spoiled by a special husband. These days, life's not a big party. Ezra fires this guard if I let the two of you ride without me."

Mrs. Waters takes the reins of her horse. "I do not want you unemployed. But Mary Stapler may not allow you to come. Her plan is mysterious."

"Not so." The mentioned woman slows her mount to a halt. "Moss is most welcome. In fact, I can't believe I did not think to ask him to join us."

The freedman looks across the grass to the closed Fort Gibson gate. "We should get going. Soldiers just shut the entrance."

The president's wife leads her friends past the palisade and along the road.

Their horses splash through the stream below and climb up the next hill into the woods.

As the trio rides through a clearing where charred remnants of Shanty Town loom on both sides, Lisa eyes the shadows and shapes in the darkness. "I'm glad Watie burned this place."

"Whiskey and women peddlers find new customers."

Mary leads further into the timbers.

***

After a lengthy ride, Mrs. Waters notices a glow in the woods. "What's that out there?"

"Our meeting. We will be there soon." The leader urges her horse forward.

As the horsemen exit the forest into a clearing, Lisa's eyes widen.

In the center of a gathering, a bonfire's flames lift red sparks into the night air.

Hooded men and women in clumps talk and watch a flatbed wagon near the fire.

Mary withdraws cotton hoods from her saddlebag and hands them to her companions. "Wear these. This is a secret meeting."

Her friend drops a covering over her head as the three dismount and tie their horses to a tree. "What is this?"

"Moss knows. Don't you?"

The fiddler slips on his mask. "Keetoowahs. The largest gathering of the society I have seen."

As the group joins the crowd, Ezra's wife notices most of the attendees wear two pins in a cross on their coats and tote handguns and rifles.

"They have grown." The freedman walks to his employer. "They call them Pin Indians."

A lanky fellow climbs on the flatbed and removes his hood. "Friends and supporters. I remove my mask so you may know me. I am Evan Jones, a White man from the Pleasant Hill Mission. You realize I am an individual of faith, so I ask you to bow your heads in prayer."

"He kept Pleasant Hill going after Jesse Bushyhead died. That's Evan's son by the wheel." Mary nods and directs Lisa's attention to a younger person. "His name's John, if I remember correctly."

"Gracious heavenly Father, we gather this night to recruit new members to oppose the inhumane institution of slavery, so vile in your eyes but so cherished in our society." Jones bows his head and stares at the wagon's bed.

"I'm a member of the Keetoowahs but not the Pins." Moss leans to Lisa's ear.

"To support opposition, we pledge allegiance to Cherokee president John Ross and the United States." The speaker raises his chin.

"John's anti-slavery?"

"Not publicly." Mary squirms. "That's political suicide. He doesn't want the Nation to be aligned."

Evan Jones whacks the butt of a rifle against the wagon's rail. "John Ross stands against humans owing others!"

The crowd cheers, and several attendees blast their guns into the sky.

A few weapon discharges become many.

Lisa surveys the audience to find who is firing.

***

From concealment in the woods, men on horseback charge into the crowd's perimeter. The riders wear masks and discharge weapons at the assembly.

People fall with wounds, and panic sweeps through the clearing.

Moss grabs Lisa's and Mary's elbows and drags the two on their hands and knees toward their tied mares. "It's the Knights of the Golden Circle! We must get you to our horses!"

An Indian collapses with a bullet in his brain in front of her.

She stops her crawl and watches blood spurt from the dead man's skull, the last beats of a Cherokee heart.

"Move! Or the next one will be you." Moss yanks her coat.

The three scramble the remaining few yards to their mounts.

As his employer climbs into her saddle, the fiddler spins and draws his pistol. It clears his holster as he fires, and an attacking Knight of the Golden Circle propels backward off his mount.

A mortally wounded attacker bounces on the ground, and his momentum knocks Mary Stapler Ross from her feet.

Blood splatters the first lady's face.

The freedman yanks the president's wife from the earth and muscles her upon a horse.

He leaps on his mare, grabs the two women's reins, and kicks its flanks. The three surge into the protective brush and tree line.

With rifle and pistol fire echoing over the foliage, Moss leaves the road.

A dead hickory tree's limb hangs from its trunk and resembles a skinny sentry with one arm pointed uphill.

Their horses follow a trail.

The leader heels his mount upward. "Hurry! We can hide under that overhang!"

At the outcrop, Lisa climbs from her horse. "You think we're safe here?"

"No. But better than on the road." The freedman scans the wagon wheel rutted way below for pursuit. "Get under there and stay quiet. I'll lose the horses."

With the three mounts, Moss rushes above the rock to concealment.

The women listen to his retreat.

"John is going to be mad. I should not have involved you." The president's spouse grabs her friend's hand.

"No. He'll be glad to find you safe." Ezra's wife listens to the silence. Weapon fire punctuates the distance.

"I knew you wanted to come. Tonight was our chance. I just picked the wrong meeting."

"Shhh! What's that?" Lisa places an index finger on her lips.

In the woods along the road, a small glow penetrates the darkness.

The women watch as the light increases and becomes torches held by riders.

With rifles in hand, the horsemen approach, and masks that cover their faces flutter in the night's breeze.

"Keep together." The lead rider's voice commands. "Pins could be anywhere."

"Watie said one of them is Ross's wife. She can't be too dangerous." A man near the rear chuckles. "You scared of Quakers?"

"Shut your mouth! I fear the president's hired guards." The leader slides a finger over his throat. "One is Frogger Bowlegs."

The name silences laughter, and the riders pass below the women.

The two huddle in silence.

When the sounds from the Knights of the Golden Circle subside and an owl hoots its lonely cry, Lisa muffles her voice. "They knew you were here."

"They knew."

"Did you tell anyone?"

"No. Just you and him."

"Who saddled your horse?" Waters focuses on her friend.

"Froggy Bowlegs. But he works for Ezra and John."

"And that killer was aware of that. You heard him."

"And he said Watie." Mary stares at her companion.

"I thought you ladies were going to stay quiet." Moss rejoins his employer. "I let the horses go. They will find their way back and lead anybody tracking away."

"Riders came along the road." Lisa points. "Six men in masks. Armed."

"Safest place is right here." The freedman looks at the trail. "You ladies try to sleep. I'll stand watch."

"Wish you had your fiddle." His employer smooths fallen leaves on the ground under the outcrop. "A soft reel helps settle my nerves."

***

Lisa's next waking moment pulls her eyelids open, and in a very dim morning light, she focuses on Moss's face.

The freedman holds a finger vertical against his lips and jerks his head toward the road that curves below them.

A wagon with a two-horse team plods into the curve, and its wheels lurch in worn ruts.

A driver sits next to an armed guard in front, and Ezra, wrapped in a blanket around his shoulders, rides in the rear. More guards follow the conveyance on horseback.

Moss readies his rifle.

"What are you doing?" Lisa grabs his arm. "That's my husband."

"I am not aiming at him." The freedman points his weapon at the trees.

Many explosions blast from the foliage on both sides of the road.

The wagon's driver falls forward between the horses as the team skitters to one side.

The jolt spills the driver's protector from his seat as another armed trailing guard goes to the earth with the impact of a discharge.

Four assassins on foot burst from the brush at roadside and attack the wagon.

The mounted rear rifleman spins and fires. He drops the weapon and struggles to draw a pistol, which hooks in his belt.

The fallen driver's partner crawls to a cart's wheel and his rifle's blast downs a second assailant before his head explodes in blood and brains.

As his handgun frees, the guard shoots a third attacker, but the fourth finishes his work with a trigger pull.

The final assassin stands by the wagon as powder smoke clears, then climbs into the bed with his gun pointed at an unarmed Waters.

From above Ezra, lips quieten her words, "Shoot him before he kills!"

"Can't. I might hit your husband."

"Froggy Bowles is going to murder him." Lisa's voice trembles.

In the carriage, the Seminole leans closer to his victim. "Not such a big attorney now? Your money doesn't stop bullets."

"What are you doing? I gave you work."

"At a poor man's wages." The eastern warrior spits in Ezra's face. "While you and your pampered wife drank brandy, I was fighting in Florida. For five hundred dollars, they bought me and sent me to this dry ground hellhole territory. This time, I didn't sell so cheap."

"Who's paying you? I'll pay more." The attorney drops his blanket.

"You north-supporting, new arrivals are going to die." Bowlegs steps back.

He cocks his pistol, feet from Ezra's forehead.

Moss's bullet impacts the assassin's chest and propels him off the wagon.

The shocked barrister, to find his savior, twists and peers at the outcrop.

"Ezra!" Wife scrambles to embrace her spouse.

"Lisa! What are you doing out here?" The man jumps from his conveyance.

"Saving you!" The two hug each other. "Froggy Bowlegs was going to kill you!"

The attorney spies the fiddler and Mrs. Ross descending the hill. "Moss! Thank God!"

"He saved your skin." The wife delights with her husband.

Waters dangles his hands in surprise. "Mary! I left John late last night. He doesn't know you're out here."

The freedman strides around the wagon.

Frogger Bowlegs bleeds out on the road.

"You made an excellent student, my friend." The dying man's lips quiver.

"And you were a wonderful teacher." Moss drops to his knee beside his trainer and pulls an enormous blade from a sheaf at his belt. "You Seminoles believe you can't die without your topknot. Tell me who hired you and I'll leave it be."

"Watie and the Treaty Party." His dying eyes flicker. "They are the money behind the Golden Knights."

# CHEROKEE REEL

## CHAPTER EIGHT — Conductor

ᎠᎡᎠᏐᎣᎢᏐᏏᎥᏯᎠᎫᎡᏇᏈᎦᎯᎦᏛᏪᏐᎦᎲᎠᏋᎣᎭᏍᎫᏩᎾᏋᎮᏂᎲᏃᏊ

The winter of 1860-61 covers Lisa and Ezra's fortress home, a fortified warehouse on an Arkansas River landing, in blustery snow.

"Compared to this, Fort Gibson was high society." His wife pulls a blanket over her shoulders and scoots her rocking chair closer to a fireplace. "Here I am at forty years old hiding in a converted cotton shed while Mary is hostess to the Cherokee Nation at Park Hill."

"Don't cry for yourself." Ezra watches the flames lick wood and sprinkle tiny red embers into the chimney. "The place had to close. Frontier's gone, and the army has no use for it."

"The fortifications were falling apart. Why must we move here instead of Tahlequah?"

"Since they murdered Judge Steel and with this slave fanaticism, business is not as good. We can't afford that big house, and if we could, too dangerous." Ezra looks at his wife.

"But Mary can!"

"Yes. She and John don't depend on this southern economy." The attorney rises and places a log in the fireplace. "The Judge's and my connections are with the federals."

"Let's move north." Lisa's voice echoes in frustration. Immature petulance ripples through its tone.

"Can't, because of your and my skin colors." Ezra stands silhouetted against the fire's light. "It's hard to start new. In this territory, to survive in business or politics, we need slaves."

"You hear the news?" Moss bursts into the room with newspapers under his arm.

The couple turns to their guard.

Moss steps closer. "The steamboat delivered fresh newspapers."

The owner of the home accepts a Hempstead County *Washington Telegraph.*

"South Carolina seceded from the union last December." He scans the front page. "Abraham Lincoln won the presidency of the United States."

The attorney looks at his wife. "Lincoln's election is why they revolt."

"What are we going to do?" Lisa's eyes widen.

"I am afraid not much." The freedman barrister clasps his wife's hand. "Except hole up here where we're safe."

"That sounds passive, unlike you, husband."

"Here's something we can change." Moss steps closer to the fireplace. "The Knights of the Golden Circle and the Pins are alike. They are shadows in the darkness that kill and ravage anyone who disagrees."

Lisa turns to the fiddler. "What do you mean?"

"I'm saying you have money. Not as much, but more than most." Moss looks back and forth between the husband and wife. "People run from this dying and crying. The poor and slaves are desperate to flee these lands. You can aid them."

Mrs. Waters wipes her eyes with her sleeve. "How? There are so many."

Moss glances at the woman. "Develop the railroad that exists."

"Against the law. In a country where legality means little, I suspect that's not an issue." Ezra nods.

"There are freedman places throughout the territory where slaves can hide." Moss studies his employer.

"But it's a loose, disorganized, unfinanced, and inadequate thing." The attorney shakes his head.

"Not organized as your freight and shipping business." The fiddler points at his boss.

"You're saying we could finance and manage escape routes for laborers?" Lisa stares at her security guard.

Moss nods. "Yes, ma'am."

Wife twists to her spouse. "If we are going to be impoverished, freeing other human beings makes it worthwhile."

Ezra gazes at the fireplace. "I don't know. It will place targets on our backs."

"More than now?" At her husband's side, she slips an arm around his waist.

"An inspiration for Moss's next reel." Her husband swallows as he fixates on the fire. "In fact, I'll call it my personal Cherokee song."

***

Several weeks later, as new snow whitens the eastern territory's landscape, Moss and Lisa guide their horses up a wooded incline.

Their mounts slip on icy rocks strewn in the soil, and the animals snort condensation in the crispness.

"How much farther, Moss?" Lisa's teeth chatter, and she pulls her heavy coat tighter. She shifts the large Patterson Colt in its holster on her hip for more warmth and comfort in her buckskin men's britches. "This cannon you taught me to shoot weighs too much."

"We'll get you one of those new percussion pistols." Moss chuckles. "They call them baby Colts."

"If we're riding in the snow at night, I'm for that."

"Shhh. The station's just over this hill." Moss heels his horse into the lead.

The two top the mound, and the land levels.

A small cabin rests against the next rise behind the dead remnants of a corn patch. Its windows lie dark, and its smokestack remains empty.

"The place is vacant." Lisa muffles her voice.

"No. These people are running. With somebody chasing for sure." Moss climbs from his horse and draws his revolver. The fiddler stands against the wall beside the cabin door and swings it open. The split log panel creaks inward.

Moss listens before stepping through the entry.

Lisa sits on her mount with both hands in the air and points her Patterson.

Moments later, Moss returns. "Everything's fine. Come. It's warmer."

Inside, Lisa's eyes adjust to the gloom.

Huddled by an unlit fireplace, a slave woman and her three young children shiver and share a blanket.

Beside the hearth, a teenage White adolescent dressed in black clothes and a heavy coat stares from under a flat-brimmed hat.

"Who are you?" Lisa nods at the boy.

"I'm the conductor." The boy fixates on Lisa's revolver.

"You are? What does that mean?"

"I oversee operations and safety." The youngster looks at Moss. "Ain't this a woman? Why is she in my station?"

"This is the railroad's banker. Watch your lip. She can help you."

"Don't need nothing from a Cherokee." The fellow jerks his head to the trembling family that shares one blanket. "But they do."

Lisa steps closer to the youngster and withdraws a small burlap bag from her coat. She offers the package.

"What's this?" The boy accepts the gift.

"Financing. There's fifty Liberty dollars in there, enough cash to run your station for six months. Get word to Moss when you want more."

"If the Knights or the secessionists don't catch me first." The youth grits his teeth. "Or a stinking slave catcher."

"Are you a Quaker?" Mrs. Waters grins.

"Yes, ma'am."

"My best friend's a Religious Society of Friends leader."

"What's his name?" The conductor tucks the financing into his coat.

"He's a her. You would not believe me if I told you." Lisa glances at the runaway slaves. "Use that cash to buy more blankets, but don't tell anybody it's Cherokee-earned dollars."

***

Throughout the winter, Ezra and Lisa's capital and organizational skills flow into the fledgling underground railroad.

As a direct result, under the suspicious surveillance of local slave holders, the Knights of the Golden Circle, and most territorial residents who lean to the southern cause, enslaved human beings discover the unfamiliar fervor of freedom.

Spring brings the sun's warmth and welcome relief from a long and frigid winter.

With an armed escort, husband and wife ride in an open carriage driven by a John Ross employee and Moss on a two-wheel marked road approach to Park Hill.

Lisa watches the white fence posts at the carriage's side flash past and enjoys the afternoon's sun and a luscious aroma of flowers. "Ezra, it's so wonderful to get away from our warehouse and that smelly river."

"Yes. It is good. Moss will stay until we're settled, but someone must continue our responsibility back home. He'll tend to business."

"He can keep escape routes open without us." The woman enjoys the smell of the Indian Paintbrush that colors the fields around the Park Hill estate. "And I'm overjoyed the president has more important duty for you."

At the entrance, Mary Stapler waits to greet her old friend. "Delighted you're here. Welcome!"

The two women embrace as Moss unloads the luggage from the carriage.

"Moss! Stop that." Mrs. Ross notices his labor. "You are family! Come with us into the house. Someone else will get those bags."

"I see you haven't changed." Ezra greets the first lady. "Is he here this afternoon?"

"My, you look handsome in that new Home Guard uniform, Colonel Waters." Mary Stapler surveys the attire.

"Thank you. And John?"

"No. He's meeting with a representative from Arkansas's Rector in Tahlequah on another crisis. Should be back for dinner."

"Crisis?"

"They expect thirteen states to separate from the union."

"Same number as the original colonies." Ezra offers his arm to Mrs. Ross.

"Their governor says Mr. Lincoln and his administration consider the territory ripe for abolitionists." Mary laughs. "He thinks we're free soilers and saboteurs."

"Eager support for the south." Moss sips his drink.

Lisa enjoys the company. "I understand Texas troops hold the military posts."

"Fort Gibson is crumbling and abandoned." The hostess nods agreement. "It's not that name anymore. When the government ceded that old fortress to the Nation, we changed it to ᏒᏍᏕ, Ke-too-wa."

"This is an independent Cherokee island in a southern sea." Lisa claps her palms.

Inside, the hostess offers the couple and Moss tea service.

"You hear the secession convention in Arkansas elected Elias Boudinot as Secretary?"

Her friend accepts a drink.

"He encourages that horrible Standhope Watie to oppose my husband." She turns to the attorney.

"I never forget the nephew." Ezra sips from his cup.

"His uncle's organizing members of the Knights of the Golden Circle into a new political group. They call themselves the Southern Rights Party. John thinks they're only guerrillas raised to protect Arkansas." Mary refills Lisa's drink and turns to Moss. "More?"

The freedman nods no.

"I am sure your husband knows the Confederate Provisional Congress created a Bureau of Indian Affairs." Ezra places his mug on a stand beside his chair.

Lisa leans into the conversation. "They appointed David Hubbard as commissioner for the secession states."

"He mentioned that." Mrs. Ross picks up the cup. "The fresh news is their War Department put that Texas Ranger, Ben McCulloch, in command of our territory."

"Resembles a good, bad wolf Cherokee story my mother used to tell us." Ezra's wife shakes her head. "But the wrong one's in charge of the henhouse."

Excited bustle at the front door interrupts the tea.

John Ross, his tall frame bent by age and supported by a cane, shuffles into the room. "The Waters! I am so glad you are here."

The guests rise from their chairs.

"Mr. President," Ezra extends his hand in greeting. "Pleased to be here at your invitation."

"Thank you for coming." The older man shakes hands. "My energy lessens every year. You are the brightest legal mind in the territory. I need you here."

"John, you look tired." Mary Ross rises. "Are you well?"

"They informed me Standhope Watie met with Ben McCulloch and Elias Boudinot in Fort Smith. McCulloch's a Confederate Brigadier General now, not only a Ranger. He and their Secretary of War promised ammunition and protection from the Pins." The president rests. "And Arkansas seceded from the union. That Texan rebel comes to Park Hill next week to talk to me."

***

Days later, John and Ezra sit in the same formal living room opposite the Brigadier General.

The officer, with a full beard and mustache of dark brown hair, flanked by several adjutants, sits ramrod straight in a chair.

Lisa and Mary listen and watch in secret from a cracked entry.

"My government guarantees the Cherokee title and possession of your entire country." The general's eyes seldom blink. "We promise to pay for the potential loss of your neutral land between Kansas and Missouri. With interest."

John Ross nods understanding. "I am concerned with justice."

"I commit to courts throughout the territory." Nothing moves except the general's lips and eyes. "You may pick representatives to serve in our Congress."

Silence looms in the room.

"We swear to protect Cherokee investments, to pay money due from existing treaties and other benefits promised by the North. If you are an ally." The soldier's expression remains vague.

He waits for a response.

Hearing none, the Texas Ranger leans forward. "In return, those who join the Confederacy may organize military companies or home guards to defend themselves in case the North invades."

Ezra leans forward. "I remind you, sir, the Cherokee Executive Council agrees to stay neutral. We will not violate our treaties with the United States."

"A man of your race speaks for the tribe?" The officer ignores the attorney.

John Ross clears his throat. "General McCulloch, federal troops within our borders is not an act inviting armed resistance."

"Why not?"

"Those soldiers are from a country with whom we celebrate treaties."

The Texan stands. "Sir, I came to my state with David Crockett, was a friend and confidant to Sam Houston, and fought for and won a nation of my own."

"Yes, you did."

"We now choose a path in opposition to the government in the North. I will not betray my people's loyalty, as you do. Good day."

The Confederates' adjuncts follow their general out of the room.

John Ross turns to Ezra. "That didn't go well."

Lisa and Mary close their eavesdropping door without their men aware of witnesses.

****

Spring changes to summer and fall, with the Waters comfortable in the security cocoon of Park Hill.

The attorney's responsibilities as a constant companion and consultant to the president allow little time with his spouse.

Tasked by her husband to check on Moss, their property and business interests, protected by men of the Nation's home guard, Mrs. Waters travels to their warehouse on the Arkansas.

Smoke rises from the river as the contingent approaches.

Lisa stops in front of her primitive fortress.

The building smokes from its rubble, and several bodies, swollen from days in the sun, lie around the porch and near the landing.

The landing's pier extends half its normal length with the rest burned to the waterline.

She stands in her carriage. "Moss! Moss!"

Silence envelopes the site.

"Massacred, Mrs. Waters." The Cherokee home guard in charge of her security stretches in his stirrups. "Two or three days ago." The man points, "But that is recent. Somebody heard you were coming and left a message."

Lisa follows the guard's point.

At the side of the charred remnants of her house, a single body hangs head to the ground on a heavy pole.

"Oh no! Is it Moss?"

The guard turns his horse and canters to the beam, looks up, and returns. "No. A young White boy."

"Pull the carriage over there."

"You sure you want to, Mrs. Waters?" The home escort shows no, and he does not urge the horses forward. "It's a sight."

"I've seen worse. Do it now."

The security man nods, and the driver moves around the corner of the burned warehouse to the ominous planted pole.

Lisa gasps as she recognizes the young Quaker conductor from the winter.

The boy's eyes stare blank, and a wooden hewn plank extends out of his side.

On the wood, in blood, crude hand-printed letters read, "Abolitionist!"

A home guard rides near his commander and offers a medallion. "Found this on the landing."

The security officer in charge examines the piece and shows it to Lisa. "It's a Knights of the Golden Circle talisman. The Southern Rights Party did this."

"Anyone find Moss?" Mrs. Water stares at the shiny amulet.

The guardsman shakes his head negative.

"Cut that poor boy loose and bury them." The owner surveys her property. "There's nothing left here. We'd better return to Park Hill."

***

As Lisa's carriage and the escorts on horseback travel, she watches the woods on both sides of the two-wheel track dirt road.

The driver sits erect in front, and several home guardsmen ride before and behind her conveyance.

Lisa fixates ahead on a dead hickory tree's limb that hangs from its trunk and resembles a skinny sentry with one arm pointed uphill. "Stop!"

The commander turns and returns to the carriage. "Mrs. Waters. We shouldn't rest here. This is guerrilla country. Southern Rights men raid Pin farms throughout these woods."

"We're not resting. Come with me." She jumps to the ground and leads up the hill. "There's a place to hide."

"That so, ma'am? What are we hiding?" The guard follows.

At the overhang, Lisa freezes. "What was that?"

A low, weak moan slips from under the rocks.

She climbs under its roof. "Moss, it's you!"

The fiddler lies in leaves, unconscious and bleeding from a shoulder bullet wound covered and pressed with a moss bandage.

"He's alive! Help me get him to the carriage!"

# CHAPTER NINE — Buzzard

DRTᎧꞳᎢᏅᏆᎥᎩᎩᎽ᎙ᎪᎫᎢꞳᏛᎳᏈ᎐ᏛᏧᎨᎥᏌᎤᏂᏗᏆᎬᏒᏋᎤᎽᎧᎿᎨᏈᏁᎤᏤᏚᎥᎠᎿᎽ

John Ross drops a letter to his lap as Lisa, Ezra and Mary Stapler frown with worry.

"Albert Pike aligned the Confederacy with the Choctaws, Chickasaws, and Creeks. We Cherokee stand alone." The president shakes his head with resignation.

"We must not enter this war." The first lady joins her husband and rubs his shoulders.

The attorney coughs. "Sir, after Bull Run, Manassas, whatever you want to call that loss, Washington may fall."

"I worry over Honey Springs." The chief executive peers into his wife's eyes. "Watie's guerrillas captured General Sigel's cannon. He's a hero of the Confederacy and our people."

"Captain Drew and the Pins retaliated." The adviser glances at his wife.

"As savages, they say." Lisa covers her lips with a handkerchief. "In the old way, by blood law, they took scalps."

"Serves Watie justice for raising the stars and bars in Tahlequah's square." The Nation's leader grimaces and turns to his consultant. "You know how I see this business. If the south wins, and the war in Virginia indicates they will, a Cherokee Confederate alliance benefits us."

"You waver, sir?" Waters firms his shoulders.

"I believe expediency requires consideration." John Ross rubs his forehead and shakes his head in resignation.

***

An actual treaty signing convenes at Park Hill in early October, 1861.

The chief executive signs for the Cherokee, and Albert Pike signs for the confederate government.

Ezra attends, assisting the president, and both wives witness the event.

"The Southern Rights Party did not take part." Lisa leans to Mary and holds her voice low. "So why is he here?" The Waters' wife sneers toward Standhope Watie, who stands with Elias Boudinot, both in uniform, within the confederate contingent. "That man paid assassins to murder Ezra."

"And my husband." Mary's words tremble.

The southern representative steps closer to the Cherokee leader with his hands under a folded stars and bars. "For the public square in Tahlequah, sir. To be raised at your discretion."

The chief executive accepts the flag, turns to Standhope Watie, and extends a hand.

His enemy freezes and looks at the emissary of the Confederate government.

The commissioned Brigadier General's body language reads accept the handshake.

Piercing eyes and harder hearts commit a symbolic act, a forced political recognition of enemies.

Lisa turns from the charade and, with lips near her friend's ear, "Opothleyohola and the Creeks will never join this."

Mary twists to her friend. "The warrior's an ally, and my husband may influence him."

"Well, I am a supporter of the Cherokee and cannot stomach this." The wife looks toward Ezra, who jerks his head with a husband's signal to exit this signing.

***

After the treaty, to protest Native American alignment with the Confederacy, Mrs. Waters increases her involvement with the fragmented but more active territorial underground railroad.

This day, with Moss, she shepherds a family of slaves through the backcountry parallel to the Texas Road.

"How's that shoulder wound?" She looks ahead at the lead mount.

"Holding well."

"Michael row the boat ashore, Hallelujah! Michael row the boat ashore, Hallelujah!" Josiah Rains with a boy child on his saddle in front sings from his heart. "Jordan's river is chilly and cold, Hallelujah! But it warms the human soul, Hallelujah!"

The slave glances behind to a trailing horse.

His wife, with a young daughter, blends her voice, "This old world is a mighty big place, Hallelujah! It got Satan all over its face, Hallelujah!"

Lisa pulls her wide-brimmed hat lower. "Do they have to sing?"

"Calms their fears, Mrs. Waters." Moss looks to the trail. "They don't have to, but it's safe enough, I figure."

"Michael row the boat ashore, Hallelujah! Michael row the boat ashore, Hallelujah!"

"Keep them moving. I'm going to ride back and make sure nobody follows." The fiddler turns his horse.

"How far to the Kansas border?" Lisa's voice crackles with concern.

91

"Few miles more. Another conductor picks them up at his cabin." Moss watches his partner's face. "Don't worry. I'll return before you exchange them."

"They put Daniel in the lion's den, Hallelujah! And he walked right out again, Hallelujah!" Josiah Reins savors the lyrics. "The reason them felines permitted that, Hallelujah, was that Daniel had no fat, Hallelujah! Waters row this boat ashore, Hallelujah!"

Lisa shifts the heavy Colt strapped to her waist and heels her horse through the brush and woods.

"Ma'am, Moss says you're a rich man's wife." The families' head urges his mount closer.

"Not so, just comfortable."

"Comfort to me and to my family is a full belly, a warm fire, and no master to make me grovel. In safety up north."

"You have a right to those things."

"Your parent was a freed slave, the fiddler claims." He studies his conductor's features. "And your mother was Cherokee?"

"Yes."

"And you were comfortable in life? How's that possible?"

"Only since I married, maybe."

The escaping father thinks about Lisa's words. "But Moss says he's a freedman. In the territory, they ain't good. Your other half must be the reason."

"My husband is an attorney and an entrepreneur."

"Entre what, phewner? Big word. I got no reading or writing."

"Means he makes money by shipping on the river and brokering cotton."

"Between the Pins and them Liberty Party boys, most of that gets burned." The slave father hugs his boy closer. "These your horses?"

"Yes."

"If I get North, Mrs. Waters, I ain't going to forget what you done for us."

"You will make it, Josiah." Lisa looks behind to assure herself no one follows. "But please, no more singing. We're not far from the road. I don't want company."

***

The party rides in silence until Moss emerges ahead. He holds a finger to his lips as she approaches.

When close, she reads the man's word, "Catchers." The fiddler points and grasps the reins of Lisa's horse.

The man urges his mount from the rough trail and pushes through the bramble with the other mounts accustomed to trailing. Their hooves splash across a creek and climb a hill.

At the hill's crest, the land flattens before a tree line.

The ruins of a burned log cabin, a farmer's home and victim of political violence, sit silent and roofless.

Charred logs form a bastion several thicknesses high.

Moss points, and the others scramble from their mounts into the enclosure.

The young slave girl whimpers, but her mother covers her mouth with one hand.

Their leader leans from his horse and passes his rifle and two pistols to Lisa. "I must hide these horses. Be back before they get here."

"But without a gun?"

"I have one. Keep these in case I'm not." Moss urges the animals toward the tree line.

Mrs. Waters turns to Josiah and offers the long gun. "Do you know how to use this?"

"Yep. Master used to have me shoot turkey for him." The slave chuckles. "It's good to hunt catchers."

The family and their protector settle behind the charred walls of the cabin in concealment and wait.

Lisa crouches in a corner and listens.

A buzzard circles in the sky overhead.

Her eyes cloud, and her mind wanders.

The bird flies low and closer. "What is your trouble, Tsalagi?"

"We hide from evil men who wish to capture and punish us." Lisa's words tremble with fear but discover air in an alternative mystic realm, for her, inexperienced and unexplored.

"Exchange with me. Fly above the ridges and view your enemies while I listen in that cabin's corner for you. I'll protect your flock."

The two transform and exchange essence.

***

*Conductor Waters flies over the cabin in a circle sweep.*

*Below, inside the enclosure fortification of burned logs, she watches a familiar woman crouch in hiding with a Colt revolver cocked.*

*A slave family of four huddles in another corner, the father with a rifle.*

*From the air, the ridges and flatlands of northeast Indian territory soil appear the same as the free state of Kansas's earth, but movement near the cabin attracts attention.*

*Lisa swoops low over three mounted men.*

A White leader in worker's clothes with two pistols, a long gun, and a bull whip wrapped on his saddle's pommel follows a Creek tracker.

The Indian leads his horse and studies the ground before his moccasins.

A third trails, another smaller framed man with a double-barrel percussion shotgun.

*Lisa lands on a dead tree limb, and the party moves along the incline.*

"Still four horses, Sarcheso?" The lead rider watches his scout.

"Yes, but they know we follow." The Creek tracker peers up the hill.

"How's that?"

"Shod mounts dig their hoof fronts into the dirt deeper when they hurry." The Indian looks at his boss. "He who helps them is a big man. He shows bigger, heavy tracks."

"Niggers couldn't make it this far without help." The catcher blows his nose on his jacket.

"They are ahead." Sarcheso grimaces at the snort noise. "Maybe very close."

The little fellow in the rear swings his shotgun toward the tree line and cocks both barrels.

"Un-cock that cannon before you blow somebody's butt to mincemeat." The leader wipes nose on an opposite sleeve. "Let's move to the ridge top."

Israel points his weapon to the side and aims at a black buzzard perched on a dead tree. "I want to blast that filthy thing!"

As if the bird understands English, it flaps its wings into flight.

*Lisa soars and returns to above the cabin.*

*"Thank you, loyal one. You may have your body back." She* circles lower.

***

Inside the log fortification, Josiah peeks over the charred wall and turns to the reincarnated woman. "I see nothing. They still coming?"

She nods from the opposite corner of the enclosure. "Just beyond the flat, working their way. I hear them."

"How many, Mrs. Waters?"

"Three, but one's a Creek." She looks over the logs for Moss. "We take them on alone. Your rifle ready?"

Josiah kisses his wife and crawls across the interior space to reinforce Lisa's position.

They wait in silence.

A head with a feather tucked in its headband peeks above the crest and disappears.

Long moments drag as Lisa and the family's patriarch tune to any sound.

Slave catcher Israel pops into view above a side of the cabin. As he swings his shotgun toward his armed adversaries, a weapon explodes black powder smoke, and a round rips through the attacker's cheek. Flesh and brains splatter the grass.

The shooter's wife screams, and she clutches her kids close.

The father drops his rifle to the cabin's dirt floor and rushes to comfort his brood.

Lisa, with her Colt cocked and clutched in both palms, leaps to her feet.

Twenty yards away, the slave catcher charges on horseback and swings his gun forward.

Her hands shake, and she fights to hold her barrel still and straight.

Smoke blasts from the attacker's long piece, and a round blows a chunk of wood from a protector log inches from Lisa's ribs.

The attacking man drops the weapon and pulls at a pistol.

Lisa squeezes her trigger, and her bullet impacts the large man's chest, which propels him backward off his mount. He lands on the ground and bounces as his horse twists away.

She stares through the smoke.

A body lies still with blank open eyes to the sky.

"Not a shoddy shot for a Cherokee woman." The Creek tracker freezes a female in fear.

She turns.

The Indian stands with his legs spread on the rear cabin wall. His revolver points at Lisa's heart.

"You're slave catching for money." Lisa fights to keep calm. "I'll pay you to let these people go."

"Conductors ain't got no funds." The scout laughs. "I'm working for a plantation man."

"My husband's an attorney and cotton broker."

"You might lie to save your own skin. But there's five of you on four horses."

The tracker's chest explodes as a bullet impacts his chest from the rear and bursts through his ribs. The fellow falls dead-eyed into the wall's enclosure.

Lisa spins toward the source. "Moss!"

She grabs a burned log wall for support and empties her stomach.

The fiddler approaches on foot at a run and holsters his Colt. "Get behind those logs. Everybody good?"

"No need. There were only three catchers." She helps Josiah's wife to her feet as the woman cuddles her terrified children.

"Are you sure?" Moss crouches inside the enclosure with wood as cover.

"I saw them coming up the hill."

"Then you stay here. I'll fetch the horses." The fiddler jumps over the charred cabin wall and trots toward the tree line.

Above the burned cabin, the buzzard circles and watches the return with the animals.

Lisa sits with her back against her fort. She stares at her trembling fingers.

"You sure you are fine?" Her savior stops at Lisa's side.

"No. I'm not. I just killed a human being. Feel sick, I can't walk."

The fiddler leans from his mount, takes her hand, and pulls.

"Your first, I expect. No time for you to be ill. There may be others. Get on your horse."

Moss and Lisa lead as Josiah, his wife and children align and trail.

The buzzard sweeps lower as the riders move away from the three dead catchers that sprawl in the grass.

As they enter the trees, she looks at the cabin.

The black carrion lands on the log wall and flaps its wings, a thank you gesture for its eminent dinner.

# CHAPTER TEN — Opothleyohola

## ᎠᎡᏔᏝᎣᎢᏍᏫᏆᎩ ᎠᎫᎬ ᎱᏆᏯᏔᎢᎦ ᏫᎥᏕᎬᎮᎭ Ꭴ ᎣᎢᎲᏝ ᏯᏪᏬᏁᏂ ᏃᎪ

The lone significant resistance to the Nation's alignment with the Confederacy arises from the president's friend and fellow natural born leader, Opothleyohola.

"Cherokee have sense like the Whites, but the Creeks have none." The chief states his enthusiasm for the culture, the industry and the advancement of his people during the late 1840s and disparages the broken-spirited emigrants of the era.

Dismayed by Ross's alliance with Pike and the south, the hold-out refused to attend the 1861 convention in Tahlequah. His faction continues to adhere to treaties made with the United States.

***

Albert Pike ignores the dissension and travels to Richmond after his triumphal merger of Ross and the southern cause.

He leaves the home guards, now called the First Cherokee Mounted Rifles, with another company of volunteers led by Ezra but under the overall command of John Drew.

They form an uneasy alliance on paper with Colonel Standhope Watie and the Second Regiment.

This allegiance receives orders to strike Opothleyohola and his village of followers at Red Fork, including aligned Creeks disparaged as useless two decades in the past.

They, full bloods and Ross-party enlistees, grumble and resist.

The Ninth Texas Calvary, aligned with Choctaw and Chickasaw mounted rifles, invade the camp and pursue withdrawing Indians to another battle at Bird Creek.

The confederate Drew's men, including officers, desert and fight for the retreating Cherokee leader.

Their remnants flee through a powerful winter snowstorm in a retreating battle for safety in Kansas.

***

On the Arkansas, Lisa waits for her husband's return in warmth and security at a concealed and secret log warehouse, another remnant of their once-thriving cotton trade.

Moss and a half-dozen loyal guards offer insurance and base themselves in a barracks next door.

The compound, with one side against a stone cliff, features a timber barricade around its perimeter.

Tucked in a valley, the fortress sits near a tributary junction on the river.

The fiddler distracts his boss's meditation of fireplace flames. "Mrs. Waters. Get your gun. Riders coming!"

She throws off her blanket and rushes across the room. From a cedar storage chest, the woman lifts a Baby Colt with holster and ammunition belt. "Hate this. I'm no female pistoleer. Why can't they just leave me alone to sing and dance?"

The wife moves to and opens a firing port near the warehouse's entrance.

The reflection from the snow in the moonlight illuminate Moss and his guards, who crouch with rifles at their posts behind its chest-high stockade.

Beyond, the dark shapes of horses move closer through knee-deep drifts.

Hot air from their mounts' nostrils form instant condensation clouds, and ice clogs breath passages. The animals struggle through the snow piles.

"Stay there! Stop or we fire!" Moss's voice rings in the frigid atmosphere.

"You hold, Moss! It's Colonel Waters. Open the gate!"

Lisa slams her firing port closed, runs, and stuffs her pistol into its cedar chest and grabs a brush near her chair. She sweeps the instrument through her long hair.

The warehouse door swings wide, and a blast of air introduces Ezra.

In a filthy, powder-stained confederate uniform covered by winter horse mane, Lisa's husband opens his arms.

They hug and kiss. "What's happened? Are you hurt?"

Moss follows his employer into the warm interior. "I'll get you brandy to thaw your stomach."

"Yes. And settle my men in the barracks. One's wounded, so take care." The soldier slips out of his heavy coat and collapses into a chair. "If we have whiskey, share with them."

Lisa drops to her knees beside her husband. "Ezra. You're exhausted."

"Opothleyohola abandoned his wagons and fled toward Kansas. My soldiers switched sides and tried to protect his rear." Ezra's eyes glaze with memories.

The soldier drifts into the recent past.

*A surgeon amputates a soldier's leg as the colonel plods his horse past the screaming patient. The victim loses consciousness in the makeshift lean-to hospital beside the road.*

*Waters rubs his eyes against the glare of a snow-covered landscape peppermint-speckled by blood.*

*The snow's glare breaks in the man's eyes as limbs of leafless stumps punch the terrain.*

*Colonel Waters rubs his eyes more, and they focus.*

*Hundreds of arms and legs, frozen, stick in the snow and replace the out-of-focus stumps the rider visioned.*

The man's mind returns to his wife. "Even the wounded were sick. Had to dig mass graves to the border."

"But you're home now. Safe."

"John Ross may have signed with the rebels, but my men won't have it." The colonel's hands shake.

His wife clasps the trembling fingers.

The man clears his throat. "Watie's guerrillas are in control. The union's moving four divisions under General Samuel Curtis south from Missouri to confront them."

"The north invades?" Lisa draws a deep breath.

"Yes. And we're going to join the Yankees."

Moss serves the officer a brandy.

The worn man gulps the liquor in a swallow.

The fiddler pours another from a glass decanter. "My guards and I can't defend this place. Guerrillas will run over us. We want to enlist with you and your men."

Waters sips his second drink. "No one dies here. We'll rest for a few days. Lisa, pack what you must take, and we wagon everything else to Kansas."

"So, I ride with you?" The wife looks at her husband.

"Yes. You are not safe here."

"I don't think I have the training to be a guerrilla."

"When we link with union troops, they'll have a surgeon." Ezra grasps and squeezes his wife's hand. "The army always needs nurses."

"How romantic! I must let Mary Stapler know."

"Might be impossible. This territory's a war zone. Ross and his government may no longer exist. Moss, how is our railroad?"

The fiddler shakes his head. "Derailed, Mr. Waters. Now, think of yourselves. Slaves will still run. With this violence, we can't help them anymore."

"I am anxious, husband."

"My concern is us, your people, John and Mary Ross, and the freedmen in the territory." Ezra slaps Moss's knee. "There is hope. Moss isn't ready to play his last Cherokee Reel."

*** 

Months later, after the snows of winter grow the flowers of spring, Lisa stands at the tent door of General Curtis's Union Army hospital. She watches Indian troops train in an open field.

Doctor Hiram Kent, chief and only surgeon for the huge, camped force, sits on a folding canvas stool with a private's foot in his lap.

A big toe extends red and swollen, with a thorn embedded under its toenail. "Soldier. We must take that out."

"Is it going to hurt, sir?"

"Expect so, but not as painful as a rebel bullet in your belly." The surgeon sanitizes a blade in the flame of an oil lamp.

"Better than losing my scalp to one of them wild Injun recruits." The private laughs.

Lisa grimaces at the reference and watches the training in the field.

White officers instruct Indian soldiers who wear misfitting blue uniforms with ridiculous small union caps atop their full-bodied, dark-haired heads.

The trainers shout, curse, and yell as Ezra, demoted to a captain in this new army, attempts to show proper cannon loading procedures.

"This shooting wagon will kill fifty men?" One Cherokee waves his sponge and rammer shaft in the air.

"Not if you don't load it! Stop waving that." A White officer grabs the pole and sticks the cleaner end into the cannon's barrel. "It ain't a flag, you dumb Injun."

"Wow!" The private in the hospital tent whistles as Doctor Kent's blade pops the thorn and half his toenail off the big toe.

"Lisa, I am done. Bandage him up for me, please."

"Of course." She turns to the patient.

The trooper inspects Lisa's face. "You a Cherokee or a nigger?"

"Shut up, soldier." The physician kicks the boy's injury, and he grimaces in pain. "She is your nurse. In a couple of weeks, she may help me cut off your leg, so show this lady respect."

The woman bandages the youth's foot, and he limps out of the hospital tent.

Doctor Kent watches the patient until he is out of hearing range and turns to Lisa. "Mrs. Waters, I know you are a friend of Mary Stapler Ross and her husband. This morning's dispatches brought news of both."

"What's happened?"

"Our troops captured the family with Cherokee records and funds. Moved them to Kansas." The physician gauges Lisa's reaction.

"Was anyone hurt?"

"No. They intend to escort the entire party to Washington. Lincoln will decide."

"If I know Mary Stapler, she'll steal the capital's social scene from Mary Todd." Lisa's mind relives better times with her friend.

***

That evening, in their officer's tent lit by candles, Ezra and his wife settle.

"That's everything that Doctor Kent knew."

"I am sure they did not capture the Ross loyalists. Or Drew's home guards and Moss."

"I hope our fiddler is safe." She dabs an eye with a handkerchief.

"We're leaving here in a couple of days." Husband reaches for his wife's hand. "A force of Van Dorn's Confederates moves into Arkansas. They believe his goal is St. Louis. We are reinforcing Curtis's troops."

"Does this mean a battle?" The woman squeezes her man's palm.

"The union can let them waltz into Missouri, but the Boston Mountains block their way. It takes time to move artillery and men over that route."

# CHAPTER ELEVEN — Pea Ridge

**ᎠᎡᎢᎣᎤᎥᎦᎧᎨᎩᎪᎫᎬᎭᎮᎯᎰᎱᎲᎳᎴᎵᎶᎷᎸᎹᎺᎻᎼᎽᎾᎿᏀᏁᏂᏃᏄᏅ**

John Ross's treaty with the Confederacy, endorsed with reticence at Park Hill, stipulates that Cherokee soldiers not fight outside their Nation.

As other treaties with the United States of America and their colonies signed over generations, this paper stands violated soon, another example of what an old Indian shaman labeled "talking leaves that blow in the wind."

Rebel native troops under a confederate battle flag and commanded by Standhope Watie amass for conflict in Arkansas.

Loyalists to Ross and most members of the Home Guard either join union forces or hide in their territorial hills.

The South's Army of the West, 16,000 men strong, moves over the Boston Mountains and approaches entrenched federal detachments near Little Sugar Creek.

Worn, without sleep and supplies, the Confederates pause.

Their aggressive officer, Major General Van Doren, splits his force on both sides of Pea Ridge and attacks. He plans to link at Elkhorn Tavern and strike the union's rear.

Over 11,200 troops in blue amass on the crest's high ground.

The rebel commander, with 17,000 soldiers in gray, expects both his divisions to reach Cross Timber Hollow. After delays, he commands McCulloch's division to take the Ford Road and meet Price.

Federal patrols detect both threats.

Curtis sends Dodge's brigade northeast on the Wire Roadway to join the Missouri Infantry at the inn.

Completely unaware of the size of each, the opposing forces approach a minor settlement near the ridge called Leetown.

***

Assisted by orderlies, Lisa sets up cots in Doctor Kent's field hospital, an insignificant building in this rural town.

Her shelter, one of a dozen structures in the hamlet, features space for twenty to thirty wounded.

Several other cabins and shelters compose the entire battlefield clinic.

For a moment, the nurse surveys the town as she waits at her clinic's entrance.

Buildings serve different surgeons as field hospitals, but the facilities appear puny and woefully inadequate.

A wagon pulls to a stop outside her doorway.

A young private jumps from its driver's seat. "I got casks of water from the creek. Where should I put them?"

"Are those what we get?"

"Yes ma'am. This trip. But I'll bring you more. The stream's only half a mile.

A spattering of rifle fire distracts.

The youngster and Lisa whip their heads in the direction of the distant percussions.

"Infantry. Doesn't sound that far." Doctor Kent stands at the building's entry and watches. "We better get ready."

The nurse steps into her workplace as the water wagon turns for a refill. "We are low on supplies. I only have bandages for a few."

"We sent for resupply from St. Louis." The doctor returns to the room. "Pray it arrives."

Unseen but heard by the two medical personnel, McCulloch's cavalry, commanded by Brigadier General James McIntosh, and an infantry brigade under Col. Louis Hebet plus joint Cherokee, Choctaw, Creek, Seminole, and Chickasaw horsemen stumble into a much smaller enemy force.

Three federal cannons shell the rebels.

A Confederate charge captures the artillery.

Two companies of the third Iowa meet an Indian ambush and suffer unacceptable casualties.

Howitzers fired blindly from beyond a tree line burst near the Cherokees who panic retreat and do not rally.

Shortly after the howitzer's distant explosions rivet Lisa and the doctor's attention toward rifle fire, the union trooper returns with a second load of water.

The boy's eyes follow the sound of cannon discharges as he jumps from the water wagon.

"More water, soldier?" Doctor Kent holds the wagon's team.

"You're going to need it, Doc. I could see fighting. Our boys are taking hell. Bunch of fellows at the river was in it."

"What did you hear?" Lisa wrings her hands.

"We got that Texas general, McCulloch! But Injuns took the south ridge. They claimed they're Watie's men. Drew's units threw away their rifles and fought with arrows! They run in packs, ignore their lines, and take scalps! No discipline, bunch of heathens!"

"Heard news of a Captain Waters?"

"Sorry. Don't know the officer."

"With the union's Cherokee Calvary."

The young soldier's eyes widen. "Them boys are in the thick of it!"

"Go get more water, Private. We're going to need every drop you can haul." Lisa points at the road out of Leesville.

A union hospital wagon churns dust and slides to a stop beside the water cart.

Crammed with wounded stacked several men deep, it delivers patients.

Orderlies unpack the bodies.

The medical corpsmen lay the dead in a row at the clinic's side. Corpses in a line grow to the width of the building.

The first injured man delivered on a gurney into the hospital's interior lies unconscious, with the skin of his forehead pierced and knife-sliced away from his skull.

Lisa gags as she escorts the stretcher to a table.

The physician leans over the young soldier. "Auugh! The poor kid's scalped!"

Helpers place more stretchers of groaning and crying men on the floor. One patient does not move.

"Tell those orderlies we can't help the dead ones!" Doctor Kent hurries from body to body. "If they're not breathing, leave them on the grounds!"

"There are so many! Another three wagons arrived." The nurse's hands shake. "What are we going to do?"

The surgeon grasps Lisa's shoulders. "Steady, woman! You're a nurse. These boys need us! And you! Do what you can!"

Lisa turns and wipes the sweat from the forehead of a young Corporal.

The patient smiles.

She realizes the youngster has no left arm.

Doctor Kent sloshes a bucket of water over his makeshift operating table and blood mixes pink as it flushes to the floor.

A new body replaces the last one, this soldier in a confederate uniform.

"Got to take this at the elbow. Nurse, my saw!"

Mrs. Waters plugs her ears with her bloody fingers to block the sound of the jagged teeth on bone.

The patient screams with pain.

***

Late that afternoon, night's concealment of suffering shades the interior of the hospital.

Lisa huddles in a corner next to a pile of amputated limbs and blubbers into her hands. She wipes her forehead, which smears several boys' blood together.

Her eyes focus on the moon outside the hospital's window.

The orb transitions in Lisa's blurred vision into a white owl.

Its wings and beak move. "The vulture and the wolf have dominion. Friends and foes rest in shared lonely graves."

Mrs. Waters feels her shoulder touched and looks up into Doctor Kent's exhausted eyes. "Nurse, it's over for the day. Find a place to hide from this. Get sleep for a few hours."

She nods, wipes her eyelids, and struggles to her feet.

Lisa stumbles along the wall with one hand on its surface for support.

She steps over union bodies and an occasional confederate to the open hospital door.

Outside, dark forms with stretchers pick men from the ground and transport them to burial wagons.

The stretcher bearers lift a youthful private from the Second Corps to the top of the body stack and dump another casualty into its last seat for a ride to a mass grave.

Lisa's tears turn to the moon above the wagon. The moisture in her pupils distorts the sky's sphere into her familiar white owl.

"Life's no Cherokee Reel." She wipes her forehead and focuses on the bird. "My sister Ella made it better. I can't help every one of these boys like her. She was good. What am I?"

The woman blinks and the bird transforms into her mother's face.

*"My little daughter, your heart cries." The woman's expression spreads love and caring through the darkness.*

*"Mommy, is it you?" The daughter's lips tremble.*

*"It is I, Ayokha."*

*Lisa's eyes tear, "She Brought Happiness. Your name carries comfort. I am the only girl left. My sisters died at the hands of White men."*

*"Bella, in that Georgia detention camp. Ella, in a brothel. Your sisters perished at the will of our own kind."*

*"I have no people as you do. My blood mixes yours and a freedman's. I live in the style of a wealthy planter. Am I my father's daughter? Do I cherish your ancestors? Who am I?"*

*"Youngest offspring, you suppress your Tsalagi heritage. You wish your father was not a slave. You strive to become a White woman, as is your friend, Mary Stapler Ross. Your eyes are blind. Cherokees murdered your sisters."*

*"What fiends could beat Ella into a grave or bullwhip Bella to her death?"*

*"You could be that person if forced. You must grow, discover yourself, recognize your native blood, and control your people's killing lust. But never abandon your father's and your husband's legacy. My daughter of your father, you have much to become."*

She Brought Happiness's light extinguishes as a black form sweeps before her luminance and lands on a corner of the death wagon.

Familiar from her meeting with slave catchers, the buzzard's expressionless pupils don't blink.

They peer.

She grabs the side of the hearse for support as her knees wobble. "My mother did not send you. Go away!"

The buzzard's gaze shifts to Lisa's hand.

Near her fingers, which grip a rail, union Captain Ezra Water's lifeless blank stare at the moon pierces the night from the cart.

Lisa trembles as she reaches to touch her husband's hair.

Matted bloody scalp slips under her fingertips and falls from his skull. Chalky bone exposes an attempted scalping.

The spouse's lips flutter and her brain vibrates. "No! Not now! How can I do this?"

She drops to her knees with her cheeks near his bloody face. "Ezra, who am I? Your wife cannot live this madness without you!"

Lisa surrenders to a mental struggle that swells her head unconscious.

A battle of physical war rages around her, but a consuming inner conflict ravages her internal multi-cultural world.

She collapses in confusion, exhaustion, frustration, and grief.

# CHAPTER TWELVE — Desertion

ᎠᎡᏔᎪᏍᏫᎢᏍᏓᎶᏯᎠᏛᎡᏉᏔᏇᎯᎩᏎᏩᎷᎦᎹᎦᏚ-ᎣᎯᎯᏛᏯᎥᏌᎥᏏᎯᏃᏋᏅᎤᏝ

Lisa stumbles and steadies her stance far from her husband's death cart. A hand braces upon a tree's trunk. Her shoulders shiver as unusual March temperatures chill exhausted muscles.

Moonlight filters through the budding limbs of the branches above and throws abstract patterns over her skirt. Splattered from the day's surgical blood, the garment dots with dark spots that mix with shadow limb shapes.

In frustrated and exhausted emotional turmoil, the shadows spin and twirl in her mind as she steadies on the rail of her stairway.

*"Who am I, Ezra?" Lisa Waters preens atop her second-story stairs and views dancing couples.*

*"You're the social queen of Fort Smith, Arkansas, my dear. No, the complete state." The queen's husband slips his palm onto his spouse's corseted waist and pulls the twenty-six-year-old onto the stairway.*

"I can't dance in a dirty dress." Lisa rubs skirt blood spots against one another with both hands.

The effort increases her breathing, and the air from her lips frosts from the uncomfortable temperature.

She holds a hand nearer her eyes in the night's luminance. "The color of my fingers say I pick cotton, but they're bloody. The red stains my other native half. No, both are mixed in war. Mother, I need you. I'm lost. Lead me to a promising land."

She sits at the trunk of the tree and visualizes her husband's face. "Ezra, my wonderful warrior. Why is your hair so matted?" Her mind wanders and eyes close.

New mental pictures form on the inside of shut eyelids.

*In Georgia, before the forced removal, Lisa watches her sisters sift through the debris of a burned log home of long ago. "Where have you been? It worried me," Bella's eyes mist.*

*Lisa's lips tremble but move in the frigid air. "Looking for a new life. Why are you here? Where is Ella?"*

*"I was walking in the fields. We have an excellent crop to sell," Older replies. "Just thinking and planning. Father did the same."*

*Lisa extends both hands. "I can help with the work."*

*"Picking is a job for slaves." The oldest shakes her head negative.*

*"Ezra does not pick cotton." She turns to her sister. "He is an attorney. And Benjamin Waters is your parent and does not tolerate slavery."*

*"But his laborers wrapped him in canvas. They moved the dead body to that old hickory tree. The one where Paw buried Grandma." The middle daughter watches.*

*"Good," the older returns. "I chose the site."*

*"Ella. We speak of slaves, our parents' death because of ownership and why you and I are not slaves."*

*Lisa gasps, recovers her senses, and flinches against the tree's trunk.*

*She struggles to both feet and stumbles to the burned remnants of her childhood home. The youngest joins the older siblings and spies something in the charred debris.*

*She lifts an unrecognizable ash-blackened toy doll from the ruins.*

*Younger sister bursts into crying. "Ma made Betsy. I was six."*

*"Be strong." Bella steps close and slips an arm around Lisa's shoulders. "Someday you can sew a new baby and give it to your daughter."*

*"Never be another! I will never have a child!" The girl throws the destroyed toy into the charred memories of life.*

*"Please, everything changes." Middle sister extends her arms. "We must stay together, protect each other, and love, if we want to survive."*

*"Why can't you shut that mouth?" The youngest sibling retorts. "Words fix nothing! You just spout noise."*

*"Bella's right. We must adapt." Ella clenches a fist. "Without a home anymore."*

*"Neither of you know!" Lisa stomps on Betsy, and charcoal dust rises from the cloth. "You both got killed and left me here alone!"*

An external noise disrupts the dream and focuses her attention.

She steadies the mind, looks around, and scrambles to concealment behind her tree.

A distance away, several union officers survey an empty field west of Elkhorn Tavern.

"Colonel Osterhaus, that knoll."

"I see it, Major. Report to General Sigel that we have found an excellent artillery position on Pea Ridge. Tell him I recommend moving the first and second divisions up Telegraph Road."

The woman stretches her arms wide and steps from behind her tree.

"What the hell?" The major's horse rears.

"How did she get out here?" Colonel Osterhaus turns his mount. "Must be a nurse. Look at that bloody dress. Take her into town."

The orderly spurs his mare, sweeps Lisa from the ground, and lifts her onto the front half of his saddle. He extends his reins and follows his officer's lead.

The union cavalrymen clatter through the night's darkness.

The trooper holds the woman.

She focuses on the soldier's skin, a darker color than her own, but worn and scarred from hard labor.

The two soldiers of different rank approach Leetown.

The major turns toward Elkhorn Tavern, the Union Army's command post.

"Take that woman to the first medical unit available, then report to your own."

"Yes, sir!" The other rider heels his horse as the officer canters to headquarters.

Too exhausted and confused to notice, Mrs. Waters rides with her escort as he turns from the road and reins his horse across a meadow and into the woodlands.

The rider slips through the trees as her protector approaches confederate lines.

Campfires glisten in the distant woods and resemble fireflies low to the ground.

The woman moans in her sleep, and the orderly's hand muffles her mouth.

***

The next morning, with her stomach supported by a saddle and her head hanging, the fleeing nurse opens her eyes and focuses on an upside-down flag that waves in a gentle early breeze. From her point of view, its flagpole points downward into the sky beyond her concealment in a brush line.

Golden light from the rising sun warms the pennant's blue field with two red and one white stripes. Stars form a small circle, and lettering reads, "Cherokee Braves."

Lisa trembles with fear as her semiconscious mind recognizes the flag of the First Mounted Rifles, Standhope Watie's confederate command.

A palm clamps over her mouth and nose, which blocks air, and she swoons into silence.

***

Moments later, morning light tickles Lisa's eyelids as she moves through the foliage.

She opens her eyes and focuses upon her escort's face, but her mind drifts in confusion.

"Michael, row the boat ashore. Hallelujah! Michael, row the boat ashore. Hallelujah!" Josiah Rains sings from his soul. "Jordan's river is chilly and cold, Hallelujah! But it warms the human soul, Hallelujah!"

The woman makes her brain concentrate on the voice. "You made it into Kansas?"

"I did Mrs. Waters."

"Help me. This is making me sick."

The freedman stops his mount and helps Lisa gain a seat behind him. "Sorry. You couldn't keep your balance. I had to carry you across my saddle."

"I'm fine. Stomach's sore. What are you doing here?"

"I joined the army, but killing Cherokees turns my stomach. I am deserting."

"And you're taking me?"

"Through confederate lines. I'll take you to your husband. My family owes you that much."

"Ezra's dead." Lisa's voice breaks. "And scalped."

"Stand Watie's soldiers, I figure. White rebels yell and shoot you but leave the skin on your skull."

"What am I going to do? I'm confused and so weak."

"I am not sure, Mrs. Waters. But I remember when you helped me."

Lisa's eyes roll and she slips into unconsciousness in the crook of Josiah Rains' arm.

She dreams.

***

*Lisa lives in the sky. Her stitched doll from her childhood's burned home waits in the middle, above the Earth.*

*The Cherokee baby, blackened by ash, hovers alone, a symbol of two cultures.*

*On her arc through the heavens from east to west in the sun's track, she picks her Betsy from the clouds.*

*Indigenous people on the ground stand in the charred ruins of her freedman father's burned farm. In fear and awe, they squint and watch her progress.*

*She lifts her dirty rag doll to her cheek. "My descendants twist their faces whenever they see me."*

*"I, as them and our folks below, am handsome." The girl toy smiles.*

*"Yes, but enslaved by the White man." Lisa holds the doll's soot-stained face before her own.*

*"Your relatives own humans!" Stuffed lips contort an accusation.*

*"I am dark as you. My father was a freedman!"*

*"The color of your skin does not matter." The blackened toy protests. "I perished in the fires of the world long ago. What counts today is the hue of your heart. You are confused and hateful!"*

*Jealous and angry, Lisa sends a great fever upon the Cherokees. Many human beings fall. Wives lose husbands and children, their mothers.*

*Lisa's anger flies westward over the grass plains and its populations to spread the carnage.*

*She exacts vengeance over the land for her doll's words.*

*Disease-surviving Indians seek help from their popular leader, Standhope Watie.*

*The confederate commander of the First Cherokee Mounted Rifles sits in a chair draped in the stars and bars.*

*"How do we stop these deaths from the fever?" Emissaries drop to their knees before their ruler, clad in the South's battle flag.*

*"The deaths of our people end when the sky woman dies." Watie touches two of his followers, and they transform into snakes, an adder and a copperhead.*

*"Hide near our ally." The soldier's voice reverberates from Georgia to the Rocky Mountains.*

*On the day after the night ends, Lisa stops to visit her doll.*

*The serpent curled around Betsy prepares to strike.*

*Its accomplice hides under the toy as reinforcement.*

*"Spiteful reptile! You enslave my baby in your curl. Free her from your oppression!" Lisa's fresh opposition, drenched with truth, blinds the snake.*

*It only spits yellow slime.*

*Lisa lifts her stuffed child to her cheek.*

*"Go, nasty thing!" She kicks at the slithered. Discouraged, the copperhead crawls away.*

*Still dying from the fever, the Cherokees bemoan their viper's failure and return to plea with Standhope Watie. "Help us, Great One! The slave doll escapes."*

*The Cherokee leader rises to his feet and sweeps his battle flag before his face. With both hands, he fans his emblem of oppression over his supplicants.*

*In the flag's shadow, a warrior shudders, confronts metamorphosis, and becomes Uktena, the water monster.*

*A lesser human within the sweep rattles into a danger-warning tailed snake.*

*"Our enemy shall die from her own earth's venom!" Watie wraps his red and white banner around his squatty shoulders.*

*"The large and fierce Uktena, with horns on its head, should succeed." A Cherokee petitioner claps his hands with delight and encourages the crowd.*

*The lesser rattlesnake wants stature and races ahead. It coils beside Lisa's doll.*

*When Lisa arrives on her day's journey across the sky, he strikes, and she falls from the heavens.*

*"Reptile, we share this earth. For this attack, you must squirm on your gut." She transforms her attacker. "And the heels of my tribe shall smash your head forever."*

*Rattlesnake in fear returns to the people, and they cower with repulsion.*

*"I promise to never bite again. I wish humans well."*

*The water monster grows angry at the usurper on its belly in the dirt.*

*It becomes so furious and venomous that wherever he looks, a Cherokee's family dies.*

*Watching the deaths, Standhope Watie spreads his arms. "You poison my loyal confederate followers. I banish your soul to walk in the afterlife with dead Yankees."*

*Without Lisa and water spirit, the people no longer die, but they must live in darkness because she doesn't trek across the sky.*

*They crawl in weakness to the leader. "Revive the abolitionist. Bring her back from Tsusgina'i. Our land has become a ghost country, which lies in Usunhi'yi, the Dark World in the west."*

*"Choose seven men to bear weapons." Watie commands. "I send them to her."*

*The tribe chooses representatives to make the journey. Each takes a box to carry one sourwood rod a handbreadth long.*

*"Find those who dance to her Cherokee Reel." Standhope Watie imitates a fiddler. "Stand outside their circle, and when the abolitionist singer dances past, strike with sourwood and place her parts in your boxes. Do not open your container, not even a crack."*

*The seven catch and put Lisa into their cartons. They close their lids, and the other dancers never notice.*

*When the group nears home, she cries out to her stuffed and stitched doll. "I move from lands where I danced with my husband. Let me return to my love!"*

*Indian hearts long for hope.*

*They soften and crack their tops.*

*With a flush sound, the future blows past them into the sky.*

*Shutting the lids, they open their packages for their Confederate leader.*

*The containers sit empty.*

*"If they kept the boxes closed," Standhope Watie adjusts the CSA (Confederate States of America) saber at his waist, "you have the traitor and we regain our soldiers from ghost country. Now, we can never recover our people who die in this war!"*

*Meanwhile, the youngest Waters girl sits on earth and cuddles her Betsy doll. She weeps for her Ezra, his allies, and every lost southern sympathizer.*

*The Cherokee desert their General of the Confederacy and send their handsomest young men and women to dance and sing for Lisa with a drum and fiddle, "Hail, daughter of the sunny south, bright banner for the free! Our hearts swell high with joy when glory points to thee!"*

*She bows her face in disbelief and ignores the attention.*

*The drummer and his fiddler change the song to her Cherokee Reel.*

*The woman hears the music, looks up at young people, forgets her grief, and smiles welcome for a better future.*

## CHAPTER THIRTEEN — Pins

ᎠᎡᎢᏐᎣᎢᏒᎣᏗᏴᎠᎫᎬᏉᏚᎯᎦᏛᏫᏛᎢᏍᎹᎢᎦᎣᏅᏚᏴᎣᏓᎣᏂᎯᏃᏉᵛ

Lisa wakens.

An old friend smiles. "Thought we lost you."

"Moss! Where am I?"

"Josiah Raines brought you in four days ago. This is a Pin hideout that you and Ezra financed. Used to be a stop on the railroad. You're safe now."

"Ezra's gone. They scalped him at Pea Ridge." The woman touches her friend's face with trembling fingers. "Why did they do that?"

The fiddler's smile fades, and his lips tighten. "War killed your husband, Mrs. Waters. But scalping's different. That's hate. The blood in your veins runs half Indian. You know why. I don't have to explain."

"Watie's Second Cherokee Mounted Rifles did it." Lisa stares at her friend.

"Against Drew's First in blue." Moss nods. "Josiah said the battle was tough on both sides. Brothers against each other. Most wanted no more killing of Indians on White man's land. Droves deserted. A few, those against slavery, joined us. Picked up sixteen men, experienced fighters."

Waters focuses on a symbol attached to Moss's coat. Two crossed pins dangle a corn husk.

"A letter came by a Cherokee courier a few weeks ago. From Mrs. John Ross." The fiddler pats her shoulder. "You strong enough to read?"

She nods and Moss steps across the small room and retrieves a paper sealed with the wax of the Nation's president. He hands the message to his ward.

"How's Josiah?"

"The fellow's with us now. Quantrill's raiders murdered his family. Remember his wife and those cute kids? Guerrillas burned his farm in Kansas, so he joined Drew's men."

"Then deserted?"

"Yes, when he found you. The man remembered the fiddler and the railroad."

"I ran too. Doctor Kent needed me, but I couldn't face the blood and dying. I helped cut off more limbs than I want to remember."

Moss nods understanding and moves to the room's door. "Curtis won Pea Ridge, but it cost union legs. These days, there's too much leg letting on both sides. Read that letter and get rest. I'll check on you before supper."

Lisa looks at the correspondence. Her hands tremble as her fingers break its seal.

"Dear closest friend. Forgive me for brevity, but I must dispatch this. We have a courier waiting. They have not executed us as traitors, for John swore allegiance to the Confederacy under duress. I fear consumption because I cough blood. For health and safety, he returns me to my parents and endures alone. How I miss the days when you lived nearby and life was without war and strife."

Lisa looks up from the letter and remembers happier times.

"I hope this finds you and Ezra safe and happy. I know the president fears for your attorney and his people, including my sons, in Colonel Drew's regiment. They have been called to fight in Arkansas. When we raised the Cherokee regiments, they committed to the defense of the territory, not action in other places. Pray for Allen. They captured him bringing supplies to the family and hold our son in a Confederate prison camp. I worry over Ezra's safety. I will write from my parents' when I can. Your lifelong friend. Mary Stapler Ross."

Lisa's letter drops to her lap, and she returns to sleep.

***

The following morning, several Cherokee Pins munch on ham and beans for breakfast as the new woman in camp joins the table. "I could use a bite of that. This stomach says I haven't eaten in a month."

Moss sweeps a hand toward a space. "Please, sit. You and your husband paid for this."

Mrs. Water's eyes moisten.

"Sorry, ma'am. If it weren't for you, this place couldn't exist." The fiddler coughs.

"I'll get you a plate." Josiah rises and steps to a pot on the fireplace. He returns with a hearty breakfast.

Lisa enjoys the food but soon notices several Pins who steal quick glances in her direction.

She swallows a mouthful of beans. "I'm the new person. What's on you fellows' minds?"

A young Cherokee leans forward. "Are you the same as Moss and Josiah?"

"No. They are male, and I am not." She chuckles. "But I under-stand. My father was a freedman in Georgia and my mother's name was Ayokha. She was a full blood."

"I fought with your husband at Pea Ridge." The youngster nods. "He was a brave officer. But I took French leave."

"He was a good man. Why did you desert your unit?" Lisa helps herself to food.

"I murdered my cousin on the other side."

The woman sits in silence. "I was a nurse in the Leetown hospital. I helped take many an arm or leg from Cherokees, Yankee and rebel. Their blood looked the same. I'm glad you said no to more killing."

"I didn't say no, Mrs. Waters." The man's forefinger flicks the corn husk that suspends from his jacket. "I still believe. I just can't shoot cousins over somebody else's property."

"Pins kill relatives on our land?"

"Hope not, ma'am. But if they're rebels, yes."

"Eat your breakfast, Willi." Moss points a spoon at the man. "Then you're going with Josiah on a fact-finding ride along the river."

After the meal, Lisa lingers with the fiddler at the table and sips coffee.

"That fellow is too youthful for war, don't you think?"

"I used to think that way, Mrs. Waters." The freedman shakes his head. "That boy lost two brothers at Pea Ridge. Before that, Watie's Knights of the Golden Circle burned his mother and father's farm a few years back because they didn't tolerate slavery. The guerrillas caught them hiding runners."

"That's a much too common story, I fear."

"I'm not worried for soldiers such as Willi. He's found his cause. But I worry over you."

"Me?" Lisa finishes her cup. "You still play the fiddle, Moss?"

"I do. Keep it under my bunk."

"I want to dance in my life. But the music in it rings sour."

"With your husband gone and the Confederates confiscating his properties, how will you survive these next few years?"

"Only need to last until this conflict ends. The union's winning. Vicksburg fell to that new commander, Grant. Ezra used to say the side that controls the Mississippi celebrates victory."

"That's far away, Mrs. Waters." Moss finishes his coffee. "Watie's a Brigadier General now, and his troops will find us. We can't huddle here to be massacred. Josiah's scouting the river. We heard they set up a small supply station, and we need provisions."

"Nor can I hide and wait for the war to end." Lisa stares into Moss's eyes. "I have a couple of hat pins if you have more corn husks."

Moss smiles. "Remember that old Patterson Colt I taught you to shoot?"

"Darn thing weighed twelve pounds."

"One man wounded at Pea Ridge had an extra Baby Dragoon five shot. It weighs less. He didn't make it, so I'll get it for you."

"Then I'm a guerrilla, armed and ready."

***

The following day, Lisa rides with Moss and Josiah along the Arkansas River. Willi guides his mount in the column of twos beside her.

"They said the depot was just around the next bend. You scared, Mrs. Waters?"

"Yes. Anyone who says different is lying or never saw Watie's Mounted Rifles."

"Or heard them yell." The youngster shudders. "They screamed crazed thunder demon yells at Pea Ridge."

"Quiet back there." A voice from ahead in the column silences conversation.

The riders stop and wait.

Lisa looks along the river's shore. In the distance, a new pier extends into the tributary and several log cabins sit on its bank.

Distant workers unload a barge and carry loads of goods into the storage buildings.

Unaware of the watching Pins, the men work under a First Cherokee Mounted Rifle flag that flaps upon its pole above the largest cabin.

The union column moves away from the river into the woods and encircles the supply depot.

Individual fighters stop every twenty yards until the storage depot lies surrounded by armed riders in a loosely packed expansive semicircle.

Lisa watches. Willi stands his mare to her left. The next Pin in line beyond him waits, obscured by trees.

By reflex action, the Calvary tightens its encirclement as they move closer through the woods.

Pistol fire on the right breaks the silence, and Lisa draws her weapon.

Her horse clears the timber, and a surprised sentry in a worn Confederate uniform whips a rifle to his shoulder.

A thirty-five-caliber percussion bullet from her round barrel Navy Dragoon impacts the guard's chest and propels him to the ground.

Willi reaches the first log cabin and runs into a Cherokee.

The rebel stumbles out with thumbs hooked to suspenders.

The young Pin spins and shoots another Confederate in the temple.

A third defender leaps and drags the boy from his horse, and they wrestle in the dirt.

Lisa fires and blows the rebel off the boy's chest.

She jumps from her saddle to the youngster's side. "You hurt?"

The youngster nods no and struggles to his feet.

Both look around the cabins.

Pins finish shooting or scalping most of the depot's workers while a few others escape into the woods.

Moss emerges with two kegs of gunpowder, one under each arm.

Lisa, with her pistol pointed inside, enters the log building before her, and her pupils focus in the dim light.

From the cabin's roof hang slabs of beef and whole pigs. She coughs in the smokehouse's raspy air.

Under a hog carcass, three slave children huddle together in a corner and tremble in fear.

"Everything's fine. No more noise. We're your friends. Nobody will hurt you." The woman walks closer and extends her hand. "Come on out. You're free now. Do you know what that means?"

Willi enters from behind and steps past Lisa to grab the girl's arm. "Out of here!"

The oldest child lunges forward and drives a knife deep into the inexperienced man's chest.

Lisa screams as her new friend falls. She hooks her hands under the youngster's armpits and drags the boy out of the dimness.

Moss supervises a final load with the last of the captured supplies and provisions.

She holds Willi's hand as he slumps his head and shoulders against a nearby trunk.

"Time to go." The fiddler steps closer. "Help me lift him into the wagon."

Josiah bends, and the two men move the young Pin, who screams and cries from pain. "No!"

"Don't hurt him, Moss!"

The youngster stops screaming with gentle placement against his tree.

"We must deliver these supplies. Too many escaped. Watie will have reinforcements here soon."

"I stay with the boy. Go."

"No ma'am." The fiddler gestures to his second-in-command. "Get the goods on the road."

"We'll return." Josiah moves his horse and the wagon's team onto the trail. "May be tomorrow afternoon at the soonest."

Lisa and Moss watch their Pin companions disappear into the trees, and quiet settles over the ravaged supply depot and its dead.

"We shouldn't be here when Watie's soldiers arrive." The fiddler stares off into space.

"Willi's passed out." She looks at her friend. "Maybe we can move him."

"At least away so we're not so obvious. Let's try to get him into the woods."

The freedman slips one arm under each of the boy's armpits, and she hoists his feet. They struggle with the weight but achieve the tree line.

"If he only fainted earlier, we could have lifted him to the wagon." Lisa catches her breath.

"I'm not doing any good here." Moss looks at his horse that stands by the cabin. "I'll do perimeter scouting. We need to know when Watie's troops come."

Willi lies under the trees in concealment, and she wipes feverish moisture from his forehead. "We'll get you back. Just don't die."

***

Late afternoon shadows stretch across the young Pin's face before his nurse twists, distracted by voices.

"Not much left, Major." An Indian scout surveys the depot with his commander. "Pin work."

Lisa peers over the brush and watches a First Cherokee Mounted Rifle detachment among the empty cabins of their supply yard. She concentrates on the officer in charge.

Lisa's mind remembers a trial.

*Standhope Watie sits with his attorney nephew, fresh from an Eastern legal school, Elias Cornelius Boudinot.*

*The defendant's eyes focus on the prosecutor's lips and words.*

*"You jurors have a prime duty." The prosecutor nods to the jury. "With the solemnity of your oath governed by the law and the evidence, you must decide Mr. Watie's fate from the merits of the case and not according to public opinion."*

*Several men seated near Lisa jump to their feet, and their cheers fade with Judge Steel's gavel. "The Advocate" reporter moves further away in her seat.*

Her movement on the bench transitions into a concealment retreat below brush, and her lips form words, "Elias Boudinot."

She peeks over the thicket a second time.

"Nothing left here." The thin-faced, mixed-blood Cherokee scout with Watie's nephew looks around the depot.

"Pins are long gone with our supplies. The cabins are good." The major directs Clemet Rogers, his Indian tracker. "Settle the men for the night. We'll ride back tomorrow."

"Yes, sir!" The scout's handlebar mustache wiggles. "Post sentries, I presume?"

"Yes."

"Track for you any day. In this war, common sense is rare."

# CHAPTER FOURTEEN — Capture

ᎠᏳᏔᏬᎢᏍᏬᏏᏴᎠᏦᎮᏋᎯᏂᎦᏫᏛᎦᎹᎭᏧᎣᎯᏋᏴᎨᏋᏁᎭᏃᏋᎣ

That evening, the First Cherokee Rifle's troopers prepare their dinner over campfires outside their looted supply depot.

Lisa weeps in silence and solitude a distance from the rebels.

She kneels near the body of her young friend.

With red bruised hands, Willi's nurse and mortician abandons the shallow depression, an attempted grave, as an impossible task in rocky soil.

She slips her fingers over the boy's eyes and closes his eyelids. From a crouch, she peeks over the brush and checks the Confederate camp.

The shadows of Cherokee troops mill against the trees, and occasional laughter punctuates the night.

Cooking food smells drift around Lisa, and her stomach growls. The hungry woman takes Willi's pistol from his belt and stuffs it in her waistband. After a last glance over the brush, she slips into the darkness.

From tree to tree, the Pin leader escapes.

At each trunk, she pauses and scans the surroundings for sentries. Soon, she intersects the two-wheel tracks of the wagon trail.

For long moments, Lisa hides in the shadows beside the ruts and observes.

Not alarmed, the escapee walks a few steps at a time, listens, and continues.

Each tree near the road looms as a menacing shadow, either a dark trunk or a rebel sentry.

One shape threatens. "Move, and I'll blow your head off, Pin."

She freezes as a Cherokee steps from the gloom with his Enfield cocked and pointed at her belly.

"Beat the Dutch! Ain't you a woman?"

***

Minutes later, his prisoner sits disarmed on a potato box with her hands bound behind her back outside Major Elias Boudinot's cabin.

Across a small fire, where coffee brews, her captor strokes his mustache and studies the captive. "You a mixed Cherokee? So am I."

Lisa squeezes her palms together. "Why don't you let me go?"

"Can't. My ancestors didn't come over on the Mayflower. With yours, we met the ship."

"Then cut these ropes and leave with me." The woman squirms on her seat. "You know that killing your kind helps the boat builders."

"Look, lady-Pin, you have no right to criticize. I'm just a country boy in a big war trying to stay alive. You do the same thing. Most manufacturers with money live north of the Mason Dixon line." The scout pours himself coffee in a tin mug. "Here, I eat regular meals. That's the primary reason for soldiering."

The guard hears a sound and jumps to his feet.

Major Elias C. Boudinot steps out of his cabin. "This the prisoner, Clemet?" The officer turns to Lisa. "You know we hang Pins. Even women guerillas."

"I hear you scalp them first." The woman stands, and the campfire's light dances in her eyes.

The man studies his captive and rubs his beard. "I remember you, Mrs. Waters, from Fort Smith years ago." The rebel nods his head.

She sits upon her potato box.

"I heard your husband fell at Pea Ridge. I might offer my condolences, but he wore the wrong uniform. In my entire legal career, I am most proud of winning my uncle's defense over him for killing James Foreman. He prosecuted well for an uppity nigger."

Lisa restrains her tongue and the rope around her wrists digs into her flesh.

"General Watie knows that, since your husband's death, you associate with an illegitimate band of abolitionists."

The nephew of the commander stares at the corn husk on his prisoner's lapel. "What do we do with Pins, Clemet?"

Rogers coughs. "Want coffee, Major?"

"I have heard my uncle voice that he suspects you and a nigger named Moss conducted escapees before the war." Boudinot nods no to the caffeine offer.

The prisoner firms her jaw as a yes to the underground railroad accusation.

"You and General Watie slaughtered innocent women and children,"

Lisa looks at Rogers. "Slave and Cherokee. Your Knights of the Golden Circle, and even Lighthorse, dealt grievous atrocities."

The officer notices the prisoner's glance at his Indian scout. "She wants a response." The major assesses his soldier.

"Rumors travel fast." The Cherokee's eyes twinkle. "But they don't stay put as does truth. Time tells that story."

"I heard you are a good friend of Mary Stapler Ross." He focuses his attention on his captive.

"Ross's wife returned to her childhood home." Lisa lowers her chin.

"With consumption." The major's voice crackles with irritation. "Lincoln freed the niggers up North, and her husband did in the territory, but that won't stand. They will elect my uncle to replace him soon."

"Because only rebels get to vote." The prisoner spits on the rebel's boots.

In anger, the officer kicks Lisa in the stomach, and she curls to the ground with pain. "Guard this guerrilla tonight, Rogers! We'll hang her at first light. I want our Cherokee troopers to watch what happens to traitors."

***

Later that night, the Pin regains consciousness inside one of the supply cabins. Her vision focuses on the bare earth of the floor. Her wrists ache and throb from tight bindings.

She moans from the pain.

"You ain't going nowhere." Clemet Rogers' voice pierces the darkness. "I'll cut those ropes. This is your last night. You deserve as much sleep as you can get."

The scout's shadow moves closer and slips a knife blade through the restricting bondage.

"How long before dawn?" Lisa rubs her wrists.

"Ten hours." The guard, against the moonlight, silhouettes in the cabin's entry. "Don't run unless you want to cheat the hangman. There's another fellow out here tonight that'll shoot you dead."

The door closes halfway and then opens.

"This ain't right." The future father of Will Rogers scratches his head.

Reminiscent of the famous son, "Stupidity got Cherokees in this mess, Mrs. Waters."

"Just come with me."

"Shame is I can't."

The entry shuts, and darkness brings more oppressive silence.

The prisoner sits alone for hours, and her mind visits her memories.

*During the extreme temperatures of the forced removal from Georgia, Lisa, as a child, watches an Indian hug her infant close and tremble from the temperature. "Help, please! Her father died from dysentery. She'll freeze!"*

*The woman lunges for one blanket carried by a US Army soldier with an armload who boots her away.*

*The man turns to the Waters sisters, who concentrate on their fire, and he moves on to the next potential customer.*

*Oldest sister Ella motions for the parent with a child to join them at their small campsite. The guest crowds beside the younger women and holds her offspring to the warmth.*

*She sees Lisa's doll. "You love your baby. That is good, but she is straw. Please take mine."*

*"What?" Lisa withdraws, and her face wrinkles with repulsion.*

*"Raise her as your own. My time is ending." The birth mother extends the child with both hands.*

*"What do you mean?"*

*"I spit blood."*

*The youngest Waters stares at the older woman for a moment and softens. "May I, Ella? She will be my sister."*

*"You can never replace Bella."*

*"Please, she's so cute." The younger sibling reaches for the slight girl.*

*"No, you spoiled planter's kid! No baby. It must eat, can't walk, needs an education."* The oldest attempts reason.

*Her words penetrate the pouty resentment and impatience.*

*After staring for a moment, she repeats a negative nod. "You're a child yourself."*

*"I wish you died instead of her! I hate you!"* The youngster retorts.

In the darkness of imprisonment, the last Waters daughter alive tucks her forehead in her hands and sobs.

Thunk!

Lisa's attention shifts to the sound from outside the cabin.

The door opens, and a shaft of moonlight stripes the earth floor.

"Moss!"

"Careful! You'll have them on us." The fiddler pulls her elbow, and she stands. "I have horses in the trees."

The freedman leads the escape.

Escapees step over a dead Confederate private that bleeds. A Cherokee war club bashed his skull.

They hug the wall and listen for danger.

Moss slides to the nearest cabin, and she follows. From one hidden spot to another, they work their way through the sleeping camp.

At the last cabin's edge, he holds his right hand in front of his partner's face with fingers extended and points.

Lisa peeks around the corner.

With his back facing the pair, a First Cherokee Rifle guard leans against the wall on one shoulder and smokes a homemade pipe.

The smell of tobacco smoke assails her nose, and she puckers to sneeze.

Before she explodes, Moss leaps and rips his knife through the sentry's neck. The soldier slumps.

Both stare at the dead smoker, a youthful Indian.

In Confederate boots and worn butternut pants patched in several places, the soldier's coat is non-regulation. The body lies thin, with cheeks drawn and pale from lack of a proper diet. A carved wooden pipe bowl smokes beside his hand.

"Come! We've made it." Moss pulls at her elbow.

"Look at that boy. He's just a young, starving, unclothed child!"

"If he got the shot, he would blow your leg away."

The fiddler half-drags his partner across the cleared space to the trees as she fixates on the teenager.

The two untie their horses from a tree.

"Don't move, Mrs. Waters." A low voice penetrates the night. "Or you, Pin. One twitch and you're a dead man."

Lisa turns to the sound, and Clemet Rogers steps around the tree with an Enfield rifle leveled. "You people won't get far."

"What do you mean?" The escapee freezes.

"We have sentries throughout these woods."

"Are you letting us go?" Lisa's jaw trembles.

"Yes. I'm helping you. If a sentry calls 'johnny cake,' you return 'cush.' Understand?"

The scout uncocks his weapon.

"I owe you, brother Cherokee."

"No, you don't. The more I fight this war, the more I realize life's what's important." He tips two fingers to his eyebrow and disappears into the brush.

The pair lead their horses through the trees. Fiddler stops and listens, then he moves further.

The escapees guide their mounts into a gully, which they follow with their heads concealed below ground level.

Their ravine leads uphill and becomes shallower as they approach a timber line.

"Johnny cake." A voice from the shadows halts progress.

"Cush." The freedman ducks behind his horse, and his companion follows the example.

"Lucky you ain't shot dead." The sentry chuckles. "Keep your heads low."

Moss turns and leads escape parallel to the trees.

Lisa wipes the sweat of fear from her forehead, and in her mind, thanks the Cherokee scout and father of the future famous twentieth-century humorist, Will Rogers.

## CHAPTER FIFTEEN — Revenge

DRTᎶᎤᎢᏏᏎᎥᎥYᎪᎫᎬᏛᏛᏇᎪ�...

Days later in camp, Lisa and Moss inventory items stolen from the Confederate supply dump.

A cabin has kegs of black powder, boxes of lead shot, stacks of blankets and winter clothing, barrels of corn and flour, and other supplies.

"Watie and the Cherokee Rifles will miss this stuff. Good raid." The fiddler pats the top of a keg.

"Productive." Lisa surveys the materials. "But we were a lucky escape. Something I want to ask."

"Why the scout helped you?"

"No. I think he was going to desert."

"Then what?" The freedman turns to his old boss.

"I know what johnny cake is. Ezra called the same stuff they ate hardtack. But what is cush?"

Moss points across the cabin's dim interior. "Saw a box over there. Only it's softened in coffee."

The two step out of the supply cabin and stand on its porch.

Beyond, the Pin guerrilla camp bustles.

Several Cherokee men gamble with rocks painted with symbols, others clean Enfield rifles, and more feed horses within a branch fence enclosure.

"Why do these fellows come to you?" Lisa watches.

"Most lost family to the Knights of the Golden Circle or Watie's raiders. They join our Pins for revenge; I think. No. Maybe it's survival." Moss tightens his jaw. "If you're not a rebel in the territory, nowhere is safe."

"This war harbors no one." The relaxed woman leans against a deck post, "Elias Boudinot, these men, Watie or John Ross, you and I."

A rider bursts from the trees and pounds along the road into the camp.

In a cloud of summer dust, the Cherokee scout flows off his horse before the pair. "Calvary coming a half mile back!"

Lisa jumps off the porch and runs for her quarters and a pistol.

Moss grabs a deerskin-headed drum from a hook on a cabin post and beats alarm with its mallet. As the signal spreads across the encampment, he exchanges the beater for a captured Enfield that leans against the wall.

The camp arms, and its cabins bristle with weapons in firing ports.

A union Calvary unit in a column of twos pounds out of the timber.

With experienced military precision, the horsemen and several wagons approach the Pins along the road into the allied fortifications.

A lieutenant stops his mount at the cabin's front. "Are you the freedman they call Moss?"

Fiddler steps to the porch's edge. "I am."

The White officer surveys the cabins which bristle with firearm barrels.

"Colonel Weer sends his compliments upon your successful action against the Second Cherokee Rifles."

The Pin leader moves off the porch. "Who is he and why do you interrupt our peaceful afternoon?"

"He commands this Indian expedition, sir!"

"You don't look Indian. Nor do these troopers."

"The contingent includes the Tenth Kansas Regiment, Allen's battery of Parrot Guns, and two recruited regiments."

Moss nods, and the young man sucks a breath. "We left Humbolt last June. Took the military road through the Quapaw Strip into the territory. Have you seen any Drew or Watie gray coats?"

"Look around you. Many of us fought for them at Pea Ridge."

"You don't fly the stars and bars, sir?"

"No, lieutenant. We switched sides. This is a Pin guerrilla camp. You and your Calvary are most welcome. We have common enemies. Water your horses and bivouac here tonight if you wish."

Lisa joins Moss with a pistol strapped to her hip.

"Afternoon." The officer tips his hat.

"You soldiers could use coffee, I expect." She looks up at the young man. "And we need fresh war news."

***

Moments later, the lieutenant nurses a clay mug of caffeine as his men refresh their horses and accept hot mugs from Moss's Pins. "Thank you. Decent water has been sparse since we left Kansas. The rebels have been poisoning the holes and ambushing patrols."

"Our scouts pick up where they camp but lack the forces to attack." Moss eyes the young officer.

"That, Colonel Weer needs to learn." The soldier slugs his coffee. "You Pins ride with us? He desires men familiar with the terrain. Where are the rebels today?"

"Near Locust Grove, raiders under Boudinot, and what's left of Drew's regiment."

"Indian mounted rifles?"

"Yes, with White rebel officers." Moss nods.

"The tribal forces at Pea Ridge went wild, no command, no organization, no discipline." The lieutenant throws the last of his coffee off the porch. "It should be easy, but we don't know Locust Grove."

"That's why you need Pins." Lisa takes the officer's cup. "I have a friend married to the president of the Cherokees. Have you heard of John Ross and his wife?"

"I believe he and his followers headquarter at Park Hill." The young officer shakes his head with resignation. "The colonel sent him correspondence asking for a meeting. He refused. His Nation signed the Confederacy, but I know nothing of any family."

"And news of the war?"

"We won an enormous engagement against Lee near Gettysburg, Pennsylvania, and Lincoln appointed General Mead as Army of the Potomac Commander."

"Lee's retreating." The woman smiles.

"But the casualties were horrific." The young officer observes his men. "Before we get too comfortable, how soon can your Pins ride with us back to camp?"

***

Three days later, Lisa and Moss follow the Calvary lieutenant.

Colonel Weer's troops, under the command of Major W.T. Campbell and conducted by Pin scouts, encircle Boudinot's confederate encampment near Locust Grove.

Fire from a skirmish engagement echoes over the woods and the soldiers as they move.

"We found the Rebs." Moss checks his long gun.

"Shouldn't we ride quicker?" Lisa glances at the union officer in front.

"We have them outnumbered. My orders are to prevent escape." The leader continues the troops' steady advance through the trees.

A Pin scout bursts out of the brush ahead. "We smashed them! They scattered!" His eyes widen as a rifle round explodes through his chest from the rear.

The fiddler slides from his horse and readies his Enfield over the pommel of its saddle.

He and Lisa protect themselves behind their mounts.

Confederate mounted rifles burst through the woods and charge guerrilla style. With reins in their teeth and pistols in both hands, they guide their horses with their knees.

Union Calvary yank their surprised and terrified mares into control.

Several Cherokee fighters pound past, fire handguns, and clatter away in desperate flights to escape.

Lisa aims and fires her pistol.

One attacker falls, catches his foot in a stirrup, and his momentum flings his body against a tree.

Another aggressive raider with a major's beret veers into the column and thrusts his Calvary sword through the troop lieutenant's throat.

The young officer's blood splatters onto Lisa's face as she aims her pistol at Elias Boudinot's head.

His eye's flash recognition as she jerks the trigger.

Watie's nephew laughs as the bullet flies over an ear, and he spurs his mount. As bullets pepper the grass around his horse, the rider escapes into the woods past the union column.

***

That afternoon, Lisa and Moss follow a summons from Major Campbell. They meet in his headquarters' tent.

In uncomfortable folding canvas chairs, the two sit before the officer's field desk.

"With the support of Pins, we captured sixty-four mule teams, a supply train, and many prisoners. I have dispatched my report to Colonel Weer, along with my description of your help." The major leans back in his wooden chair.

"Thank you, sir." Moss nods. "My men and I delight in any Watie defeat."

"Yes. I am sure you do. Two other issues need your attention." The White officer studies the pair across his desk. "Many Cherokees in Drew's regiment invited capture. They want to switch alliances."

"That does not surprise me." Lisa leans forward. "We do not wish to fight against our own."

"But you are not Cherokee, ma'am." The officer's eyebrow raises.

"Half, sir. My father was a freedman."

"Congress stated slaves employed against the union were free in sixty-one. Last year, another act freed those owned by men who supported the Confederacy." The officer lifts his eyebrows.

Lisa nods understanding and agreement.

"In January, Lincoln issued the Emancipation Proclamation." The major coughs.

"But you don't include Drew's troops?" Moss stares.

"Many of them claim slaves. These people's allegiance beyond themselves and their families is suspect, even to each other."

"I hear your words." Lisa settles into her chair. "But is there a question?"

"I do not wish to ignore the tribe's value as fighting men. Do your Pins accept these troops of unreliable loyalty?"

"We welcome the reinforcements." Moss grips his palms.

"Those disloyal to the union cause soon drift away. We have limited provisions to support those who stay."

"Which our supply flow through Kansas and Missouri can correct." The officer nods.

"Then, sir," the Pin leader grins, "I believe we agree."

"Contingent on my second issue." Major Campbell stands and steps to a map behind his field desk. "We need further help. My colonel directs me to take our expedition deeper into this territory infested with Watie's guerrillas. I am ordered to examine the positions of the enemy south of the Arkansas River."

Lisa and Moss watch the officer as he points at a primitive map. "Confederates control the west from Fort Davis."

The Pin leader points. "And this one?"

"I intend to occupy the Cherokees' decayed Gibson fortifications and wait for reinforcements."

"Good."

"Here is President Ross's headquarters at Park Hill. Do you know how many soldiers he controls?"

Moss looks at the map. "Couple hundred men. Two artillery pieces."

"When Weer arrives, we will dispatch a company to capture the president." The major glances at the pair seated before him for approval.

Neither respond.

After a moment, Lisa clears her throat. "The union plans to hang him?"

Campbell laughs. "No! You misunderstand. My orders are to escort him to Kansas. They can parole him to join his family in Washington."

Mary Stapler's friend expels her captured breath. "They are safe?" Relief floods her being.

***

The union's plan succeeds with the help and intelligence provided by Moss's Pins.

The expeditionary force they command disbands after its completed mission.

Later that year, after parole, Ross establishes residence in a two-story home on South Washington Square in Philadelphia.

He spends his time in the capital and develops a personal relationship with President Lincoln.

The leader's interests stay with his people.

From the seat of government, the leader influences the affairs of his Cherokee Nation.

As fall fades, the war decimates the land. It rages with guerrilla fervor throughout the territory.

Lisa and Moss hide in the hills with their Pins, no longer protected by a large union troop presence.

"We got supplies before the expedition fell apart." She smokes a pipe with her back against a cabin's wall.

"Weer stands trial in Leavenworth." The fiddler leans on his rifle and watches the sun set over the trees. "They claim he was a boozer, abusive and violent with his officers. To me, it smells of deceit, not alcohol."

"What are they doing with his troops?" Relaxed, she blows circles of smoke that hold their form and drift.

"The Indian brigades moved north of the Arkansas. Drew and his soldiers protect the president's holdings at Park Hill. South of the river is Watie's."

"Which leaves us the only union force." She draws on her pipe.

"Yep." Moss drops to his knees. "Their guerrillas destroyed a hundred hogsheads of sugar at Daniel Ross's store. Then Watie called a general council at Tahlequah and elected himself principal leader of the Cherokee." The freedman laughs. "Nobody came out of hiding in the hills to vote against him."

"He was the only candidate." Lisa coughs over her pipe. The vapor drifts in the air and her eyes follow its movement.

In Lisa's view, the smoke flashes white hot at its base.

The center of the camp disintegrates in an explosion.

"Artillery! Where are our scouts?" The leader jumps to his feet as another cannon ball destroys a bunkhouse.

Panic sweeps through the encampment, and many flee the barrage.

From the opposite side, Cherokee Second Mounted Rifle guerrillas attack.

"They're coming from everywhere!" Lisa leaps to action.

Riflemen charge through the cabins on horseback and indiscriminately fire upon Pins.

"The woods!" Moss points.

"I don't have my pistol." She looks for a flight route.

"Go now!" The freedman, with his weapon, blows an attacker off his horse. "I'll rally the men!"

She runs for protection and concealment in the trees. She dives into the underbrush and crawls.

To escape, the woman rolls into a runoff ditch and scrambles along its course deeper into the woods.

Behind the escapee, in the Pin camp, several more cannon charges explode in symphony with rapid rifle and pistol fire and muffle the screams of dying Cherokee, both Union and Confederate.

From the gully, Lisa scurries through trees until she reaches a massive eastern Red Cedar with its trunk against a large rock. She uses the stone to climb into the tree's thick branches and squirms from branch to branch high near its top. Concealed from the ground, she catches her breath and listens to distant carnage.

Her Pins and their protection in numbers perish at the hands of an Elias Boudinot-led and Standhope Watie-planned surprise attack.

Lisa muffles her desperation as she sobs in hiding, cradled by the thick branches of her eastern fir.

***

Late in the night, she wakens and grabs a tree limb for unnecessary support.

Two horsemen move below her perch.

"Got any bark juice, Harry?"

"No booze." A second voice trails the first.

"Why are they searching for this woman?"

"Major B says she's a Pin hard fighter." The man slaps his hip. "Packs a pistol."

"Don't that beat a drum. She disappeared. But we sure captured that other nigger, that one they call Moss."

"Better yet, we shot or scalped the rest of them Pins. Good day's work." The two chuckle.

"Old Stand Watie may promote us both."

"Not both, just me, I figure." The lead rider pushes on through the brush.

Lisa hides.

***

The next midday, a shadow sweeps across the sun and she looks.

A black shape circles.

"Are you my buzzard? The one I fed bodies?" She squints.

152

Carrion bird sweeps closer to the earth and swoops to the ground over the next rise.

"Guess not." She chuckles. "It must be after a dead rabbit."

Nothing disturbs Lisa's hiding place the rest of the day or throughout the following night.

***

As the sun rises, Lisa climbs from her tree and assesses her peril.

Barefoot and weaponless in men's pants and a cotton shirt, without a hat to protect her skin, the woman steps from her protection and walks away from her safe concealment.

She stops, looks toward her Pin encampment, and shades her eyes with her hand.

Several hills beyond, buzzards circle above the remains of the camp and its bloated dead bodies.

154

# CHAPTER SIXTEEN — Restoration

## ᎠᏣᎢᏐᎣᎢᏏᏍᎣᏆᏯᎠᏨᎬᏈᏚᎯᎢᎣᏊᏪᏛᎴᏆᎹᏄᎯᎣᏅᏎᏲᏗᏇᏙᏏᏂᏃᏊ

For days, Lisa wanders into the territory's wilderness. Her bare feet bleed from sharp rocks and thorns, and her lips crack for water. She shades the eyes and searches the sky for buzzards, but no black shapes threaten.

"Keep moving. Half that blood on these stones is Cherokee. This is your land! You're home!" The woman stops and sits. "Why work against the soil? Foolish! Embrace your heritage. You are a child of this earth."

The wanderer spots dead stalks of river cane along a dry runoff rivulet and forces painful feet into movement. She selects a straight shaft and a stone. Impact with a sizable rock splits the object and leaves a crisp edge.

The half-Cherokee scores the tube, and it breaks.

The woman tucks the makeshift knife into a pocket.

Using a smaller diameter rod as a punch, Lisa hollows a larger stalk and smooths its interior with sand and a ramrod reed.

Nearby, she spots a clump of yellow thistle and harvests a fluffy leaf.

With a tip of the cane, the woman rubs the end to a point.

She ties the fluff to the tube with a torn strip of cotton from her shirt.

Lisa repeats primitive tool manufacturing and soon pockets a half-dozen darts.

With the blowgun, this hunter moves uphill and follows the dry-stone rivulet. Her eyes scan the landscape for food and water.

An unfortunate rabbit hops from under a bush and freezes with curiosity over the intruding human.

With care not to startle the prey, Lisa slips a dart into the hollowed cane and lifts it to lips. The force in her lungs blows, and the arrow flies true.

The meat jumps upon impact and limps several yards before a last breath.

The proud hunter retrieves the weapon and carries the carcass by hind legs as she continues up the hill.

Near the top, a freshwater spring source for a snow-melt-enhanced rivulet streams from under an outcrop and fills a small bowl.

A limited overflow dribbles out of the basin, and several yards of rocks in the gully show darkness from the moisture.

Lisa drops to her stomach and laps the water with her hands.

She rolls onto her back and watches dark winter's coming clouds drift across the late fall sky. Her gaze turns to the deciduous trees on the hill. Leaves are brown and orange with a touch of yellow. A few detach in the breeze.

Satisfied, the half-Cherokee sits up, withdraws the sharp stone from her pocket. The hunter field dresses and cleans the rabbit.

Below the spring, another outcrop juts from the earth and offers a protective roof over an animal's created den.

Near the small cave space, Lisa finds a dry fallen tree branch split from its trunk with a clean level break.

On this flat surface, she cuts a straight channel in its center with the sharp rock. She hollows the line into a shallow, thin groove. With another soft wood stick carved to a rounded point, the fire-maker rubs the tool in the track.

Next to the apparatus, in front of the den under an outcrop, Lisa gathers twigs and dry leaves, then crumbles more kindling.

To generate enough heat to kindle a flame, she presses two crafted parts together with force that her size and weight musters.

From one end to the other, back and forth, the stick against the baseboard shaves slivers of wood. Tiny embers from friction ignite the shavings.

Lisa blows on the sparks within the debris and adds smashed fragments of dry leaves. The tinder ignites into a flame that crackles with kindling.

Soon, a rabbit roasts over the fire pierced by a branch spit supported by another limb fork anchored with a stone. She gathers more firewood for the night.

Blackness engulfs the woods, and the wind changes from a breeze to a brisk propeller of leaves across the landscape.

The woman, with rediscovered Cherokee survival will, curls in the den underneath the protecting outcrop behind a fire.

Her ravenous stomach enjoys the cooked rabbit while darkness descends.

Wolves howl in the distance and attract the half-Cherokee's attention.

The lonely call reflects the emptiness within her soul and increases her isolation.

The animal's song lulls eyelids into sleep.

***

*Those lids flutter as Lisa, now a twenty-six-year-old, preens atop second-floor stairs and enjoys the color riot of whirling couples who promenade.*

*Hoop dresses spin in unison around women who follow leads by prominent Native American, mixed-race, and Anglo men—formal but uneasy guests.*

*Ezra Waters, a rising star in the political and financial center, joins his wife. "When you invited both factions, I didn't think many would come."*

*"Why not? People love to dance a reel." Wife strokes her husband, "But you saved me. With no slaves, you found waiters and musicians."*

*Music inspires animated gowns, hand fans, embroidery bonnets, and flushed faces.*

*A violinist, guitar strummer, and rhythm man on spoons, talented freedmen hired for the festivities, create the melody around a pianist.*

*Indian territory Treaty Party representatives and upscale new-arrival guests mix with the gateway to the west's society.*

*Fort Smith and Gibson army officers, wealthy Arkansas River shippers, and prosperous rice and cotton plantation owners socialize, hosted by the town's burgeoning legal establishment.*

*As oil and vinegar, opposing political position supporters do not intermingle, but cluster with others of similar affiliation.*

*They sip raspberry brandy, support each other's opinions, and eye those with disputing points of view.*

*The actual host couple steps onto the stairway to join the guests.*

*Lisa scans the people. "I see no one from the northern route."*

*"And your sister isn't here," Ezra slips a hand around his wife's waist.*

*"Celebrity enlivens a party. They flock to meet the Cherokee Rose. But I'm worried. I haven't heard from Ella in months." Lisa holds her gown's hoops forward to descend the stairs.*

***

Heads turn from political arguments, and as the sleeper wakens, yellow hate-filled eyes stare at the hostess with blood lust and unnatural soulless malice.

She faces slanted pupils that pierce the darkness outside the den a few yards beyond the flames.

The survivor scrambles to add wood to the blaze and reinforces the arc of heat at the shelter's opening.

Wolves cringe away from the brightness and pace back and forth.

As Lisa's combustion expands with new fuel, she grabs a flaming branch and hurls it into the wolf pack. Several wild dogs jump and cry as sparks splatter legs and paws.

Satisfied danger has passed, she settles into a safe and comforting enclosure.

Her mind shifts to words from the dream. "They flock to meet the Cherokee Rose."

With her sister's memory of how Ella could let nothing starve, the sister throws the remains of the cooked rabbit over the fire to the hungry dogs.

Their thin torsos with ribs through skin fight each other for nourishment.

Next dawn, the sun warms the sleeping quarters. Lisa wakens and adds her remaining timber to the fire's coals. The woman stands before the arc bed and stretches.

Wolves no longer wait outside the protection. She walks uphill and slaps spring water over her face. With cupped hands, she enjoys a morning drink.

***

After several nights in the survival den feeling falling night temperatures, Lisa summons the courage to return to investigate the Pin camp.

With a constant awareness of vibrations from the woods, she approaches the site one tree at a time.

No sounds penetrate the woods, and the air carries no evidence of recent Second Cherokee Mounted Rifles.

The ground's occasional hoof prints appear old and filled with leaves and natural debris.

The cabins of the Pin camp emerge in Lisa's vision from concealment. Most sit as roofless shells blackened by fire but cool and smoke free.

Human carcasses lie on the ground, unrecognizable as past fighters.

Swollen to shapes distorted as people, unburied men sprawl in the open, eaten by carrions and covered with maggots.

Lisa wipes tears from her eyes as she walks amid the carnage toward her cabin.

Inside, she searches through dumped flour kegs and ransacked supplies of the main room.

Under a burlap corn sack, she notices polished wood. Beneath lies Moss's undamaged fiddle and bow.

The woman drops to knees and hugs the musical instrument. Her thoughts shift to times long ago.

*Moss steps to the fireplace and captures his violin, where it leans against the brick. He sips his brandy, lifts his talent to a chin and strokes a soft melody.*

*She listens and sways to the rhythm. "The whiskey in a drunkard's cup is never meant for me," her mind invents the words to flow with the music.*

*"You have a wonderful voice." Moss's notes pause. "Keep going and try that again." He tucks the instrument under a chin and slides the bow across strings.*

*"The whiskey in a drunkard's cup is never meant for me." Lisa's eyes moisten as her emotions release memories of her sister. "It kills*

*my body and my soul and is a sight to see. I must abstain from all these things to free this Cherokee."*

*Moss holds the last note, and the song floats in the warm interior air. "A Cherokee Reel, Ms. Lisa. Your heart shapes the words, and this Louisiana rice-field fiddle makes the melody."*

The woman smiles at the memory and tucks the instrument under an arm.

She steps through the pillaged cabin to a separate chamber.

As its door swings open, clothing, including winter garb, lays flung on the floor. Women's things unfit for a guerilla to confiscate as contraband or for personal use include moccasins and a woman's size pair of boots.

She scans the room for other items.

Near one corner, a small wooden crate sits undisturbed.

Lisa jumps to open its lid.

Within lies a pistol, holster and belt loaded with cartridges.

Below the contents, other ammunition covers the box's base.

She pulls on the foot protection, straps the handgun to her waist, and gathers a load into a large burlap corn bag.

With lifesaving discoveries, the survivor leaves the Pin death grounds and returns to the spring- fed outcrop's shelter.

As she walks through the woods, she munches on kernels retrieved from the cabin.

A rustle from the woods attracts attention, and she pulls the pistol from its holster and ducks behind a tree. "Come out where I can see you! I'm armed, but I won't shoot."

No answer returns from the brush, but more branches move.

Lisa cocks the Colt.

A saddled and bridled US Calvary mount jerks with reins entangled in the thicket. Its eyes follow Lisa's moves as she releases the hammer of the weapon and struggles to free the horse.

She stands by its head and offers a handful of corn, which the animal chomps.

*****

Lisa's time in hiding transitions fall into winter.

The nights grow colder, spit rain, and later, moisture that drops at night hardens into ice.

During these days, Lisa explores the hillsides around the outcrop on horseback, including several returns to the devastated Pin encampment to collect useful left-behind tools and supplies.

One trip produces an Enfield rifle found upon a rebel casualty, along with the soldier's ammunition.

Another scouting foray higher in the hills discovers an abandoned but undestroyed cabin tucked against an outcrop near a hilltop.

The cabin's appeal includes proximity to a natural spring.

The explorer transfers the weapons, horse, gear and gathered items to the more secluded protection.

Temperatures fall, and winter winds sweep from the north.

Lisa completes a final scavenger return to the old Pin encampment.

Satisfied that she collected everything useful abandoned by Watie's Mounted Rifles, the woman settles into the cabin.

With a fire in the hearth and a fresh deer butchered, portions spit-roast over its flames. The rest of the meat cures in a barrel of salt brine.

Lisa sits on the soil floor of the room and opens Moss's violin case. She retrieves a fiddle, tucks it under her chin and slides the bow across strings.

She grimaces at the sound but attempts the note again with a slight change that improves the timbre.

Hours later, as snow settles outside the cabin and the horse stomps in its attached lean-to, the determined musician falls asleep with the instrument in hands.

***

Several nights after the fiddle practice, the mare snorts and thumps, which wakens the dreamer from thoughts of proficient music creation.

Lisa grabs an Enfield from against the cabin's wall near the fireplace and slips to a firing port window. She lifts the opening's cover and examines a full-moon-lit snowscape.

Frozen trees stand as sentinels around the clearing, and the snow sparkles, resembling stars in reflected moonlight.

At the clearing's edge, three shadowy shapes protrude from the whiteness.

They do not move but anchor in the ice as miniature obelisks.

Other than these forms, nothing else threatens.

Lisa closes and secures the firing port. She opens the cabin's door and points the rifle.

"Name yourselves!"

Small dark forms turn and, with clumsy steps in the snow, retreat.

"Wait! I will not shoot."

They stop.

"Come closer!"

The three tiny figures move toward the cabin.

Lisa moves outside and recognizes two girls and a bigger boy. The youngster carries a rolled deer skin over one shoulder and holds their possessions embraced in both arms.

"What are you children doing out here?"

"I ain't no child, lady." The youngster comes closer. "I'm eleven. My name's James."

"Of course. Who are these girls?"

"My little sisters, Elizabeth and Lucy."

"You're Cherokee?" Lisa sets the butt of the Enfield on the cabin's porch.

"I don't believe you are." The boy's voice trembles.

"I am, but that doesn't matter. You and your family get warm here. I have venison leftover from supper."

## CHAPTER SEVENTEEN — Judaculla

ᎠᏕᏍᏆᎣᎢᏎᎣᏞᏴ ᎠᏦᎬᏰᏈᎠᏲᎦ ᏔᏪᏍᏈᏣᎷᏔᎦᏋᎧᏅᎯᏝᏯᎾᏔᎾᏂᎻᏃᏈᎤᏉ

Lisa sits before the fireplace and watches her rescued Cherokee children sleep under piles of abandoned Confederate blankets.

The young boy and his sisters rest with the intensity of the exhausted and deprived. Their peace reflects their warm bodies and satisfied stomachs.

The two girls remind the adult of her own siblings, and she remembers.

Winter no longer imprisons.

*Lisa's full-blooded mother, her older Ella and Bella, along with family friends, dance individual appreciations of spring in a crosswise framed circle firepit.*

*Four logs, each in a traditional cardinal direction, enclose a ceremonial bonfire square.*

*Slave women mingle with the siblings and Indian wives, unusual but comfortable and reflective of the preferences of the event's host.*

*The individuals wave sticks with colorful strips attached to their tips.*

*A floating visual riot of primary color ribbons mix and float with the smell of flowers and an aura of equality in the air.*

*From the corners of the fire's pit, long branches of pine extend above the wives, the colors, and the sparks. A quad-pod, tied by rope at the top, anchors the limbs and dangles more bright colored straps and fresh yellow ripe cobs. In the breeze, they swing in rhythm with the celebrants.*

*Lisa's middle sibling, Bella, a shapely to a White man's eye sixteen-year-old, mimics her older sister's dance moves with tentative steps.*

*She concentrates on her instructress but cannot suppress her indecisiveness and insecurity as she notices several men's stares that follow her movements.*

*Lisa, fourteen, appreciates the men's reactions. The teen glances at Ella, admires Bella, and laughs. Younger twirls toward a mature youth of her age who stares, enthralled. The girl rattles leg shells and enjoys flirting.*

*The boy steps forward, and the inexperienced girl, flush with experimentation but cautious, slips behind others and blends with dancing forms.*

*Exploratory teaser security distances from her adolescent target. Across the fire pit, Ella, the oldest, points with a censuring glare. Youngest sibling winks, giggles and waves ribbon sticks. The mature daughter of the three slows pace as the younger girl dances nearby. "You are fourteen years old. Act that age. Don't pretend you are older."*

*The immature dancer flips ribbons in her sister's direction. "At least I'm not a biddy without a beau."*

Lisa remembers her families' Corn Ceremony during happier times.

The young Cherokee boy warm in blankets stirs, wakens, and rises.

A forefinger to lips reminds the youngster of his sisters' sleep.

James folds his blankets, slips moccasins on his feet, and follows the adult. They sit by the fireplace, and he inspects a pan of hot corn pone.

"Have breakfast." The cook impales a patty of the fried dough with a knife while bacon grease and cooked bits within the bread fill the room with aroma. "Where are your parents, James?"

The youth accepts the blade-born meal. "I don't know, ma'am."

"Call me Lisa."

"My father is a soldier with Drew's regiment, and he's been gone since I was nine and a half. Mother and us kids lived in a lodge near Crooked Creek way up in the hills. Mom said we had to hide from guerrillas. Week ago, they came, and we went for the woods. I became lost, and we wandered a couple of days before it snowed."

"Your mom?"

"Hope she escaped. Last I saw, she had Paw's old hunting musket, but I know we ran out of black powder."

"I'm pleased you found me, James. I live here alone and can use company."

"You don't know glad, ma'am. It's the way I felt when we first spotted your cabin."

"You and your sisters stay here, and when the weather clears, we'll go look for your mother."

"I doubt she's still alive. The guerrillas count my Paw as an Indian Blue Belly, and you know what they do to them."

"I know. But you can't give up hope." The woman hugs the boy. "We Cherokee have optimism."

***

Several days later, Lisa, with a rifle, and James, dressed in an oversized confederate coat, slip through the woods on foot and hunt fresh meat.

The young man spots a deer in a clearing. Both hunters conceal themselves, and he points.

His leader nods recognition, and the two creep closer.

A six-point buck kicks small patches of remaining snow and grazes on exposed brown winter grass.

The animal moves and lifts its head often to survey the meadow and its surrounding timbers for peril.

At wood's edge, the hunters huddle behind a lightning-split tree trunk, and the adult extends the barrel of her gun over the gap to steady her aim. One eye peers along the rifle's length and centers its sight on the prey's shoulders.

James coughs, and she twists to touch her lips with a forefinger. The boy's eyes dance with hunting excitement.

Lisa moves aside and leaves the weapon on the tree trunk. "You choose the shot."

The youngster grins and cuddles the rifle against his shoulder.

He pauses, looks at his hunting partner, and bows his head. "Unetlanvhi (ᎤᏁᏝᏅᎯ u-ne-tla-nv-hi, Creator God), I ask to take this deer to feed my sisters and my friend and want a sign it grants me a life."

The woman smiles and remembers.

An arrow thuds into the ground a few feet from the prey.

James focuses on the instant and pulls the rifle's trigger.

The deer in the meadow jumps from the impact of the bullet. It stumbles a few steps and falls in the partial snow.

Lisa holds the young man's arm and his impulse to retrieve the kill. "Wait. That came from somewhere."

"My mother says it's permission from Unetlanvhi." The boy peeks over the stump.

"See the movement over there?" A forefinger points at a solitary figure that emerges from the opposite tree line.

The shape moves on a slight hill toward the carcass.

"Somebody hunting with a bow is not a Cherokee Mounted Rifle." She stands and leads the youngster from their concealment.

The man stops and waits.

The pair of hunters approach.

Their competition notches an arrow into the string. "I have one left, so don't come closer."

"And I have plenty of ammunition." Lisa levels her long gun at her waist. "We mean you no harm."

"You shot the buck, but I need the meat for my kids."

"Put that dart in your quiver and you can have the deer." The hunter shifts her rifle barrel to her shoulder. "Where is your family?"

"We live in a cave. The Mounted Rifles burned our cabin."

"Why?" The woman grits her teeth.

"My place was a stop on the underground railroad."

Aware of the process, the ex-financier chuckles. "I used to be a conductor. James and I have a large home with a good supply of provisions. You're welcome to bring your kin and stay with us."

"I don't want a handout, but I lost my youngest daughter in that last temperature snap. She froze to death in our cave."

"My offer's not charity. Watie's raiders roam these woods. There's safety in numbers." The hunter raises her rifle. "I only have this and a pistol."

The Cherokee father lifts his bow. "I can make more arrows. I'll skin this deer. Then I'll go get my wife and kids."

Lisa nods. "Good."

"I know another family, John Graywolf. They hide in a temporary lodge near my cave. He's a President Ross man. The two of us build homes, and he has an Enfield. What do you say if I ask him to join?"

"I don't own my meadow. Unetlanvhi does. He and his weapon are welcome."

"We'll make rooms with shooting ports." The father turns to the animal carcass.

"I'll help you dress that meat since we shot it. Not a poor shot for my young fellow." Lisa pulls a knife from its sheath on her belt. The action opens her coat and exposes the Colt strapped to her opposite hip.

The Cherokee man notices the pistol, smiles, and nods his head at the youngster. "Save the rack. Your first set of antlers is special."

James beams with pride.

***

Weeks later, the Waters sister smokes her pipe on the porch of her cabin in the late afternoon and watches the two recent male additions to her group chop notches in tree logs with Pin camp recovered axes.

The several-log-high cabins stand near each other and in a line with Lisa's.

The Cherokee father's wife sits and strings sinew through fresh holes to make new moccasins. Her children play with Elizabeth and Lucy, and they skip over ground patches of snow.

James helps the men with cabin construction.

"We can never repay your kindness, Lisa." The mother ties a knot and looks at her handicraft.

"No need. You know how lonely these hills are."

"Yes. I felt it in our cave. But you've done more. Food. Supplies. Tools. None of these things did we have."

"Which once belonged to our fighters and our enemies. I just gathered them and put them to use." Mrs. Waters chuckles.

"My husband says you were married?"

"To a good man, an attorney. We once had a fine house in Fort Smith, but they confiscated it in the war. Then he died at Pea Ridge."

"I am so sorry." The woman leans closer and extends her craftsmanship.

"Moccasins? For me?" Lisa accepts the gift, slips off her boot and slides her foot into comfort.

"They look big." The wife laughs. "Let me tighten them."

She stands, shifts the pistol on her hip, and pops her pipe against the porch to empty the ash in its bowl.

The mother with the moccasins screams, and Lisa twists with a chilling rebel yell reverberating in her ears.

Three riders with pistols and rifles, Second Cherokee Mounted Rifle guerrillas, charge the camp from the woods.

Panicked hands lunge for her Enfield, which leans against her cabin's wall.

The lead attacker fires his pistol, and a round whistles past the Indian father's ear.

On one knee, Lisa pulls the trigger, and the raider yanks back off his horse with a bullet through his heart.

Second commando avoids the first's loose animal and aims for the resistance.

The fighter moves her firearm quicker, and the next guerrilla falls forward.

The engagement allows the third rider a moment, and he fires his handgun at close range.

A projectile explodes wood chips from the porch's post near her shoulder as she grips the barrel of her long gun and swings at the man's head.

The butt of the rifle impacts the attacker's face, and his momentum against the heavy weapon tears his chin from the skull.

Blood splatters Lisa's cheeks.

The dead man falls, and his horse trips on the deck's corner. He sprawls on the ground.

With red rivulets on her forehead, Lisa watches the mount regain its feet uninjured.

The animal snorts and stomps.

She looks at the wife beside her on the porch.

The Cherokee mother huddles with her arms around her knees and sobs in fear.

The fighter turns to the woman's husband. He stands with his jaw hanging open and his eyes wide.

The man's hands shake and his lips tremble. "You are the Judaculla! Unetlanvhi protects!"

Lisa steels her spine and shakes the stricken Indian by his shoulders. "Gather the guns from those bodies." The shaken defender spins to the teen. "Get in the cabin. These guerrillas don't travel in threes. There are bound to be more. Move!"

Inside, the woman fighter and the others station themselves at gun ports.

With more pistols and rifles, both men plus the youth now defend their home, armed.

Two wives and the children huddle in one corner where Elizabeth and Lucy stare with wide eyes at their grown-up big brother.

He offers a cloth wipe to his benefactor. "There's blood on your face, ma'am."

"Thanks." Lisa cleans her forehead.

She lowers her voice. "What's a Judaculla?"

The young man glances at the others, who peer through firing ports and pay no attention. "It's a Cherokee warrior, a slant-eyed fighter giant that defends our people and the land. Nobody kills it."

"Believe me, a Reb ball can end my time." Lisa looks through her observation port.

Nothing moves. The defender closes the opening and returns to the boy. "But not today, I don't think." Her hand pats the boy's shoulder. "I have too much powerful help."

174

## CHAPTER EIGHTEEN — Recruitment

### DRTᎦᎣᎢᏚᎣᏒᎩᎪᎫᎬᏋᏁᏗᎯᎱᏉᎳᏫᏕᎱᎶMᎲᎥᎣᏐᎯᎫᎩᎮᏖᎸᎾᏁᎯᏃᎥᏅᏬ

Four months after the attack by three Cherokee Mounted Rifles on Lisa's secluded cabin, spring floods the territory's hills with recent growth, fresh green leaves, and welcomed warmth.

Families who hide in the ridges discover the commune by accident or hear of its existence as an enclave of similar believers and recognize defensive strength in numbers.

Eight cabins cluster together without windows, but each bristles with sealed firing ports.

A corral has a dozen horses next to an equipment shed for saddles and dry hay.

The expanded clearing around the village features tree stumps, cabin construction reminders.

A ditch dug in the soil and lined with rocks carries water from the nearby creek to a hand-constructed basin within the cabins' square.

Smoke rises from a smaller log smokehouse where meat hangs and cures.

The beginnings of a corn patch's furrows show recent and promising agricultural development.

In the warmth of a fresh spring, children play chase around the cabins, and their parents work, aware Lisa's outriders will warn of potential danger.

Their commander, in her cabin, practices the fiddle.

"You know, ma'am, you're getting better."

"Lisa, please, James. Not ma'am."

"Yes, Lisa ma'am." The boy cleans his pistol, the same weapon fired that missed his leader and scattered chips from her porch's posts months earlier. "I can tell it's a tune. Play that again, and I'll sing."

She rosins her bow and begins afresh.

The young man's voice fills the cabin in symphony with the music. "Away down south in the land of traitors, rattlesnakes and alligators, right away! Turn away! Right away! Right away, move away! Where cotton's king and men are chattels, union boys will win the battles, right away! Turn away! Right away! Right away, come away."

The Cherokee father from the deer hunt swings the cabin's door open. "Mrs. Waters, a fresh addition arrived. Says he knows you."

"Is that so?" The musician places Moss's violin in its case and stands.

From a peg in the wall, she removes her pistol holster and straps the weapon around her hips. She steps through the exit and her eyes adjust to the brightness.

"Good to find you!"

"Josiah Rains! You got away!" The woman hugs her old friend.

"I did! A bunch of Cherokee Mounted Rifles ain't going to kill this freedman."

"Come. You can stay. We build barracks for fighters without family."

***

Later that day, Lisa sips coffee on her porch and renews her friendship.

"You know what happened to Moss?" The escaped slave drinks from his clay mug.

"No. Last I saw him, he told me to run for the trees as he took on Watie's guerrillas. I don't expect he made it." Lisa's eyes moisten.

"He did, but they captured him." The large man sniffs the steam from his coffee. "I heard he's in a Confederate prison camp, Camp Ford in Texas."

"Never been there." Lisa studies the woods around her camp. "It's not possible to free him. Too far."

"I understand the camp is bare ground, with over five thousand of our boys crammed into a stockade." Josiah shakes his head. "Reb troops ain't in much shape on the battlefield. I expect nothing for their prisoners."

"Moss is a powerful man." Lisa stares into the air. "I wish we could help him."

"Try prayer." The ex-slave holds silence for a moment. "Never seen you pray, Mrs. Waters."

"To whom? The White man's Christ? My mother's Creation God, or Jefferson Davis? I don't believe President Lincoln or Grant could save Moss."

"I took up their religion." Josiah chuckles. "Christ wasn't the color of General Lee. He was the same as us. Maybe He can."

"I am glad to have you back." Lisa finishes her coffee. "Stand Watie's guerrillas terrorized these hills far too long. We're stronger. He has to pay for every orphan. You're an experienced fighter, and I need the help."

"Vengeance is mine, sayeth the Lord." The ex-slave sighs. "But revenge might tickle my bones. If the Judaculla can't avenge us, nobody else will. The union ain't interested in these hills or anybody that lives here."

"My men call me that. I'm not mythical or a slant-eyed giant." She swallows her heritage as sour cod liver oil. "I am a half-Cherokee freedman's daughter with a loaded Colt on my hip."

Josiah recognizes the woman's isolation. "Federal troops pulled out of Tahlequah."

She listens.

The ex-slave shares more news. "They went with General Rains and Jo Shelby to recover lead mines.

"How about Watie?"

"He evacuated Fort Gibson and the territory for Kansas and Missouri where the fighting was."

"The people who lived there?" The woman holds the tips of her fingers to her lips.

"Nothing's left behind except gloom, apprehension, and dead bodies."

Lisa lowers her head for a moment. "He won't stay gone."

The woman displays more situational awareness than Josiah expects.

She gazes into the distance. "Every group of thugs in the woods claims to be Second Cherokee Mounted Rifles."

***

Days later, the leader rides at the head of a six-man unit through the hills and stumbles upon a burning cabin.

James, along as a scout and tracker, takes part in his first patrol.

The smoke from the fire rises white and wispy, evidence the flames burn from coals and blackened logs.

The youngster pulls his horse next to his leader. "Twenty raiders did this. Tracks are everywhere. But the rain last night softened their edges. Cabins burned yesterday; I expect."

"Good scouting." Lisa turns to her Pins. "See if anyone survived. James, stay with me."

The men search the clearing around the cabin ruins and the woods.

The other pair rides together, and the leader pulls her mount to a stop.

A Cherokee hangs by one foot from a tree limb.

The boy gags and vomits off the side of his saddle.

The corpse's eyes bulge. From a knife slit at her throat to her crotch, a lung and intestines hang. Flies swarm upon the meat.

"What person did this?" James looks at his leader.

"One who hates." Lisa pats the boy's shoulder. "You will never do this to another human."

"I swear."

"Thank you for not calling me ma'am."

The two turn from the grisly sight and navigate through the trees toward the cabin where a Pin rides to meet them.

"No survivors. We found four dead, a farmer and three children."

"And a wife in the woods." Lisa jerks her thumb in the air. "Let's get our livestock watered, then we'll track these devils."

"Must have been twenty guerrillas?" The guerrilla looks at horse tracks.

"Think six of us can catch them?" The leader stares at her follower.

"With the Judaculla, we will." The horseman turns toward the cabin and its water well.

***

As the moon rises to its apex, the group pushes through the woods.

James, beside his lead, sways on his saddle.

"Stay awake. Sleep and you might lose your scalp." The woman nudges the boy's shoulder.

"I'm not sleeping. Are we going to ride through the night?"

"We are. They're camped and don't know we're coming." Lisa's eyes glint in the darkness. "That mistake will catch them."

"But I can't see their tracks is this gloom."

"No need. We've got four Cherokee who can."

As the sun turns the sky gray before painting the clouds yellow at its rise, Lisa and her Pins surround a group of Watie's guerrillas.

Without sentries posted, the rebels sleep near several spent campfires, unaware others circle.

The Judaculla raises her pistol into the air and swings it forward.

The outnumbered horsemen attack from four sides.

Wakened by surprise, the troops lunge for weapons.

On horseback, the attackers fire as they charge through the encampment.

Lisa spins her mount for a second push and surveys the conflict. Many Cherokee Rifles lie shot in their beds.

A wounded horse thrashes on the opposite side of the group, and young James struggles to his feet from the fall.

A Watie guerrilla raises his war club above the youngster's head.

The Pin heels her horse's flanks and charges.

She fires from horseback, and the heavy weapon falls from the attacker's hand as the inexperienced young man cringes. The leader yanks her reins and her horse slips and slides on its haunches to a stop.

Two guerrillas avoid the sliding mount as the Judaculla leaps to the boy's side.

She shoots and eliminates one attacker. Her knife blade flashes as she spins and drives its steel shaft deep into the second man's chest.

The woman cocks her pistol and twists to meet more adversaries.

Her Pins finish the surprise attack massacre and turn to their leader.

The four fighters brandish their rifles and pistols in the air in victory.

"The Judaculla! Judaculla! Judaculla!" The men chant.

Lisa wipes blood from her cheek and points at her men. "You are the Judacullas!"

They slap each other's shoulders and hop into a frenzy.

"Judacullas, Judacullas, Judacullas!"

The woman returns her attention to her youthful companion.

The young boy sits with his knees spread before him, his eyes wide with fear, and trembles.

She drops beside the youngster and engulfs him in her arms. "You are unhurt. Don't feel afraid. They're dead."

James's hands tremble, and sobs slur his words. "Not them. It's you!"

***

Days later, exhilarated by her defeat of Watie's guerrillas, the Judaculla meets with Josiah and her leaders in her camp cabin.

Before her, on a hewn log eating table, rows of crossed pins with a suspended corn husk lay. The actual symbols display an addition. Between the fasteners and their leaf, a square of Watie Mounted Rifle skull skin shows evidence of the recent victory.

Lisa picks one set. She holds it high for the group to view. "This is our new symbol of war. Wear this badge of honor! With this slice of your enemy on your chest, pledge loyalty to President John Ross and acknowledge him as principal chief of the Cherokee Nation!"

The men cheer.

"Swear to dispense death to pro-Confederate traitors and even our Indian brothers who support and ride with Standhope Watie and the Southern faction!"

The fighters in the cabin raise weapons above heads.

"Judacullas! Judacullas! Judacullas!"

The large ex-slave steps forward, and Lisa pins a badge on his chest. "And I honor Josiah with the first pin. Judacullas do not have to be Cherokee, only enemies of the stars and bars!"

The group within the room cheers, claps, and surges to the table for their badges.

After the excitement, their leader plans the next action. "We are stronger and grow our numbers daily. These fighters and their families need food, clothing, and arms. No more living off the land. Union troops have pulled out of the territory except for Drew's Second that guards Ross's estate and his remaining family."

Josiah leans over the table and points at the map on its surface. "They are here with a group of men."

He sweeps his fingers over most of the northeast part of the Nation. "Watie controls our areas except this camp. With General Gano and his Texas Brigade, he captured a federal train with food and clothing for two thousand troops, plus a hundred fifty wagons and mules."

"We know where they store supplies." Lisa stares at her right-hand man. "Pick their weakest supply depot and we'll take it."

The ex-slave looks at the Judaculla, smiles, and nods approval.

## CHAPTER NINETEEN — Honey Springs

ᎠᎡᎢᏏᎣᎢᏍᏲᎨᏯ ᎠᏌᎬᎥᏣᎯᎦᎤᏉᎤᏍᎫᏒᏍᎷᏘᎦᎣ ᎣᎯᎲᏚᏯ ᎥᏔ ᎣᏏᎭᏃ ᏍᎦᎤᎥ

Josiah climbs from his horse and stands before Lisa. "Watie moved seven wagons of supplies to your old place on Cain's Creek."

Lisa, on her cabin's porch, teaches James the Syllabary. "Guarded?" She slaps her buckskin-clad leg with a pointer stick.

"No. Only five Cherokee Mounted Rifles."

"Good. Prepare the men. We'll raid them tonight." Teacher turns to her student and points at the first symbol, a D. "Ah."

The young man studies the image. "Ah."

She switches to a T. "Ee."

The boy repeats the sound, "Ee."

"Someone told me you knew Sequoyah?" The ex-slave slips his hat off and wipes its interior hatband with his neckerchief.

"Met him once. My family camped our wagon for a night at his cabin on the bayou. An old medicine man with me was his friend."

"They say he was brilliant." Josiah takes his horse's reins.

"He was. I was young. The man's pipe smoke impressed me."

"I'll ready ten men. That should be enough. Are you riding with us?" Her second-in-command leads his horse away from the porch but stops.

"They'll do better with their Judaculla." Lisa nods yes and points at the next symbol.

"Why do I need to learn to read and write if you kill our Cherokees?" The youngster stares at his tutor.

She lowers the pointer. "Before the war, we were more literate than White people, James. And I don't shoot our own, just rebs."

"That so?" The young man crosses his arms. "They call you the Judaculla because you teach them our language?"

The teacher sits beside her pupil. "Our people split, but most side with the Confederacy. You know that. Many of our Pins and others, as my husband who died at Pea Ridge, support Abraham Lincoln. Half of me is Indian. The other half the president set free. It's for my second fraction that my Cherokee blood fights."

"Do you?" James studies his chest with his chin low.

"Then what do you understand?" Lisa slips her arm around the boy's shoulder.

"I think you enjoy killing too much."

***

Late that same night, the leader, Josiah, and her Pins, with their horses in the woods, look along a decline to Cain's Creek.

Several empty wagons, each turned upon its side, shape a sporadic defensive wall and surround three log structures. Smoke drifts from the cabin's smokestacks, and two guards lounge and puff pipes on each side of the enclosure.

"We can charge. We have them outnumbered." Josiah keeps his voice low.

"No. I had a talk with James." Lisa heels her horse forward. "Give them a chance to surrender."

"I'll ride with you." The ex-slave nudges his mount.

"No. They'll think it's an attack."

"They can't tell you are female. That guard fires first, talks later."

"Stay here." She moves ahead. "If I have trouble, hit fast."

As she approaches and sees the sentinel notice, she reins her horse to a stop. "Cherokee brother. I will not shoot."

The sentry lowers his rifle. "Don't come closer. What do you want?"

The fighter climbs off her mount.

She walks a few steps. "I offer you a chance to surrender. I am the Judaculla. My men wait in the woods."

"I see your grim corn husk."

Aroused by the voices, a second Cherokee peeks out of the first cabin. "What's going on, Eli?"

"Got a Pin out here." The guard's voice breaks.

"What's he want?"

"Ain't a he. The witch wants us to quit."

Josiah and the mounted guerrillas emerge from the timbers, and the Confederates' eyes enlarge.

"General Blunt and the Army of the Frontier captured Fort Gibson. I think you should surrender your arms." Lisa controls her voice, and its calmness connects.

***

As the sun warms the horizon, she and her Judacullas guide seven confiscated supply wagons. They move through the woods in a line from one clearing to the next.

Josiah rides at the side of a wagon driven by an Indian rebel.

The Pin's leader reins her mount near the opposite wheels.

The Confederate chews a plug and eyes the ex-slave as they travel. "The Yankee Army of the Frontier has nigger soldiers, the First Kansas Volunteer Infantry. You know that?"

The large freedman looks at the driver. "And white troops."

"General Cooper's men are Creek, Cherokee, Chickasaw, and Choctaw." The rebel spits and tobacco stains the wagon's bed. "With the Texans camped at Honey Springs, we'll take Fort Gibson."

"They say the rebs brought leg irons to march prisoners to Fort Smith when their reinforcements arrive." Second-in-command looks across the wagon at his leader.

"Lincoln's 'Grand Strategy' is to defeat the enemy at every opportunity." She pats the pistol on her hip. "I don't expect a Blunt to serve a picnic for those Texicans at Fort Gibson."

The Confederate driver spits. "Troops aren't loyal. This Cherokee won't fight against my own. How do you earn one of those pins to wear?"

The Judaculla looks at the man. "After we get these wagons back to camp, our guerillas reinforce Blunt. You want a corn husk, switch sides."

***

Weeks later, in the middle of the night, Lisa and Josiah travel together at the head of a column of guerrillas in line with General Blunt's troops.

Rain drenches the force's movement along the Texas Road near Chimney Mountain.

She pulls a blanket closer to her neck as water drips from her hat. "They think Standhope Watie's with the Texans in camp."

"That's what they say." Josiah wipes moisture from his forehead.

"The many times we've fought his men, he's never been there." The woman feels for her pistol. "I want to get him in range for James and the orphans."

"Supposed to be over three thousand rebs camped at Honey Springs. You'll never see him."

A rifle discharges from the front of the column.

Josiah stands in his stirrups to peer into the night.

The distant discharge becomes a barrage. "Sounds as if our advance men ran into Confederate scouts."

As the morning sun breaks the horizon, more skirmish action penetrates the fresh air forward.

The Judacullas collect with other federal forces on the Texas Road.

A union mounted messenger rides along the side of the thoroughfare. "The main johnny line is a mile ahead. Orders are to rest. Get food. Fill your canteens. Blunt says fighting before noon."

Many troops, including the volunteers, refresh their water from rain in the road's depressions.

"We just heard Colonel Watie's cavalry are moving toward Webbers Falls." Josiah fills his jug. "They say it's a diversion, and we missed him again."

"Someone said several units of Texans are with his contingent." The woman mounts her horse. "And we're going to that ridge up ahead."

***

By mid-morning, Blunt's force in two columns, one to the left of the Texas Road under Colonels William Phillips, and the other on the right commanded by William Judson, face the Confederate's line.

Lisa, her second-in-command, and their Judacullas supplement regular troops from Indian territory as infantry.

Opposite, 5,700 men wait in Brigadier General Cooper's rebel battle formation. The Choctaw, Chickasaw regiments, and two squadrons of Texas Cavalry wait in reserve.

"Look, Josiah! A fourth of them don't have firearms!" Lisa points. "And only four light battery pieces."

"Those without will pick up guns when the dying starts." The ex-slave checks that his ammunition remains dry.

The rebels' cannons roar, and explosives fall around the federal's artillery.

They reply with case shot, shell, and solid balls.

A Confederate Mountain-Rifle with a small explosive load, one of only eighteen manufactured at the Tredigar Iron Works of Richmond, and three twelve-pound howitzers, targets the First Kansas Volunteer Infantry Regiment.

These freedmen and union enlisted escaped slaves face the Twentieth and Twenty-Ninth Texas Cavalry.

Lisa and Josiah from horseback watch federal twelve-pound Napoleons, with two six-pound and four twelve-pound howitzers, blast.

The rebel artillery aims their precision long-range mountain-rifle field piece on union officers who occupy open ground beyond the battle line.

The mounted troopers, at Blunt's command, dismount and fight as infantry.

Both lines exchange barrages for over two hours.

Lisa and the Judacullas hold the federal left.

In the high brush of the creek's plain, both sides sway with close contact.

The Judaculla pops up from concealment in the grass to fire her Springfield.

In front, a Texan yanks the trigger of an Enfield pointed at her head. The weapon misfires.

Josiah, beside his leader, blasts the Texas cavalryman into oblivion.

"Wet ammunition!" The ex-slave pulls her to the ground concealed in the brush. "The rebs are coming! Too many of them!"

Colonel James M. Williams of the First Kansas Infantry screams. "Fix bayonets! Take that artillery!"

Aware of no quarter if captured because of their skin color, the infantrymen attack the Texans.

The leaders and their Judacullas, lined with the Federal Second Indian Home Guard Regiment, surge forward and thrust themselves between the lines.

At once, Lieutenant Colonel John Bowles commands the local troops to return to their place in the battle line. The Pins retreat.

A Texan officer hears the fallback command and assumes the Federals run. "Don't let them get away, boys! Attack!"

The Texas Cavalry surges to within fifty paces of the Kansas Regiment's center before they volley with Springfield rifles.

A rebel color bearer falls, but another raises the stars and bars, only to stumble again.

The position north of Elk Creek retreats, and the Confederate Texans regroup to defend its bridge as they move their artillery.

First Kansas attacks, but the Texas Calvary holds the crossover long enough for their units to escape, but they suffer heavy casualties.

"They're escaping!" Josiah directs his men toward the strategic water crossing.

"The Choctaws and the Chickasaws cover their retreat!" She points.

"They run toward the Honey Springs Depot!" Her second-in-command turns to the Judaculla. "We need our horses!"

Federal fighters pour across the bridge onto the brushy prairie.

They follow the Confederate flight on the Texas Road.

Lisa gathers her Judacullas and waits for her men's' mounts.

***

Early that afternoon, she rides with her small force into the burning buildings and supply dumps at Honey Springs, set ablaze by the retreating rebels.

The Pins extinguish flames, and their leaders survey quantities of flour, sorghum, salt, and bacon.

"This engagement's done."

The ex-slave looks for enemies.

"Orders are bivouac for the night." Lisa turns her mount.

"Nothing to capture on the prairie. Fort Gibson, in federal hands, is our reward." Josiah spits.

"Maybe." She wipes her hatband. "I want to beat Standhope Watie. The Home Guard against his men. Here, there was no winner, union against rebel. Both bands of Cherokees lose."

# CHAPTER TWENTY — Aftermath

DRTᎦᎧᎣꞌiᏚᎣᏅᎩᎪᎫᏋᏗᎠᏨᎭ ᎭᏖᏬᏇᎷᎥᎢᎽᎥᏍᎷᎦꞌᎤᎮᏝᎩᎠᎾᎿᎭZᏋᎣᵛ

Days after the union victory at Honey Springs, Lisa and Josiah ride together at the head of their mounted Judaculla column of twos.

The battle-weary elements of the Home Guard and First Kansas approach Fort Gibson.

The Texas Road hosts legions of Cherokee refugees, hundreds of elderly men, women, and young children, Confederate- and union-affiliated, who separate for the troops and pull carts loaded with pitiful possessions to the side.

Lisa watches an old woman stumble, and her blood splatters rocks on the wheel-pressed furrows. Burst blisters on her bare feet re-swell and stain her trail.

She twists to her second-in-command. "Look at them. They are not human anymore."

"Widows and war orphans. The union's setting up refugee camps along the Red River." The freedman shakes his head. "How will they feed them?"

"They ordered Kansas exiles back to their home state." The woman gazes at the refugees. "They say over seven thousand Indians camp at Fort Gibson."

The troops move out of timber onto the prairie.

Extending in every direction, makeshift lodgings and temporary tents plus hand-constructed shelters crowd the land.

"This is not the place I remember." Lisa observes the anguish of humanity.

They approach a federal field hospital with several tents on both sides of the road.

A physician drags his weary feet from one military cot to the next and attends Union and Confederate wounded and dying.

Cherokees, Choctaws and Chickasaws, sick, suffering, and sprawled in the canvases, await the physician's attention.

Lisa reins her horse to a halt. "Doctor Kent!"

The surgeon turns to his name and attempts to focus. "Do I know you, sir?"

She whips off her hat. "From Pea Ridge?"

"Sorry, I am worn out. Who are you?"

"Waters! Ezra's wife from your field hospital."

The physician stumbles and grabs her leg for support. "Lisa. Of course, I remember. You lost your husband. He was an excellent officer." Kent shakes his head. "I am just so tired, and you're a nurse. Can you aid?"

She dismounts. "Yes. These are my men. We will help."

The doctor looks at Josiah and the Judacullas. "Thank God. We have so many patients. They need so much."

The Pin leader glances through the hospital. "And these refugees?"

Kent peers at her second-in-command on his horse. "With your people, I might get a catnap."

Days pass as the group treats the wounded in blue, empathizes with the displaced evacuees, and consoles injured Confederates.

A First Kansas Private grimaces as Lisa wraps a fresh bandage around the man's chest. "Sorry, soldier, you were lucky. Another inch and that Reb ball killed you."

"See those scars on my back, ma'am?"

"Yes. You must have been a slave. Those are from a whip."

"They are. After that, I ran for the state line on the underground railroad, and then Mr. Lincoln let me join the army."

Lisa swallows. "My sister died of that punishment in a Georgia internment camp."

"Sorry. I have never been there. Too many cotton plantations. You ain't a freedwoman, are you?"

"No. Father was a freedman. Mother was Cherokee."

"My old master was your kind."

She ties the man's bandage.

"His uncle's now that Confederate colonel we whupped at Honey Springs. You heard of Standhope Watie? His nephew, Elias C. Boudinot, owned me. Gave me these scars."

"I know both men."

"They both are mean killers. Talk was the old man beat a Cherokee woman to death in Fort Smith while my overseer watched."

Lisa freezes and stares at her patient. "An Indian girl?"

The soldier nods. "That's what they say. A loose woman, a pleasure toy."

"When was this? Were you there?"

"No, just heard it. They said the prostitute didn't want the colonel's attention. You understand? And my owner was drunk. But he watched the beating."

"Do you remember her name or when this happened?"

"The dead Indian's? No. Now that you ask, I'm not even sure she was Cherokee. Maybe it was a Creek or Mexican. That was a long time ago."

Doctor Kent walks near the two. "Many fresh patients coming. Can you and your Judacullas set more cots? These soldiers are union but prisoners from Fort Davis. The rebels used them as slaves."

Afternoon wagons pull into the tent hospital camp.

Each carts Indian and slave cargo. A few men climb from their conveyance, but more starved, skin and bones humans lie or sit, too weak or injured to move.

The Pins unload the victims and carry them on canvas stretchers to cots.

Kent operates a triage on each wagon. "Get that one to surgery. His leg's too infected. Take that man to tent three. Son, are you able to walk?"

Inside, Lisa moves from one cot to the next. "Soldier, what's your name?"

"Billy."

The Chickasaw adolescent's eyes open wide. "You're a woman?"

"A nurse. Do you have kin for us to tell?"

"My hip took a Reb ball at Honey Springs before they captured me. They got no doctors at Fort Davis. My family can't help me now."

"I know. But we'll write them after you pass. Tell them you died a hero."

"Thank you, ma'am. Name's William Johnson. Please, my mother, Hattie, in Teshatulla. Is this a dying place?"

"Yes, son. I'll get word to your mom." Lisa stands and moves to the next cot.

***

After the sun sets and the Judacullas light oil lamps in the hospital tents, the nurse completes her tour of doomed boys.

She meets Doctor Kent as she ducks out of the canvas.

"How you holding up, Mrs. Waters?" The physician hands her a cup of coffee.

"Better than those poor souls in there. Most ask me to write family in places that don't still exist."

"This war's not leaving them anything worth coming home to. That's a fact." The surgeon swigs his drink. "Over there, number five tent," the doctor points, "I send those that no longer are workable."

"What do you mean?"

"Brain damaged, crazy from war, blind, burned bodies and souls." The physician drops his chin. "We can't treat them, but most of them will live. But not a life we want."

"There's a couple of hours left in me." Lisa gulps her coffee. "I'll see if I can help."

She ducks under the entry flap.

A hand grasps her ankle. "They coming, Jack! Listen to the yells. We ain't got a chance. Run!" A bleary-eyed, crazed face with unfocused pupils shakes Lisa's foot. "Them Texans will slap us slaves in leg irons!"

The Pin leader drops to her knees. "I'm an attendant. How can I help?"

The ex-slave's eyes roll back into his head. "Hear them yell. We lost. Take me away!"

"Soldier, what is a nurse?"

The man releases her ankle and points across space. "Make me gone! As he is!"

She looks at the man's point.

On the opposite side of the tent, shirtless, with hundreds of scars crisscrossing his back, a large slave trembles on his hands and knees in a fetal slump.

"Moss. No!" She stumbles over the dirt floor to her old friend. "It's Lisa."

"No, massa! Don't whip me no more." The form cringes away and stuffs his head against the tent's canvas wall.

She reaches to her friend's shoulder, and he slobbers. "Yes, sir! I do it! Whatever you say, I did it."

Nearby, two Judacullas lower a drooling patient onto a cot.

"Need help here, men. Move this fellow to a private tent. Next to mine."

The Pins nod obedience to their leader.

***

Several days later, Lisa, Josiah, and Doctor Kent sit at an army table and enjoy a breakfast of cornmeal mush with cream and maple syrup, griddle cakes, and tea.

"Wish we had peaches." Second-in-command spoons his meal.

"I offer my pension for an orange." The surgeon licks his fingers.

There is a commotion in the hospital.

Josiah stands and peers across camp. "We're going to have beef."

Livestock kicks dust as herders move cows.

"No telling what price the army pays." The physician shakes his head.

"For stolen cattle." Lisa watches the herd. "Looters pillage those creatures from within the territory and sell them to contractors who resell to us. The Cherokee lose again, and more starving refugees flood Fort Gibson."

"You and your followers should get into the contractor business." Doctor Kent winks at his nurse.

"Only with rebel cows." The Judaculla leader smiles. "What we can do is done. Josiah and I will take our Pins back to camp soon."

"Lisa, I couldn't have survived Honey Springs and these refugees without you and your men." The surgeon sets his fork on the table and offers his tea in a toast gesture. "Our army should award you a medal."

"The union just needs to win this war." She lifts her teacup. "Anyone wearing these pins will hang if we lose."

"This battle gives us control of the territory." The doctor clicks his cup against Lisa's.

He twists to Josiah. "Here's to victory."

"Standhope Watie and his men are still alive." The woman shakes her head.

"Mostly running to Texas." Josiah nods. "Our camp's much safer." The man looks at his leader. "When do you want to move out?"

The nurse stares at the surgeon. "Do you think Moss is safe to travel?"

"You may have to cage him as an animal." The doctor returns the look. "There's nothing I can do to help him."

"Never." Lisa shakes her head. "You do not know the fighter he was."

***

Weeks later, the head of the Pins cleans her pistol on her cabin porch and watches the fiddler, who huddles against a post on the opposite side.

The shell of the prior leader extends his arms over his knees, and his bare feet rock his body in a slow, repetitive motion.

197

His eyes stare into space without focus.

James steps out of the cabin's door and looks at the ex-Pin founder.

The adolescent Cherokee boy walks to the porch and sits with his back against the cabin wall. He studies his companion. "Your name is Moss?"

The youngster moves closer. He sees no response. "Do you know I'm here?"

"Why don't you come over here?" She beckons. "He doesn't want company."

The young fellow joins the Judaculla at her weapon cleaning table. "Did he ever speak?"

"Yes." Lisa nods her head. "That man created Pins and the underground railroad. He plays an outstanding fiddle."

"As well as you?"

"No. Much better. More, a violinist."

The teenager looks at the hulk, then enters the cabin.

He returns with the strings and bow and walks across the porch. "Mister, I enjoy your music."

The man doesn't move but continues to stare into the air.

"Could you play?" The boy extends the instrument. "Mrs. Water's song?"

The mass of a human shows no response.

James shakes his head and sits near Lisa.

She grips the boy's shoulder.

"No need. That fellow is the Cherokee Reel."

## CHAPTER TWENTY-ONE — J. R. Williams

**ᎠᎡᎢᎣᎤᎥᎦᎧᎨᎩᎪᎫᎬᎭᎮᎯᎰᎱᎲᎳᎴᎵᎶᎷᎸᎹᎺᎻᎼᎽᎾᎿᏀᏁᏂᏃᏄᏅ**

Josiah interrupts Lisa's breakfast.

A Cherokee cook serves wild onions with eggs and a side of blueberries.

"Judaculla, we intercepted a rebel with a union dispatch."

"When?" Lisa swallows her mouthful and looks at James' smaller siblings who share the table. "Girls, eat your food, not just sweet fruit."

"Last night." The man smiles at the youngster and his sisters. "He had information I thought you should see."

The leader and her Pin lieutenant step outside the cabin, and she settles into a porch rocking chair to read the documents.

The messenger waits for her reaction.

After a few moments, she stands. "You announce it to the men. The other requires action. What happened to the person with these?"

"Dead. Our scouts took them off his body after they intercepted."

"That means no one got this except us?"

"I suspect so." Second-in-command nods.

"If Watie's brigade plans to capture the J. R. Williams, this warning never reached union troops. They don't know of his plan. It's up to Pins to stop him."

Josiah steps off the porch.

"Gather the men for your announcement, then how soon can we ride?"

"Mid-afternoon. We pull in the outriders."

"Call them." Lisa stares above the camp's clearing in the woods. "We can be there by late tomorrow."

"That steamboat will be at Fort Gibson by nightfall." The big man shakes his head. "Pleasant Bluff's further along the Arkansas. I don't believe we'll arrive in time."

"Do what you can. Get us moving quicker, but I want the men to hear your announcement as a group." Lisa claps her hands in encouragement.

Second-in-command trots toward the camp's barracks and family quarters to summon the Judacullas.

She reenters her cabin as the young ones finish their eggs.

James smiles at his little sisters.

"They did well, ma'am."

"Not ma'am. Lisa."

"Yes, I hear you."

"I'm leaving for a few days. Our boys have business on the river." The acting mother hugs the two girls. "Everything will be fine. I'll be back soon."

The youngster stands. "Fighting, you mean?" The boy's face becomes serious. "There's something I must show you before you go."

He leads the woman to the children's sleeping corner in the cabin. He lifts the edge of his mat and withdraws a deerskin that encloses their possessions.

"I remember you had that when you came into camp. I told you I did not want your things." She smiles at the boy.

"You rescued us that day. Today you go off to fight." James looks up at his benefactor. "I'm afraid you won't return."

The woman coughs and gathers the teenager into her arms. "I will come back home. You take care of the girls until I do."

"We can never repay you." He turns to his deerskin roll. "I want you to have something valuable."

The boy unrolls their possessions.

She eyes a short heritage belt piece of sun-bleached gulf water seaweed adorned by hand polished shells and beads.

James lifts the item. "My mother gave us this. She said it came from Selu. An old medicine man entrusted it to her for safekeeping before I was born."

Lisa examines the partial heirloom. "I can't take this. Do you know this piece is an heirloom?"

"My mother's gift to my sisters and to me."

"Yes, but it's much more. When I was a young girl, they forced my sisters from our home in Georgia, and after Bella died, my big sister and I came here with an old medicine man. He spoke of this that you have."

"Mama said it was a shaman that gave it to her."

"This is important to the Cherokee people. It is one-seventh of a sacred heritage belt. Someone in each clan got one. Your mother was special."

"And you are, as well." The boy offers the item. "Please, take it as a thank you for what you have done."

Lisa crosses her hands and arms. "I am not worthy. I'm only half-Cherokee."

James's eyes tear, and moisture drops form at their edges.

"You will honor me more by keeping Selu's belt for your clan. Someday the people may reunite these pieces." She softens her refusal. "You and your sisters are my own children. That gift given to me is a generous thank you." She hugs the boy.

He smiles. "I am not a child. I want to ride with you."

Lisa's mind floats with the words to the ice-and-snow day when they first met, but her concentration returns to her adopted household.

"You are not. This is your home now, and you are head of your family. Stay here and protect them."

The young man looks at the beaded belt. "My sisters and I look to the future. But this icon is not ours. We don't have a woman to lead in the Cherokee way."

"Yes." Lisa stares out the cabin's window. "You and your girls will someday consider this your home. So, in your honor, I cite this place my valley, Utugi Uweha (ᎤᏚᎩ ᎤᏪᎲ u-tu-gi u-we-ha)."

James smiles. "She has hope. That is a good name."

***

Later, the Pin Judacullas gather in the center of the named encampment, armed and provisioned for several days away from camp.

Less than one hundred union committed guerillas form a military group outside their cabins.

In the field, this band of unrecognized fighters, freedman and Cherokee, brothers and relatives, bound by a common cause, present a small but potent Calvary unit.

Lisa stands beside Josiah on the porch of her headquarters cabin.

Moss sits at the porch's opposite end and stares into space while mounted men seethe before him.

"We have reliable information that Stand Watie's rebels attack an important supply steamboat." The large leader raises his fist into the air. "We move to prevent that action!"

The freedman and Indian fighters cheer.

"But before we ride, the government in exile has adopted a new declaration." Their second-in-command pauses as the crowd settles.

"Any Cherokee who holds slaves owes a one- to five-thousand-dollar fine."

Several whoops rise from the troops.

"The official who doesn't enforce this act loses his job."

The riders cheer, and several discharge weapons.

Lisa steps forward.

"The Judaculla!" the mounted soldiers chant.

"In this territory, we can free few! People who support the union own workers. Most of us let our humans go long ago." The leader looks at Moss, but he shows no response.

"Many of you men were once owned. Today we ride against owners. Freedmen ride with Cherokees! Against General Standhope Watie and his First Regiment!" She leaps from the porch to her horse and leads her fighters from the encampment headquarters.

***

The following afternoon, their advanced scouts locate rebels.

Lisa and Josiah halt their column as a scout bursts from the brush. "Judaculla! He has cannons with four hundred troops across the river!"

"Can we see from the top?" She points.

The advance rider nods yes, and she heels her mount up the hill, followed by her second-in-command and James.

The trio observes Pleasant Bluff, a small rock jutting into the water below a bend of the Arkansas and the Canadian mix.

From their position, in full view, Confederates man cannons.

In concealment within the trees and the brush at the riverside, Watie's troops hide in ambush.

The Pin leader twists to James. "Do you think you can ride to the mouth of the Illinois?"

The youngster nods with pleasure at his new adult status.

"Warn Colonel John Ritchie's Second Regiment that rebs wait near the Canadian. Tell him we have one hundred Pins." She pauses. "But careful, you watch for rebels. You understand me?"

The young man grins and prods his horse into the woods with his heels.

Lisa turns her attention to the river.

In the distance, a stern-mounted paddle wheeler powered by a wood-fired boiler churns water. Steam billows from its stack, and the wheel splashes the Arkansas.

The boat rides low, with its cargo of a thousand barrels of flour and fifteen tons of bacon.

The load travels to Cherokee refugees from Kansas and Missouri, who wait protected by Union troops at Fort Gibson.

Its military load includes Sharps rifles and new revolvers.

"There's the Williams." Josiah points at the river.

Confederate cannon blasts from the bluff interrupt the steamboat's progress.

Two ineffective balls splash neat the steamboat, but one smashes its smokestack, pilothouse, and boiler. An explosion splits the boat apart, and steam burns deckhands and crew.

The Confederates open a rifle barrage from shore.

In chaos, the Williams's executive officer and crewmen steer to the north bank opposite Watie's position, and guardsmen on its rails return rebel fire.

To Lisa's and the Judaculla's astonishment, the steamboat's captain and officers desert in the boat's yawl and defect to the Confederate side of the Arkansas.

The two-masted sailboat slides into sand, and the boat's key crewmembers hold their hands high in surrender.

Rebels on horseback swim and board the abandoned steamboat.

Leaderless guardsmen and armed crew lay their weapons on the boat's shattered deck.

With horses and ropes tied to the vessel, the mounts tow the wreck to its final sandbar rest under the Confederate cannon's bluff position above the south shore.

As Lisa and Josiah watch, the soldiers unload the boat's cargo onto the bar.

Many Cherokee load food on their mares for their starving families.

Despite threats from their commanders, troops desert with their loads into the woods at river's bank.

Remaining rebels pack mules and several wagons with supplies and arms while others prepare their artillery for movement.

Lisa watches the short rum-barrel shaped Stand Watie in his faded and dirty Confederate officer's uniform wheel his mount among his fighters and shout commands.

Rifle fire from the opposite side of the river interrupts the pilfering.

Bullets from the Union's Second Regiment disrupt loading and force the looters into a hasty retreat.

Lisa turns to Josiah. "Ritchie's troops! James must have found their camp."

"Should we attack?" Second-in-command waits for direction.

"Yes. The odds are better now. Destroy Watie's force!"

***

That night, encamped in a clearing in the woods, the Judacullas celebrate their accomplishment. The fighters add logs to a central bonfire, drink fresh water, and enjoy slabs of pork.

"The Arkansas rose. I've never seen so many barrels of flour and bacon as floated off that sandbar." Josiah chews his meat.

"That food's for our hungry families." She shakes her head. "But they escaped with their cannons."

"Hundreds of his men deserted."

"To go home and feed their children, but they will return." The Judaculla stares into the night's darkness. "But he got away with those Sharp rifles." She paces near the bonfire. "And I'm worried for James. The boy's not returned."

"Here come our scouts." Josiah spits a piece of tough sinew into the fire. "They might have word."

Several riders enter the camp with a Confederate prisoner over the rear of one horse.

The men ride to their commanders and dump the prize at their leader's feet. "An officer. We shot his rebs."

The major rolls onto his back with his hands tied behind and struggles to rise. "You're the Judaculla?" The man stares in wonderment.

"Elias C. Boudinot." Lisa steps forward. "I did not know you were with your kinfolk."

"Not uncle. Brigadier General Stand Watie. They promoted him in May." The man's eyes glare hatred.

"String this slave owner to that tree over there." The leader points at a strong, low limb. "Put him on a barrel."

Judacullas drag the bound rebel and encircle his neck with a hangman's noose.

They throw rope over the bough and support Boudinot's boots on a small wooden keg with the line taut and tied around its trunk.

The men turn to their commander.

She grabs a burning branch from the bonfire.

The woman steps to the prisoner.

"What's Brigadier General Stand Watie's next move, Reb?"

"That's major, you Pin vermin."

Lisa presses her torch against the support below the officer's feet until its slats smoke and flames appear.

"This will take time to collapse. If you answer my questions, we'll cut you free." She throws her igniter back toward the bonfire. "What's your uncle's next move?"

Boudinot looks at the wood below his boots as its panels crackle and pop. "The general's going to attack the capital in Tahlequah and destroy John Ross's home at Park Hill."

The questioner nods, but her thought changes. "You were with your uncle in Fort Smith many years ago. He beat a woman to death with his pistol."

"What? What are you asking me?"

"You heard. Were you? What handgun did he use?"

Boudinot balances on his perch as one metal band that secures its bottom snaps.

The barrel shakes and flames lick the officer's boots. "Yes! Yes! I was there. He beat a prostitute! With his Patterson Colt!"

Josiah steps near Lisa's ear. "Our scouts say they captured the boy. Watie's got him."

Lisa stares at the rebel on the disintegrating stand for a moment.

"Cut him loose." She turns to her second-in-command. "Send someone into the general's camp. Tell him we have his nephew, who we will hang if they hurt James. I want to talk a trade."

# CHAPTER TWENTY-TWO — Confirmation

ᎠᎡᏔᏐᎣᎢᏍᎰᏔᏯᎪᏎᎤᏓᎢᎢᎤᏫᏍᎠᎹᏏᎥᎰᎭᏚᏯᎾᎬᏅᎲᏃᎤ

Overnight, uncomfortable, Lisa tosses on her mat and dreams as the Judaculla's campfire burns to coals.

Remembrances in her mind shift to a party in Fort Smith long ago.

*Mary Stapler Ross enjoys a tidbit nibble and points her fan at a guest whose icy stare follows John around the room. "And that shorter stocky fellow, I don't believe he supports my husband."*

*"You can tell? That's Stand Watie, an old settler, plantation owner, a New Echota signee." Lisa's voice quivers. "They lead different sides of this political talk, but he shook hands with your man in Washington after signing that treaty."*

*"Not so tonight." Mrs. Ross watches the opposition leader.*

*The stocky fellow nods to several followers and presses a path to the door without acknowledging his opponent's presence.*

Lisa turns a fresh shoulder to her hard sleeping mat, and her mind continues its dance with memories.

*Outside her Fort Smith home in a rain and snow mix, a short, stocky rider dismounts, looks at his companions, and then steps onto the Waters' porch. "This place is owned by an attorney. They could have runaways inside, but if they do, careful. He's a protégé of Judge Steel."*

*The intruder draws a Patterson Colt revolver from his belt holster.*

*The mounted officers on horseback draw pistols or check their powder before they rest the stocks of their long guns on knees.*

*Their short and stocky leader pounds on the front door with the butt of his pistol and waits.*

*Lisa opens the door and peeks out, "Gracious! Ezra, it's Standhope Watie. Sir, what could you want this early? More raspberry brandy?" She sneezes into her fist against the bitter temperature. "How did you enjoy my party the other evening?"*

*"Morning, Mrs. Waters." The man removes his hat and water drips onto the porch.*

*Ezra, without his rifle, joins his wife. "Mr. Watie. This is irregular. Who are these fellows, and what brings you to my house?"*

*"They are Lighthorse under my command. We're trailing escapees from the Vann plantation."*

*"You don't need that big gun, and you're dripping water." Lisa swings the entrance open. "Come and get out of the weather."*

*The intruder holsters his Patterson and turns to his party. "You fellows stay here."*

*They pause in the foyer at the base of the stairs.*

*Atop in the darkness with both percussion long guns, Moss waits.*

*"Slaves ran from plantations west of here near Webbers Falls. I'm looking for a group moving east, and Lighthorse chase the others. You folks heard or seen runners tonight?"*

*"Why, goodness no." Lisa pulls her robe tighter around her throat. "You know we don't even own servants."*

*The wet, stocky man pauses. "Or harbor any?"*

*"Against the law." Ezra's voice steels.*

*"Now Ezra, no grumpy barrister attitudes this early in the morning." She beams at their visitor. "Please, sir, tell your men to tie their horses in the stable, and I'll make everyone chicory coffee. It's fresh off the boat from New Orleans."*

*Standhope Watie stares at the lawyer for a moment and glances at the hostess. "No, thank you, Mrs. Waters. We must move on and finish our work."*

*Ezra closes the door and draws a deep breath.*

Lisa rolls over on her camp mat, wakens, and frets in half-sleep throughout the rest of the night.

***

The following afternoon on Pleasant Bluff over the Arkansas, the Pin leader and Josiah wait upon horses as the burned and abandoned hulk of the steamboat J. R. Williams looms in shallow water.

"This place is ghostly." Her second-in-command scans the shore on both sides.

"Nothing left." She mimics his scan. "The Home Guard took what the rebs didn't."

"Curious that the general chose here to meet."

"Smart." The Pin turns her attention to movement on her side of the river. "Federals never expected a return."

"Do you think they will come?" Josiah looks at his leader.

"Standhope Watie believes in his family. He moved his wife Sarah to Texas with their four younger children. Saladin, his eldest son, is a captain and rides with his father." Lisa nods. "He won't abandon his nephew, either."

"Most Confederate Cherokees have fled the Nation for refuge in Chickasaw and Choctaw camps. The union controls most of this territory. This war's winding to a close." Josiah rests his wrists on his saddle horn. "Why does the old man keep fighting?"

"Why do we?" She peers at her companion.

"Because Watie won't quit. While rebels walk these woods, your and my kinds live in danger."

The commander looks at her second. "What kind is that?"

"You know, Mrs. Waters."

"No, I don't. I am the daughter of a freedman and a Cherokee. Now I'm a Yankee-loving Pin guerrilla. What do you call me, Josiah?"

"You're the Judaculla, a patriot and a lifelong champion of my people. And you keep fighting because Moss sits in silence on your porch."

"He does. That rebel camp in Texas must have been horrible." Lisa watches the woods along the river's bank.

"Worse. They knew he could never submit."

"Those scars on his back are not his story." She looks at Josiah. "The ones on his soul are deeper."

"You have not bathed him." The man grits his teeth. "You don't see the worst."

"What are you saying?" The woman focuses on her companion's words.

"We don't know how much the rebs did to him. They castrated him."

"What?"

"You heard me. The guards at Fort Davis were Texans. They calmed his fighting spirit as they fix their Texas bulls."

Her memories of the champion flood her mind as she swallows. Her eyes tear.

Moisture blurs her vision as two riders in Confederate uniforms emerge from the woods that crowd the river's edge.

The rebels ride toward the Judacullas. They splash through shallow water at the sandbar.

"Lisa Waters. These last years, my troops fear the Judaculla." Stand Watie chuckles. "Had I known who the demon warrior was, I could have pissed on your myth. Who is this nigger with you?"

"My second-in-command, Josiah Rains."

"You love them darkies. Married one, lived with that abolitionist fiddle player. What was his name?"

"I'm not here to exchange insults with you. Where's my James?"

The Reb turns in his saddle and points to the woodlands behind him.

A Confederate guides a horse out of the brush. The youngster sits upon the mount and waves.

The general stares at the Pin leader. "And my nephew?"

Lisa jerks her chin toward another Cherokee who steps from the woods with Boudinot at the end of a rope with a hangman's knot around his neck.

Watie nods recognition as he draws his Patterson Colt and points the weapon. "What if I just kill you now, Judaculla? Save a Confederate firing squad's time later."

"Because my men in the timbers will splatter your blood over this bluff." The Pin grits her teeth.

The man uncocks his pistol. "You might enjoy watching that."

She nods and smiles. "Make the exchange."

The rebel commander waves in the air and his trooper moves his prisoner toward the Judaculla with Boudinot.

When the two meet, they switch prisoners, and both disappear into the foliage.

"Remember when your nigger playmate prosecuted me for James Foreman's murder?"

"You were guilty."

"Jury said I was innocent."

"When you beat that Tsalagi girl to death in Fort Smith after your trial?" Lisa fingers her handgun.

"You draw that weapon, and my men will spread you over this sandbar." Watie's piercing eyes focus on Lisa's firearm. "And I enjoy watching."

"Answer me."

"I don't remember what happened back then."

"In Hattie's whorehouse. Boudinot said he was there and watched you pistol whip her."

The uneasy man shuffles upon his mare. "That wasn't a Tsalagi, just a nigger whore."

"That woman was the removal's Cherokee Rose and my sister."

Watie turns his mount. "From the northern route?"

"I swear to what you believe in," Lisa's voice trembles, "while my blood rushes red in my veins, I will watch you die a worse death than hers."

In spite, the dangerous fighter spits on Lisa's leg. "I told you at the Foreman trial, I'm watching you, Mrs. Waters, and dreaming of poking you and sweet Mary Ross someday."

The Confederate Brigadier General laughs as he rides away.

# CHAPTER TWENTY-THREE — Exhaustion

ᎠᏗᏌᎣᎢᏍᏚᏆᏯᎠᏣᎮᏇᎷᎠᏂᎦᏫᏍᎶᏣᎹᎪᏓᏥᎣᎻᎭᎫᏯᎣᏖᎣᏂᎭᏃᏆᎣᎥ

Elizabeth and Sarah run to greet James as the Judacullas ride into the encampment's clearing. The girls squeal and laugh as their brother slides off his horse and hugs his little sisters.

Unnoticed on the porch, Moss turns and watches the family reunion. His lips twist at the ends in a gentle smile.

"Josiah, better dispatch outriders. Watie may track us." Lisa slings a leg over her mount's rump to firm ground.

"Sure, but I don't think the old man's desertions leave enough soldiers to move his cannons, much less follow."

"Can't blame his men." The leader hands the reins of her horse to a Pin and hangs her pistol belt on a peg near the cabin's door. "Most have families without flour and bacon. The rebels still control the people's brains, but stomachs demand attention."

"Watie won't surrender. That steamboat had more than food and clothing." Josiah looks toward Moss. "With weapons, he'll find men."

"Yes." Lisa's eyes follow her second-in-command's. "I only hope they don't attack here."

The fiddler sits with spine against a porch post. Hands prop his head on elbows supported by knees.

Lisa greets Elizabeth and Sarah. "Girls! James is home, and he's a hungry young man. Let's go fix dinner."

This salmagundi  family laughs and chatters as they enter.

Josiah leads the remaining Pins and their horses toward the troops' household cabins, garrisons and corrals.

Happy families greet returning warriors as many unsaddle mounts that stomp, eager for grain.

Outside the cabin and alone, Moss stands and stares at the barracks and the livestock pens.

He steps with purpose across the porch to Lisa's pistol belt.

The freedman fiddler withdraws the revolver, pulls its hammer, and inserts the barrel into his mouth.

"Lisa! Can we have blueberry corn pone?" Sarah's voice floats outside from within the cabin.

"No! I want fireplace squash!" Elizabeth expresses her wishes.

"We captured bacon," James interrupts. "To celebrate this homecoming!"

Moss uncocks the weapon.

The man returns the revolver to the holster.

He turns and shuffles to a seat against a porch post.

***

Several days later, a Judaculla outrider pounds into camp with new intelligence.

Josiah reports the information as his commander plays dolls with Elizabeth and Sarah. "We captured Watie's plan. The general attacks Tahlequah."

"Send a dispatch and warn the Union troops at Fort Gibson." Lisa holds a home-made straw baby. "How soon can we move to protect the town?"

"By morning." Josiah pats Elizabeth's head.

"I'll be ready." The woman extends the toy to Sarah. "What's her name, Pretty Eyes?"

The second-in-command moves to the cabin door.

His commander twists. "Tell James to stay here this time. In case something turns bad, I don't want these girls to be alone."

The freedman steps out the door.

Sara hugs the doll. "This is Betsy. I love her so."

Lisa's mind clouds, and thoughts sweeps into the subconscious. *The mental cloud becomes snow that falls around a gristmill, a stop on the northern route from Georgia.*

*A cemetery's marker stones stand atop a hill, sentinels on watch, and the gray shapes dot white against the gray, as guards.*

*"We are fortunate. There's a graveyard beyond the mill. We can entomb baby Betsy today, as is the custom." Dideyohvsgi, the medicine man, nods a head.*

*"Cherokee custom? Betsy's actual mother never had a grave," Lisa mutters. She raises a voice in protest. "Her spirit coughs on the trail with us, or maybe Tesali just left her in the woods for the wolves."*

*"We bury the child because we loved her." Lisa's older sister Ella pulls the youngest sibling into her arms. "Not because her parent couldn't care for her."*

*"In a Presbyterian cemetery?" She questions. "My Betsy died of their curse; they even named the pox after their chickens."*

*"Yes, a grave on non-Indian lands, but buried by Cherokee hands." The oldest rises. "Burial takes a White man's permission required by his law."*

*"And how do you pull that off?" Lisa snaps with immature insensitivity.*

*"I'm not sure, but it's my duty to try." The Waters clan leader steps away from the fire. She marches through clumps of other campfires toward the gristmill.*

Lisa's mind returns to the Pin cabin and the young child with a straw Betsy. "Yes, Sarah. You love her, and I do as well. You and Elizabeth are family now. I have no others."

"Did you have brothers and sisters as I do?"

"Yes, and I loved them very much. I was the youngest, as you. Their names were Bella and Ella."

"But no boys?"

"No. You are very lucky to have a brother."

The girl stares at the woman. "I think we are fortunate to have you."

"I am delighted." She hugs the child.

***

Two days later, the Judaculla and the mounted Pins stand horses on a ridgeline and watch Tahlequah burn.

Flames in the center of town rush black smoke clouds into the sky and brighten the evening.

"Watie burned the capitol." Josiah rises in his saddle.

"No sign of rebel troops." Lisa stands in stirrups and leans forward with a hand on a pommel.

"We got here too late." He settles on his mount.

"Hates John Ross. I suspect he rides to Park Hill even if the president's up North." She glances at the second-in-command.

He nods agreement.

"That's only five miles to the south. We can be there before the moon rises." The leader looks at the horizon and turns her horse toward the executive's home.

Judacullas arrive in time to watch John Ross's house burn.

A massive, two-story, white residence with Doric columns supports a classic Greek portico and smokes black ash and flames from four windows on each side.

Lisa and Josiah ride through corpses of Sixth Kansas troopers.

Bodies of the Second Cherokee Mounted Rifles charged with security for the Ross home and property clutter the ground.

One federal casualty moves and groans.

Second-in-command slides off his horse and lifts the soldier's head. "What happened, Corporal?"

"Are you reinforcements?"

"We're Pin guerrillas."

"Too late. Rebs attacked. Caught us by surprise. Captured William Potter Ross and Daniel Hicks. Slaughtered everyone." The fighter dies in Josiah's arms.

The second-in-command lowers the soldier's shoulders to the ground and looks at his commander. "Every time we close on the man, the Reb escapes!"

"Willy is John's nephew. The president needs to know Watie has him." The leader surveys the destroyed property from her horse. "Dispatch a rider to Fort Leavenworth. He needs to learn they burned this place."

She glances at the devastation and turns to the return road toward Tahlequah.

As the Judaculla and the Pins ride in a column of twos and approach the city, an advance scout joins the main body. "Watie's men wait in ambush between here and town."

The leader raises one hand, and the column stops. "How many?"

The Pin shakes both shoulders. "Not sure. There are at least twenty Cherokee Rifles."

Josiah peers at Lisa. "We can wipe out a force that small."

She turns in her saddle to the man. "Any artillery?"

The young rider nods. "No. Or any leaders. It's a group left behind to ambush."

"Brothers against each other again. I don't appreciate the opportunity." The leader reins her horse and looks along the long column of Pins. "Encircle them. Give every fighter a chance to surrender. If they want to switch sides, that's fine. Those who won't, tell them to go home to wives and children."

"Pass Company A those orders." Second-in-command points, and the scout nods understanding before he guides his mount into the column.

The leader waves, and the rows move.

"We never catch that devil when we can take him." Lisa eyes the surrounding woods. "He's slicker than Robert E. Lee."

"President Davis and their Congress thanked the general. The man's a hero." Josiah chuckles.

"That was before the surrender to Grant." She pulls a hat lower on her forehead. "But Watie hasn't quit."

"And won't without force." Second-in-command clicks his horse forward.

"So, this Cherokee civil war rages." The Judaculla shakes her head. "Our men's families hide in the hills. Crops must be planted, cattle need calves. Locals have paid the cost of the conflict, and it's time to reap the profits of peace."

"Watie's no threat now." Josiah nods.

"He's a menace to me forever." The leader guides her horse away from Tahlequah and the column of Pins follows. "But you're correct. He no longer has the strength to do war except burn buildings in defenseless towns. When we return to camp, encourage the men to go home."

***

Days later, safe within the Pin encampment, Lisa watches James chop wood for winter while Elizabeth and Sarah play tag and stack firewood.

Moss sits with his back against a post and stares into space.

She enters the cabin and returns with Moss's violin and bow.

Perching on the stoop, she tucks the instrument under a chin and draws strap over strings.

Her voice floats in the fresh air. "Two brothers on their way, one wore blue, and one wore gray. As they marched along their way, fife and drum began to play, all on a beautiful morning."

James leaves the woodpile, and his sisters join the young man at Lisa's feet.

Lisa eyes Moss's shoulders for movement, and then continues. "One was gentle, one was kind. One came back, one stayed behind. Cannonball don't pay no mind if you're gentle or if you're kind. It don't think of the folks behind or of a beautiful morning."

He does not move.

"Two girls waiting by the railroad track, one wore blue, and one wore black, waiting by the railroad track." Lisa leans closer to Elizabeth and Sarah, "For their lovers to come back. All on a beautiful morning."

The girls blush and squeal.

James laughs and returns to work.

Moss sits and stares at the woods beyond the clearing.

# CHAPTER TWENTY-FOUR — Vindication

ᎠᏣᎢᏍᎣᎢᏍᏍᎢᎩᏯᎠᎫᎬᏛᎯᏗᎠᎵᎦᏣᏪᏍᎶᎬᎷᎡᎦᎮᎠᏍᎯᏍᎩᏎᎦᎯᎦᏎᏄᎭᏃᏈ

Lisa Waters, forty-two years old, tired, and emotionally spent from guerrilla warfare, gathers the Pins for a final general muster in September, 1865.

Over three hundred Cherokee men, freedmen, and escaped slaves gather around a flatbed wagon where she stands with Josiah.

"Your Judaculla speaks for the last time to this fighting unit." Second-in-command steps aside.

Lisa stiffens the back and surveys the Pins. "In a few hours, you courageous brothers will live in history. You heroes of many hard-fought fields return to firesides from which you have been so long absent. Today, you muster out of service. The cause of freedom respects and appreciates that your blood soaked these Cherokee lands against those who own other human beings."

A rumble of agreement ripples through the assembly.

"That sacrifice frees every man, woman, and child, despite the wish of others. I know you will stay vigilant as we build the future with no further bloodshed and united with our Union brothers. Vigilance welcomes peace."

The men applaud.

Josiah steps forward. "Return to your lives. Take your wives and children home. On June 23, Brigadier General Stand Watie surrendered and signed articles of surrender at Doaksville in the Choctaw

Nation. He is the last Confederate general officer to surrender. Rebs threaten no more!"

Cherokee, along with freedmen and new freed slaves, fire rifles in the air and churn on horseback in celebration.

Josiah turns to Lisa.

He withdraws a letter from his belt. "A Union dispatch rider this morning brought correspondence from President Ross."

***

Later in the day, in the privacy of her cabin, she reads.

John's words in his voice vibrate in her ears as if the Cherokee leader speaks. "Steamer Iron City, Five miles below Van Buren, August 31, 1865. Dear Mrs. Waters, I journey to Fort Gibson from Washington to attend a council in Fort Smith on September 8 to represent loyal Union Cherokees."

Lisa's mind remembers another steamboat on the Arkansas but reads more.

"Fondly, I remember days when your husband's wisdom proved most useful and respectfully ask that you serve as a delegate. After a three-year absence, I approach my country, people, my children, relatives, and friends. My only wish is that my beloved wife Mary was at my side and not the victim of consumption. You were her close friend, and she penned a letter before she passed, which I have included in this dispatch."

The warm, loving face of the first lady smiles in Lisa's mind.

"The plan is to stay at the Murrell house near Park Hill until I travel to Fort Smith. Please show a willingness to join the delegation by return missive. Respectfully, John Ross."

Lisa leans back in a chair and gazes out the cabin's open door.

Unaware he is visible, or that anyone is within hearing distance, Moss plays a fiddle outside, sad notes, but music.

The Judaculla smiles and turns to the second letter.

Hands shake as she unfolds the parchment.

"Dearest Lisa," the words on paper blur with moisture in the woman's eyes, "In bed on a bloody pillow in this cold land of my childhood, I remember the warmth of your life and our love for one another. How I wish I could see you once more. The physician just left the bedroom with my husband and his body language says that limited days upon this earth remain."

Lisa dabs an eye's moisture with a sleeve.

"I most wanted to write and tell you that your friendship is my fondest memory. The president is returning to Cherokee lands soon, and I am sure that I will not be able to go with him. I suggested he seek your council and plead that you accept the task. I have heard you struggled during the war at home for our noble cause and ask you to continue that effort with the peace."

Lisa, for a moment, focuses on Moss's sad song but returns to her letter.

"You asked me once to never speak of your sister's death, and I did not. In return, please counsel my beloved husband. His health declines. Be my soul near his side. In love, Mary Stapler."

Fresh tear drops spot and smear the signature on the paper.

Lisa twists to the sounds that float through her cabin's door.

"We are coming from the cotton fields, we're coming from afar; we have left the plow, the hoe and ax and gone off to a war."

Moss's voice rings weak and resonates with helplessness.

"We have left old plantation seat, the sugar and the cane, where we work'd and toil'd with weary feet in sun and wind and rain."

Moss plays his fiddle and sings in the yard as his tone strengthens. "We have left our chains behind us, boys, the prison, and the rack; and we've hid beneath a soldier's coat the scars upon our backs."

Lisa, with Mary Stapler Ross's letter, stands in the open cabin doorway and observes the fiddler.

"We'll teach the world a lesson soon if taken by the hand, how the night shall come before tis noon, upon old Pharaoh's land."

Moss turns and realizes she watches.

He pauses the lament.

"Wonderful. So long since I enjoyed your voice and music."

"Nu-, nun-, not t-, t-, tal-, talk. O-, o-, on-, only si-, si-, sing." The big man's chin quivers.

Lisa nods, and wetness fills her eyes.

He lifts the fiddle and sings. "By the heavy chains that bound our hands through centuries of wrong, we have learned the hard bought lesson well, how to suffer and be strong. We only ask the power to show what freedom does for man; and we'll give sign to friend and foe as none beside us can."

"I hear and understand. Soon, I travel to Fort Smith with President John Ross to represent my Union supporting Cherokee half." Lisa folds a fist over the heart. "You and Josiah come with me and serve in my father's memory."

***

Days later, the ex-second-in-command Pin reins a team of four horses that pulls a loaded wagon off the road over rocky terrain. The wheels lurch over a stone. "This was once a hunting trail."

"Still rough." Lisa sits beside the driver.

"Isolated place, but Moss remembers traveling through from the underground railroad." He glances to the rear where the fiddler, James, Elizabeth, and Sarah sit on burlap bags of flower and salt pork. "One of the former escape stations is over that rim."

"Away from normal pathways. That's good." Lisa looks at the ridge ahead. "Our people will be safe here."

"But I should stay behind for security. Take Moss on the trip."

"Josiah, you earned representation."

"So did he. The fiddler can't guard this place." The wagon's driver shrugs. "A few Reb renegades, including Watie's Cherokees, don't understand who lost the war. With James and I, the girls will be safe."

"I'm the one who should stay." Lisa rubs a sore forehead. "Watie murdered my sister, and his troops killed Ezra. If there's trouble, this pistol should settle the issue."

"The president requested you. He doesn't need others." Josiah smiles.

***

Several days later, she sits cross-legged on the floor of the cabin in front of James, Elizabeth, and Sarah.

"Do we have to do this?" The girl pouts.

"You speak the language but can't read or write a word. In school, Presbyterians only taught English. I had to learn. A man father knew created these symbols."

She dips a down plume quill into a small bottle of black ink in a brass and tin soldiers' carrying case. The instrument forms the Cherokee Syllabary ᎦᎦ "sa-sa" and repeats the shape that resembles an inverted capital English A with a round top.

"Sah, sah." The teacher points to the feather. "Goose. Go first, James."

"Everybody's heard of Sequoya. Did you know him?" The teenage boy accepts the pen and draws the symbols below the instructor's example.

"Met the great man when I was your age. With my sister and old medicine man." Lisa watches the writing. "I remember the smoke from his long pipe most."

"Sah, sah. Goose." Big brother hands the point to Elizabeth, and the girl imitates the sibling.

"See, I can do it." The pen passes to Sarah.

As the brother sees youngest sister form the letters, he smiles and turns to the teacher. "The war ended. Reading and writing will become important again, don't you think?"

"Yes, you need an education, a career."

"I want to stay here, to hunt and fish and roam these woods."

"Of course. But the war changed everything. You did not know my husband, Ezra. He was an attorney. Studied law with a Judge in Fort Smith. President John Ross depended upon his counsel." Lisa looks at Sarah's quill work. "Very nice, Sarah."

"I never met any judges." The youngster folds both arms and frowns.

"That's not what I am saying, James." The older woman focuses. "You aren't the only one who needs a career. My and Ezra's money is gone. An income is necessary."

"Where did it go?" The young man lifts hands, palms to the sky.

"The war spent it."

"But your side won. That doesn't make much sense."

"I didn't win, the Union did. Whites were the real victors. People such as Josiah, the Judaculla, and the Pins helped them win. Most people around here were rebels." She massages her forehead. "A few say President Lincoln wants to help the south recover. The papers call the effort reconstruction."

"Even for Cherokees?"

"Yes. And freed slaves."

"What does that name mean?"

Lisa pats Sarah's head and climbs to her feet. "Means to look for opportunity."

"I don't understand." James stands.

"New things from the war come. Railroad commerce is an example. The territory has no railways." The Judaculla looks out the cabin's door and gazes at the woods beyond the clearing. "Someone will build tracks along known Cherokee passages and travel ways, such as the California mail and stage route."

"Or north and south on the Texas Road?" The young man's eyes sparkle.

"Which intersect at Crossroads, on Choctaw soil in Confederate loyal land." Lisa smiles. "But the woods are here. New tracks will need ties."

# CHAPTER TWENTY-FIVE — Delegates

DRTᎪᏫᎣᎥᏚᎤᏒᎩᎪᎫᎬᎥᎮᏗᎮᎭᎦᎤᏪᏓᎮᎬᎷᎭᎤᏗᎥᏗᎮᎮᎯᎠᎭᎫᏪᎥᎨᏅᎥᎢ

$F$all leaves turn to early color as Lisa and Josiah travel through eastern territory. They bounce in ruts on the journey from Fort Gibson to Smith.

An elevated seat above the wagon box cushions the rocky route as it exits woodlands of the Boston Mountains' foothills, twelve miles from the Arkansas River, into the flats around Mackey's salt works.

Lisa watches an old Cherokee man kick a hole in an abandoned, charred hollow log utilized to pipe saline water from the springs to rows of enormous metal cauldrons.

Many of the bowls, used to boil the liquid and leave the mineral, show holes from Confederate destruction to prevent Union access to the commodity.

Shells of blackened, burned wagons used to haul the finished product to another scorched house sit with the kettles.

The two pass the remnants of a massive enterprise.

Lisa visualizes customers who buy the salt and shovel it into wagon beds, bags, or barrels.

Her mind remembers the river and Moss supervising crews loading the same product in sacks onto Ezra's boats, destined for markets in New Orleans.

"Josiah, I miss the fiddler." She turns to the wagon's driver.

"Better he stays home with James and the girls." The operator clicks his tongue as four mules snort in response. "You are enough for the grand council to accept, even if invited by John Ross."

"What are you saying?"

"In the old days, women accepted, most welcomed, leadership, but the war changed that."

"Oh." Lisa nods. "But my Cherokee Pins followed."

"You were their Judaculla."

"And now I am not? They should listen to Stand Watie's opinion."

Josiah smiles. "It's more than you are a woman. You forget your freedman father."

"I don't ignore father's people, but mother's have much to gain as well. I remember starving on a frozen Mississippi riverbank while White soldiers roasted meat."

"The old Reb general has no thoughts on that. He was a New Echota signee and migrated earlier."

Lisa smiles. "The roast was Confederate beef. They say he and the other rebels are boycotting the conference."

Josiah points ahead. "Someone's camped up there."

She turns attention to the road.

Outside a worn army surplus tent, a White man stands and studies a map on a temporary wooden counter.

Geological survey implements on tripods and burlap bags of equipment surround the table.

An unsaddled horse, tethered, grazes beyond the canvas, and a Spencer fifty caliber leans against the pavilion.

The fellow looks up and steps to the weapon as Lisa's wagon approaches.

"Good day, sir." She waves as Josiah pulls the wagon's team to a halt. "No need for that rifle. We are harmless."

The White man cradles the firearm in the crook of an elbow. "My name's Oliver Weldon. I'm an engineer doing mapping, a US geological survey of Indian Territory. What's your business so far from civilization?"

"We travel to Fort Smith. Lisa Waters, and this fellow is Josiah Raines."

The surveyor returns the Spencer to rest. "Can't be too careful. The war's not over long. Lot of homeless rebels around, not to mention a few wild Pins. But I see you're a Cherokee. Once served with a group of their soldiers."

"You work for the federal government?" Lisa's voice remains friendly. "This is the first mapping I've seen since the war."

"Yes. The fighting's over, and I lacked work. I was a captain with the twenty-second Arkansas Volunteer Confederate Infantry. But the United States needed a surveyor."

"May I look at your map?"

"Sure. I'm proud of my skills."

Lisa jumps to the ground and joins the engineer at the table.

"Railroads are expanding into the territory." Weldon points at the topographical sketch. "Most promising routes are along the Texas Road, the Shawnee Trail, and the California route."

"What's that gray shape in the south?" Lisa's curiosity intrudes.

"Coal deposits at the crossroads. Railways want fuel."

"That's a huge parcel of land." Lisa glances at the engineer. "On Indian property."

"Yes. Companies will lay tracks through there." Weldon nods.

"May I buy this map?" She looks at Josiah, who watches from the wagon and smiles.

"I gave a duplicate to a war buddy of mine in Fort Smith but will sell one to you. Ten federal dollars, no Confederate script." The engineer rolls the design.

"Heading there. Might run into him."

"My friend served with Stand Watie. His name is McAlester. If you meet J. J., tell him I expect to be out here another couple of weeks, but I said hello."

"Mr. Weldon. I will."

***

The following day, Lisa and Josiah approach the town from the east.

Their wagon rolls onto a ferry over the Arkansas River, and the large fortification, with a multi-story soldier's quarters fronted by columns from ground to roof, looms between the water and the bluffs.

The land beside the fort bustles with people swollen by delegates from the Cherokee, Chickasaw, Choctaw, Creek (Muscogee), and Seminoles.

As Lisa and Josiah guide the mules into town and search for a stable, she observes a raucous crowd surrounding a speaker on a wagon under a shade tree with fall color leaves.

The Pin second-in-command turns wheels to a livery keeper as the speaker's voice howls from under the foliage. "This conference is to reestablish government relations with Injuns who fought as rebs! I say string them high!"

Several Choctaws pull the speechmaker off the bed.

They replace the fellow with their representative.

The new speaker waves both arms for attention. "Albert Pike, Confederate commissioner to Indian territory, forged agreements in 1861 with us, as well as the Comanche, Wichita, Osage, Shawnee, Seneca, and the Quapaw. He lied!"

Lisa and Josiah walk toward the excitement.

The orator jerks a hand at the neck, a hangman's imitation. "Can Andrew Johnson hang everyone?"

A freedman jumps onto the wagon bed and pushes the southern sympathizer aside. "Lincoln gave the right to vote! We fought the battles! Spilled our blood! Choctaws and Cherokees can't own this fighter no more!"

Smoke billows from a pistol as the speechmaker grasps a hole in the chest and falls.

The crowd erupts into a mob fight.

The two visitors run across the street to avoid the conflict.

"This is ugly." Josiah dusts his hat on a knee as the two approach a Cherokee desk worker. "Is this the Hotel Main? President John Ross has a room?"

The host nods confirmation.

"Please inform the gentleman Mrs. Waters has arrived. We will wait for a response."

"Sorry, that's not possible."

"Why?"

The clerk jerks a thumb toward Josiah. "That man is not welcome in this establishment."

Lisa pulls her pistol from its hip holster and jabs the barrel under the Cherokee's chin. "I suggest you listen and serve your customers." She cocks the weapon's hammer.

"Yes, ma'am." The clerk's voice cracks and sweat pops from pores on the employee's brow.

He gasps for air as the weapon uncocks.

The man glances at Josiah and hurries for the stairway to the second floor.

The two wait in Hotel Main's sitting room. Both, unaccustomed to the comfort of opulent surroundings, fidget in stuffed chairs.

After a brief interval, the tall, stately stature of President Ross, in a knee-length topcoat and top hat, fills the room's doorway. The man's hands tremble. His shoulders slump with age and the weight of forty years of service to the Cherokee Nation.

Lisa stands, and her companion follows the example. "John, wonderful to see you."

The statesman steps into the room with a cane's assistance. "So good of you to come. Know of Mary Stapler?"

"Yes." She nods in respect.

Ross extends the greeting. "You must be Josiah. Your reputation for military leadership precedes this visit. The union owes our veterans gratitude."

The Pin shakes the Cherokee leader's hand. "Thank you, sir."

The tired leader steps to a stuffed armchair, seats his length, and leans his cane against a chair arm. "Please sit." He gazes at his wife's best friend. "The heart is heavy. Beloved Mary left far too soon. I was at the bedside, and before she passed, one of her last utterances was appreciation of your friendship."

Lisa's eyes mist.

The sitting room stays silent for a long moment.

"She told me of your sister's murder. Said she swore to never tell anyone but wanted me aware." John Ross removes an embroidered handkerchief from an interior topcoat pocket and wipes below the eyes. "The murderer escaped?"

"Let's say no one arrested the killer." Lisa leans forward in the chair. "We know who did the killing, but with many Cherokee murders, justice is political. A fellow that worked for Ezra saw the act. His name is Moss."

"I remember the man. He was a guest for a short time at Park Hill."

"Yes. The same. But he spent over a year in the rebel prison camp at Fort Davis, unconquered. The guards whipped his back to a pulp and castrated the man. He still works with me, but little remains. His mind wanders."

The president shifts his cane from one chair arm to another. "Not news I want to hear. My biggest mistake was allegiance to the South's cause for too long." He looks at the second-in-command. "My son served with the Third Regiment of Federal Indian Home Guard, those men who switched sides from Colonel John Drew's rebels."

The Pin nods.

"Allen died in a Confederate prison camp." Ross twists to Lisa. "Could Moss name your sister's killer?"

She shakes a chin negatively. "Not in that condition. But I know the fiend who pistol whipped her to death."

The leader straightens.

"Yes, sir." The muscles in her jaws twitch. "The murderer admitted the act, considered brutality a badge of honor."

"Who?"

"When the Pins attempted to save the John B. Williams, the beast met Josiah and I on a sandbar. His nephew was there and confessed under stress. Uncle was proud of the deed."

"Standhope Watie?" The president leans back.

Lisa nods.

"Your life is in danger. The general never forgets."

"Or forgives. So is yours, sir."

"But mine has been throughout this war." Ross chuckles. "You are fresh."

The Judaculla jerks toward her companion. "That's why Josiah protects."

John Ross's tone turns to business. "The general and the Confederate faction boycott this conference. I do not expect that to continue. The stakes here are too high."

"And those are?" Lisa's voice changes.

"United States Commissioner of Indian Affairs, Dennis Cooley, negotiates a post-war status treaty with the tribes, including the new arrivals."

"The western part of Cherokee territory becomes a federal dumping ground for those plains removals out west." Lisa eyes John Ross's top hat.

"As was the eastern half for immigrants when your sister earned the people's adoration." The president smiles.

Lincoln's friend claps weak hands and points. "Stand Watie and the Confederate sympathizers won't allow any treaty to be negotiated without a say."

"Feelings are hot. There was a shooting at a rally outside the hotel." Lisa looks at Josiah.

"Everything is tenuous and volatile." Ross watches for reaction. "We should keep controversy as low-key as possible for a favorable treaty."

"I agree."

"Temporarily set aside your hatred for southern sympathizers, even the justifiable contempt for Watie."

Lisa squirms in the chair.

The Nation's executive looks at Josiah and then returns eyes to his wife's friend. "I want you to be a delegate. Your level head and blood mix work well. But there is a problem."

"Which is?" She glances at the Judaculla's second-in-command.

The head of the nation coughs. "You are female."

Lisa stares at the president of the Cherokees as if the gentleman cursed.

"Sir!"

John Ross leans forward. "These are modern times. This is the nineteenth century. In the East, women fight for rights and representation. Which they deserve. But in Fort Smith, Arkansas, a woman's thoughts and opinions do not carry equal weight."

"That's not a solution." The Pin leader flushes red-cheeked. "It's an indictment."

"The answer is pants!" Ross points. "Wear them."

"Your voice is deep and hoarse from the war. You sound like a man." Josiah leans back in a chair with both palms extended forward for safety. "Cut the hair shorter?"

# CHAPTER TWENTY-SIX — Oklahoma

## DRTᏯᏫᎣᎥᏚᎧᏉᎩAJEᏋᏘᎯᏨᏫᏯWᏛᎡGMᎯᏕᎣᎥᎻᏚᎩᎮᏪᎾᏔᎻZᎯᎣᵛ

September 8, 1865, US Commissioner Dennis N. Cooley pounds a gavel on a wooden podium in Fort Smith's military barracks, the same room that becomes Isaac Parker's courtroom years later.

Behind the desk, federal officials Elijah Sells, Superintendent of Indian Affairs, and Colonel E. S. Parker (no relation to the hanging judge) sit and stare at the delegates who crowd the chamber.

Cherokee, Chickasaw, Choctaw, Comanche, Creek, Osage, Quapaw, Seminole, Seneca, Shawnee, Wichita, and Wyandotte tribal representatives fill the place.

Many eye the stiff military representative at the head table, Colonel Parker, a Seneca Indian who served on General Ulysses S. Grant's staff and recognized author of the final surrender terms signed by Lee at Appomattox.

President John Ross heads his Union-affiliated-without-southern-sympathizer competition, and Lisa, with shorn hair and dressed in a man's suit, sits in her chair nearby.

Eastern territorial tribes, in business attire with coats and stiff collars, separate themselves from the western contingents who dress within their traditions.

Neckties maintain a narrow aisle between themselves and anyone with a feather or moccasins.

A loud "bang-bang" of Cooley's gavel stresses command from the podium, and the audience settles into chairs.

"The United States of America declares this conference open!" Cooley, dressed in a black suit and a bow tie around white collars that point upward on each side of his neck, twitches a heavy mustache.

His words reverberate through the room. "This meeting renegotiates treaties between the Union and those tribes who aligned with the Confederacy. Your rebellion gave up your tribal annuities and interests in the lands of the territory!"

John Ross leans to Lisa's ear. "Unexpected. Sounds as if they have new attitudes, or seek revenge? Radical and startling for those of us still loyal."

"You who entered treaties with the rebels give up your rights and protection from the government." Cooley's eyes flash vengeance. "We may confiscate your property!"

The delegates erupt with angry protests and catcalls.

Cooley nods to Colonel Parker, and the officer, with military precision, steps to and opens the meeting room's door.

Union soldiers with shiny new Springfield rifles file in and stand at ease along the exterior walls, spaced six feet apart.

Force quiets the place. Members of the western tribes eye the troopers' weapons.

"Defeated rebels must meet seven conditions demanded by the United States of America before discussions." The Commissioner of Indian Affairs thrust his chin forward.

"What are those?" Someone in the back penetrates above the delegates and their grumbles.

"One! The tribes are required to set up permanent peace and amity between themselves and the federal government!" Cooley slams his gavel on the table, and the sound overwhelms dissent.

Lisa leans to John Ross. "He means we embrace murderers such as Stand Watie?"

The president nods. "And our Choctaw neighbors. See the delegate in the top hat?"

"Resembles a fat Abraham Lincoln."

"That's Allen Wright, the Choctaw's principal leader." The Cherokee covers his chuckle with one hand. "Thinks he's more important than the rail splitter ever was."

"Two!" Cooley points at the Comanche delegates. "Those who rejoin the Union swear to aid this government in keeping the peace with the plains tribes."

Their representatives jump from their seats and stalk past nervous soldier guards outside the room's door.

"Three! Everyone abolishes slavery and frees laborers from captivity." The Commissioner ignores derision and catcalls from the audience.

"Four! Freedmen incorporate into your clans equal with tribesmen."

The room erupts, and Cooley pounds his gavel.

A Cherokee delegate leans close and yells to John Ross loud enough to be heard over the clamor. "Watie will never agree!"

"Five! Territory tribes must surrender portions of their lands to resettle others from Kansas! Order! Let there be quiet!"

Union troopers with rifles in hand push and shove attendees into their chairs.

"Six! Whites may not live within tribal land."

The crowd bursts into cheers and hurrahs.

"Seven! The United States will organize a single governing entity for residents."

Hoorays turn to derisive hisses.

"These are the terms of peace required by the Union!" Cooley slams his gavel.

"Mr. Commissioner!"

"The Director of Indian Affairs recognizes Allen Wright, Principal Chief of the Choctaw Nation."

"Sir! Distinguished delegates. One government for the tribes requires a new name for these lands."

"Oh no, here we go." John Ross elbows Lisa.

"As leader of the most prominent tribe, I propose an original title to be used by our common governing body, taken from two of my language's words, meaning Land of the Red Man." Wright doffs his top hat for effect. "I nominate the glorious nom de guerre, Oklahoma!"

Attendees except Choctaws leap upon their feet with objections.

Lisa's mentor stands. "Mr. Commissioner."

"I recognize John Ross, president of the northern faction of the Cherokee Nation."

"I wish to point out that merged government diminishes our individual tribal identities and is a scheme we should oppose." He looks around the group for support. "I object to the term 'northern faction.' We are not of multiple factions. We are of one proud culture with a long heritage."

A voice drips hatred. "Your father was a White man!"

"Sir! My mother was a full-blood Cherokee! Further, I am the elected president of the Nation!"

"And Stand Watie is the accepted leader of the Confederate Cherokees!"

"Restore order!" Cooley pounds his wooden table.

Federal troopers push into the delegate crowd to force compliance with another White man's treaty.

***

That evening, Lisa and John Ross sip tea in the sitting room of Hotel Main.

The president slumps in his chair, worn and exhausted from the day's debates. "My Mary is not proud of her husband today. He is old and tired of politics."

She remembers. "Mary's pride for your forty years of selfless service to the Cherokee Nation overrides this temporary setback."

"Thank you. The issue is not history, but my capabilities." He yawns and covers his mouth with a fist. "I didn't represent my people well, and the southern group wasn't present."

"You need rest. You should go to your room."

"I believe I will."

"Let me help you. Here's your cane."

John leans on his protégé as the two move through the sitting room's doors toward the lobby's stairs.

Lisa glances at the door.

Josiah stands outside and motions for her to join him.

She nods recognition and helps the president through the last steps to the staircase.

The exhausted statesman grasps the stair's rail. "I can make it from here. I cannot accept help further. My male ego won't allow it."

"Even though this establishment's guests see me as a man, sir, my female soul understands. Good night."

Lisa turns and strides to the Hotel Main's doorway.

"Over here." Josiah's voice beckons.

The two confer in the shadows of a gazebo near the hotel entrance.

"Is the place where you're staying comfortable? I rest guilty on a bed in the best inn in town." She watches the building's lit windows, which cast rectangles of luminance on the ground.

"It's a room above the stables off the street." Josiah grins. "Where they don't shoot uppity freedman."

"I'm sorry. I need to be with him. He has aged since I last was aware, and he doesn't admit it, but his health fails."

"Not his condition that worries. It is yours."

"I am fine."

"Not what I mean. I heard two drunk Cherokees, ex-confederates who rode with Watie, brag how they await their opportunity to assassinate the Judaculla."

Lisa turns her full attention to her second-in-command.

"They had money and a bottle. Doing heavy drinking behind the stable where their horses are."

"I suspect the general paid them. Should I wear my Colt?"

Josiah chuckles. "Not tonight. They were too drunk. I will keep my eye on them. If action happens, I'll warn you."

***

The following morning, Lisa waits in Fort Smith's barracks for the conference to meet. Most delegates mill around or cluster in groups of similar opinions, but the seats at the front table stay empty.

Union soldiers with bayonetted rifles rim the room at intervals.

A Cherokee sits next to her. "Sir, President Ross has not arrived yet. Was he detained?"

"Good morning." She holds her voice low and deep. "I don't know why he isn't here."

"My apologies." The delegate looks at the door. "I thought you were part of his staff."

"No. I am a representative. The name's Peters. Pleasure meeting you."

Commissioner of Indian Affairs, Dennis Cooley, and his entourage sweep into the room and seat themselves in the front.

"Who speaks for us if Ross isn't here?" The man elbows his seatmate.

"Is a speech necessary?"

"Yes. To object to incorporating ex-slaves into our tribe."

"Not I." Lisa's voice cracks. "I'm for it."

The moderator stands and pounds his gavel. "Order! This day's business will begin."

The attendees settle into their seats.

"Many of the tribes oppose freedmen in their midst. My government requires this condition before peace talks meet. In the spirit of understanding, we accept statements from those that urge otherwise. Who wishes to speak?"

The delegate next to Lisa jabs an elbow into her ribs. "John Ross was our speaker. As a member of his staff and his protégé, it's your responsibility."

She peers at the jabber and the other delegates, who fixate upon her.

She swallows and stands.

"Who rises in the Cherokee tribe?" Cooley points.

"Ezra Peters, Commissioner, special assistant to the president."

"Go ahead."

The short-haired woman in pants looks at the faces in the room. "Representatives of the United States of America, honored territorial delegates, my distinguished colleagues. I rise this morning in the place of our most experienced political leader."

Attendees burst into applause.

"The question before us held inviolate by federal officers is we must accept freedmen into our midst as members despite their lack of Indian blood."

A frustrated crowd hisses and boos.

"For peace and acceptance into the Union fold for our territory and its inhabitants who chose alliance to the southern cause in the recent conflict," she pauses. "I remind you the surrender at Appomattox settled this issue. That is not in doubt."

A rumble of disapproval sweeps the assembly.

"John Ross, to keep the treaty integrity of agreements with the Union, resisted overtures from the Confederates. Popular opinion swept the territory into the war on the losing side. Battle split Indians against freedman, and animosity survives today."

Most delegates grumble but agree.

Lisa waits for calm. "President Ross was a Northern troop's captive early released upon an oath of fealty to the United States. James, Allen, Silas, and George, his sons, served in the Third Regiment of the Home Guards. Allen fell prisoner three years ago while delivering needed supplies to his family. He survived various prison camps but died a detainee last year. Confederate guerrillas attacked the residence of John Ross's daughter. Jane and her husband Andrew Nave perished. This confirms the president's fidelity!"

People sit upon their hands.

Lisa pauses and surveys the audience. "After forty years of service to his people, President Ross, who lost his beloved wife Mary a few short months ago, pleads for a quick and permanent reconciliation with the United States government."

The conference's stillness palls the room as Lisa sits.

After a few moments, Commissioner Cooley breaks the wake. "Delegates. It has come to my awareness that John Ross, President of the Cherokee Nation, must abandon his plan to attend the sessions of this conference because of health issues. He returns to Park Hill this afternoon and will live with relatives at the Murrell house. His replacement is Second Chief Lewis Downing."

No delegates respond in any manner to the announcement.

Cooley smiles and slams his gavel on the table. "I adjourn our business for this day."

As the attendees file without comment from the room, one steps close. "Mr. Peters. Have you heard the news from the southern Cherokees?"

Lisa shakes her head.

"The ex-rebel Choctaws, Creeks, Seminoles, and Chickasaws hold their own council with Stand Watie."

"Where?" She turns to the whisperer.

"South. At the Armstrong Academy in the Choctaw Nation, away from Pins." He responds in the arrogant manner and style of Cooley, the powerful conference moderator.

# CHAPTER TWENTY-SEVEN — Rejection

ᎠᏚᎢᎰᎠᎢᏍᏲᏝᏯ ᎠᏎᎬᏇᎯᎵᏣᏫᏛᎵᏓᎹᏗᏏᎣᎯᎲᏚᏯᎾᏣᏁᏂᏃᏑᎤ

The following day, September 10th, Lisa breakfasts with three men, a morning meeting in the Hotel Main.

Lewis Downing, chosen replacement for John Ross, sips coffee across the table.

His secretary and bodyguard complete the four-person seating.

"I understand you served as Company F's and S's Chaplain in the First Cherokee Mounted Rifles?" She looks at her colleague. "And fought with the Confederates at Pea Ridge?"

"Yes, I did, Mr. Peters." Downing places his cup on the surface. "Many brave men died in that battle."

"Including a friend of mine, an attorney adviser to John Ross named Ezra Waters." His wife, in disguise, coughs into her linen napkin.

"Sorry to hear that. I've heard of that lawyer and his influence with the president but never met him." Lewis Downing signals a freedman waiter for more coffee. "After Flat Rock Creek in '62, as most of us except Drew, I joined the Third Regiment of the Indian Home Guards. The Union made me a Lieutenant Colonel and designated John Jones its chaplain in Phillips's Brigade."

"An admirable unit." Lisa watches the attendant pour fresh drinks.

"Yes, thank you." Downing nods to the servant. "President Ross suggested this meeting. He told me you are a close friend and adviser, but my aids find no evidence of Union service, Mr. Peters. Curious."

"I led a force of Pins throughout the war affiliated with the North."

"Guerrillas?" The minister clasps his hands together on his lap.

"Yes."

"I am an ordained Protestant who came to the territory with the forced removal in Bushyhead's detachment." The preacher puffs his chest, pulpit style.

"New arrival, as many of us."

"Served as Flint Baptist Church's pastor after Jesse died."

"Admirable."

The politician's jaw tightens. "Much you irregulars did was an affront to God."

"Including both sides. War is offensive to Him by definition, sir."

"But we are now united, Mr. Peters. We have a common problem, these Cooley requirements for the renewal of relations with the federal government. We cannot deny most fought for the south."

"You did, Mr. Downing." Lisa stares at her breakfast's host. "I did not."

He shrugs. "These government stipulations result from my actions?"

"No. Permanent peace and amity between the tribes, assisting the federals in keeping the truce, abolition of slavery, incorporation of freedmen, surrender of Western land to resettle Kansas people, a merged territorial government, and no Whites living on Indian lands sounds more than your fault."

"We don't have the power to resist. Those I represent are most interested in maintaining tribal identity, plus no ex-slaves in our Nations or institutions."

Lisa stands and places her napkin on the breakfast table. "I serve at the request of John Ross. The war which I fought and suffered through was to incorporate freedmen into our culture and state. My father was a freedman. Without President Ross and with leadership of your mind, I must resign my responsibilities as a delegate."

Lewis Downing stands. "So be it, Mr. Peters."

She turns and marches out of the Hotel Main's breakfast room.

***

Josiah waits across the street. He steps from the boardwalk and meets his leader. "You're fuming, and that was a brief meeting."

"Who am I, old friend?"

The second-in-command glances over his shoulder at people within hearing distance. "Ezra Peters?"

She yanks off her hat, throws it into the dirt and ruffles her cut short hair. "I'll tell you who I am not! I am not a fictitious politician. Don't even know who that name is. Worse yet, he doesn't realize who I am!"

"You are a leader, the daughter of a Cherokee and an ex-slave." Second-in-command picks up the brim and slaps dust from its surface. "That's who you are."

"No. The Cherokees reject freedmen such as you and my father. I fought a war to include fighters! I'm not the Judaculla of my mother's people."

Her friend offers the clean headgear. "You're not White as Commissioner Cooley and the rest of the rule makers. So, the daughter of a freedman is what's left."

The woman stops in the street. "Get our wagon. It's time this freedman's girl goes home and tends to family!"

Lisa waits on a wooden bench under the shade of the same tree that greeted her arrival in Fort Smith.

She watches several dusty wagons escorted by armed and mounted men approach the Hotel Main.

Many riders wear Confederate issue butternut blouses.

Street traffic churns near the arrivals, and a young boy runs with excitement past Lisa's shaded seat.

"Stop!" She grasps the child's arm. "What's going on over there?"

"Them's the Southern Cherokee delegation with Stand Watie. Let me go. I got to tell my mom!"

"Your mother?" She releases the boy's sleeve.

"Yeah! She wants a separate Nation where we can keep our slaves!"

"That will not happen, son."

"You don't know! Somebody important is over there, General Watie!"

"No, I'm not a Cherokee." Lisa smiles. "Only a freedman's daughter."

The boy jerks away. "You're touched, Mister. I have eyes. Leave me alone."

***

As darkness gathers miles from Fort Smith, Lisa's and Josiah's mules plod along the road home.

"It was him, Mrs. Waters." The second-in-command searches for a campsite.

A roadside clearing beckons.

"Elias Cornelius Boudinot was with him." He guides the team into the space. "Their people want the United States to pay to relocate freedmen."

"Cooley will ignore that. They think of the tribes as one surrendered Confederate entity."

"Imagine so." Josiah pulls the reins and slows the mules. "But this freedman fought a war to stay here. I'm not going anywhere. You ready to settle for the night?"

After a supper cooked over an open fire, Lisa settles into a primitive bedroll made from wool US Army issue blankets on the bed of the wagon. She listens to Josiah arrange more bedding on the ground under the side for his comfort.

Later, as the moon spreads light throughout her campsite, she wakens. She pulls her covers off her shoulders and sits upright.

Two small round orbs glow outside the encampment and blink.

The woken woman feels the wagon's bed until her fingers find a lumpy object near her head.

She uncovers her holster and slips her pistol from its bedroll.

With a weapon, she investigates the phenomenon.

A bobcat rests on a rock nearby.

With distinctive black bars on its forelegs and a dark-tipped, stubby tail, the cat sits as if it waits and doesn't move as Lisa stands on the ground.

The woman looks through the wheel spokes at a shadowy lump.

Snores show Josiah.

Her visual investigation sweeps to the dying embers of their wood cooking fire that smolders like the cat's eyes upon the rock.

The wary investigator steps from the wagon toward the animal, which remains motionless without fear and watches.

"Bobcat, shoo, go away."

The feline rests and stares.

"Leave us in peace. When I was little, an old medicine man told me stories. Of you. He claimed to understand and speak your talk. Was that true?"

The wild one does not move.

"Guess it wasn't. And I sure don't. It shows the true Cherokee I am."

The animal's whiskers twitch, and the fur upon its neck stiffens.

It jumps from the rock to the ground and retreats several yards before it twists to watch.

"What do you call for, Bobcat?" She follows and nears the cat. It scampers thirty feet along the roadway that borders the wagon.

The creature stops, sits, and peers.

"You wish me to follow you?" She approaches the animal as it pads farther, then jumps into a clump of trees and disappears.

Lisa investigates. The foliage and brush where the vision vanished show no movement. No orbs glow as wild eyes in the night.

She freezes and allows her pupils to adjust to less moonlight.

Muffled thumps from the trail distract from the animal search. The woman drops to her knees for concealment.

Beyond her, two dark forms become horsemen whose metal shoes plod in the dirt surface.

"Hold up, Pete." One form reins its mount to a stop.

The second imitates his partner's action. "Light ahead. Embers of a campfire."

"Figure we just caught up with them." A muffled voice responds. "They're Judacullas. Careful, Pins are dangerous, but I bet we found them asleep."

"General Watie said it's a woman." Pete's tone quivers. "I ain't ever killed a female. Have you?"

"I rode with Quantrill, fool. Quiet. Don't wake them."

Both riders dismount and tie their horses to a tree near Lisa's concealment.

On foot, the two assassins approach the campfire's embers and the dark shadow of the wagon beside the road.

As the men walk beyond hearing, Lisa muffles the sound as she cocks her pistol against her stomach and steps from the brush.

Quantrill's man motions Pete to separate.

Each assassin slips near opposite sides of the conveyance.

With pistols ready, they lean into the darkness under canvas.

"Ain't no Pins here, Pete."

"Because I'm behind you, you Quantrill bushwhacker!"

The gunman spins to attack Lisa, and she pulls her pistol's trigger.

Smoke blasts forward, and her bullet blows a hole through the Confederate's neck and shoulder.

The second killer jerks to help his partner as Josiah's long gun's round hurtles the assassin's body to land on its back with one arm in the campfire's coals.

Josiah struggles from under the wagon to his feet. "They had us. You saved my life again, Judaculla."

"This cockroach needed killing. He rode with Kansas bushwhackers." Lisa nudges the corpse on the ground with her bare foot. "Don't know the other killer except his name was Pete."

"You knew they were coming?" Josiah drops to a knee and examines the body's face. "This fellow is not one of those boys I was watching in Fort Smith."

"I heard them talking up the road. They said Watie sent them to kill a couple of Pins." Lisa's voice trembles.

"Same question. What tipped you?"

Lisa peers at the full moon and then stares at the moonlit route where the bobcat disappeared.

"I'm not sure. Something in my Cherokee blood warned me. But for safety, it's time to return to Utugi Uweha. My boy and the girls are safe without threat from Watie there."

Josiah studies the woman. "She Has Hope. Why do you call it that?"

"Two of the men who mean the most to me live there."

"And so does my family." Josiah's eyes mist. "Days for killing are in the past."

The Judaculla grips her friend's shoulder.

The second-in-command grasps the comforting hand. "This freedman becomes a husband and father."

# CHAPTER TWENTY-EIGHT — Baggage

ᎠᏰᎢ ᏎᎣᎢᏍᏬᏎᎭᏯᎠᏤᏍᏝᏈᎦᎭᎦᏉᏪᎦᎨᎹᎻᎨᏍᎣᎲᎫᏯᎦᎡᎦᎾᎭᏃᏝᎤ

Later in the safety and security of Utugi Uweha, concealed from her southern Cherokee enemies, fall transitions into winter.

An early unseasonal snowstorm, a predictor of the harsh season to come, blankets Lisa's refuge in a coat of clean, white, impermanent self-confidence.

Lisa sits in a rocking chair in front of the fireplace with several candles that illuminate a wrinkled from reading months-old copy of the Cherokee Georgian newspaper.

James rests a knee on the hearth and adds wood to the room's fire while Sarah and Elizabeth knit nearby.

"I wish Josiah were here to read this." She attempts to divert the worker from stoking.

"That paper's from July." The young man returns a metal poker to a rack. "Old news."

"Takes time to get here from Georgia. But freedmen should be celebrating."

"How come?"

"On the nineteenth, the Cherokee Nation signed a reconstruction treaty with the United States in Washington." Lisa pats the newspaper on her lap.

"That's a long way from here." The young man brushes away the information. "Only construction Josiah's interested in is a new pen for hogs."

"It grants citizenship to freedman and their descendants and gives each person 160 acres."

"That will get his attention. You want me to ride up to his place when the snow stops?"

"No. I suspect he'll visit soon. Have you checked Moss today?"

"He only sits and plays the fiddle in the old Pin barracks."

"What songs?"

"Slow, sad tunes." James shakes a head. "The man's waiting to die."

"Hush. He's younger than I am." The woman winks at the youthful man. "He was resolute as you before the war."

"That war's long done. What's happening after has nothing to do with the fellow's fiddling."

"Hear you well." Lisa lays the newspaper on the floor by the rocker. "I'm worried over other things. Our food supply runs low. Need supplies. We'll go up the river, buy pork and corn. Want to go?"

The younger's eyes dance with excitement, an obvious yes.

***

Days later, Lisa, sitting atop the wagon with James at her side, guides a four-mule team along a muddy snow melt trail. Wind flaps the edges of a canvas cover over wood sides where rope ties cloth to frame.

She wears a long dress with sleeves under a heavy Union winter coat with a wrapped wool blanket top layer. A wide-brimmed hat perches atop a scarf that warms ears and neck.

James, bundled, props a rifle's stock upon worn federal boots and steadies the weapon in a cotton cloth-swathed hand.

Lisa's pistol in a holster, with an ammunition belt wrapped around its girth, lies on the seat with the buckle tucked under her hip. Two long guns rest on the bed behind the driver's bench.

"With the fighting over, why the weapons?" James shifts the rifle from one foot to the other.

"Railroads and commerce bring settlers and more people as they did in the Western territory. Not as dangerous in the East." The driver pats her passenger's back. "But Cherokees from both sides of the war still hate each other. Farmers used to be slaves in these hills."

"The new treaty settled that."

"Freedmen got the vote. It granted amnesty for those who fought for the South. Allotment divided tribal lands. People don't like the agreement. Most think the purpose was for railroad's right of way through farms." Lisa watches a trail of smoke rising from a distant ridgeline.

"I'm for tracks and locomotives." James chuckles. "It's 1866. Civilization runs on steam, so this treaty's a good thing."

"A former medicine man I grew up with called treaties talking leaves. Soon as signed, the wind blows the terms away."

"That same shaman? You told me." The youngster spies the smoke rising several miles in front of the mules. "Look, something's burning up ahead."

"We'll explore that way."

The wagon sits a short while later on the crest of the second hill. The two view a shallow valley.

Swollen by the season, a small snow-melt creek surges through the flat land.

A modest, crude-built log cabin lies near the water's bank with a chimney that smokes and provides a hint that the place supports life.

Around the home, the earth shows evidence of last year's planting, but winter months erase any trace except rudimental furrows.

A corral behind has a mule and a milk cow that huddle together in a corner under a primitive shed roof for warmth.

Lisa clicks reins on her mules' rumps and descends a rutted path that disappears under patches of dead fall grass but leads by the residence.

As the wagon stops, the heifer in the corral bellows and warns the cabin's occupants.

"What do you want out there?" A male's voice breaks the silence.

"Name's Waters, and my friend is James. Looking to buy corn or bacon."

"Got none of either. Keep moving!"

"Many thanks." Lisa pops the mule's reins and turns the wagon. "We'll move."

"Wait! You a woman?" The words within the cabin soften.

She stops the mules.

"Nobody else is in the back?"

"Empty for cargo."

A middle-aged Choctaw opens the cottage's door and steps into view. Work-blistered hands grip a long gun.

James lowers a rifle waist high and points the barrel at the armed farmer.

"Whoa there, young fellow. This here rifle's just for show. Ain't got no powder or bullets."

The owner props the weapon against an exterior wall. "You folks brought any food you want to sell? I'll trade for flour or corn."

A Choctaw mother and three daughters emerge from the darkness beyond the door.

Lisa stands in the wagon. "Mister, if you help unhitch these mules and fetch water from that stream, we'll fix a big dinner and you can keep your goods."

The girls, one teenager and two youngsters behind the mom, smile as if it's Christmas.

The older girl's eyes lock with James's, and she blushes.

***

After a meal, the farmer's family sits with the guests in front of the fireplace in the cabin.

"That sure was good cornbread, Mrs. Waters." The wife grips both fists tight and shakes them in emphasis. "Lordy! Been three months since we had bread made with real milk!"

"That cow in the corral was mooing when we got close." Lisa pulls a long-stem pipe from her pack and stuffs its bowl.

"She's dry. No grain or corn for feed, and the winter grass turned brown. She moos, but sometimes it's more of a bellow." One of the farmer's girls crawls closer and watches the visitor light tobacco.

"Papa's going to cut its throat and butcher her for meat." A second girl squirms beside the sister. "Don't want that. Paw says we must, to eat through the winter."

The smoker blows rings, and the youngsters poke forefingers into the drifting circles.

The oldest ignores the trick and steals glances at the male visitor.

The young man smiles.

The pipe smoker studies the male parent. "This is a decent piece of land with fresh water. But you folks don't appear to be doing so well."

The freedman coughs and clears his throat. "First couple of years, fine. Choctaw men, not Cherokee citizens, were welcome. Everybody was hiding from the killing. My father escaped guerrillas and fled Kansas. The war changed everything."

"What happened?" Lisa offers the man the smoke.

"Southern Calvary raided twice." The host draws on Lisa's pipe. "They took what they wanted, except the girls. Both were in the woods picking berries first time. And upstream looking for basket canes the second."

"Lucky you and the wife are still alive."

"Since the war ended, nobody." The farmer returns the lengthy smoker. "You folks are the first visitors besides a crazy Baptist minister who stumbled in on foot last summer. He said the Cherokee and the Choctaw settled with the Union. Now I can vote and live lawful in my Nation."

"That's right." She nods. "Same for freedmen. Long time coming."

The group sits in silence, and flames from the fireplace play light across faces as Lisa's smoke ring dissolves.

"We drove the wagon from the hill this afternoon. Something took your crop?" She looks at the farmer.

"Yes. The White man's skin-colored caterpillars, this long." The man extends forefinger and thumb less than an inch apart. "There were spots on the backs. Red and dark brown."

"Seen those. A flight destroys corn."

"Night-flying, yellowish-tan moths with black wavy bands across both wings took flight." The farmer shakes his head in remembrance. "And left nothing."

"How will you make it through winter?" Lisa glances at the farmer's wife.

"Won't. That brings me to something I must ask."

"You can have everything we brought. It's only a few days' supply."

"No hope out here. Don't have the resources or strength to go someplace new." The man clears his throat. "We'll stay here and accept what comes, but save the children. Take them with you."

"No. Can't do that." Lisa's eyes moisten at the edges.

"Keep them. Better than starving."

"You don't understand." She looks at James, and the youngster's stare penetrates her soul. "Yes, the two of us have a wagon, four mules, and food for days, but the war drained us as well."

The farmer clasps both hands together palm to palm with fingers upward. "They are good workers."

"I have no wish to separate family." She stands. "I have federal dollars left and search for supplies to buy. We will return and take you people to our valley. There, we can get through this winter. Can't promise more than that."

The farmer lunges forward and kisses Lisa's feet.

# CHAPTER TWENTY-NINE — Rattlesnake

## ᎠᎡᏛᏙᎣᎢᏍᎣᏫᎩᎠᏛᎬᏫᎢᏆᎯᏛᎾᏫᎤᎵᏆᎹᏛᏲᎣᏣᎲᏛᏚᏎᏆᏯᎲᏒᏙᎤᎲᎿᏃᎩᎤ

That night in the corn farmer's small cabin, Lisa tosses and turns on her sleeping mat. She awakens, sits up, and gathers the warm US Army blanket over both shoulders.

The family sleeps in peace across the room, and James curls in comfort near her feet, wrapped in two blankets.

She slips through the darkness and cracks the shelter's door.

A full moon illuminates an unhitched wagon.

Four mules sleep standing together. With front hooves tethered, the animals rest, and one, a sentinel, turns a head to look as the entry creaks.

Lisa's breath fogs in the night's temperature, and she steps into the air.

Fallow corn rows stretch away and emphasize the bleakness of the approaching winter scape.

Above the horizon, the seven stars of the Pleiades cluster form the tail of the Cherokee Rattlesnake constellation.

The half-Indian woman's memory drifts in the night to childhood confinement by the Georgia militia before the northern trek to the territory.

*At midnight, older sister Ella lies on the grass with Lisa and the medicine man family friend, Dideyohvsgi, around a campfire, one of many within the forced encampment prison.*

Peaceful, well fed, no wall conditions soften Lisa's present mind. But past individual encounters with the Georgia militia affront her dream sensibilities.

She watches other families and remembers a missing middle sister.

Groups she envisions in the camp miss members passed from sickness, malnutrition, or broken souls. Wisps of smoke, sparks, and small red embers rise from heating fires, but on this night they resemble funeral pyres.

A flutist plays in the distance, accompanied by a banjoist who sings, "Old man, old man, your hair is getting gray. I'd follow you ten thousand miles to hear your banjo play."

Lisa's head sways in rhythm to the tune. The flame's light dances in her eyes and reflects bitterness and anger.

*She stares across the fire at an older sister, who gazes in return.*

*"I failed again." Ella's voice cracks. "That army captain molded my fear easier than pottery clay."*

*"Old man, old man, you live to hear me say." The song drifts over the two women. "I'd follow you ten thousand more to walk another day."*

*"Stop blaming yourself. They were military," Lisa empathizes, "with the power." Her eyes stare into the sky and focus on the tail of a specific constellation.*

*Dideyohvsgi follows her gaze. "That's the Rattlesnake. It tells me elders will avenge your sister. Be at peace."*

*The youthful woman smiles disbelief at the medicine man.*

*"Mother earth sings a 'Death Song' as that flutist plays, because of the severity of the violations against her." The shaman shifts weight and settles into the story. "It restores everything when the sacred people who are the keepers of truth emerge with the strength*

*to overcome the white-eyed monster."*

*"The Georgia militia?"*

*"Monsters don't terrorize Tsalagi only here, child."*

*"Everywhere?" Lisa's eyes enlarge.*

*"The stars above in the Rattlesnake hold time and un-time within grasp for eternity. The outline is always the serpent. When, where, and how changes and transforms with movement."*

*"Into a frog or something?"*

*"No. The transformation is not the shape but the addition or subtraction of elements upon the snake." Dideyohvsgi stares at the Pleiades. "These things tell the tales of the universe."*

*"Even for me?"*

*"Yes, long before the White man discovered Turtle Island and the people, elders warned of monsters with pale eyes. One monster crossed the Eastern waters with evil and terrifying power. It destroys Tsalagi. The spirits of animals and trees wither. Beautiful lands lie devastated with a weak heartbeat."*

Lisa gazes at the Rattlesnake described above in the night sky. Her thoughts remember.

*"The monster devours children tribe by tribe." Dideyohvsgi, so many years ago, points at the sky's lights. "Even those who survive will be dead since they have no connection to ancestors. The land sings a death song due to harsh conditions."*

*The youthful Lisa looks up at the medicine man. "Can this happen to me?"*

*The elder wraps the child in both arms under Georgia's night sky. "When the monster happens, children look into hearts and face annihilation. A keeper of the truth emerges strong enough to overcome the power of the white-eyed beast. She restores the land to strength. With leadership, the offspring of the tribes of Turtle Island guide the people to the right way."*

*"And what happens then, Dideyohvsgi?*

*"Races live in peace." The shaman closes both eyes and turns to the girl. His lids open. "The spirit of the animals and trees returns to health, and the white monster fades into distant memory."*

In the present frosty air underneath the Rattlesnake, Lisa wonders at the words of the medicine man years before under the same stars.

After a few long moments in the moonlight, the night gazer slips back into the farmer's cabin for sleep.

***

Two days later, she and James direct mules and wagon along a wheel-rutted road.

"This evening, show me the Rattlesnake." The youngster looks up at the afternoon sky.

"I will." She pats the youngster's shoulder.

"That old healer, Dideyohvsgi. You talk of the shaman often."

"Yes. He was father's best friend. But more than that. I didn't realize what the man was until I got older." She nods at her companion.

"More than a medicine man?" The youth's eyes question.

"Yes. He was the soul and heart of the Cherokee people. At least he appeared that way."

"Don't know of real shamans anymore." James clicks the wagon's reins as the team slows.

"That's true." Lisa sighs.

"Why is that?"

"In the Rattlesnake myth," Lisa's gaze sweeps the horizon, "one keeper of the truth emerges strong enough to overcome the power of the White-Eyed Monster. She restores the land to health. With that leadership, the children of the tribes of Turtle Island lead the people to the right way."

"That's you?"

Lisa laughs. "No. Maybe my sister could have if she lived. I am one of the originals. There's too much weight on these shoulders."

James chuckles and guides the team around a bend.

They stumble upon a tent encampment.

A dozen or more US Army surplus military canvases scatter through a large meadow in the woods.

A freshwater stream intersects the camp, and loaded wagons group in clusters within the compound.

Cherokees and a sprinkle of Whites mill around campfires, and the approaching wagon presents no threat. Most do not notice its arrival.

One woman in a long dress and bonnet steps forward and meets Lisa.

"Hello travelers." She waves as the driver slows the mules. "What are a woman and a youngster doing out here alone?"

Lisa ties the team's reins to the bench. "Want to buy supplies. Think anyone has spare to sell?"

"There's no law, no respect, life's worth nothing out here." The greeter wipes both hands with her skirt. "You folks take a terrible risk."

"The name's Lisa, and this young fellow is my ward." The driver climbs from the wagon. "We farm a few days from here but run short of supplies. Need to buy for the winter."

"I'm Sallie. This is Evan and his son John B. Jones's camp. Our Baptists move to Tahlequah."

"Heard of the Joneses and the Keetoowah Society. The family's forming the Downing party to defeat Lewis against W.P. Ross."

"Right. You an ex-Confederate?

"No. Pro-Union."

The greeter waves an arm. "Then someone will sell supplies for federal dollars."

***

As the sun sets that day, the two buyers load a last keg of flour upon the wagon.

"That was a lot of freight!" James rubs a sore arm.

"Enough for the winter." Lisa ties the barrel to the wagon's side. "But come Spring, crops need to get in the ground. We spent the Union's Pin fund."

"Don't forget to pick up that farmer's family." The young man nods agreement.

"You liked the daughter, Emily. I could tell."

The young man concentrates on covering the cargo with a canvas and straps the edges to the wood frame. "Cherokee and Choctaw do not mix. Never have."

Sallie approaches the wagon's tongue. "Stay here for the night and leave in the morning. Join my family for supper?"

"Thank you." Lisa smiles. "I believe we will."

After the meal, outside Sallie's tent, Waters sits on a barrel beside the family's campfire. James lies on the ground, and the hostess, with a brother and husband, settles on crate chairs, smokes pipes, and stares into the flames.

"The pro-Union faction signed the treaty." Sallie repeats gossip. "The ex-Confederates sent a delegation, but the government didn't recognize them."

"Did the group send Stand Watie?" Lisa's interest perks.

"No, his son Saladin and nephew Elias Boudinot, along with John Rollin Ridge, Richard Fields, and William P. Adair."

"Glad the Federals sided with the Ross factions." The smoker pulls a pipe from a coat pocket.

"You realize the president died in August?"

She drops the smoke and sits in surprised silence.

James rolls over upon an elbow. "In Washington?"

"At the Medes Hotel on the first day of the month." Sallie turns to the young man.

"After fifty years of service to the people." Lisa's voice vibrates deep and reflective.

"Newspapers quoted him." The hostess stands, enters the tent and exits with a paper.

She reads, "Not one act of public life rises to braid me. I have done the best I could, and today, upon this bed of sickness, my heart approves of my actions. And still I am John Ross, the same of former years, unchanged." The reader gazes at the listeners. "Isn't that something?"

The woman glances at Lisa, who drops her head into both palms and sobs.

Sallie looks at James.

"She knew the president well. His second wife was her best friend." The young man moves closer and extends an arm around Lisa's shoulder. "Morning comes early. I suspect it's time to prepare mats to sleep under rattlesnake stars."

# CHAPTER THIRTY — Stagnation

## ᎠᏣᏍᎣᎢᏍᏙᏞᎩᎠᏎᎬᎢᎢᏗᏝᏫᏍᏣᏅᏈᏎᎣᏏᎥᏚᏓᎥᏎᏂᏃᏎ

After several days of travel, Lisa encourages her mules over the last ridgeline before Utugi Uweha, the Pin encampment.

The adopted farmer's family rides in the wagon's cargo bed with their meager possessions strapped to the top of supplies purchased from the Baptists.

James and the teenage daughter of the farmer hang their legs off the rear of the wagon and smile at each other as the team plods into Lisa's She Has Hope Valley.

Cabins abandoned by Judaculla families at war's end now appear occupied.

Smoke drifts from chimneys, and thin, malnourished livestock occupy the corrals.

"James, we've only been gone a week, but it looks as if we have visitors!" Lisa calls to the rear.

The young man's attention focuses on his seat partner.

Mules step forward and pull into the small settlement.

A man with a familiar gait greets the valley's owner.

"Josiah!" She stops the approach and stands. "So good to see you!"

"Mrs. Waters! I was worried. They said you went to find supplies, but it's been a week."

"Not much out there to buy. I have flour and bacon, but not enough to last through the winter. Glad you're visiting."

"Not short term. I hope to occupy the old cabin." The man points at the camp's Pin accommodations. "Many of these men brought families. They need the same."

"I cannot feed my own." The Judaculla surveys the camp. "Federal dollars are gone."

"They can't support theirs. Rebels burned most homes and ate the livestock." Second-in-command assists the commander as she steps on a spoke hub and jumps to the ground. "You're not much better off, but, as in the war, they figure as a group we're stronger."

Children play outside cabins, men chop firewood, and women hang wash to dry on porches.

"The place isn't strong without Union support." The leader firms her spine.

"Our fighters are Cherokee and freedman. We've faced tough times." Josiah dusts his hat with a knee slap. "Together."

"Agreed. Brave and strong, no doubt. We can sell the livestock." She steps onto the planks of her cabin and spots the fiddler with his back to a post. "And how's Moss?"

"The same. Plays his fiddle and sits on the porch." The man rubs a hand over his forehead.

"Lisa, where are we going to put our newest arrivals?" James holds his girlfriend's palm. The parents stand behind the wagon and eye the encampment.

"Picked up these folks." She sweeps one finger toward the group. "Can you make space to live?"

"For a while." Second-in-command turns to the family. "At the rate people are coming, our accommodations won't last long."

"Understand." Feeling the protective urge of a mother, the Judaculla looks at the young man. "Help our newest friends get settled."

James nods approval at the suggestion.

***

A land decimated by years of battle and strife belches ex-Yankee fighters as the Southern-sympathizing population persecutes dissenters.

Over weeks, the Pins create capacity for more returnees.

In the territory, a few defeated rebels with means sharecrop for sustenance. The privileged few hire others to support the remnants of a pre-war economy.

Yankees or rebs, many starve.

***

The wintry winds of November push an ice storm in December over the encampment.

Food becomes more scarce.

Lisa, wrapped in old and threadbare US Army blankets, rocks in front of the fireplace. A blue norther blizzard rattles the windows.

James's youngest sister, Lucy, coughs, sweats, and shivers, sick on a pallet near the fire.

The older, Elizabeth, sits beside a wooden bucket of water and swabs the younger's forehead to cool fever.

A massive form, Moss wrapped in blankets, looms at a window on the porch outside and fills the space with a shadow.

"Does he have to stand there?" James glances at the hulk. "Makes me nervous."

Lisa stops rocking. "The man's not dangerous. He's broken by the war and won't come into the warmth. He protects the family."

The young man shudders. "A guard dog. They broke him for sure. But he hovers like a vulture for a meal."

"Eating is all you talk about!" Elizabeth throws a cloth into a water bucket. "Food is you. Meals we don't have!"

"Hush." Lisa intervenes. "That's not what your brother's saying. Your stomach speaks instead of the heart."

"Don't talk! Me! Because I'm a girl!" The sister stamps a foot on the floor. "While he just sits here and complains. Tell him to go hunt a rabbit!"

The woman steps to and hugs the older boy. "There's ice on the ground. Your brother hunted every day last week."

"But shot nothing!" Elizabeth stares condemnation at her sibling.

"No game." The young fellow jumps to both feet. "None of the men got meat except Josiah. He shot his horse. You've been eating it!"

***

Several days later, the settlement leaders confer on the front porch, and both shiver in the temperature.

"I have a small sum of Pin money left. Not much, but maybe enough to buy food for a week." The Judaculla stares at the camp's barracks and cabins, snow covered, nearby. "Too many mouths to feed."

"You want me to go buy supplies?" The freedman follows the woman's gaze.

"Better you than me."

She extends a newspaper. "This came in with a new arrival. A special convention amended the Cherokee Constitution back in November. Freed slaves may be citizens if they choose."

"Long coming." The man accepts the paper. "Citizenship is good, but something to eat is better."

"I think the South won the war." Lisa grins. "No one would sell when I went to buy. This buyer was from the wrong side."

"A freedman does better? Is that the suggestion?"

"Yes."

Josiah opens the newspaper and reads aloud, "Native-born Cherokees, Indians, and Whites legally members of the Nation by adoption, and freedmen liberated by a voluntary act of former owners or by law, as well as free colored persons who were in the country at the commencement of the rebellion and are now residents or who may return within six months from the nineteenth day of July, 1866, and their descendants, who live in the limits of Cherokee land, are deemed to be citizens."

"Understand?" She reaches for the newspaper. "Sellers consider me a traitor."

"You might be right." The man surrenders the news. "We ate my horse, but your mules can still pull a wagon. I'll leave in the morning."

Lisa turns to enter the cabin but stops. "Take James."

"And you?" Josiah stares at the Judaculla.

"No. My place is here with the men. As an ex-Yankee fighter, my Cherokee enemies hate me. Freedmen also don't need me. My family are the girls and these starving Pins." She nods, enters, and closes the wood-slat door.

*** 

Early the following morning, Lisa attempts a hug, but James shies away.

"Too old for that." He climbs onto the wagon beside Josiah.

"Unless it's Emily!" Elizabeth waves from the cabin's porch.

"Take care of your sister. Hear me?" Brother blows a kiss.

"Good luck, men. Find food to buy."

"We must, Mrs. Waters."

"If you can't come back before spring, don't bother." The Judaculla slaps a mule's rump and pulls forward.

Lisa watches the team plod out of camp.

Just before the wagon disappears into the surrounding woods, James turns and waves.

His proxy mother throws a kiss in return, and the two men merge with brown bramble. The road enters a winter's trunk and limbs skeletal entanglement.

Elizabeth and her sister retreat from the chill into the cabin's warmth.

The half-Cherokee daughter of a freedman remains in silence on the porch and listens to winter's wind as the season engulfs the senses.

Air rustles dead branches and stirs debris around the cabins and barracks of the Pin sanctuary. Slim whiffs of smoke slip from chimneys and show life within the buildings, but ice outside suggests its fragility.

Along the road by the last quarters, something moves and attracts Lisa's attention.

A dark, blanket-wrapped form steps from the encampment and trudges after the wagon. The man carries a fiddle case.

"Moss! Where are you going?" Lisa cups both hands around her mouth, but the call drifts away in the wind.

The musician plods forward against the north's blast and follows the earlier wagon's mules.

Lisa's question call returns and slaps her face, unheard.

The Judaculla gathers her skirt above ankles and runs to and around the corner of the nearest cabin to the corral.

She stops and falls to both knees.

The enclosure stands empty, and snow sweeps across the ground's surface.

She looks to the quiet cabins and back at the road.

Moss is out of sight.

Lisa sits alone.

After a few minutes, she strains to stand and steps to the closest cabin's porch and its door. With a clenched hand, the visitor raps knuckles on the entry's wood.

Only the wind answers.

Icy fingers push a latch and swing the entrance open wide enough to step into the dimness.

A shaft of light sweeps across the room's dirt floor.

Illumination shows the face of a thin Cherokee woman.

"Oh my, the Judaculla. Wake up, Henry." She shakes the husband's blanket wrapped around both of the Pin's shoulders.

The man does not move.

Lisa glances to the cabin's corner where two emaciated children cling together for warmth.

At the man's side, she drops to knees onto the floor and feels for a pulse. "Henry's dead, mother. Have these babies eaten in days?"

"No. He's asleep." The parent shakes the body's shoulder. "Wake, husband. The Judaculla wants you to fight the rebels again."

"He was a good fighter." The leader straightens. "But I wish he had been a better father. Your kids are starving."

"There's no food. Josiah shared his horse, but we are so many. He's gone to find supplies. Henry can stay here until something to eat comes."

Lisa stands, and her eyes swell with tears. "I didn't know food was this serious. You and your man can wait, but I'll take the children to my cabin. Please?"

The Cherokee Pin woman nods. "Henry told me the Judaculla saves her men."

The leader gathers the two youngsters into arms and carries the little ones out of the cabin.

***

Later that day, Lisa loads her meager supplies into a burlap sack and divides the provisions between the cabins and barracks.

She repeats upon departure from each stop, "Hang on, ration this food. I go today to find more."

After distribution, Lisa straps a pistol and holster belt around hips, takes a long rifle from pegs above the fireplace, dons her heaviest union coat, and covers its blueness with a Cherokee blanket.

She glances around the space for useful items, slips a pipe into a pocket without tobacco, and pulls James' sisters into a hug.

"Can we come, Lisa?" Elizabeth hugs the only parent she remembers.

"No. I don't even have a mount." She kisses both on foreheads. "I asked the others to take care of you girls until someone returns. Be brave."

The surrogate mother leaves the cabin and the Pin encampment.

Her feet follow Josiah's wheel ruts.

***

As darkness descends along the route and the trail disappears, Lisa's feet and toes find the wagon's traces by touch.

Dark trunks of trees crowd both sides of the primitive road in transition to a hunter's pathway, and stark leafless limbs reach out to grasp each other for comfort and warmth as a blue norther howls a chilling call.

Lisa stops and washes the mouth with water from a US Army canteen, then swallows. The traveler reaches into a coat pocket for food.

Fingers feel nothing, and she remembers those shared supplies.

With a Cherokee blanket wrapped around neck and shoulders, the woman trudges for several days without a destination, led by numbing toes that sense a wagon's ruts.

***

At night, the north air whips through ears and resonates their lobes as she rests. The norther's tone rings deep but weak, much weaker than a remembered voice.

The dying words of another devoted to the Cherokee soul ride the speaking wind. *"Not one act of public life rises to abrade. I have done the best I could, and today, upon this bed of sickness, my heart approves of my actions. And I am John Ross, the same of former years, unchanged."*

"And I, Mr. President, acted in civic affairs with you and Ezra. But people scorn father's heritage and drive me to embrace it. I have given my finest, but leave illness and starvation sewn by war. My soul favors the efforts. And I am Lisa Waters. The same wife of the attorney and daughter of Ayokaha and Benjamin, as in former years, unchanged."

A crack of lightning splits a nearby oak trunk, and Lisa's rest transforms into a feverish stumble to regain the route. She falls to knees.

"Save me, John Ross!"

Large hands grip shoulders and pull the sufferer off the road.

"Shhh. It's Moss. Let's get off this trail. You are the sick and helpless one this time."

"You're speaking!" Lisa collapses with fever and coughs from the depths of both lungs.

Stress and exhaustion complicate gasps for air afflicted and weakened by pneumonia.

# CHAPTER THIRTY-ONE — Recovery

ᎠᏗᎢᎤᎣᎢᏍᎤᏓᎤᏯᎠᏓᎬᎤᎮᎠᎢᎦᎾᎳᏓᎷᎬᎷᎠᏅᎤᎣᎢᎯᏚᏯᎾᎢᎤᏂᏂᎻᎰᎤᎥ

Lisa wakens under a temporary lean-to roof constructed of small limbs and thorny bramble and its openings stuffed tight with winter debris.

Several spots leak and drip moisture into the space, but the angle of the logs protects occupants from the chill of the wind.

Moss, bundled in a worn US Army coat and federal issue blankets, adds gathered sticks and broken branches to the coals of an established campfire.

He notices Lisa move and nods.

She struggles to an elbow. "Old friend, you spoke. That means you are better."

"I'll never be well, Lisa."

"Understand. The war. That prison at Fort Davis. Want to talk?"

"No."

"Hate Confederates as I do?"

"No."

The couple sits in silence and stares into the campfire's flames as chilly rainfall pelts the overhead protection.

She pulls knees to chin and tightens a blanket. "I am not coughing. Must be better. How long did I sleep?"

"Two months." Moss's voice disappears under the staccato of rain drops.

"No!"

"Look at the buds on the trees." Moss peers at the land from the relative dryness of the hand constructed shelter. "Spring wakens these woods."

"You fed, nursed me those days and nights?"

"Grubs, bats, and lizard soup."

"The Pins are starving back in camp. I must get them something." Lisa slaps a stick in the fire's bed of coals.

"Yes." Moss twists toward the nearby road and stares. "Your tribe has food, rebel provisions, paid for by blood but fit to eat."

"Cherokees will never share with a Yankee Pin, much less a half-freedman's daughter."

"Slaves who want to be counted as citizens return to the territory." The man watches the flames. "They are free and too poor to go anywhere else. Think they can help?"

"Not much. Those people feed brothers who fought for the cause." Lisa shakes a head in appreciation. "Most are starving, as well."

"General Watie returned from the Choctaw to Honey Creek. He's rebuilding a home and is a hero to the people. He doesn't starve." Moss looks away from the fire toward the north. "They got food there."

"You never lacked a direction." The Judaculla lifts her burning branch from the coals, and its smoke drifts with the warmer wind from the southwest.

"The general's place is northeast. I suggest we confiscate supplies." The fiddler pulls blankets tighter against shoulders and shifts weight to a recline. The man falls asleep near the campfire.

***

Many days later, the two walk closer to the Kansas-Arkansas border. Both use rugged hewn sticks to steady as they force a path through rough terrain.

Moss stops and extends a hand's palm to earth.

Lisa grasps her walking stick with both hands and supports a tired frame as she stares toward Moss's point.

Several hundred yards ahead, a whiff of smoke rises above the naked treetops, not a wildfire but controlled, a camp or cabin sign.

For an hour, they creep through the brush until log structures become visible through the trees.

The nearest cabin's chimney sits without smoke. Beside its walls, an empty wagon rests with no sign of oxen or mule team.

"That's mine, Moss." Lisa elbows her companion. "Josiah must be here."

"Doesn't mean he's alone. Don't call out. This ain't his place for sure."

"Take this." She slips the long gun strap off a shoulder and extends the weapon to the fiddler. "We need to get in closer."

As the couple sneaks into concealment behind the Conestoga, muffled voices rise from the second cabin.

Several horses and Josiah's mules huddle together in a small corral at the opposite side.

"He's not alone." She twists toward her partner.

"The brand on those animals is CSA." He ducks under the wagon's bed and extends a rifle barrel through the spokes of a wheel.

"Those mounts mean three rebels." Lisa pats her friend on the shoulder. "I'll go back through the woods. On the other side, I'll make a racket. Shoot well when the door opens."

The man nods understanding, and she retraces a path into the safety of the trees.

She moves through the brush to the entrance.

With the entry in view, the Judaculla pulls a pistol from a hip holster and cocks the firearm pointed toward the building.

At the corral, she stops and lifts a dead branch from the ground. With the limb, she whacks the flank of a CSA horse, and it jumps and kicks in protest.

The mounts in the enclosure grunt and whinny as Lisa scrambles to a door view.

"Something's bothering the horses." A familiar voice rises from within the cabin. "Go check, Luke."

"Yes, sir."

The appointed scout opens the entry and steps onto a planked platform.

Moss's rifle's round rips through the man's chest and hurls his carcass off the wood to sprawl on the ground.

Lisa waits at the corner protection, with pistol cocked and ready.

Silence engulfs the interior but breaks as a second man in worn Confederate pants slides on the stomach through the door with a weapon extended toward Moss and the wagon.

She fires at the ex-soldier's back, and the bullet shatters the target's spine an inch above the shoulders. She cocks the pistol and waits.

"You men out there, hold your fire." Elias Boudinot's call reverberates from the interior. "Shoot and you'll go to Hell for me killing a young Cherokee man."

The voice steps out the cabin's door, dressed in a black business suit, with a captive hooked by one arm to chest for protection. He grips a revolver in his second hand.

"Don't, Moss! That's James!"

"Damn right! Stop shooting or the boy's dead." The Confederate looks at the woman attacker. "You too, mister."

"I am not a man, Elias Boudinot. I'm Ezra Water's wife."

"The Judaculla!"

"The war's ended." She holds the pistol level at the two as the young prisoner stares, petrified with fear.

"Not yet. You Yankee nigger lovers think you won, but my people have the peace." Standhope Watie's nephew edges away with back pressed against the cabin's wall and drags the captive as a shield.

Lisa steps onto the porch and follows.

At the corner, the escapee pushes the prisoner toward his adversary.

 She drops the pistol to catch the traumatized young man.

The general's kin leaps to the corral and vaults its fence inches before Moss's second round blows splinters off a post near the target's head.

He leaps upon a mount bareback, and the horse crashes through the enclosure's rickety rails.

With a whoop, the escapee races toward the woods and freedom.

The Judaculla comforts her charge as Moss joins both on the porch.

"You hurt, Mrs. Waters?"

"Lisa! You came!" James trembles, with hands tied behind his back.

"Where's Josiah?" She slides a knife from a belt sheath and cuts the prisoner loose. "Sure you're all right?"

"They hung him."

The woman looks at the fiddler.

"Said he was an outlaw raider during the war. Called him a murderer and a thief." The young fellow slips the rope that binds both wrists over bruised hands. "And an escaped slave! When we asked to buy food, they threw us in lockup near Honey Creek. Two months after that, the one named Boudinot remembered Josiah. They took him to the woods and hung him from a tree. Kept me as a hostage. They were trying to find you!"

"You're safe now." Lisa hugs the youth with both arms.

"How am I going to explain to Josiah's kids?" James shakes a head as he looks at Moss. "They don't have a father anymore."

"Won't have to explain. I will tell his wife what a great hero he was. They need to know, to remember." She feels the young man's forehead. "You're hot with fever!"

"I'm ill." He rubs both wrists. "They kept me tied most days. Brought me food and water, but no one came close."

"Moss. We aren't going anywhere for a while. Can you get wood? This cabin's freezing. We've got a very sick young man."

***

Two weeks later, Lisa wipes fever sweat from James's forehead, then gazes at the fireplace. Her mind wanders to an earlier time.

*A different fire, where Lisa's family lounges, glows in the darkness, one of hundreds within a Fort Wool collection center before the forced removal.*

*The bustle and din of daytime disappear.*

*Fear of disease fades. Insecurity of life prevails.*

*Serenity and peace prevail, and a thousand fireflies flicker.*

*Night's natural light show announces early evening.*

*Lisa abandons the circle of luminance to catch a firefly in cupped hands.*

*Returning, she sits and peeks into the captured lantern. Inside the darkness of both palms, the green-white glow of the insect's tail dims but blinks to illuminate anew.*

*"You will highlight the night as a star," she coos.*

*The medicine man, Dideyohvsgi, and her older sister Ella enjoy watching the happy young adolescent.*

*"She is that firefly." The shaman opens a hand and clenches it shut, then repeats the move. "Shine, then fade, only to blink again."*

*"Such a small thing to light the darkness." A younger sibling peeks at her captive.*

*"But you are brighter." The matriarch of the family hugs the spontaneous girl. "With glitter that improves our days!"*

*Lisa allows the insect to escape, and they watch the star soar.*

*The firefly hovers in the sky above the congregate of a once proud Nation reduced by civil strife to homeless clans clustered and forgotten by a larger land and nature-consuming cross-continental expansion.*

The strange night light blinks out in the woman's mind.

She wipes James's forehead. "Don't fly away. Stay."

The experienced nurse drops a wipe into a pail of cool water, rubs tears from eyes, and strains to stand. She speaks in native Cherokee: "The Lord bless you and keep you; the Lord makes his face shine on you and be gracious to you; the Lord turn his face toward you and give you peace."

***

Two days later, the group prepares to return to the Pin encampment.

Lisa's wagon sits loaded by the first cabin where Moss used spokes as a firing platform.

James lifts a last keg of flour onto its load.

He turns to Lisa. "You quoted from the White man's Bible. That surprised me, Mrs. Waters."

She coughs in the wintry morning air. "I read much of the book this winter. It makes more sense than the stories of water beetles an old shaman used to tell me."

"Just perplexed me." James nods. "I think of you as Cherokee."

"My skin is darker than yours." The woman smiles. "My father was a freedman, remember?"

"His ancestors didn't know the White man's book."

"True. This winter's been tough, and their holy words don't give the answers."

The surrogate son chuckles. "Ain't none."

"Got to be. We have a wagon load of Confederate furnished supplies on the way to save a union sympathetic Pin encampment from starvation." Lisa nods. "That is very near an answer."

"Maybe so. But listen to my words." The youth's gaze shifts to the horizon. "We are both Cherokee and must keep searching."

## CHAPTER THIRTY-TWO — Premonition



$L$isa's party returns to the Pin encampment with supplies. The journey pauses late in the afternoon.

Their mules pull the loaded wagon from woods into a meadow west of Standhope Watie's Honey Creek. The grassland stretches to a small ditch that bubbles water.

"Over there, see him?" James pulls at her elbow as she reins the team.

Lisa turns and looks in the direction of the point.

Across the prairie, a tall, thin White man in a slouch black hat holds a stick with legs spread apart. He steadies the rod vertical to the ground, unusual for its dark and light painted sections. Motionless, intensity maintains verticality of the staff.

She guides the wagon toward the statue.

As they approach, the image remains still.

Moss, on a box of corn in the wagon's rear, reaches for the rifle at his feet. "Careful, Mrs. Waters. This is General Watie's country."

She stops near the figure, who pays little attention. "My name's Lisa. You need help?"

Without moving his staff, the statue's lips move. "No, ma'am. Unless you and your friends are wild Injuns."

"Why you're standing out here?"

"Surveying for the Union Pacific."

"That so?" She rests her mule's reins on her lap. "You have to stand so still?"

The surveyor breaks his stance and turns to face the wagon. "Not now. Johnson just waved. He got the reading." The stickman points into the distance.

She twists to follow his direction.

At the opposite side of the meadow, another White fellow holds a palm high, next to a tripod, several hundred yards away.

"I've heard of the Union Pacific railroad." The Judaculla waves as well. "Don't people call it the 'Southern Branch'?"

"We're looking for the best route from Fort Riley through Gibson on to Texas." The surveyor pulls a handkerchief from his pocket and wipes his brow. "Our crews on the Kansas border are ready to run track."

"You know this land is Cherokee." Lisa touches Moss's shoulder as he shifts his rifle to his knees.

"Federal treaties with the tribes got voided. The 1866 treaty allows construction of two rail routes through here, one north and south, the other east and west." The worker stuffs his handkerchief into his pocket. "We're surveying the first."

"I heard the people in Kansas lost their lands to the railroads. Cherokee aren't interested in giving up land." Lisa reaches for a CSA canteen by her feet. "You want a drink?"

The surveyor recoils from the military mark on the container. "You folks guerrilla bandits? We have nothing worth dying to steal."

"Ease your mind. We found this thing. No rebels here." She hands the man water. "We're hauling supplies to a union camp west of here."

"You got any bacon?"

"Salt pork."

"I'll get Johnson over here. We could use some, and he has our per diem funds."

Lisa retrieves her drinking vessel. "May not sell you any. Your railroad will change these lands, maybe even our lives."

"Yes, lady. Iron rails are inevitable and good." The surveyor eyes the rifle in Moss's lap. "We see poverty out here. This is going to boost your economy, put food in people's mouths."

"Believe you are right, mister." Lisa ties her reins and jumps to the ground. "You wave for Johnson, and I'll unpack salt pork. If you don't object, we'll camp here for the night and fix cornbread for dinner."

"Never turn down a woman's cooking!" The surveyor raises his staff above the head. "If my partner says no, plunk him with this."

***

After dark around a campfire, Lisa, Moss, and James rest on one side, and the surveyors sit on equipment boxes.

Several pack mules tethered nearby munch grass with the wagon's mule team.

"You need a Conestoga." The young man watches the surveyor's animals.

"No." Johnson glances at their livestock. "Where we go, you often can't get wheels. Too rough."

"Must be interesting work." The youth shows more than casual interest.

"It is, son." The first surveyor swallows his last bite of cornbread and eyes the empty black iron skillet. "But you need education, lots of math."

"Mrs. Waters has maps from years ago, before the war." James looks for acknowledgment.

"An official exploration." She nods confirmation.

"An Indian territory US Geological Survey?" Johnson's interest perks. "By an engineer named Weldon?"

"I'm not sure." She lifts her black heavy pan and cleans its iron. "Sounds correct, but that was years ago."

"If you want to sell that map, the Union Pacific line pays good money." Johnson volunteers.

"Why's that?" Lisa packs the cooking utensil.

"He never made it back. Got bushwhacked by rebel guerrillas, we think. Others said somebody murdered him in Fort Smith." The rail employee nods. "His work is valuable, especially to the railroad."

"Thank you, sir, for the tip. When we get home, I'll check and see if I still have it." She turns to the expert. "Where can I sell it?"

"UP (Union Pacific) offices at Fort Riley."

"Mr. Johnson, your information's worth a pan of cornbread."

"Which was mighty good, Mrs. Waters. I sleep well tonight."

***

Later in the evening around campfire coals, the men snore.

Lisa and James whisper as they try the same in blankets under their wagon.

Moss snores in another makeshift bed wrap near the tethered mules.

"I'm worried for Emily and my sisters." The youth props his head in one palm with an elbow on his blanket. "We've been gone far too long. Spring is here."

"More concerned with her than her parents and the girls, I suspect?" Lisa rolls over to face the young man.

"No. I miss my sisters. Remember them playing."

"I was insensitive."

"Three months since we departed. Winter's fading." James pulls his blanket tighter around his shoulder.

"Be another five or six days before we can get this wagon to them." Lisa's voice's tone carries concern. "Food was gone when I left. By now, they abandoned the place."

"That's what worries me the most." The youthful man drops his cover off his elbow. "Josiah tried several stops at farms. Nobody had goods to sell. They were starving, and game was hunted to nothing."

"That I understand." Lisa settles on her mat for more comfort. "Too many people to feed, plus our Cherokee war wasn't so civil."

The following day, the young man drives the mules along an ancient trail toward Lisa's Utugi Uweha.

He smiles at a napper at his side. Against a corn bag, the sleeper bumps over ruts. Moss grunts with the lurches.

The teams enter a thicket overgrown on both sides of the trail, and trees crowd their tops into a canopy.

A flash of light to the wagon's left attracts the mule driver's attention, and he twists.

The source is gone.

A draft of wind sweeps through the tunnel in the foliage.

"You see that?"

"What?"

On the wind, "Hacaw! Hacaw!"

A raspy raven's call floats in the breeze.

"Didn't see anything. Let's get moving." Moss settles into his seat.

James flips his reins, and they flap with the sound of bird wings on his mules' rumps. The animals increase pace beyond a hypnotic plod.

As the wheels turn around a bend, in the tree tunnel ahead, a dark shadow waits beside the faint trail.

"I see that." The older rider grumbles.

The younger and the wagon approach, but the form holds its place.

One of the team snorts and its ears flatten against its neck.

"It's spooking the animals." The driver leans back on the reins.

A withered Cherokee with no visible weapon in a filthy and worn union kepi pulls black suspenders that support oversized dungarees and snaps them against the ribs of a malnourished chest.

The mules stop before the sound as if from its influence.

James glances into the rear bed. Lisa snores, unaware movement stopped.

"You are a medicine man?" The fellow's voice cracks to match his lips.

"No, not a preacher either." The young driver rests the team's reins in his lap. "You want one?"

The ancient smiles and several of the gaps where teeth should be whistle. "No. I want your strength. You can add years to my life."

"You need help or something? What are you doing alone?"

"I hunt."

"We've been on the road for weeks. Nothing moves, not even a rabbit, much less a deer." Moss leans forward and inspects the hunter.

"That's not what I kill."

"Is that right? What then?" The young man stares.

"Hearts."

James reaches to his feet and picks up a long gun. "None of those, either." The youngster clicks the mule's reins. "Make way, sir."

The form keeps pace along the side of the road. "You are moving? To where?"

"The valley where I live."

"Why?"

The operator watches the fellow. "This wagon's full of supplies for its people."

"Food?"

The teamster nods affirmatively and turns his attention to the route.

The elderly Cherokee's voice trails his path. "I hunt."

The driver looks back.

The vision no longer stands by the side of the ancient hunting trail.

James twists in his seat to Moss.

The freedman shakes his head. "When I was young, my grandfather talked of an old Cherokee who reminds me of that one. Not good. He told tales of legends, things called Raven Mockers. They flew with the wings of bats or crows."

The youngster checks behind the wagon.

Nothing follows.

The companion at his side pulls a blanket tighter around his shoulders as another draft of wind flows through the tunnel in the trees.

On the wind, "Hacaw! Hacaw!"

## **CHAPTER THIRTY-THREE — Catharsis**

### ᎠᎡᎢᏐᎣᎢᏍᎣᏗᎥᎩᎠᎫᎬᎤᏍᏚᎯᎢᎦᏫᎦᏞᎬᎹᎤᏒᎣᏂᎲᎴᎩᎣᎫᎴᏂᎭᏃᎤᎧ

Two days from their Pin encampment home, James drives the supply wagon with Moss awake and seated at his side.

Lisa semi-reclines in the rear and watches the primitive road, more a hunting trail, move below the back wheels.

The driver pulls the mules to a halt.

"What's the matter?" The Judaculla turns and looks forward.

"A Cherokee basket, see it?" The fiddler points.

She focuses on the object more than a hundred yards away.

A double-sided reed container with a rock on its top leans on a short, forked stick. A small pile of brown moss sits under the box, and several feet beyond, a rabbit pays no attention.

"Fresh meat tonight." The freedman pulls his rifle from the rear of the wagon.

"Somebody's trying to catch it." The young man cups a hand over his forehead to block out the sun.

"First game we've seen in over a month!" The fiddler hands his protégé the long gun. "My eyes are not as good anymore. You take the kill."

With the rifle, James slips from the driver's seat to the ground and props its barrel steady on the front wheel. "Tough shot, Moss."

"Don't miss, boy. My stomach wants fresh meat for supper."

The marksman pulls the trigger and feels the recoil.

He peers along the road, and his rabbit target collapses.

"Good shooting!" His companion extends an open hand slap to the shooter.

The young man claps the fingers.

With the weapon, he springs onto the wagon's seat.

As they watch, a quick, dark object bursts out of the scrub and retrieves the kill.

"Get these mules moving. A wolf's got our dinner!" Moss pops the flank of the animal before him with a palm.

At a gallop, the team rushes forward, and the driver yanks them to a stop near the Cherokee basket.

With the rifle, he jumps from the wagon and charges into the undergrowth where the prey disappeared.

His friends follow the youngster's chase by sound.

The noise stops.

The two wait.

"You think that wolf attacked him?" Fear furrows the fiddler's voice.

Lisa slips her pistol from her hip into Moss's hand. "Better go check."

"Mrs. Waters! Come here." James's call floats from the bramble.

She strides into the winter brown underbrush several yards.

The young man waits with Emily in his arms.

The girl's body, exposed through a ripped and tattered dress, curls in a fetal clump within strong shoulders that support her weight. She shivers. Her eyes stare, and she clutches the dead hare with the teeth of a blood-stained mouth.

"She's freezing and terrified." The fiddler tries to lift the bloody game from her hands, and she jerks it to her chest.

"No! Mine!" She hisses a water moccasin's warning.

"I'll get a blanket." The Judaculla turns for the wagon.

When she returns with the warmer, the younger trembles as she babbles to James.

"Those who stole each other's food got executed. They ate our horse and then vermin. We devoured our dogs, cats, rats, everything." The young woman's panic, tears, and defensive chatter slur her words. "I ate dead men's boot soles!"

"Shhh, Emily." His comfort rocks the fear aside. "I'm back."

"Why did you leave?" The girl pushes his chest. "We searched the woods for snakes and roots. Everyone looked ghastly and pale. Nothing's the same!"

"We have supplies in the wagon." The young man cuddles the trembler.

"Don't need them, you fool! You can never understand. Everybody's dead! You abandoned me! Father dug corpses out of graves, and I ate them!"

The older woman drops to her knees beside the teenager. "Oh no, you didn't."

Emily slaps her across the face. "You condemn me? It's your fault."

The Judaculla steps backward, nurses a split lip, and gives the pitiful victim space.

"I licked up my father's blood from the floor. One of your precious Pins butchered him!"

She spits red from her own mouth as she covers the hysterical youth with a Confederate States of America issued blanket.

***

Two days later, Lisa drives the mule team along the road into her once proud Pin sanctuary.

Moss sits on the seat beside her with James.

Wrapped in warmth and tied by rope for her safety, the injured mind lies in the back, and her insane hatred stare never leaves the young man.

The woods around the cabins and barracks display signs of spring, an occasional tree bud, a green tip of a weed above the soil, but silence hangs heavy over She Has Hope Valley.

Lisa pulls to a stop at her own cabin.

She climbs from the driver's seat as Moss jumps to the ground with his rifle at the ready.

The Judaculla steps upon her porch, draws her pistol, and approaches her door.

With the weapon's barrel, she pushes, and the wood creaks as it swings inward. Nothing moves in the darkness.

The broken window and light from the opening illuminate the mess in the interior.

Furniture lies smashed.

The room's contents appear destroyed by a tornado.

Trash and household items lay everywhere.

Nothing is un-ransacked.

Lisa steps through the debris to a corner of the cabin.

She searches the floor and spies a roll of paper loose but undamaged. The owner bends and retrieves the document.

Holstering her pistol, both hands spread the map.

Satisfied the Weldon study showing the coal deposits in the Choctaw Nation are intact, she rolls the item and tucks it under her arm.

"Anyone in there?" Moss watches the Judaculla step out and nod in the negative. "Any remains?"

She shakes her head and steps off her porch.

James strides toward the nearest cabin.

The fiddler follows with the wagon.

At this entrance, as it swings open, Lisa stares into the dim enclosure.

She holsters her pistol and backs away from the opening.

The Pin veteran of war and the Pea Ridge battlefield hospital nurse bends at the waist and vomits.

"You did that!" Emily screams hysteria from the rear of the wagon. "Those are your people!"

Moss turns to the younger man. "Make her stop screaming."

"No. Leave the girl alone." Lisa wipes her mouth with her hand. "She's right."

***

Several days later, a White stranger on a road-worn mule dressed in a black suit with a string tie around the collar approaches. His stained and well-traveled shirt waves an Abraham Lincoln style stove-pipe hat. A wooden cross hangs around the traveler's neck on a leather strap.

The camp's leader sits in a slat rocker on the porch of her cleaned cabin and watches the rider approach.

The preacher rides past two rows of fresh graves and the cool ashes of a huge but burned-out bonfire.

"Hello!" he calls.

"Osiyo, tohitsu?" she returns.

The minister stops his mount before the portico and dismounts. "I am well in Christ, to answer your question. Isn't thank you wado?"

"It is."

"May I say you don't appear Cherokee?" The visitor dusts his stove-pipe.

"Or do you a Christian." She smiles but keeps fingers near the pistol at her belt.

The caller laughs. "Then what?"

"An undertaker."

"Which you must be, ma'am, from those fresh graves beside the road."

From the cabin opposite, Moss steps around the corner with his long gun.

Lisa flicks her chin, and the fiddler returns to his own business.

"I'm just a circuit preacher. Of the Baptist faith." The fellow holds his hat in front of his stomach with both hands. "A hungry voice for God willing to say His words over graves in exchange for a meal and a stake of salt pork to take on the trail."

"I believe you've found a congregation, sir. Sit with us and speak in the morning before you leave."

"Much appreciated, ma'am. When do we eat?"

***

After supper, Lisa sits on the porch with her feet on the ground and smokes her long stem pipe.

Moss sits at the opposite end with his back against a post and plays scales on his violin.

The Baptist joins them from within the cabin. "Mrs. Waters, that was a priceless meal. I thank you for your hospitality."

"It was not without cost, Pastor. Those fresh graves you pray over in the morning contain troubled souls who paid with lives for your food."

"That so? Do you want to talk of it?"

Lisa sits in silence for a moment, and then draws and expels a lung full of smoke. "Does your God forgive humans for the cruelty and pain they inflict upon themselves and others?"

"My Lord sent his only Son to die a cruel death at the hands of his enemies and forgives those assassins according to my Bible."

"Makes an easy out?" Moss lowers his fiddle.

"Well, no." The speaker rubs his chin. "He excuses, but it requires repentance, change, and faith in his Child, Jesus Christ."

"That's asking too much." The fiddler spits and turns away.

"Another condition for mercy is to forgive." The minister delivers his message.

An unforgiving freedman shakes his head.

The Baptist looks at the Judaculla. "Do you need absolution?"

She swallows and steels her backbone. "My sister was murdered after I refused her sanctuary; my husband paid for my selfish beliefs in war time; I led many gullible souls to bloody deaths. I have murdered, thieved, tortured, and hated. Enemies fear my name."

"My goodness! Repent these sins and reserve your space in God's kingdom."

"Is it a White's place?"

"White? Yes, the purity of drifting clouds, the clean cloth of salvation."

Lisa stares at the preacher. "To enter, must I forgive Standhope Watie?"

"The confederate general in Honey Springs? I baptized him several months ago. He has something to do with this?"

"Yes. That man is an anti-Christ. You dunked a demon who eats your liver and laughs!"

***

As dawn breaks the following morning, the Baptist missionary leads Lisa, Moss, and James in a slow walk.

They travel through the many graves on the opposite side of the rutted trail.

The young man carries Emily, wild-eyed and tied within a blanket.

307

The preacher stops and stares at the rising sun. "God brings warmth and light to these departed souls this morning. Praise be to Him." He turns to James. "This young woman you carry, I did not meet her last night during dinner."

The girl's protector nods. "Her parents and sisters lie in a few of these graves."

The pastor strokes the young woman's forehead. "She acts troubled."

Emily snarls and catches the pastor's hand with her teeth.

As he yanks his fingers away, she bites, and blood colors the man's knuckles.

"My! She's wild." The man of God wipes the injury on his pants. "Is she a Comanche?"

"No." Lisa steps between the two. "She needs your God's forgiveness, but her mind does not grasp repentance. Let this go. Tend to my dead."

"Your graves? What do you mean, sister?" The Baptist stares wide-eyed. "Did you kill these souls?"

"No, but I abandoned them during a time of dire need."

"I don't understand." The pastor takes her fingers and presses them together for prayer.

"They were my charges who starved a slow death."

"And they ate each other!" Emily burst into hysterical laughter. "My father fed me my mother's ribs!"

The Baptist drops Lisa's hands as if they are diseased and contagious. He twists toward the accuser, aghast. "What?"

"And I licked her blood off my fingers!" The young woman sputters and drools.

"What is this place?" The minister backs away from the others. His body shakes as he extends palms forward for protection.

Lisa stares at the Baptist.

The man runs for the road and his mule.

The Judaculla drops to her knees in the middle of the fresh graveyard.

Moss watches the preacher run. "Want me to stop him, Mrs. Waters?"

She nods no and motions for the others to kneel. "Rising sun. These poor people are free of fear. We plea to the wind for relief from our pain."

The devastated woman lifts her chin, and the air stirs her hair. "I caused these bodies to rot here. They are dead and do not remember. My mother's kind lies here. So do my father's. Their survivors consider me their enemy. With time, do they forget?"

Warmth and sunlight flood her face.

The breeze tickles her ears and creates faint words, "Gadooossdi hada (ᎦᏙᎤᏍᏗ ᎭᏓ ga-do-oo-ss-di ha-da, What did you say?)

"I said I do not know who I am. Am I Cherokee or freedman, a mother or murderer?"

The soft wind calms.

Lisa's knees buckle.

She sits on the ground. "I only want to live in peace." Her lungs cry wrenching tears.

# CHAPTER THIRTY-FOUR — Progress

ᎠᎾᏓᏍᏏᏍᏗᎭᎸᏯᎫᏕᎾᎱᏁᎭᎵᏡᎳᏪᏍᎶᏣᎹᏰᎥᎤᎯᏎᏯᎣᏖᎸᎾᎭᏃᏔᎤ

Time eases the horror of winter's starvation.

The graves across the road from Utugi Uweha rest well-kept and tended. The camp in the meadow surrounded by woods bustles.

Moss, James, and several others hoe weeds in corn rows that display knee-high, healthy plants.

A freedman father and his older sons build a food storage cabin connected to barracks used by Pins.

More recent constructions expand the number of buildings in the complex, the most imposing, a large log single-room school-house.

Inside, Lisa stands before a dozen children between six and twelve, eight freedman, and several Cherokee. She holds a stick in the air.

The students in unison call, "One."

She extends the wood a second time.

"ᎤᏃ Sa-quu."

The teacher holds an object in each hand.

"Two, ᎹᏟ ta-li."

And the practice expands, "Three, ᏦᎢ tso-i; four, ᎤᏴᎩ nv-gi; five, ᎯᏍᎩ hi-s-gi."

The door opens, and the extra light that floods the room dims, blocked by Moss's enormous form. "Wagons coming out of the trees, Mrs. Waters."

The tutor lays her visual aids on the table.

"They have US Army mule teams. I think you should come."

The instructor turns to her students. "Children, that's enough for today. You have an early release."

Moss steps aside to avoid the children's rush for the door.

She follows the big man out of the schoolroom and into the afternoon light.

Canvas-covered Conestoga wagons with US stamps on their cloth, pulled by four-mule teams, approach along the rough and grass-grown road.

"Been over a year since we had a visitor, Moss."

"And you're not running for your pistol."

"Maybe not, but my stomach's fluttering as if I should."

The two wait.

The first wagon stops before them. Its driver extends the hand brake forward. "Afternoon. Hot day under this canvas." He pulls a neckerchief from his pockets and wipes sweat from his forehead.

Lisa steps closer. "It's been a while since anyone visited. I see these are Army mules and wagons. You just passing through our valley?"

The freedman on the bench stuffs his cloth in his pocket. "This is a medical unit from Fort Smith and the Fourth Military District."

The woman looks at her companion. "Sorry, not familiar with that division."

"Under the Reconstruction Act, passed by Congress two years ago." The teamster smiles as the wagons that follow brake to a stop.

"What are you doing out here?" Lisa coughs, and the driver notices.

"Planning to set up a health unit. That cough persistent?"

A physician joins the group from the caravan's second wagon.

"Good afternoon, folks. My name is Doctor Kent. This is a mobile dispensary from Fort Smith."

"Elijah! Look at me." She takes off her hat.

The older Army specialist in a major's uniform stares for a moment. "Nurse Waters!"

"It's me, major."

"So glad to see you." The man opens his arms and hugs his friend. "Do you live way out here?"

"Long story. Why not camp for the night? Join us for dinner. We can feed you."

Kent looks at Moss and beyond to the cabins, where adults work and children play. "You have plenty of mouths to satisfy. The army has provisions to share."

***

After the meal, on her porch, Lisa enjoys her pipe and fellowship with her friend from Pea Ridge. "What brings you so far from Fort Smith?"

"We have a full medical hospital in these wagons, Nurse Waters."

"Why?"

"General Edward Ord, commander of the Fourth Military District, ordered a field unit to serve freedmen and others in the territory."

"Out here, we are unaccustomed to positive attention from the government." She looks at Moss, who sits on the porch at the opposite end. "Unless they ask us to fight and die."

"Tragic, yes. But the Reconstruction Acts changed that, I hope." Dr. Kent watches the woman blow smoke rings. "Ex-slaves welcome our care, but we haven't established credibility with others. Most Cherokee hate Yankee soldiers, including the doctors."

313

"A few stayed loyal to the union." James steps out of the cabin onto the porch. "Us and other Pins. But it made nothing better."

"Can't be sure, young man." The physician smiles. "This country lost over fifty-three thousand fine men at Gettysburg alone. The war took a generation away on both sides. They did not perish with futile deaths. This country's changing."

"Doctor, there's no country out here." James sits beside Moss.

"Point taken." Dr. Kent turns to his host. "We tried to set up our unit near Honey Springs."

"Sound military thinking." The young man elbows the fiddler.

"Many freedmen tenant farm tobacco there for Standhope Watie and Elias Boudinot, but conditions weren't right." The physician ignores the sarcasm.

"No surprise there." Lisa coughs as her lungs clog with smoke.

"Those rebels make good money off their tenants. They get a tax immunity from the '66 treaty." The surgeon rubs a fist into his opposite hand. "But not forever. Law protects them, but it's a new slavery. The union won't allow that to continue."

"Only way to stop Watie is with a gun." Lisa fidgets.

The doctor, in silence, considers his nurse for a long moment. "At Pea Ridge, you were a junior assistant sickened by violent death. You lost your husband and still helped me care for horrific casualties." He swallows and thinks before his words. "You've changed. What happened?"

"Cruelty and inhumanity. Watie and hundreds of others." She empties her pipe's bowl against the side of her porch. "This compound looks peaceful to you, Elijah. It's a place of refuge and hope now, but its history is war, starvation, and degradation that you cannot imagine."

"I know you well enough to recognize you need to change that legacy."

"Yes."

"And I want to help you carry out reform." Dr. Kent stands.

"I must move forward." Lisa rises to face the union physician.

"How do you plan to do that, Mrs. Waters?" The surgeon smiles.

"Only education can lead to the future. I started a school here for everyone."

"Reconstruction requires a health clinic, for anyone." The scientist extends his right palm. "Our army budget will rent a part of this compound for use. Federal money supports your establishment."

The woman looks at Moss and James, who nod in agreement.

"Agreed?" The union physician glances at the two men.

"To the future." She shakes the officer's hand. "And you might as well start now."

"What do you mean?" He cocks his eyebrows.

"I want you to meet your first patient."

***

Moments later, Lisa opens the wooden door to a cabin near hers. She steps into the dark interior. Doctor Kent and James follow.

"Who are you?" Emily's tone trembles in the darkness.

"Open that wide, son." The physician leans forward toward the young woman's voice. "I am Elijah. They tell me your name's Emily."

"No, my name is mother eater. That evil girl died and lost her heart to a Raven Mocker."

"Mrs. Waters told me your story. I can help you."

"She is one." Disturbance chuckles, but the laugh chokes with tears. "An evil spirit."

"Then I'll ask her to step outside." Kent jerks his head at Lisa, and she retreats out the cabin's door.

"You can't make it right. My hand must."

"How?" The physician's voice softens.

"By killing myself. Untie me. Then I restore peace."

"Not tonight. But soon, I promise."

"I don't believe your words."

"Goodnight, Emily." The man motions for James to step outside the cabin. He follows where Lisa waits and closes the front wooden door.

"Poor woman. I can help her."

"How?" The young man steps closer.

"Not by applying modern medicine." The expert shakes his head in the negative. "Current medical studies conclude female sanity is brain stability in the face of overwhelming physical resistance."

"This nurse thinks that science is ridiculous." Lisa chokes a laugh.

"Medicine expects women to have a mental breakdown during their lifetime."

"Because we are different from men?" She draws a deep breath.

"Yes." The doctor glances at the cabin's door.

"That's ridiculous!" The Judaculla slaps both hips.

"It is." Kent returns his attention to the ex-nurse. "I don't follow the logic. It secludes, debases, and degrades women."

"Yes, it does."

"Mental health institutions today do not rehabilitate the ill but only lift the burden off ashamed families and try to quell disturbance."

"So, what can you do for her?" James intrudes.

"I am not sure. War injuries are my specialty, and one wound I saw often was psychiatric. But I have no training with that injury." The doctor pauses for a moment. "We will try simple talk. I will meet with Emily, untie her, and empathize, counselor to patient, several times a week. Let her heal herself."

"How can I help?" He touches the doctor's arm.

"By doing the same, James. She needs human interaction, not imprisonment in that dark cabin."

317

# CHAPTER THIRTY-FIVE — Engagement

**ᎠᎡᎢᎣᎤᎥᎦᎧᎨᎩᎪᎫᎬᎭᎮᎯᎰᎱᎲᎳᎴᎵᎶᎷᎸᎹᎺᎻᎼᎽᎾᎿᏀᏁᏂᏃᏄᏅ**

Lisa's agreement with Doctor Kent and the union's outreach to freedmen prospers.

Her enclave of civility, health care, and inclusive education grows.

Years pass and dissolve Cherokee Confederate politics as family sympathies step aside and bow to more modern but traditional love of children.

The matriarchal society seeps from the depths of mistrust and hidden wartime sanctuaries into Lisa's school and Doctor Kent's health clinics.

Moss and James find purpose within the camp.

The fiddler hulks around the perimeter as a security guard and children's education cheerleader.

The younger teaches English and the Cherokee language to tribal and freedmen children. In addition, he attends to a frightened and reclusive Emily.

With time, he accepts the general management of the school.

He evolves into logistics for the Army-financed hospital.

Doctor Kent's clinic opens every Monday, and the young man brings his ward for help.

This morning, they both sit as the physician listens to the girl's heart with a stethoscope. He hangs the scope around his neck and pulls a stool to face the couple.

"You had tremendous mental trauma in your life."

Emily shifts her weight in her chair. "Yes, sir. But our talks have helped."

"You are a young woman, and as far as my skills read, you are in excellent physical health. Why are you so tired? Your friend tells me you seldom come out of the darkness in your cabin."

She looks at the tattletale. "You told him that?"

"I did. He's trying to help you. The doctor is the only person able."

"Nobody removes my guilt."

"I can't cure those who refuse aid." The physician pats Emily's shoulder. "But I don't believe you are one."

"How do you see me?"

"Physically fine. But in your head, things are not." The man smiles.

She nods agreement.

He takes her hand. "New concepts are being adopted in medicine. Today's medicine considers the brain an organ of the soul. Human behavior is neurological, more than philosophical or religious."

"I don't understand." Emily bows her chin.

"I have seen similar cases who survived battle but remained wounded in their thoughts." The army battlefield surgeon rubs his forehead.

"Am I injured in that way?"

"Yes. Because of war experiences, dealing with daily life remains difficult. The past fogs your actions because of trauma that you never forget."

"Is this unease a wound to her brain?" James focuses his scrutiny.

"Yes. I believe so."

"Will she get well, Doctor Kent?" He stares at the physician.

"No surgery or medicine in my profession helps her. There is little I can do." The therapist pauses. "But you are different, if you are willing."

"I am."

"This girl needs time to heal, and it requires daily attention. You are that medication."

"I don't understand." Her protector queries the healer.

"With calm, peace, tranquility, comfort, and security, thoughts mend."

The Cherokee looks at Emily, his Choctaw dependent. "These things I will try to offer." He takes the girl's elbow, nods thank you to Dr. Kent, and strides out of the clinic into a new life.

***

The following morning, James tracks through the dew on the grass before his new love's home with a burlap bag of corn. He steps to her door and leaves the bag. On top of the traditional gift, he places his prized possession.

The young man retreats and observes from concealment around the corner.

Early day passes while the observer fidgets.

Midday, Emily opens her cabin and peeks. She sees the package, recoils, and shuts her wooden entrance.

The suitor waits and watches.

After a delay, wood slats swing open a second time.

Curiosity investigates and focuses upon the item lying on the burlap.

A short heritage belt, a piece of sun-bleached, gulf-water seaweed adorned by hand-polished shells and beads, sits on top.

She smiles but does not see James.

The budding woman picks up the gift and the bag of corn and closes her cabin's opening.

He waits in concealment.

Smoke rises from the chimney, and within an hour, the sweet smell of fresh cornbread escapes.

A new man saunters to the portico. As he steps upon her porch, the entry swings open.

Emily stands in with a black pot of hot bread extended with cloth-pad-protected hands.

The suitor enters the cabin.

They consummate the engagement ritual.

***

Middle of the same week, James and Moss breakfast outside with Lisa and the doctor before school and clinic opening, an informal management meal.

This morning, the leaders gather under a redbud, seated at a US Army portable mess table on folding chairs with canvas backs and seats.

The Judaculla and Dr. Kent eat with the young man at one side and the fiddler, the other.

The group enjoys bacon, biscuits, and fresh chicken eggs prepared to order and served by military cooks who work from a chow hall cabin.

"Doctor, this unit's food is a special surprise result of our agreement." She crunches a slice of fried ham.

"A little primitive way out here." The physician smiles. "But our supplies arrive."

"Think the railroads will improve that?" James forks a mouthful of scrambled eggs.

"The '66 treaty opens Cherokee land to a north-south and an east-west route. I hear the Katy prepares to enter the northern territory." Moss jerks a thumb in the general direction of northwest.

Lisa shakes her head at the fiddler. "Be as it was in Kansas, the Tribes lost their homelands to railroads. The freedman in me wants to keep our own."

"I worry. We lose our culture and way of life." James finishes a biscuit.

"They are coming. It's inevitable." The woman smiles at her surrogate son. "Could be an economic boost."

"The Katy drove their first spike on June 6." Doctor Kent quotes recent troop dispatches. "My report says from the northwest, the road will pass through Muskogee, and they plan to cross the Red River by Christmas of '72."

Lisa leans forward. "That's south of here."

"You're thinking of something, Nurse Waters." The army healer pushes back in his chair and chuckles. "I can tell."

"Yes, sir, I am. James and I talked years ago." She watches her young schoolteacher attend to her words. "That railroad's going to eat up ties, and we're in the perfect location to meet that appetite."

"Sounds good, but I am not a business type." Doctor Kent stands. "Time to open my clinic."

"Take care of your patients, Doc. You other two drink your coffee and let me find something in my cabin. I want to show you an interesting study."

"Sure thing, Mrs. Waters." Moss reaches for the pot as the Judaculla trots toward her home.

Moments later, she returns.

"I've seen that before." James sits his hot drink on the table.

"But times have changed." Lisa spreads Surveyor Weldon's map before the men. She points to the gray section in the lower middle part of the eastern territory. "That shows coal deposits. Railroads run on fuel. We know two things. First, the rails need wood to lay rail through Cherokee land. Second, they must fire their engines to pull their cars. We can offer both."

"How do you figure that?" James shakes his head. "That gray is Choctaw property."

"Coal can wait. I see us providing railroad ties. Plenty of timber around here, but we don't have a sawmill." Lisa studies the map. "Steam locomotives power railroads, and they are changing everything. If I must go to Boston, I'll cut logs."

"It doesn't give anyone the right to take coal from other countries." James shakes his head. "And this takes money, lots of union greenbacks."

"Emily is Choctaw." Lisa stares at her surrogate son.

The young man focuses in return. "And she is a broken soul that lost a family."

"Yes. But we are her adopted clan." Ezra Water's wife envisions the future. "And she's our access to tribal coal."

# CHAPTER THIRTY-SIX — Negotiation

## ᎠᏓᎢᏍᎣᎢᏏᏍᏎᏂᏯᎠᎫᎬᎥᏉᏗᎯᎵᏍᏭᎣᎦᎶᎬᎹᏏᏮᎣᏱᎯᏛᏯᎦᎵᎦᏂᎮᏃᎠᎣ

Weeks later, Moss reins a mule team and guides a wagon north to Arkansas. Fifty-one-year-old Lisa Waters, in a man's business suit and a wide-brim planter's hat, sits at his side. Luggage, supplies, and provisions ride in the conveyance's bed.

The mules plod alongside the Cairo and Fulton track and approach Crossing's Union Station and Yard Office, where the course turns north beside the rails of the Little Rock and Fort Smith Road.

A steam locomotive belches black smoke, and the Judaculla flaps one hand in front of her face to clean the air.

Moss reins the mules to a stop before excited people who disembark the train's passenger cars.

A wild-eyed young man spots the woman. "Which way into town?"

She points north along the tracks. "What's the excitement, Mister?"

"Hanging in the morning. Ain't you heard?" The blood-thirsty fan stares as if she is a back country nobody. "John Childers hangs for murdering Raeburn Wedding. I need a place to stay tonight."

"You're welcome to ride." She sweeps a hand toward the rear of the wagon.

The fellow eyes the mules. "Don't think so. Faster on foot. Much obliged!" He trots away and jogs north.

Lisa watches for a moment before another burst of smoke obscures the view. "Moss, these infernal engines change everything." She coughs. "Including how to cut railroad ties, I expect."

"What do you mean, Mrs. Waters?" The fiddler fans pollution.

"We're looking for a steam saw." She waves through the soot with her hat. "Water power is out of date."

The driver clicks the reins and guides the mule team behind the station.

They turn north toward Fort Smith and mix with the trainload of ghoulish potential pedestrian spectators for the impending execution.

As the wagon moves into the frontier municipality of Lisa's youth, the tenacious social and economic population center appears transformed during her adulthood.

She observes a far different post-national conflict society.

Construction booms throughout the city.

Buildings, business and residential, appear, driven by economic growth and reconstruction spending.

Southern attitudes prevail. Efforts by the federal government dump tinder on hot coals. Racial turbulence radiates under a placid surface.

As Moss enters Main Street, the mules join others on horseback and in wagons.

The Judaculla watches buildings and signs on both sides of the thruway.

One catches her attention, and she pulls Moss's elbow and points.

The sign, painted on wood, reads, "Elias C. Boudinot, Attorney at Law."

"Tobacco farmers must need extra income." Lisa settles the wagon's seat and gazes along the line at the town's nicest hotel. "Keep going. Can't afford that place. I stay with my people."

The fiddler turns onto a side street, and street foot traffic changes from prosperous businessmen in shiny boots and wide-brim hats to plebeian freed workers and various indigenous laborers and lounge-abouts.

Establishments without advertising signs out front cater to customers and offer meals, whiskey, and accommodations.

Moss guides the team into a stable where an older man meets the mules.

The stableman wears worn dungarees with no shirt, and old whip scars crisscross the fellow's shoulders. "In town for the hanging tomorrow?"

"No, sir." Lisa stands in the wagon and stretches. "On business. Will you board these animals for a few days?"

"Sure can. A night and three days in advance. Six bits."

She pulls the coins from a pant pocket and hands the money to the attendant. "A recommendation for a place to stay?"

"Betty's, a block on the left along the street. Ain't marked, but you won't miss the smell of food. Best corn on the cob in town. Magic tastes in their butter churn."

"Much obliged." The customer flips another coin.

"You a man or a woman?" The stableman unhitches the mules and eyes his patron. "Don't matter. I can tell. You're a Choctaw, right?"

"Is that important?" Lisa digs in a rear wagon pack.

"Not in this stable. But watch where you might stay. Since the war, Indians sleep in our part of town."

The Judaculla removes a pistol holster from the packed gear and straps the belt around denim-clad hips.

The stableman fixates on the weapon. "Or go wherever, with that hog leg."

She turns for the stable's street entrance.

The mixed-race woman and Moss step outside into the afternoon sun's stroked street.

"What's next, Mrs. Waters?" The fiddler shades eyes with a palm as he looks both directions along the street.

"Not sure. Need to buy a steam-powered sawmill and ship the equipment into the territory, plus find a person who knows how to run and maintain the machinery. Hire that expert and sell our business idea to the railroad. Our budget might buy a saw blade."

"Not real promising." The freedman shakes his shoulders.

"Let's begin with something controllable. Find Betty's and try churned butter corn on the cob."

***

Later, Lisa and her companion push back their places from a lengthy shared table, one of three in the meal room at the establishment.

Each long surface hosts a dozen chairs, and an assortment of non-White diners use those seats to finish a hearty, tasty feast.

"Fine cooking!" A plump gentleman with black hair and eyes that show appreciation behind eyelids indicating Asian descent leans back in a chair. "Can't beat this food. You folks in town for the hanging?"

"No." Lisa nods agreement. "To purchase a steam sawmill."

The dinner partner laughs. "They are lying around Fort Smith?"

"We know the machines are new. May have to go to Boston or somewhere." She tolerates the man's clumsy humor at her expense. "Or wherever. Steam's the future."

"Need more than a mill. A sawer who knows how to harness that power ain't in this town." The man attempts to contain laughter, but cannot. "Lots of cash that'll cost, sir. No eating here with those kinds of funds."

"We're looking for investors."

"No factory, no operator, no money. What do you have, Injun?"

Lisa's blood surges in the temples, and lips lie, "A contract for railroad ties with the Missouri, Kansas, and Texas."

The room falls silent. Everyone hears the rash claim.

His questioning, laughing tone changes to respect. "The Katy's a good line. Your sawmill need a cook?"

***

Lisa and Moss exit Betty's onto the street to walk off excess dinner.

A small-frame freedman from the dining interrupts. "Excuse me. The name is Haley. Couldn't help but overhear a while ago at supper. I know where there's a steam sawmill for sale."

She stops. "Not sure I believe you. Where?"

"Up the Arkansas at Clarksville. I worked for a man named Jackson who invested his life's savings into a new boiler mill. Then died. Heart gave out. The wife wants to sell."

The Judaculla turns to Moss. "Forget that hanging in the morning. Let's hitch the mules before sunrise."

***

Next day, Lisa sits at Mrs. Jackson's kitchen table and sips coffee.

"You have a contract for railroad ties with the Katy?" The White woman sawmill owner pours a cup of strong, dark liquid from a hot pot.

"Yes. Mr. Haley said your husband passed. We were reluctant to intrude. But we are sorry for the loss."

"No matter, Mrs. Waters. This is business. Not many potential buyers for a three-bed steam-powered plant in Arkansas exist. And I wish to sell. My late husband's contacts in Georgia kept a mill with that much capacity busy. Without him, the place is a liability, and I want to visit my sister. Poor woman lost a plantation in that butcher Sherman's march to the sea. We need to join my brother in South Carolina."

"Understand." The Judaculla sets a cup on the table. "What is a fair price for the mill?"

"I talked with my husband before he died. Seven thousand dollars is the number." The seller glances at the potential customer and reads a reaction. "But I wish to move soon, so six."

Lisa coughs. "Problem is that I have no sawer with steam experience."

"There's my husband's right-hand man."

"Pardon?"

"Josh trained, but never had the title."

The buyer sits in silence and considers the thought. "All right. If he accepts employment, what you ask is a fair price."

"That's an agreement." The White woman smiles. "Dependent upon payment?"

"Certainly." The Judaculla grins. "With Josh's signature, I will return to Fort Smith, have an attorney draw up the papers, and come back with the money. Agreed?"

"Within a week for cash?"

"Yes."

***

On the return to town, Moss loses his calm demeanor. "You promised that woman six thousand dollars in seven days!"

"Afraid so."

330

"Where will you get the funds?"

Lisa elbows her lifelong friend. "Heist one of the big banks? Find a high-stakes poker game? Rob the Katy with Jesse James?"

"The guy that hung this morning was a robber." The fiddler calms. "May make town for the burial."

"I do sound like a bandit, but we're not traveling to Fort Smith. The trip will push these mules hard, but the railroad's field headquarters on the state border is two eighteen-hour treks."

***

After heavy travel over rough roads, Lisa sits across the desk from Major Seth Andrews, Construction Superintendent for Kansas, Missouri, and Texas. The office, a temporary constructed headquarters, sits miles within Cherokee territory.

"Mrs. Waters. Assistants say you claim capability to supply ties for Katy's order?"

"Yes, sir. With a steam-powered sawmill that will be operational soon."

"Have you seen our specifications?"

"Yes. Read them."

"By hand, lumber crews hew several hundred a day, not near the required total. The demand is much higher and is the only reason I agreed to talk today."

"Mr. Andrews, how many daily?"

"Construction needs 3,250 ties per mile and builds three miles every twenty-four hours. That's 10,000 units every morning." The superintendent taps a pencil on the desk.

"Supply depends on the price." She shrugs.

The construction foreman squirms. "Say forty cents apiece?"

Lisa leans forward. "Major, my sawer claims a hand-hewn product costs you eighty. We will meet the demand for fifty a tie, thanks to the mechanized results of steam power and a three-bed mill."

The superintendent studies the half-Cherokee. "Indians do things in nature's time. The Katy has a railroad to build and a tight schedule. The road offers two bits per piece for every 10,000 ties delivered to our construction point daily. Only forty a unit for less quantity or regularity. That contract can close today with supply commencement in one month."

Lisa leans back in her chair. "We accept your requirements, sir."

Major Andrews chuckles. "Mrs. Waters, this line commits to modern performance."

"Thank you."

"You are the only female who has ever done business across this desk. I am struck by that fact. A Cherokee at that."

"That is unfortunate."

"Deliver this contract, and I swear to agree to change that circumstance."

***

Two days later, Lisa sits in a loan officer's reception chair.

She glances at the bank's entrance and re-reads the reverse writing on a glass window.

The lettering forms the words "First Arkansas National Bank" in large print and "Chartered, 1866, under the National Bank Act" in smaller.

From within the banker's office, loud voices float from under its door.

"Mr. Boudinot, unless you post further collateral, this lender must demand immediate payment."

"Our business flourished with the 1866 Cherokee tax immunities!" A familiar voice stresses.

"Your uncle supported the Confederacy." The banker's tone increases urgency. "The United States' new agreement canceled those privileges."

"And may I mention to the First Arkansas National Bank that I, along with attorneys Pike, Johnson, and Butler, present the case before the Supreme Court in only sixty days? We refuse to pay tobacco taxes on product made in the Cherokee Nation. Watie is exempt by the 1866 treaty!"

"I am aware of that case. If the firm loses, the government confiscates your crops and lands, which are pledged as collateral for this loan."

A moment of silence allows Lisa to pull her hat's brim low over the forehead and face.

Elias Boudinot's voice does not quiver. "Ninety days. A short extension. While the Supreme Court decides. You owe the general that courtesy. He was your champion during the war."

"The old man lost. You are an influential attorney at the forefront of railroad expansion through Cherokee territory." The banker pauses. "Don't mess it up to save your uncle's tobacco farm dream. The plant doesn't do well in rocky soil. You know that."

"Ninety days?"

"Against my better judgment. But no longer."

"We lost the war, that's right. But the conflict's over, and veterans must stick together."

A moment later, Elias Boudinot closes the office door and, without a glance at Lisa, exits the building.

***

The banker soon follows. "Yes, ma'am, I can see you now."

She settles on a seat, still warm from the body heat of her arch enemy.

"How may I help you?"

"The name is Mrs. Waters. I want a fifteen-thousand-dollar business loan."

The bank officer coughs. "Not to start a tobacco plantation, I hope. That much money could fund several farms."

"No. I want to buy a steam-powered sawmill and make railway ties for the Katy railroad."

The businessman relaxes in the chair and crosses arms on the front of his chest. "Sure, Mrs. Waters, but I recommend something more feminine. An enterprise women excel at, with a much smaller price."

"Fifteen thousand dollars. That investment is three days of gross sales."

The financier leans backward. "What guarantees this credit?"

Lisa extends the contract. "Major Seth Andrews, Construction Superintendent, Kansas Missouri and Texas Railway signed this."

The man reads the document.

He hands the paper to the woman. "Mrs. Waters. This is remarkable. The bank will offer whatever financing necessary to meet any needs."

## CHAPTER THIRTY-SEVEN — Buckllucksy

ᎠᏣᎢᏏᎣᎥᎢᏍᎣᏈᏯᎠᎫᎬᏫᏈᎠᏓᏌᏈᎣᏫᏍᎡᎬᎹᎯᏍᎣᎯᎲᏂᏯᎮᏠᎲᏂᏃᏍᎠᎣᴜ

Before dawn, Josh, the sawer, moves inside the Utugi Uweha sawmill.

From a night fire, he lifts a burning stick and steps to a flat steel load of wood chips and saw blade debris. The flame lights the shovel's contents, and the man dumps the hot coals into the first boiler.

Two freedmen and a Cherokee shovel more fuel into the furnace from an immense pile of sawdust, bark, and splinters.

Josh ignites more boilers as the men stoke three fires.

Soon, smoke puffs from chimneys as the manager checks a pressure valve.

The mill, an imposing wood-frame building, houses the machine and its workers. Steam forces everything. A powerful primary engine powers the line shaft that drives the log carriage, and the head rig circular blades extend one from the base and the other suspended offset and overlapping. It turns the adjustable edgers.

The lower fundamental cutter features a fifty-two-inch blade with vicious-appearing sharp, flat edge claws.

Concentric circles emanate from its drive shaft. Sliced timber polished the shiny rings.

Its smaller, forty-eight-inch top saw only engages extra-large logs.

A twin-cylinder, steam-powered winch pulls the tree trunks to the deck.

The third vertical engine powers a conveyor belt that empties sawdust from below the head rig.

Its fourth driver propels a cut-off blade.

Outside, a spring-fed mill pond serves a dual purpose. The water cleans dirt and debris from the pieces that arrive in wagons with collapsible sides.

This early morning, they line up with the mule teams and drivers loaded with logs from Moss's cutting program.

The first wagon, at the sawer's signal, drops its side, and a load of tree trunks roll into the pond.

A Cherokee loader selects a trunk and clamps his pick's pointed claws to secure the raw material. Suspended on a heavy chain, the bed winch pulls the massive log from the water onto the saw's cutting surface.

With long picks, two freedmen handle the mass.

The row of raw materials awaits the blade.

Josh checks the pressure gauge, which reads 160 as the sun breaks the horizon.

The metal machinery transitions its color from a dark gray-blue into a warmer sunlight-influenced orange-brown.

"Steam's at pressure!" the sawer calls.

A railroad whistle blows. The signal opens operations for the day.

"Stand free!" Josh screams, and operators, one at a time, but at the top of their voices, respond. "Clear!"

"Clean!"

"I'm good."

"Mill in motion!" The overseer cups a hand to his mouth, and his words warn the other workers.

Metal cranks awaken from the night, steam puffs from exhaust pipes, and the conveyor tightens. Belts surge into action and power the various machines.

Josh and a Cherokee carriage setter load a log onto the bed and secure the timber.

The iron surfaces carry the wood to the saw, and the blade chews its first cut.

The supervisor signals the Indian to set the railroad tie depth for the next slice.

In a matter of minutes, loaders stack thirty or more finished railway supports into waiting transport wagons that carry over 500 per trip.

***

Unknown to the production foreman, or to Lisa Waters, two men on horseback watch from concealment in the woods.

One rider wears old, worn, and filthy Confederate pants tucked into battle-tested boots. His butternut shirt hangs out of his britches.

The second observer, a Cherokee but in cleaner, newer clothes, watches Lisa's steam production with a pair of field glasses.

"This is that Pin camp we looked for during the war. They raided us twice, but we never found their base." The dirty Confederate spits to the ground near of his mount.

"Could be, but now it's a sawmill. They're making railroad ties, thousands of them, by modern power." The other man chews tobacco as he studies the terrain through binoculars. "Don't see any weapons or guards." He turns his horse. "Come. It's a three-day ride. We need to report to Mr. Boudinot."

***

Within Utugi Uweha Sawmill's valley near the road, its owner steps through her cabin's door, dressed for work.

She stretches her arms and greets the morning.

Warm, reassuring sun rays paint her face golden as she turns to a sound from her home's corner.

"ᎣᏏᏲ (o-si-yo, hello) Lisa. ᏙᎯᏧ (to-hi-tsu, how are you?)" Her surrogate son smiles.

"ᎣᏍᏓ (o-s-da, good) James. ᏂᎯᎾ (ni-hi-na, how about you?)

"ᎭᏩ (ha-wa). Have you been to the mill?

The woman shakes her head.

She looks across to the three boiler stacks that belch dark smoke. "I don't care for that black debris. It makes She Has Hope stink."

"Smells of Katy Railroad dollars, you mean?"

"No. When I was a young girl with my sisters Ella and Bella, everything smelled. Then it was my father's fresh cotton. Causes me to think and reminds me of my parents' murder."

James points. "Here comes the fiddler."

Lisa waves as two riders approach. "ᎣᏏᏲ (o-si-yo) Moss."

"Morning, Mrs. Waters," The freedman dismounts. "Your sawer expects twelve or thirteen wagon loads of ties today. We have enough wagons and mules, but he says his mill men are getting more experienced. They will make fifteen to twenty by the end of the month."

"Do we have the drivers?" The owner looks at the estimator.

"No, ma'am. Freedmen don't take to sharecropping. But they're eager to work at your wages." He pats his mount's shoulder. "I expect no trouble hiring as many as we need."

"Sounds good." Lisa pulls a long pipe from her belt. "Moss, you've been with me the longest, so you're in charge. I'm going to be traveling for a few months, maybe longer."

"You are?" Moss's brows wrinkle.

"Yes, sir." She stuffs and lights tobacco in her pipe's bowl. "In a month. James and I have business in the Choctaw Nation."

***

Days later, Josh carries a new kerosene lamp and walks, as every morning before daylight, along the road from his cabin to the sawmill.

This dawn, he turns to the rustle of branches in the woods that surround the encampment and holds his light high. "Must be a deer." He steps onto the worn path that leads to the mill. Another sound from the timbers attracts his attention.

A rider upon a black horse blends with the darkness as he moves from concealment into the pre-dawn grayness.

Josh runs for the sawmill building with his lamp swinging and lunges through a door.

Several Cherokee and freedmen workers wait within the room.

"You!" The boss points at a young fellow. "Run! Get James or Mrs. Waters."

The young man dashes out the entrance.

The manager leaps to an opposite side window.

Outside, six other dark shapes on horseback maneuver their mounts to surround their defenses.

In position and encircling the sawmill equal distances apart, the horsemen become clearer as the sun's rim peeks above the horizon.

The rider threatening Josh's view wears old, worn, and filthy Confederate pants tucked into battle-tested boots. His butternut shirt hangs out of his britches on one side.

With a pistol on each hip, the man carries a trapdoor Springfield, designed as an inexpensive method of converting rifled muskets into breach-loaded weapons.

The design change improves its rate of fire from three shots per minute to over eight.

The threatening horsemen appear well-armed.

Sacks with eye holes conceal faces.

A burlap-masked footman lights his torch with burning pipe tobacco and moves from rider to rider, lighting individual torches.

Josh twists to his workers. "Find weapons to defend us. Shovels, picks, anything. These ghosts may ignite the building, but the machines won't burn. Don't let them breech the walls."

From the old Pin encampment, a dinner bell peals a security breach.

"The kid made it." The supervisor jerks a thumb to the alarm, then returns to the window.

A bullet chews a chunk of the windowsill frame above his forehead.

As he ducks, the boss spots a rider moving closer with a torch. "Get low, men. They're coming!"

Rifle and pistol fire rip holes through the lumber slats of the walls, and deadly lead ricochets off the iron carriage and boilers.

A flame spirals through the window and lands near the sawer's boots.

He jumps to retrieve the threat and throw it outside, but its heat ignites trash and shavings on the mill floor.

A hooded horseman bursts through the entrance, and once in, his mount spins.

Its rider plummets off a side of his saddle as a furious freedman's shovel swings and impacts its target.

Dragging the rider by one boot caught in a stirrup, the horse panics from the flames and lunges through the entry for escape.

A volley of pistol and rifle fire from camp employees rousted by the bell overcomes the hooded attackers, and the riders give way.

They flee toward the wood's protection.

"We're here!" Lisa yanks Josh to his feet by an elbow. "Get our workers out! The roof's burning!"

***

Later, as midday approaches, the owner, Moss, and James stand with a group of sawmill employees and armed off-duty supporters in the sun. They watch the last flames lick the remnants of the building.

The sawer shakes his head. "We're out of business for a few days. The equipment's made of iron. Replace the belts and we'll be running while we build a new building around us."

"At least nobody died." Lisa draws a deep breath. "And they didn't burn the tie stockpile. We have plenty to supply the Katy for a week."

"I can have this mill operational in three days." Josh nods. "But what keeps those raiders away?"

"We do." Moss's voice crackles with determination.

"Moss." The Judaculla glances at her friend. "Ex-Pins out there need work. Hire them. I want a security force around this camp, an army."

"Yes ma'am. You still plan to travel south?"

"I do. Nothing's changed here. To me, it's the same as during the war." She turns and strides away from the mill toward her cabin.

***

Ten days after the raid, James drives a shiny new black carriage pulled by two matched grays into the modest settlement of Bucklucksy, Choctaw Territory.

Dressed in her men's cotton shirt, denims, and buckskin coat with a wide-brimmed planter's hat, Lisa sits beside her younger driver.

341

Not strapped around her hips, a pistol in a holster on the floor at her feet dangles from a belt of cartridges that wraps the weapon.

Emily, wrapped in a blanket behind James on a travel trunk, stares into space.

"There, the third cabin. Sign says Reynolds and Hannaford Trading Post and General Store." Lisa points. "Pull up."

The young driver ties the carriage's horses to a hitching rail outside the establishment.

A large White storekeeper steps from the front door. "Good day, travelers. Welcome. My name's Captain James Jackson McAlester."

"Captain?" She grabs the gun, jumps from the carriage, and straps its belt around her hips.

"Yes, sir." The big man imitates a salute.

"Which unit?"

"Twenty-second Confederate Volunteer Infantry under General Watie. Did you serve?"

"I was a union nurse at Pea Ridge." The Judaculla rests a right hand upon her pistol.

"Excuse me, ma'am!" McAlester's voice booms and carries to several people who step from other buildings to inspect the newcomers. "No offense meant. Your hat and clothes confused me. This store welcomes every customer!"

"None taken, Mr. McAlester." Lisa waves toward her traveling companions. "This young fellow is my associate, James, and the young lady is Emily. You served under Watie?"

"Yes, ma'am. The last general officer to succumb in that terrible war. Should have done it a year earlier. How can I help you?"

"Everyone in the territory's heard of him." Lisa helps her ward off the rear of the carriage. "They say the old man is tobacco farming around Honey Springs in Cherokee country."

"Haven't seen our southern hero since the surrender." The storekeeper eyes Lisa's new and expensive wagon. "I was told the government closed his place for nonpayment of taxes. This is a fine conveyance with a handsome team. May I ask your business?"

"My name's Lisa Waters. I own the Utugi Uweha Sawmill. We're looking to gain land, expand our operations as the railroad moves south."

"You know the A and P's laying track for an east to west crossing." McAlester watches for Lisa's reaction.

"I heard, but I'm contracted with the Katy."

"You're Cherokee. You must be Choctaw to buy property here."

"Our partner is full blood." Lisa jerks her head toward Emily.

"Come on in and make yourselves comfortable. I'll get my wife to work up lunch. If you're interested in land titles, we know what's available." The storekeeper opens his front door.

"You purchasing? But you're White." She pauses entry into the general store.

The entrepreneur laughs. "Yep, Scotch Irish. The wife's full-blood Chickasaw."

***

Emily stands outside and pulls her blanket tighter over her shoulders. "Must I go in there, James?"

The young defender steps closer and slips an arm onto the girl's shoulder. "Of course not. We can either stay or take a walk. We can do what you want."

"Just give me a moment. These people are staring."

Her protector glances at bystanders curious over the new arrivals.

"They are, but not at you. We're newcomers. Curiosity."

"I am sure that's right, James. But wait and let me calm before we enter."

343

# CHAPTER THIRTY-EIGHT — Anthracite

DRTᏯᎣᏬᎢᏚᎠᏈᎩᎪᏨᎬᎯᏈᎠᏂᎡᎤᏫᏍᎡᏳᎷᏃᎢᎠᏈᎢᏎᎥᏯᎣᎵᎯᏅᏏᏅᎯᏃᏋᎣ

Lisa studies Major McAlester's map of the Bucklucksy region of Choctaw Territory spread before her on a wooden surface.

The store's owner and operator points to different mapped locations. "My understanding is tribal leaders will sell most of this."

She focuses on the display.

The ex-confederate notices the attention. "I purchased, or let's say my wife has bought or claimed, these properties outlined with dashed lines. Most of the lands are still available."

Lisa conceals familiarity. "This is a fine map, the best I have seen."

"Thanks. From an old friend of mine. Served together in the war. He was a surveyor for the government."

She points to a gray in the lower middle part of the eastern territory. "And what does this shading mean?"

"Unexplored? Unmapped? Not sure."

"Major, this is from Oliver Weldon, an engineer doing mapping for a US Geological Survey."

"Yes, my good friend. Saved my life during the war. You knew him?"

"Met the man during the study and bought a copy of this."

"So, you know what the gray means?" McAlester straightens and stares at the guest.

"Your purchases are parcels of those lands." She grins across the table.

"Why do you wish to obtain that property?" The host smiles in return.

"Coal deposits."

The man nods. "Near here, the A&P (Atlantic and Pacific) will have tracks."

"Which provides access to markets."

The major chuckles. "Which means we are competitors. Friendly, I hope."

Lisa's hand rests on the pistol at her hip. "I led a Pin guerrilla unit during the war. You rebels called me the Judaculla. That doesn't bode well for friendship."

"Mrs. Waters, your side won. I served with General Watie, and the old man surrendered after the war's end. His heart never gave up. But this soldier was sick of the bloodshed. Nobody wins wars. I am only interested in the future."

"I agree, Major."

"Perhaps we should partner. Choctaw law designates that mineral discoverers can claim for one mile in each direction and have the right to lease to another party." The White store operator rolls the map closed. "I am claiming coal land as I am financially able, but as you see on the document, not fast enough. To declare, the claimer must show actual deposits. Most are not on the surface. That takes mining exploration money, more than this old soldier has. You appear a businesswoman who understands the value of resources."

"Sorry to decline the offer. I have partners, James and Emily."

"What you discover, or buy, will be owned by her. Understand? If she finds another partner, that young man for instance, you have no interest in the mineral rights."

"Won't happen." Lisa smiles. "The Katy paid one cent per ton royalty to the Choctaw Republic for years but now agrees that discoverers, including Chickasaw, receive higher royalties. Called a discovery lease. The A&P must cooperate because their roads burn coal."

"Do you understand what's at stake here?" Major McAlester nods at his newest competitor.

The competition displays a poker face.

"Elias Boudinot is influential with both railroads. But not Watie. Tax problems. He and his uncle parted company."

The entrepreneur offers a handshake. "You have this officer's word, and I need the same from you, that wartime feuds will not interfere with business."

"Sir, you do not know the history." She grits her teeth, and enamel grinds.

"I have a past also, with the last Reb general officer to surrender." The major chuckles. "He's broken and tired. Some say most days he wanders around touched and confused. Sometimes he doesn't even realize the war is history."

The Judaculla unstraps a pistol and lays the battle symbol on the map before the two. "I'm willing to set aside ancient feuds. That's a commitment."

***

Months later, from a fresh, milled-wood office in Perryville near Bucklucksy in the heart of coal country, a sign reads, "Utugi Uweha," (ᎤᏍᏫ ᎤᏪᎭ in Syllabary, u-tu-gi u-we-ha, She Has Hope) Mining Company.

The business stands in the competing village with Reynolds and Hannaford's general store.

Inside, Lisa lounges in a wooden chair and listens.

"Slope or drift mines intersect seams near the surface." Josh, the sawer from the mill, attempts to keep the boss interested. "Sawmill people become miners with picks and shovels. They need the work. The mill's only operational a few days a month."

Lisa nods agreement.

"A black powder man blasts holes in the rock. We load the broken coal into tie wagons and cart the goods to the Katy. Problem is the water level. Blow or dig too deep, and liquid flows into the hole. Pumps are expensive. Our operation lacks systems for pumping, ventilation, and extraction. But the business owns boilers for steam power, and I know how to adapt the machinery."

"Hold on, Josh." Lisa through the window. "You learned from that trip to Pennsylvania, but you are way ahead of me."

"Don't understand."

"Can't mine without discovery rights." She turns attention to the sawer. "McAlester left Reynolds and Hannaford. They stay interested in stores and trading posts. The company bought his ownership, which gives the man more capital. Our emphasis must be to discover and claim fresh coal seams before he does."

"Mrs. Waters, I'm a machinery person. My interest is steam. Frankly, doesn't matter if it's a sawmill, coal mine, or something new, such as a powered carriage."

Lisa ridicules. "Or a flying boat!"

The sawer stares at the boss. The amusement mystifies.

"Find and hire a black powder expert, Josh. James and I will discover the seams."

***

Days later, the two principals, each with a work wagon and crew, study a copy of the Weldon map.

"A seam should be over that rise." The young fellow scans the terrain that lies before them.

"Think you are correct." She stares in the same direction. "Let's take the workers over there. If we're right, you analyze that one, and I will probe outward."

Both wagons move over the next ridge.

As six-man work groups stop, with individual shovels, mixed freedman, Cherokee and Choctaw jump to the ground.

Lisa shows a spot for each unit to burrow into topsoil.

Soon, diggers work in a hole until a shovel clinks instead of clunks. Its blade impacts black rock, not the red territory soil.

The worker clenches a fist in the air and whoops a success call.

The explorers concentrate on the positive sample and discover a coal river several feet below the surface.

As the cavity expands, the laborers follow the mineral.

"Keep those fellows on this, James. I'll take the second team and try that other location. Think it's just beyond that tree line."

Lisa's protégé nods, and she loads the crew and pulls a wagon in pursuit of another discovery.

***

As the afternoon approaches, Lisa rejoins the young man. "Two excellent finds today!"

Both tote chunks of coal in a modest pile on each wagon's bed.

"This seam runs that way four feet below the surface." The youngster points. "Spot-checked holes for a quarter of a mile."

"Wonderful! I marked both on the map." Lisa's enthusiasm shows in body language.

Nearby, a digger crew cooks small game on spits over a fire.

"Let me show you something." She climbs from the driver's seat. "Your men shot a couple of rabbits?"

James glances toward the flames. "Yes. Said they wanted fresh meat instead of our provisions."

Lisa selects two chunks of coal from the back of the wagon and carries the rocks to the cooking fire.

She places both in the fire's wood coals.

The diggers who cook watch.

The mineral ignites.

Men step closer and elbow each other in amazement.

"Interesting. It burns. No surprise. So what?" Her surrogate son watches the flames.

"No extra smoke. See? These claims aren't bituminous. The stuff's anthracite."

"Which sells for a higher price?" The young man understands.

"And is unusual." She claps both hands in pleasure. "Typical discoveries in this field are the cheap stuff."

James notices several of the diggers view the fire. "Watch the men. Many have never seen rock burn."

"Look at the faces." Lisa's mind remembers sister Ella as the siblings toil to erect a lean-to in the snow before the night's temperatures envelop the Mississippi river's east bank.

*The older stops and gazes across the water. Most of the deportees pitching camp stare with hands by sides.*

*Stretching before, frozen at banks with ice to the center, a majestic national waterway symbolizes the gateway to the west. A wide channel flows in the middle.*

*A huge White man's boat belches heavy smoke from two smokestacks. Columns, doors, and windows punctuate each level. Music floats across the Mississippi's waters, and golden light glows from the boat's decks. A large American flag flies from the bow of the craft. In the back of the flatboat, a massive wheel with horizontal paddles strikes the icy water. It lifts ice blocks until they slip and splash into the torrent.*

*Ella and Lisa watch the boat churn past and around a bend. They look at each other, shake heads with awe tinged with jealousy, and focus on the night's camp.*

***

Lisa's thoughts return to the present. "I know the feeling. I've seen change before."

"The diggers don't understand why they dig rocks. Maybe burning coal explains." James turns to his boss.

She concentrates on the job. "Leave the supplies and the crews out here with one wagon. You and I can take a load into town. In the morning, the three of us file a discovery claim."

"Do we have to include Emily?"

"She's our Choctaw." The woman glances at the young man. "You or I don't have to go, but her signature is necessary."

"She does not want …"

"What?" Lisa's voice tinges tense with concern.

"Her mind is afraid of people."

"Got to get over that." The concerned mother and business-woman grabs her surrogate son by both shoulders. "Too much at stake for childish fears."

James shakes from her tight grasp. "Her terrors are not foolish! I can't believe you can even say that. You were there when we returned to Utugi Uweha! You saw what happened to her family."

"I did, my boy. But I didn't let it consume my life."

"Because you weren't there to live it." The young man clenches his fist.

"Emily lived and is with us today because of you and me. We saved our valley."

"Nothing was ours. It was yours." The defender firms his backbone. "Even these coal seams! They are not Emily's or mine or these miners'. Don't you see? It's for you. You never notice that I've changed. Emily is with me. You are not!"

# CHAPTER THIRTY-NINE — Misfortune

ᎠᏤᎯᏍᎤᎢᏍᎤᏏᎧᎠᏧᎬᏲᏩᎯᎦᏆᏤᏈᎶᎤᎧᏝᎬᏲᎤᏍᎤᎤᏤᎦᏃᏌ

Lisa sits across a desk from Major Seth Andrews, Construction Superintendent, Kansas Missouri and Texas Railroad, in his office, a brick building across the state line several miles into Cherokee territory.

"Mrs. Waters. I recognize you met our demand for ties."

"Yes, sir. And you can depend on the same results for coal."

"You have proved yourself a dependable business." The major coughs. "But the matter is not mine. As you know, the Union Pacific completed track east and west. With Katy rails north and south, we have healthy competition and opportunity. It is not public, but we sold our tracks to them, and the company transfers me."

"My competitor in Bucklucksy controls that crossing. My headquarters are in Perryville." She leans forward with concern.

"Which is now a UP station." The major nods. "They are renaming it McAlester."

"Which leaves your reliable railroad tie turned coal ally abandoned." The woman slams a fist on the desk.

"Out of my hands, Mrs. Waters. But, in appreciation for your help to lay the Katy line, I offer advice."

"Contracts are better, but I'll listen."

"That other mining company overextends. Too shallow pockets. He's in control of seams but has no production capacity. Produce fuel, and the railroad will buy your supply. They have no other choice."

* * *

Weeks later, Lisa and James survey the operations with Josh, the steam aficionado. An explosion cracks a coal seam as the two watch from a safe distance. Black dust and rock fall to the ground.

"I see you hired a powder man." The owner protects her mouth and nose as pollution from the blast drifts.

"Blasting powder's not so clean." James coughs and protects his breathing.

"That will make at least a dozen wagon loads." Josh fans the smog away from the face. "A day of digging for twenty men."

"Railroads pay over four dollars a ton." Lisa shakes her head. "Profit margin's nothing compared to railroad ties."

"Slope mines don't work. Need to follow these seams deeper, but the water table's too high." Josh looks at the younger supervisor. "Steam-driven pumps could keep the shafts dry enough."

"Future growth." Mrs. Waters turns the wagon. "Right now, slopes are filling the wagons faster than McAlester's. That's the only thing important. James, did you get that property bought?"

"Yes, ma'am."

"Good." She nods. "Since the new road named the place after the competition, I'll call this part South Town."

"Rider coming." Emily's man points at an approaching horseman. "Think it's Moss."

The fiddler reins a mount to a halt next to the wagon.

"What's the hurry?" Lisa pats the horse's nose.

"News, Mrs. Waters." He catches his breath. "Thought I should tell you. The Union Pacific signed an exclusive contract with McAlester. The agreement finances his efforts, and the coal goes for eighty cents a ton."

354

"People won't accept that. I'm not the only one holding exploration leases." She looks at her younger assistant.

"Might be a good thing. To stop blowing holes over the countryside." He wipes black dust from a darkened forehead.

"Better get back into town." The boss pops the reins on the team's rumps, and they move forward.

Moss trots his horse and follows the wagon.

***

As she guides the horses into McAlester, the team steers away from an angry group of Choctaw and Cherokee miners who shout and wave handmade signs in front of McAlester's mining offices.

"Stop the Union Pacific! Coal belongs to the people!" A protestor waves a sign.

"We have a right to work! In every mine!" A freedman shakes a fist at the office.

"The White man's not our tribe! He steals the land!" Another man throws a rock at a window and glass sprinkles the ground.

"Things are getting out of hand." James leans to Lisa. "Get on to our offices."

"Times have changed since the war." She turns the wagon southward. "None of these men carry weapons."

"But those do." Moss points.

A dozen riders in a line with burlap bags over heads block the angry mob from the McAlester headquarters. Each anonymous rifleman has a pistol strapped at the belt.

The mounted men's leader fires a handgun into the air. "Go home! Mining is southern prosperity. The Union Pacific is that cash! Disperse now!"

The crowd quiets. A few individuals slip away.

"Get out!" The masked rider clubs a freedman with the butt of a rifle. "If you don't support the UP, you'll get the same as this nigger!"

Lisa clicks the reins on the team's rumps, and the wagon retreats.

"How can they do that?" James twists in the wagon's seat to watch the violent riders mill at the entry to the company and intimidate protesters. "McAlester's not even Choctaw! This is native land!"

"I'm not one either." The driver hurries the team. "And you're a Cherokee who works for me."

"That's right! You're only half!" The young man's emotions override his mouth. "Both of your companies blast holes in our ground. The money's dirty with coal dust."

"Enough, James." Moss trots his horse beside the wagon.

"But Emily's a full blood." The woman controls the response.

"And hates this. She wants to go home!" The surrogate son watches the violence behind. "We should turn around and help those folks."

"Don't be a fool." The experienced fighter clicks the team faster. "We're unarmed. Helping is a good way to die."

***

A week after the disturbance, in private, James and Emily, with Moss as a witness, join in marriage, officiated by a traveling Baptist clergyman.

After the last words, the fiddler shakes his friend's hand. "It will disturb Mrs. Waters when she learns of this."

"Because we own the coal leases?" The newlywed grips the freedman's palm.

"No, boy. Because you did not include your mother. To her, you are a son."

"That so?" His eyes flash. "That was true once. But, since the war, she's changed. Only money counts."

"I hear you. And understand why you believe that. This old man has been with her since the beginning. My mind won't think that way."

***

Several days later, Lisa, Moss, James, and Josh stand on the front boardwalk of the She Has Hope Coal Company in South Town with a dozen Choctaw, Cherokee, and freedman miners.

The owner steps to her dependable Judaculla second-in-command so that words stay private. "Sure the word got out we're hiring?"

"Yes. This is the response."

She shakes her head and turns to the assembly. "Thank you for coming in today. This company must hire three hundred workers. You are a dozen. Why do others not need work?"

"UP has an exclusive contract with McAlester. Where do you think you're going to sell coal?" A large-boned freedman steps forward.

"He cannot produce enough to satisfy the UP's demand. This company will take advantage of that weakness."

A Cherokee miner joins the first. "We supported the North in the war. But most miners fought for the rebels. Union soldiers are not welcome on crews. Not fair. We won and want to work."

The speakers look at a third who accompanies the others. "I'm a Choctaw. Two nights ago, scum cowards in hoods burned my pig pen because we work for you. I came today because I refuse to run!"

"Men, I understand." Mrs. Waters extends both arms for attention. "This company needs to hire over three hundred miners. Without you, coal stays in the ground."

"McAlester holds the contract. He's our only choice." The large-boned freedman crosses biceps over his chest.

Lisa looks at James, who stares at the ground.

She turns to Josh, who glances away.

Moss greets her gaze with a placid smile.

She coughs into a hand. "Men, practicality says go talk to my competition." Mrs. Waters lowers a chin. "I can't hire miners, so I must."

***

The following day, the owner of She Has Hope Mining sits across the desk from the major in the McAlester office.

"I had no choice other than contracting with the Union Pacific." The company's proprietor holds both palms in the air. "As the industry expands, slope or drift mines on surface seams that need little capital become exhausted. Picks and shovels to extract coal, even with black powder to blast, are too slow. We must dig below the water line. That requires large amounts of investment for new systems of pumping, ventilation, and extraction. It means steam power, which costs money I don't have. Had to sign."

"And sell cheap. This I understand." Lisa nods. "But why not hire workers that were Union fighters?"

"Who told you that?"

"No one. My employees can't hire onto your crews."

"Mrs. Waters, the day we met, you and I gave our word." McAlester stands. "You said 'I led a Pin guerrilla unit during the war. Rebels called me the Judaculla. That does not bode well for friendship.'"

Lisa nods.

"And I replied that strife is done. I served with General Watie. The old man gave up long after it ended. Fact is, I don't believe his heart surrendered."

McAlester extends an arm for a handshake. "Then I added, 'I was sick of the bloodshed. Nobody wins wars. I am only interested in the future.'"

"I remember, Major." Lisa looks at the man's extended palm. "These men who ride at night with burlap bags over faces report to you?"

He shakes his head negative.

"To Watie?"

"No one answers to the old general anymore. He's touched and wanders around Honey Creek lost most of the time. His family suffers. These night terrorists are the new South's threat to peace and prosperity."

She shakes her competitor's hand. "I believe you, Major."

"Thank you. She Has Hope Mining did well."

"I came south to control the coal industry in the territory. That failed. Your company succeeded. But I manage large acreages of discovery and surface property that needs work." Mrs. Waters leans forward. "I offer the mineral rights for sale."

McAlester smiles. "I understand those leases are not in your control. They belong to a Choctaw by the name of Emily and her spouse."

The surprised woman reacts by leaning backward. "What husband?"

"You didn't know?" The coal man chuckles. "Yes. She married that foreman, the one named James. They own the assets you want to sell."

360

## CHAPTER FORTY — Abandonment

ᎠᏣᎿᎣᎢᏍᏬᏆᏯ ᎠᏤᏫᏆᏰᎯᏦᎤᏫᏗᎧᎹᏭᏍᎣᎯᎲᎫᏯᎮ&ᎾᏗᏃᏴᎤ

"Why shouldn't we take McAlester's offer?" James slams his fist on the wooden table inside his small home near Lisa's coal company office in South Town.

Emily jumps with a nervous reaction in her chair. The surrogate son and Lisa face each other at opposite confrontational ends of the kitchen's eating surface.

Moss leans against the wall behind his boss. "Because the buy is pennies on the dollar!"

The mining's operational owner slams her fist against the wood. "You don't even know how much money our diggings cost us!"

"Because you run everything! You must be in total control! Because you allow nobody close! Ask the fiddler, he knows."

"These two got married?" Lisa looks at her old musical friend.

"Yes, ma'am."

"Why didn't you tell me?"

"Because they asked me for secrecy."

She turns to the young fellow. "Why, James? I raised you as family since I found you and your sisters that day in the snow."

"And you let them starve to death with your followers!"

"Stop it! Please!" Emily bursts into tears. "Both of you." Her head collapses onto her crossed arms.

"I want you out of my house." The man glares at his surrogate mother. "I want you out of here, out of our life."

"Who paid for this place?" The Judaculla stiffens her back.

"I did, every penny, with money I earned working for you! Now get out!"

Outside the modest home, the Judaculla's anger spins to the fiddler. "If you work for me, no more secrets, no matter who makes you promise. Do you understand?"

"More than anyone, Lisa." Moss smiles.

She pauses and takes a deep breath. "That's the only time you ever used my first name."

"Because I remember your sister, Ella. You are much alike."

***

That same evening, her resentment attempts sleep disturbed by the day and painful dreams.

*In her mind, dressed in a ball gown, she moves onto the rear doorstep of her Fort Smith home and lifts the hem of her hoop dress above the soil.*

*A woman lies on the dirt with her back against the house wall. She cuddles a whiskey jug. Her hair hangs in strings from a worn woolen hat, and her clothing stinks of alcohol and trail dust.*

*"Ella!" Lisa's voice breaks. "You're drunk!"*

*"Not near enough, little sister." The sibling waves her empty H and H labeled bottle in the air. "Got any liquor?"*

*The younger drops to her knees. "You know you can't handle booze. Where's Dideyohvsgi?"*

*"The old shaman died in Georgia. As I should have." The drunk's giggle bubbles on her lips. "Guess his last words?"*

*"Ella, how can I help you?" Lisa grasps her sister's hands.*

*The woman slobbers and laughs. "Nothing near that. My hero stuck an eagle feather in my hair and asked me who am I?"*

***

"Mrs. Waters, waken."

Lisa's shoulder rocks with Moss's gentle shake. She responds, "Do you have an eagle feather?"

"A what? You here with me?" The fiddler's voice remains low but vibrates with urgency. "Our miners warned us. The masked riders saddle mounts and raid James's house tonight. Get your pistol. I've got two rifles. Meet you in the front."

Minutes later, the Judaculla and her musical friend stand their horses in the shadow concealment of a building's wall near the young man's home.

The residence stands well-lit by over a dozen torches that encircle, held by burlap head draped men.

One slings a brick through a front window and the glass's crinkle as it falls sounds like breaking lake ice. "Come out, you Yankee loving sons-a-bitches! Your coal leases ain't protection now!"

Another terrorist spurs his mount close and throws his torch. The opening flares light as flames ignite interior curtains.

The brick thrower heels his horse closer. "Choctaw Nation don't let blue belly Cherokee and Choctaw whores run our mines!" He slings his flame through the air and reins away laughing.

Lisa's rifle sights follow the burlap head of the rider.

"Hold that shot." The fiddler touches the woman's elbow. "Too many of them. But they're not organized. Nobody's guarding the back."

As the front of the house smolders and licks sparks, the pair ride around South Town buildings to the rear of the burning home.

Unseen, before the rescuers get in position, a shadow helps another hide behind a water barrel. James's arm over Emily's shoulders guides his wife.

The young couple slips away.

They escape into the safety and darkness of the night.

***

Lisa and Moss halt near the home's back.

"Hold the horses. I'm going to bring them out." From her saddle, she leaps through the building's open entrance.

Inside, the front of the home burns, and smoke curls along ceilings.

She hurries from room to room as the heavy vapor lowers.

Satisfied that no one remains, the Judaculla struggles for the rear and escape.

With a cough and a gag, overcome by soot, she collapses on the floor. Her mind succumbs, and her body stumbles toward a distant illusion, a tune from a violin.

Moments later, the fiddler secures her arm and pulls the woman to safety.

He loads her limp form across his saddle.

With her horse in tow, Moss spurs his mount from the flames and gas.

Lisa coughs and gags as her head dangles and her chin bounces against a hairy horse belly. "Nobody in there." The lather on the shoulder tastes salty. "They got away."

Her friend reins to a halt. "I'll pull you up. You're fine to ride."

***

Three days later, James and Emily sit in the seat of a loaded wagon at the Utugi Uweha Mining Company.

Lisa and the fiddler stand on the boardwalk entryway.

She fidgets, uncomfortable with the encounter, and the fiddler's eyes tear.

"Are you sure you must go?" Lisa's voice rings tentative and soft. "The company's defunct, but we've been worse."

"Emily and I must discover our own peace, away from Yankee rebel hatred. We need a life where Cherokee and Choctaw don't constantly disagree, where we can raise kids of all races without disgusting monikers."

"That paradise doesn't exist." His surrogate mother leans against a porch pole.

"Then we create it." The younger woman smiles at her spouse.

"But not as a front for a land grab." James firms his shoulders.

"I am not sorry we took care of you." The matriarch continues to look at her son. "What must I do to change your minds?"

"Stop being Lisa Waters." Emily stutters her words.

"That's enough." The husband grasps his wife's hand. "Don't make it harder than necessary."

"Let's go." The youthful woman sighs.

"Donadagohvi Moss. (ᎤᏃᏓᎦᎰᎢ do-na-da-go-hv-i, Let us see each other again.)

Fiddler touches his hat brim with an index finger, and James flips the team's reins.

The wagon pulls away from the couple on the porch.

Old friends watch their young ones move out of South Town.

The fiddler takes the bow and instrument from its case at his feet. He draws across string, and the fiddle plays sad notes.

"Where do you believe they're going?"

"Don't know, Mrs. Waters. They consider everywhere better than here."

***

Weeks later, the musician steers his own Conestoga over a rise and out of a forest of tree stumps that open into the Utugi Uweha valley.

The missing trees change the aura of the place from one of natural encroachment to less inviting, ragged exploitation.

Lisa sits beside the driver of the loaded wagon as four mules pull its iron-rimmed wheels across the stream near the sawmill.

From her perch, the mill's walls settle deep in long grass, and vines creep along seams toward windows. The old path to the mill's entrance lies obscured by fresh growth.

A large stack of aging, grey instead of light brown railroad ties extend on one side of the mill, and its collapsed end lies in rubble.

"Where are my workers?"

"They only work the saws a couple days a month, Mrs. Waters." The wagon driver moves past the factory toward the cabins and slat structures. "Josh should be around here somewhere. Most of your men farm when the mill's not running."

Moss leads the team to the front of Lisa's small, two-room home.

The silence and stillness of the valley overwhelms her as she steadies her feet and legs on the ground. She looks, then turns to the wagon and pulls her long pipe from behind the wagon's seat.

Lisa removes a pouch of tobacco from her vest and attempts to load her pipe's bowl.

Hands shake, and she dumps more on the earth than into the smoker.

"Let me help you with that." Moss steps close and prepares the indulgence.

The woman draws deep and expels a stream of smoke. "Not sure I can start again?"

"You named this valley She Has Hope, Mrs. Waters."

"Yes, I did." She jerks her head toward a noise from one of the old cabins near her house. "What's that?"

The pair leaves the wagon and investigates the banging.

They enter a cabin.

Josh, with a hammer, pounds on a pipe.

Next to the sawer, four iron wheels at the corners of a wood frame support a small boiler and drive, with two belts extended to their axle.

"What are you doing?" Lisa shouts to override the pounding.

The man jumps at the unexpected voice.

His demeanor shows relief when he recognizes the interrupters. "Glad you're back."

"What is this?" She moves closer.

The sawer steps aside and sweeps an arm and hand toward the machine. "I'm working on a steam wagon."

"A what?" Lisa hooks her thumbs on her hips.

"A boiler propels the apparatus." The inventor smiles, excited by his progress.

His boss stares at the contraption for a moment. "I pay for the time you take to play with that thing."

Josh's smile disappears. "There's no sawing for the mill, Mrs. Waters. But if this works, it will replace horses and mules. Don't you see the possibilities?"

"I fire you!  Get your stuff, including this junk, and leave my property!"

The steam man stiffens his back. "Fired? After what I've done for you?"

"You heard me!"

"I'll take my engine off your land, and good luck with the business." The angry ex-employee strides past the pair out the door. "And I recommend you switch to something simple. Try farming!" He slams the entrance as he exits.

***

The following morning, Lisa sits on her front porch, smokes her pipe which Moss loaded and stews over the run-down condition of her valley and its sawmill.

"This place lacks attention, much less work, for months."

"You were gone a long time, Mrs. Waters."

"The sawmill's a business, not my plaything."

"It is, ma'am."

"If I left you in charge, would my mill look this terrible?"

"I am not sure."

"I don't understand."

"A lot in this world confuses me, Lisa."

## **CHAPTER FORTY-ONE — Explosion**

ᎠᏣᎢᏍᎣᎢᏌᎣᏗᏯᎠᏤᏫᎮᏗᎭᎢᎦᏫᏍᎦᎺᎦᏮᎣᎯᎮᎷᏯᎩᏔᎠᏂᎭᏃᎤᏉᎤ

Early fall color tinges the foliage that dangles from new growth shoots on many of the stumps around Lisa's valley and its sawmill. She stands in the afternoon shade of an oak beside the mill house's west wall and shades her eyes with a hand.

Moss moves along the road in a lead wagon laden with tree trunks trimmed of branches. Others follow, loaded, but with mule teams driven by hired Cherokee and freedman teamsters.

Lisa waves as the load splashes through the stream that crosses their path and flows into the floating pond of the mill. As the raw materials approach, she evaluates the quality and quantity of the goods.

The fiddler drives to the water.

The owner meets and holds the lead mule of the team. "Good Katy lumber! Those make great ties."

Moss stands in the front. "Not that road anymore, Mrs. Waters. These logs are for the Union Pacific, but no matter. It's work for the mill."

"It is." She steadies the mules. "We got lucky with them replacing old tracks."

"Bring up those teams!" The fiddler waves his arm at the other drivers, and they maneuver into a row behind the leader. "Unload this first."

Men from the others, with long-handled wood movers that feature pointed hooks on an end, yank the top log from the apex of the wagon's pile.

Once in motion, gravity pulls, and it splashes into the pool, followed by the next tree trunk.

Lisa watches the work and smirks satisfaction. "Good thing we got the contract. Tough getting through this winter without it."

Her friend points at the color on the oak beside the mill. "Leaves turn color early."

"I wish we could have saved those in the valley. I miss my forests."

"You men take care!" Moss points at two inexperienced freedmen atop the wood stack as one shoves a log into motion with his foot. He turns to the boss. "I'm worried. These workers we hired have no experience. Without Josh, it's risky."

"He trained our first crew." She nods. "We can train these."

"I hear you, Mrs. Waters. But the man knew everything steam."

"We'll be fine, Moss."

"So, you'll fire up the boilers in the morning?"

"Before dawn, as the sawer did." Lisa rubs her hands together. "That load of coal we ordered from McAlester came in two days ago."

"He used wood."

"We have to send wagons to cut timber." She pats Moss's shoulder. "Need our trees for railroad ties, not boiler kindling."

"Ayaeee!" A Cherokee handler catches his foot between logs as one rolls into the washing pond.

A group of workers gather around the injured man as the supervisors help.

Lisa feels the man's ankle and lower leg bones. "Broken. Couple of you men carry him to my cabin. I'll set and splint it."

"I forget you were a nurse." The fiddler smiles.

***

Before dawn the following morning, the boss woman carries a kerosene lamp and moves inside the Utugi Uweha sawmill.

Two Cherokee workers with large, deep shovels wait at the base of a coal pile dumped into the mill through a window.

From kindling, the mill's owner selects sticks that look dry and combustible. She makes a small stack in the first boiler and starts its fire.

A Cherokee with a shovel joins her, where she adds pieces of the black rock, and her flames grow.

As light from the blaze flickers color on Lisa's and the loader's faces, the men dump shovels of fuel into the cauldron.

Soon, the two Cherokee employees throw more into another opening on a second pile of sawdust, chips, bark and splintered debris.

Lisa checks a pressure valve.

Steam rules everything.

She inspects the large primary engine that runs the line shaft drive for the log carriage. A head rig circular saw extends from the base, and an added cutter offsets and overlaps.

The sawer walks the main, which powers the adjustable edger saws.

A lower cutter, with a fifty-two-inch blade and sharp, flat edge claws, displays concentric circles emanating from its shaft. Each shines, polished from cut timber.

The forty-eight-inch top saw hangs available to engage extra-large logs.

A Cherokee loader selects the first log and clamps a pick suspended from a heavy chain, and the pick's pointed iron spikes secure the raw material. The bed winch pulls the trunk from the pond.

With the mill's boilers powered and to pressure, a twin-cylinder tool draws the tree onto the deck.

A third vertical engine powers a conveyor belt that empties sawdust from below the head rig.

A fourth drives a cut-off saw.

Outside, the spring-fed mill pool cleans dirt and debris from the raw timber.

The wagons in line, with collapsible sides that this early morning uploaded logs from Moss's tree cutting, wait.

With long-handled clamps, two freedmen roll the trunk into the row that awaits the blade.

Moss checks the pressure gauge, which reads 160 as the sun breaks the horizon.

"Steams up!" Lisa calls.

A steam whistle, like a railroad locomotive, blows. It signals daily business opening.

"Stand clear!" The freedman yells, and operators, one at a time at the top of their voices, respond. "Clear!"

"Clear!"

"I'm clear."

"Mill in motion!" The boss cups a hand to her mouth. Her words warn the workers.

Heavy metal cranks wake from the night, steam puffs from exhaust pipes, and the conveyor belt tightens.

Belts surge into motion and power the various machines.

Lisa and a Cherokee carriage-setter load the log onto the bed and secure the wood. The iron carries the raw material, and the blade chews a first cut.

The mill's owner signals to set the railroad's tie depth for the next slice.

In a matter of minutes, loaders stack thirty finished railway crossties into waiting transport wagons that carry over 500 per trip.

The Utugi Uweha sawmill produces after its long rest and profitless inactivity.

***

Later in the day, Moss checks a gauge. "Mrs. Waters! Pressure's building in boiler one!"

"You men slow the coal!" Lisa gives a thumbs-down to her loaders.

After a pause, the fiddler rechecks, smiles, and waves.

"Come on, I need a smoke break." The boss motions to her old friend.

Outside the mill, he loads Lisa's pipe with tobacco. "What caused that pressure to rise? It neared the red line, Mrs. Waters."

"Don't know for sure." She draws pleasure into lungs and puffs lazy rings. "But I think it's coal. The stuff burns hotter."

The conversation ceases with a calamitous crash from the last wood wagon.

With its side dangling broken, logs roll off the wagon's bed and bounce upon the ground. Workers from the other wagons converge at the accident, and their bosses jog to help.

"What a mess!" Lisa directs her inexperienced crew. "Get a rope and unhitch one of the mule teams. Pull this timber back on the bed."

The woman spins toward a massive explosion behind her. Her mouth hangs open.

A huge chunk of iron bursts into the mill's gable and spirals as a giant saw blade. The piece decapitates the oak tree beside the mill as the building's walls swell and erupt in flames and steam.

Moss drops to his knees and stares.

Wood slats, gables, and conveyor belts, along with spinning blades and mangled torsos of bloody workers, fly in the air's expansion from the explosion. It resembles a volcano's lava against land encounter in splats across the pond and surrounding terrain.

"No!" Lisa scrambles toward the tragedy.

Inside the burning debris of her building, its owner holds her hat over her mouth as she coughs in the smoke and attempts to help.

Several bodies, Cherokee and freedman employees, hang from twisted metal remnants of the boilers and machinery.

Wood slats and coal rock burns and tortures iron and flesh.

Moss grabs his boss and pulls her from the tragedy before the roof collapses upon the interior.

***

Two days after the explosion, Lisa buries her dead.

The cemetery across the road from her cabin complex and at the opposite end of her valley from the devastated sawmill site displays seven fresh-dug graves.

A small group of family members and friends stand in bunches near individual holes, and quiet whispers ripple through the grieving.

"The cause is unknown. Someone said low water." A voice speculates.

"Our men's mangled bodies lie in the debris." Another trembles. "See that oak? Flying metal chopped its top clean."

Moss and Lisa walk in front of a mule team that pulls a wood wagon with seven stiff burlap-wrapped remains. Three appear smaller and only contain body parts.

The makeshift hearse pauses at individual holes where family members or friends unload their members and lower the wraps into darkness with ropes.

With the transport unloaded, Lisa and Moss stand before the assembly.

"These workers died horrible deaths. They fill this cemetery with tragic endings. Good men and women end here. It is a symbol of my shame. I named this valley Utugi Uweha because years ago I had hope. Now, I have none. Many who lie here's only transgressions were belief in my ideas. Their end is a tragedy, one that will follow me the rest of my life."

The gathering is quiet for a moment.

The valley's founder breaks the weight. "This is not for me! I am finished, and I stand here alive. These do not!"

"Let this doomed place haunt you!" A Cherokee and his wife stalk off from the graves.

Several others break from the group and move toward the road out of the valley. "This place is a memorial to the Judaculla. A dealer in death!"

Lisa looks up at her friend's freedman face. "Moss?"

"I'm not leaving you, Mrs. Waters."

"But you don't call me Lisa." The founder of She Has Hope drops her chin upon her chest, and her eyes swell with tears.

# CHAPTER FORTY-TWO — Finality

ᎠᏡᏥᎤᎢᏍᎤᎭᏴᎠᏒᎬᏛᏞᎠᏫᎦᏬᏩᏖᏒᎬᎷᎪᏯᎶᏃᎭᏐᏴᎿᎮᎳᎭᏃᏇᎤ

Months later, in November 1873, Lisa Waters, fifty-four years old, without a working sawmill or income and with her fortune lost in her coal mining experiment, approaches winter with little hope and less security.

A norther blows through the blackened shell of the destroyed mill where the woman sits on the fragment of a machine.

She pulls a Cherokee blanket tighter around her shoulders against the temperature.

The woman's ears fill with music and the polite chatter of a party long ago.

*Most guests turn to a couple, new arrivals.*

*Ezra extends a handshake. "Mr. President. Welcome to my home and to Fort Smith."*

*"And to your United States of America. It's far from Tahlequah." The dignitary removes his black top hat.*

*"May I introduce my wife, Lisa?"*

*Ross sweeps his hand toward his companion. "And this southern beauty is mine, Mary Stapler."*

*Attired in an ornate, eastern fashionable gown, a striking twenty-year-old clings to her famous older spouse and smiles at the hostess, one of the few in the party near her age. "I am so pleased to meet the social queen of Fort Smith. John, why don't you and Mr.*

*Waters work the room? Do your politics. She and I must become friends." She turns to her new acquaintance. "My husband loves to entertain. Particularly his people. We were married in Philadelphia, and I was raised a proper Quaker by my family in Brandywine, without slaves. They tell me your waiters and musicians are hired freedmen?"*

*"Yes, my Ezra was born a slave. He rejects the condition."*

*"And I understand you are half? With my childhood religious training, I appreciate your point of view, but I am aware this territory demands, should I say, an attitude adjustment."*

***

Lisa trembles and returns to her station in her destroyed mill and stares at the limbs of the oak above the black rafters of her roof. They thrash in response to the wind.

Unnoticed, Moss, in a heavy coat, sits on a tree stump and watches from across the log pond. He shifts his weight and the bulk of Lisa's pistol at his waist. Both the freedman's hands grip the barrel of his rifle, and he rests his chin on his palms. His eyes fixate on the destroyed structure and follow any movement.

Lisa continues to stare at the large skeletal tree. After a moment, she gazes at the skin of her own hand and wrist. She compares the oak's surface.

The half-Cherokee freedmen's daughter groans as she stands and steps several feet to the remnants of the coal pile that fueled her boilers. She reaches and scrubs her hands in the black dust and powder.

Now differently complected, she stares at her new skin color, and her mind drifts.

***

*In front of her primitive fortress home, the building smokes from its rubble, and bodies swollen from days in the sun lie around the porch and near the landing. Its pier extends less than normal length, with the rest burned to the waterline.*

*Lisa rises in her carriage. "Moss! Moss!"*

*Silence envelopes the area.*

*"They've been massacred, Mrs. Waters." The Cherokee home guard in charge stands in his stirrups. "Days ago. These men are bloated." The man points, "But over there, that is recent. Somebody knew you were coming and left a message."*

*Lisa follows the guard's point.*

*At the side of the charred remnants of her house, a single body hangs upside down on a heavy pole planted in the ground.*

*"Oh no! Is it Moss?"*

*He turns his horse and canters to the upright, looks up, and returns. "No. The body's a young White boy."*

*"Driver, pull the carriage closer."*

*"Not sure you want to, Mrs. Waters." The home guard signals no to the teamster. "It's not a pretty sight."*

*"I've seen worse. Do it now."*

*The inspector nods, and the conveyance moves around the corner of the burned warehouse to the ominous pole.*

*Lisa gasps as she recognized the young Quaker conductor from the winter. His eyes stare blank, and a wooden hewn plank extends out of his side. On the wood, crude hand-printed letters in blood read, "Abolitionist!"*

***

The word rings in Lisa's memory.

As she sits and reminisces in her destroyed sawmill, unseen, a broken old man on a mule flies a Confederate battle flag from a pole that he props in his stirrup and emerges into She Has Hope Valley from the tree stumps.

The stars and bars flap in the north wind against a rusted Patterson Colt in a worn CSA holster at his waist. A Confederacy issued Enfield converted to a shotgun rides in a long sheath belted to the rider's saddle.

Engrossed with her thoughts and wallowing in self-examination, Lisa's mind continues to drift.

***

*A voice from the past floats through the sawmill's debris. "We are coming from the cotton fields, we're coming from afar; we have left the plow, the hoe and ax and gone off to a war."*

*Moss's song rings weak and resonates with helplessness.*

*"We have left old plantation seat, the sugar and the cane, where we work'd and toil'd with weary feet in sun and wind and rain."*

*Moss plays his fiddle and sings as his tone strengthens. "We have left our chains behind us, boys, the prison, and the rack; and we'll hide beneath a soldier's coat the scars upon our backs."*

*In her mind's eye, Lisa watches the fiddler sing.*

*"We'll teach the world a lesson soon if taken by the hand, how the night shall come before 'tis noon, upon old Pharaoh's land."*

*Moss turns and realizes she observes. He pauses his lament.*

*"It's beautiful, Moss. So long since I enjoyed your voice."*

*The big man's chin quivers.*

*Lisa nods, and wetness fills her eyes.*

*Moss lifts his fiddle. "By the heavy chains that bound our hands through centuries of wrong, we have learned the hard-bought lesson well, how to suffer and be strong. We only ask the power to show what freedom does for man; and we'll give sign to friend and foe as none beside us can."*

***

Lisa shakes away the memory and looks up to focus on the few remaining leaves of the half-oak above her head.

She prays. "Oh, Unetlanvhi, whose voice I hear in the wind." A leaf drifts from the tree and brushes the woman's nose. "Your breath gives life to the world."

The woman stands and extends her fingers to the uninviting sky. "Listen to me. I need your strength and wisdom."

Several more leaves drop and swirl toward her head. "Let me walk in peace, and prepare my eyes to behold the leaf fall."

Lisa turns and drops to her knees. "Make my hands respect the objects you have made and my ears sharp to hear your voice in the wind."

She transcends to her mother's culture and beliefs. "Ready me wise so I may understand the words you have taught my people."

*The sound of a galloping horse, the sound of hooves on a historical harpsichord, beckons Lisa's attention.*

*A Tsalagi warrior dressed in black leggings, breechcloth, and deerskin vest approaches.*

*"Aid me to stay calm and strong in the face of what comes for me." She trembles.*

*Her eyes search the ground. "Let me learn the lessons you have hidden in every leaf and rock."*

*She picks up a stone and prepares to defend against the charging Cherokee.*

*Lisa drops her lump of coal. "Support my pure thoughts, actions, and intent to help others."*

*The attacking warrior's pupils glow red, and his sockets flash white.*

*The half-Cherokee woman's terrified soul prays, "Use me to find compassion without hate overwhelming me."*

*She throws her arms up to protect her skull. "I search for strength, not to be greater than my brother, but to fight my greatest enemy."*

*The helpless human peeks through her protective hands.*

*The attacker's horse rears with its front hooves flailing inches from harm.*

*Its rider transforms to a wild-haired, crazy-eyed, buckskin-clad woman wielding a Cherokee hatchet.*

*Lisa's own reflected image flashes fire from her lips as she screams, "Who am I? I am my greatest enemy!"*

***

In the stumps across the sawmill's pond and near the road into the valley, resolute, an old Confederate general guides his mule with knee pressure and reins between his teeth.

The lapels of his worn and dirty rebel coat flap in the wind below a tattered but gold-braided star, and his pants tuck into battle-abused boots.

As the officer moves toward his target, he heels his mount to a faster pace.

He looks to his right, and his mind envisions a line of Cherokee Confederates with rifles and bayonets at a charge. They jump stumps and pound through long grass.

The attacker turns to his left and waves encouragement to three artillery pieces that maneuver in his vision through the stump dotted terrain propelled by lathered teams.

"Hold up there! You don't want a gut shot." Moss, with his rifle pointed at the rider, obstructs progress.

General Standhope Watie leans back in his saddle, reins between teeth, and his mule stops from the restraint. "What's this? Get out of my way, Nigger!"

"That filthy banner's not coming into my valley!" Moss steps in front of the mount.

"Boom!" The shotgun blasts smoke and buckshot near his mule's ear.

Metal balls tear into Moss's chest and neck, and the force of the round throws his body backward onto his back with his shoulder against a tree stump.

With his saddle near vertical, the general slides across his cantel.

Gravity grips, and the animal kicks its front hooves. "Enemy artillery! Charge, Boys!"

Watie grabs his pommel, attempts to stay mounted, but the elderly man's grip fails, and his mule punts fragile ribs mid-fall.

Lisa's dreams congeal into the sound of the shotgun's blast. "Moss!"

The old rebel general struggles to his feet with one hand protecting his side. "Come on, Brothers! Attack! It's a Pin camp. Bring up the twelve pounders!"

The commander draws his Patterson and waves the weapon toward the enemy.

In his eyes, a company of butternut-clad soldiers with rifles rise from the tree stumps behind him and press their charge.

Lisa stumbles out of the sawmill's ruins and scans the view before her. "Moss!"

The general hears her call and spies the unarmed woman beside the burned mill. "Follow me!"

At a fast limp with one hand pressed against his ribs for pain prevention, the attacker discovers his battle flag on the ground.

He stops, retrieves the banner, glances at his defenseless foe, and throws the stars and bars back into the dirt and dust. "It's the Judaculla! Attack!"

Lisa grabs an old, charred log pick near the pond as her foe stumbles forward.

She lifts the pole in her defense.

The general points his Patterson Colt at her head. "Surrender! Disarm your Pins!"

"There are none, you fool! Just you and me and that pistol you used to beat my sister!"

"What?" Watie pauses, his mind attempts to adjust to reality. "You're not their leader?"

Lisa's eyes flash with hatred. "I am! I bring Hell upon your house!"

He pulls the Patterson's trigger, and the rusty revolver explodes.

The weapon's long barrel splits, metallic corn husks shucked from their ear.

Back pressure propels the revolver's cartridge cylinder into several chunks.

A hot metal shrapnel impacts the general's forehead, and his knees buckle into his boots.

The last hero of the Confederacy to surrender to Union troops collapses into unconsciousness at the feet of Lisa Waters, his lifelong nemesis, a freedman's daughter and legacy of a Cherokee mother's pride.

# CHAPTER FORTY-THREE — Antithesis

ᎠᎡᏔᏐᎣᎢᏒᏐᏆᎩᎩᎠᏨᎡᏉᏢᎠᎻᎦᎳᏪᏍᎦᎷᎬᎻᎠᏒᎣᎯᎲᏚᎩᎾᏋᏏᎾᎯᏃᏪᎤ

The following morning, Lisa sits cross-legged on a Confederate battle flag a short distance from Moss's grave digger.

With both hands, she points her cocked Pin pistol at General Standhope Watie's chest as he digs in a hole.

Her finger trembles on the weapon's sensitive trigger.

Watie gasps breath from the exertion and slams the blade of his shovel into the soil. "Shoot me, Judaculla!"

He leans on the tool's handle and his fingers shake.

The man clings to the wood. "I need water."

"Dig, Reb. You get a drink after you get Moss's grave done."

She grimaces. "And after you dig a second one for you."

"I'm dizzy, can't. Too old for this." The Confederate sits on the rim of the hole. "No sleep." He rubs his wrists. "The rope around my feet was too tight."

"Crack!" A bullet from Lisa's pistol ricochets off the blade's sheathing of the gravedigger's shovel and impacts the hole's wall.

Dirt and rock splatters the old man's boots as he jerks them from danger.

"All right! I'm digging!" The general throws a load of soil then discards his trowel. "I don't dig graves for niggers."

"His name was Moss! Say it!" Lisa aims at the prisoner's forehead.

"Moss." Watie sneers. "Nigger Moss!"

"Blam!" Lisa's bullet rips through the flesh of the rebel's thigh, and he screams in pain.

His knees buckle and hips spin.

Elbows catch the weight of the fall onto the grave's edge.

The man stabilizes and looks at his attacker as if she is his friend. "Love you, crazy woman! Look what you did. Can't dig no grave now with a shot leg!"

Lisa stands. "Can you with two bum legs?" She cocks her pistol.

"I'm bleeding!" The general imitates his company bugler. "Ta-da-da! Tot ta-da, ta-da! Call the regimental surgeon!"

The Judaculla picks the stars and bars from the ground and flings it to the wounded prisoner. "Tie that rag around it."

Watie grabs the banner, rips a strip from its cloth and wraps it tight over his leg wound. "Your slug went clean through. No bones broken."

"That's good for you." The woman returns to her cross-legged perch. "Means you can keep digging."

The Reb spits. "You ain't no different from me. You got lucky and ended on the winning side."

"And I'm the same as the body you bury. But my mother was Cherokee." Aloha's daughter glances at Moss's burlap-wrapped form in a nearby wagon.

"Blood has nothing to do with it." Watie plants his shovel blade and pushes it with his good foot. "In Fort Smith, you hated me because I protected myself."

"You claim beating my sister to death was protecting yourself? Or hiring assassins to kill my husband and me? Burning my home?" Lisa's voice rings with a tint of hysteria.

"That woman you call your family was a paid whore that stole my money. The rest was war. You led marauders. We called Pin guerrillas murderers because you butchered and pillaged my men and their families." Watie throws a shovel load of dirt out of the grave. "They named you the Judaculla, not me."

"True, but a difference between us made me right."

The general stops shoveling.

"I'm not a racial or social bigot." Lisa's voice penetrates the old man's ears with purpose. "This fellow you're burying was good, a musician, a fiddler who loved the poor, the disposed, the helpless victims of your twisted mind. That stands as his legacy. What's yours? The red and white banner you tear?"

"I know abolitionists, you cherish niggers. We ain't talking about him. We're speaking of you and I."

"He and I are the same."

"That so? He used his people for selfish goals? To collect wealth? Ran off his family and friends?"

"Moss never did that."

"Then you're not similar. You are the Judaculla."

"And you, the last general officer to surrender after your perverted ideals lost the great war, are a hero?"

Watie jerks to attention.

He executes a left-face to the ripped banner on the edge of Moss's grave, and salutes. "O, I wish I was in the land of cotton. Old times there are not forgotten. Look away! Look away! Look away! Dixie Land." He turns to Lisa. "Your nigger ever sing or fiddle that one?"

She lunges forward and slaps the general's ear with the weight of her pistol.

The tired man collapses unconscious.

***

387

Three days later, the captor drives a mule team and wagon along the rutted dirt road to Honey Creek.

Bound in burlap and tied with rope, Standhope Watie feels the wagon's iron rim wheels impact every stone.

"Driver!" the general grunts with each bump. "I will report you to the brigade's surgeon if you hit another rut!"

The Pin leader looks at the cloth-wrapped torso in the rear. Red blood stains a leg.

"Doctor? How far to the field hospital?" The captive rolls to a side where he can view the injury. "I'm hurt. Wounded. Took a Yankee ball in the calf. Bleeding! But you ain't cutting off my leg."

"Shut up, back there. You're not going to a surgeon."

The old man's eyes focus and his thoughts clear. "Blue Belly! Am I a prisoner! These stars mean you're dealing with a general officer. I expect to be treated as one."

"You will be." Lisa handles her wagon over a rut and its bed bounces. "I'm taking you home."

"Shoot me, Judaculla!" The venerable man reclaims his mind. "Nothing for me at Honey Creek! No money! No future, just my family who needs food! Murder me now!"

"Not going to, Watie." She guides her team to hit another bump. "I will hang you from the back of the wagon with a rope. When I lash these mules, your people can watch your eyes bulge out. Hope they pop!"

"Damn Yankee!" The prisoner spits in Lisa's direction. "A Blue Belly Cherokee's much worse!"

"Remember that when kicking for breath!"

"My troops will hang you too." The man smiles and his eyeballs glint as a snake's. "We are the same, you and I. Murderers, no better than Quantrill! Take me home, shoot me now, no matter. You'll see yours!"

"But you first!" Lisa hits a stone in the road, and her cargo groans with the bump.

"I want a trial. No, I demand one. These stars are a General in the Confederate States of America. The Confederacy deserves justice." The old man's mind drifts. "But my people remember me. Cherokee will talk of my life for generations."

"You had your court hearing. For James Foreman's death."

"I know of Jefferson Davis and John Ross. But don't recall that name."

"You killed him, as many others." The woman turns her attention to the road. "A corrupt judge got you off, but tomorrow, for that killing, for my sister Ella, and for all Cherokee Pins, you're going to hang."

***

The following afternoon, under a stout tree on a hill above his home and bankrupt tobacco plantation at Honey Creek, she fits a rope around the general's neck. He sits in the back of her wagon. She throws the other end over a limb above her head and catches its frayed terminal knot.

With her weight, The Pin leader tugs the cable, and Watie coughs as his noose tightens.

"On your feet, you woman killer!"

Still wrapped in burlap, with the hangman's loop pulling him upward, the old man struggles and regains his stance on the wagon's bed.

Lisa jumps to the ground and ties the executioner's cord to a tree's trunk.

The hangman strides to the Conestoga's tail and draws her pistol.

She fires three rounds into the air.

The mules hitched to the wagon shift back and forth with the discharges.

Watie rocks in his burlap-wrapped black Confederate boots.

The Pin leader watches the buildings of the tobacco plantation below.

Several people exit doors and look around.

A stout female points up at the hanging.

The Judaculla strides to the fidgety mules, takes their reins, and slaps the lead animal's rump.

Her team surges forward, and the wagon's bed slides from under the prisoner's feet.

A noose tightens with black boots several inches from the ground. He kicks, and his face puffs pink, then blue.

Lisa's mind flashes to the day prior.

Her mental vision watches Watie smile and his eyes glint like a snake's. "We are the same, you and I. Murderers. Worse than Quantrill! Take me home, shoot me now, no matter. You'll get yours!"

She draws a deep breath as her thought race.

In reality, she sees the mature man's pupils bulge.

Her brain blurs vision. The figure jerks to attention, does a left-face to the ripped banner on the edge of Moss's grave, and salutes. "O, I wish I was in the land of cotton. Old times there are not forgotten. Look away! Look away! Look away! Dixie Land."

He turns to Lisa. "Your nigger ever sing or play that one?"

***

The Judaculla whips her knife from the sheaf at her belt, lunges to the strangling human, and with its razor-sharp blade, cuts the rope inches above the hangman's knot.

Watie's burlap body falls, and his captor loosens the noose.

The general sucks in breath through blue chapped lips.

"Moss played a Cherokee Reel, you useless, pathetic donkey patty, not your blood-stained murder hymn!"

With her boot, she shoves the poverty struck, lost, unhappy, and senile symbol of the Confederacy toward the pitiful, impoverished remnants of his life.

His wife and adult children struggle up the hill to rescue him.

Lisa Waters turns, climbs into her wagon, and lashes the reins across her mule's rumps.

Her head jerks backward as the team canters away from Honey Creek, the past, and the Judaculla, into resurrection.

***

A month later, big, soft snowflakes fill a dark sky as she sits on the driver's bench and peers through barren tree trunks at a small log cabin in a valley.

Words and fiddle music float in the whiteness above the trees. "Let us pause in life's pleasures and count its many tears. While we all sup sorrow with the poor, there's a song that will linger forever in our ears. Oh, hard times come again no more."

The woman, alone in the winter landscape, searches for a source. "Tis the song, the sigh of the weary. Hard times, hard times, come again no more. Many days you have lingered around my cabin door. Oh, hard times come again no more."

She recognizes the words and melody of Steven Foster, popular with her generation.

The actual singer and fiddle player sounds more immediate and personal. "While we seek mirth and beauty and music bright and gay, there are frail forms fainting at the door."

Little light escapes through windows of the cabin in the valley shuttered against the temperature, but smoke drifts from a chimney.

In the snow to the woman's left, a dark shadow plays a fiddle and sings lyrics, "'Tis the song, the sigh of the weary. Hard times, hard times, come again no more. Many days you have lingered around my cabin door. Oh, hard times come again no more."

"Moss! Is that you?" Lisa stands in her wagon.

"'Tis a sigh that is wafted across the troubled wave. 'Tis a wail that is heard upon the shore. 'Tis a dirge that is murmured around the lowly grave. Oh, hard times come again no more." The shadow drops from a back-legged stance to all fours.

The woman collapses on her wagon's seat and watches a black bear pad tracks of retreat into the snow between the trees.

She turns and focuses on the cabin in the valley.

***

The wagon moves closer.

The place presents a prosperous aura with a corral, two horses, and several mules.

A Conestoga rests beside the fence with its bed covered by inches of wet snow.

Beyond the animal enclosure, a smokehouse, half in the ground, displays a trail of foot tracks from its entrance to the cabin's porch.

Lisa clicks her reins, and her team pulls.

She watches the home draw larger as she moves around its corner onto the ice before its front.

The door opens a notch, and warm light sweeps a stripe across its wood slat portico and over the clean whiteness.

Emily steps into the illumination with one hand supporting a pregnant, swollen belly.

She stares at Lisa. "Who are you?"

"Not the woman you knew. I'm the same freedman's daughter from a Cherokee mother, but I've forgotten and forgiven. This woman wants to greet this Spring with open eyes and a healing heart. I'll leave if not welcome." The wagon driver's voice vibrates low and unassertive.

"Come out here." The expectant mother opens the entry wider. "You must receive someone."

James steps to join his wife.

Lisa removes her hat for recognition and shakes it to clear the blizzard's weight.

Behind her surrogate son, on the cabin's wall, she eyes a short heritage belt piece of sun-bleached gulf-water seaweed adorned by hand polished shells and beads.

The young man moves onto the porch. "I remember when my sisters and I came to your cabin out of a snowstorm. Now you return to mine. You are the only mother I know. Come in and get warm."


## THE BEGINNING

# ACKNOWLEDGEMENTS

**ᎠᎡᎢᎣᎤᎥᎦᎧᎨᎩᎪᎫᎬᎭᎮᎯᎰᎱᎲᎳᎴᎵᎶᎷᎸᎹᎺᎻᎼᎽᎾᎿᏀᏁᏂᏃᏄᏅ**

The author acknowledges the following contributors to this book:

My wife, who enabled endless hours of research and writing time.

Ella Waters, my paternal grandmother and Dawes Roll signee, who inspired my interest in all things Cherokee - even though we never met.

Ed Fields and Mary Rae, who teach the Cherokee online language classes from the Cherokee Nation. And their language department for expanding my interest in our culture, syllabary and speech. The author reccommends their book, *Journeying Into Cherokee*, for help and encouragement learning the Cherokee Language.

The author, Grace Steel Woodward, who introduced me to Cherokee history through her book, *The Cherokees* published by University of Oklahoma Press, Norman.

# ABOUT THE AUTHOR

ᎠᏣᎢᏍᎣᎢᏍᎤᎵᏴᎠᏌᎴᏉᏫᏆᎠᏝᎾᏭᏛᎣᏟᎹᏄᏫᎣᏌᎲᏎᏴᎥᏖᎾᏏᏃᏊᎤ

ᏍᏆᎲ ᎲᏚᏝ

Thank you for reading *Cherokee Reel*. I hope you enjoyed the book and ask you to recommend it to your friends.

That recommendation is important to spread Cherokee culture, history, and language awareness.

I am a citizen of the Cherokee Nation and work daily to learn our Class IV language and our history's nuances.

Married for over fifty years with two children and four grandchildren, I live in Grapevine, Texas. Other than writing, my interests include painting in oils and watercolors, making short films, plus anything that makes my grandchildren happy.

ᏩᏙ (Wa-do Thank you.)

James A. Humphrey

## ALSO BY JAMES A. HUMPHREY

ᎠᏩᏔᏬᎣᎢᏍᏬᏢᏴᎠᎫᎬᏫᏀᏝᏌᎯᎦᏈᏪᏗᏊᏪᏗᎦᎹᏀᎷᎣᏅᏀᏛᏌᏴᏋᏰᏁᎯᏃᏋᎥ

This historical novel, *Cherokee Reel,* is book three of the Cherokee Trilogy, the story of the extended Waters family from 1779 through Civil War Reconstruction.

The other two are:

*Cherokee Rock*, the first book, tells an epic story as exploitation sweeps westward over the Appalachians in 1779 and engulfs a Tsalagi boy who loses his mother to smallpox, allies with a mentor squirrel, and trains as a shaman. A tribal fountain-head, Cherokee Rock, shelters his growth to manhood. Through decades of pestilence and war, with a Freedman blood brother, he battles a malignant medicine man for their peoples' hearts. The life-long enemies collide in an epic revelation.

*Cherokee Rose*, the second book, tells the epic story of Benjamin Waters's half Cherokee daughter, Ella, who after his death battles pestilence, bigotry, alcoholism, starvation and a record cold 1838 winter during a forced removal led by white profiteers and her father's murderer to Indian Territory. On the trek, she earns her people's respect and adoration as the Cherokee Rose, then illegally jumps her land allotment and faces a white jury in a trial that sets national precedents for Native American rights.

All three historical novels are available for purchase at www. cherokeetrilogy.com or from Tsalagi Books, tsalagibooks.com

ᎦᏫ (Wa-do) Thank you.